AMBULANCE
GIRLS
AT WAR

Deborah Burrows

AMBULANCE GIRLS AT WAR

EBURY
PRESS

1 3 5 7 9 10 8 6 4 2

Ebury Press, an imprint of Ebury Publishing
20 Vauxhall Bridge Road,
London SW1V 2SA

Penguin
Random House
UK

Ebury Press is part of the Penguin Random House group of companies
whose addresses can be found at global.penguinrandomhouse.com

First published in the UK in 2019 by Ebury Press

www.penguin.co.uk

A CIP catalogue record for this book is available from the British Library

Hardback ISBN 9781785034640

Typeset in 12/15 pt Times LT Std
by Integra Software Services Pvt. Ltd, Pondicherry

Printed and bound in Great Britain by Clays Ltd, Elcograf S.p.A.

Penguin Random House is committed to a sustainable future
for our business, our readers and our planet. This book is
made from Forest Stewardship Council® certified paper.

To the Burrows gang, Em, Lucy, Nigel,
and to Jacob, Olive and Sunday, who are simply grand.

CHAPTER ONE

Thursday 23 January 1941

'My God, Maisie,' said Celia. 'The whole world's on fire.'

I hit the brake hard and the ambulance shuddered to a stop in a cloud of bitter smoke that made my eyes sting. The buildings on both sides of Theobald's Road had gone up like tinder in the incendiary attack earlier that night. Now they were vivid and pulsing pinnacles of fire flickering red and pink, lapped at the centre with tongues of gold and green and purple and blue. Fire hoses coiled and twisted over the road. A dozen or so firemen, black shapes silhouetted by the flames, held gushing hoses that writhed in their hands, as if trying to escape their grip and flee the inferno. The ground was awash with water, reflecting the scene as a shimmering melted-copper lake.

A sheet of fire covered the narrow side street in front of us, cutting us off from the wounded men we'd been assigned to pick up. The chit that Jack Moray, our station leader, had handed to Celia before we left the ambulance station told us that there were four firemen to take to hospital, all badly wounded when a wall collapsed. Our patients were tantalisingly near, on the other side of the fire.

'Bit of a sticky wicket, this,' said Celia. Beautiful, upper-crust Celia Ashwin was acting as my attendant that night. She glanced at the chit, then back at the flames.

'What do you think?' I asked. 'Should we try to get through?'

'We *are* in the Studebaker,' she replied.

1

I knew what Celia meant. The Studebaker was a tough, reliable ambulance. If anything could take us through that wall of fire, the Studebaker could.

There were many dangers, though. The petrol tank might explode. A tyre might rupture in the heat. An unseen hazard could cause a puncture. The road was awash with water and dangerously slippery. We'd be driving blind through choking smoke. I could lose control of the ambulance and crash into a burning building.

We were both well aware of the perils we faced.

The fires around us roared like an express engine as the wind picked up, and a stream of sparks rose high into the sky and fell around the ambulance like shimmering fairy lights. Larger clumps of burning stuff, paper and rags floated past in the heated air.

'Look at that,' said Celia. She pointed to a fluttering pigeon vainly beating singed wings as it fell in a lurching descent. It landed in a puddle beside the ambulance and lay there, shuddering. Another singed pigeon soon joined it.

'Should we ask the firemen how deep they think those flames across the road are?' I suggested. 'And if the ambulance could make it through?'

Celia shook her head. 'They'll tell us not to do it. Say we're girls and it's too dangerous.'

'They may be right,' I replied.

'We're girls, certainly. But I think it's up to us to decide if it's too dangerous. I think we should risk it.'

'Ye-es,' I said, 'but you quite like danger, Celia. I've seen you take ridiculous risks.'

Celia gave me a smile. 'That was the old me. Haven't you noticed? I've changed. I'm very careful nowadays. One might even say cautious.'

'Why the change of heart?'

'I now own a parrot. The responsibility of parrot ownership makes me resist the temptation of stupid heroics.' She gave a laugh. 'And Dr Levy would be absolutely furious if I were to die stupidly, after he did so much to save my life the other day.'

'You really think we could make it through?'

'If we're fast enough.'

'So your plan – your only plan – is for me to drive through the fire really, really fast.'

She eyed the galloping flames that blocked our path and gave me a wry smile. 'The Studebaker's a good girl. She'll get us through. Back up a bit to get a run up, put your foot to the floor and go like the wind.'

It was madness to attempt it. But beyond the flames lay injured firemen. I stood in awe of the Fire Service men, who risked their lives battling the infernos, even when they knew that the light of those fires made them an easy target for high-explosive bombs. You'd swear that they never heard the bombs whistling, thudding and exploding all around them as they stood firm, directing water from hissing hoses into the heart of the fiercest blaze. They had become my exemplar of bravery. And too many had paid the ultimate price.

Not these ones, not if I could save them. I shoved the gearstick into reverse. The Studebaker complained with a shrill metallic shriek but she backed up smoothly enough. I stopped about a hundred feet from the fire we had to drive through. We hastily wound up our windows, although we knew there was no way to stop the smoke pouring in, because the box body that had been attached to the sedan had no doors, only curtains at the back.

I shoved hard on the clutch, slammed the gearstick into position and pushed the accelerator pedal down. The Studebaker took off with a roar and I saw the horrified faces of firemen as we raced past them into the conflagration.

By the time we entered the fire the accelerator pedal was flat on the floor. Thick smoke filled the cab and I prayed that the road didn't bend as I was driving blind, acting on instinct. The engine screamed its protest at the speed, the air grew hotter, the smoke thicker. Debris banged on the roof, as if demanding entry. Hot tears streamed down my cheeks from my stinging eyes. I tried to take only shallow breaths of choking air, but my protesting lungs forced me into sharp painful coughs. Then the ambulance began to slide. My heart hammered painfully as we slewed to the right. I clung to the steering wheel, twisted it in the direction of the skid and prayed. The wheels gripped tarmac and I swung the ambulance to what I hoped was the centre of the road.

And then we were through, into clear air. I eased my foot off the accelerator and slowed to a stop. I felt light, empty, shattered.

Celia grinned and squeezed my arm. 'Stout fella,' she said.

'Let's not tell Moray about this,' I replied, in a shaky voice. He would be furious that we had taken such a risk with one of our precious ambulances.

'Quite,' she said, nodding. 'He'd just say we were showing off.'

Fires raged in the narrow street, worse than those on Theobald's Road. The leaping flames at times reached twice the height of the houses they devoured and all was bright as day and hot as summer in the French Riviera. Firemen were silhouetted against the roaring red and gold, rushing around with hoses that squirmed and wriggled as they spewed futile streams of water. The men's steel helmets reflected the firelight gleam.

Celia touched my arm and pointed to a small group huddled together in the portico of what had been an ornate building but was now a burned-out shell. Some lay on the ground, others sat with their heads in their hands, or rested on the wall behind. They all looked weary and some had obvious injuries.

A warden ran up to the ambulance and peered in my window.

'By God, you're a pair of girls,' he said. 'That was brave, to drive through the fire.'

'How many casualties?' I asked.

'How many can you fit?'

'Four stretcher cases,' said Celia, in her clear upper-class voice. 'At a pinch we can squeeze in another three, if they're willing to sit on the floor between the stretchers.'

'Can you take five on the floor?' He waved behind him, towards the huddle of wounded men. 'That building is about to collapse and there's no shelter once it does. And they want to dynamite the building opposite to try to stop the fires spreading.'

Celia and I exchanged looks. 'We'll do it somehow,' she said to the warden, and pushed open her door. 'Let's go and get them.'

When I stepped out of the ambulance to join her, it was like entering a blast furnace. I mopped at the sweat on my forehead with my sleeve. Under her tin hat, Celia's face was brick red, dripping with sweat and flicked with black smuts and ash. I assumed I looked as bad.

Celia grabbed a stretcher to pull it out of its rack, gave a shrill yelp and shook her hand frantically, as if it were burnt.

'What happened?' I said.

She rolled her eyes, annoyed. 'The metal is too hot to handle. We'll need to use our sleeves as mittens.'

I pulled down the sleeves of my shirt and jumper to cover my hands and helped Celia to remove the stretcher. Even through a layer of cotton and wool, the metal was hot on my hands. We carried the stretcher to the injured men and laid it on the ground. I covered its metal frame with a blanket and we began to check our patients. A fireman groaned when I touched him. My quick examination revealed a penetrating stomach wound and quite severe burns.

'Name?' I asked. 'Address?'

His lips were tightly compressed, probably with pain, and his face was wet with perspiration, but he managed 'John Breen' and gave me an address. I wrote it on a tag that I tied to his wrist with some string. The tightness around his mouth eased as he lapsed into unconsciousness.

We lifted him gently on to the stretcher, pulled our sleeves down again and picked it up. Once Mr Breen's stretcher had been carefully slid into its rack, we got out another and went back for the next patient.

It wasn't long before all nine patients were in the ambulance. Celia sat on the floor with four men, who all had varying degrees of burns and abrasions. John Breen and the other three, more severely injured men lay on the stretchers. Our ninth patient was a big fireman called Ed Goshawk who had a broken collarbone and arm injuries along with the usual burns. He was so big that it was easier to put him beside me in the cab.

The warden looked in at my window.

'Get out of here quickly,' he said, pointing at the ruin where the men had sheltered. 'I think it'll collapse soon.'

'Will you be all right?' I asked.

'I'm getting a lift,' he said, gesturing towards a fire truck that was parked nearby. 'We'll be right behind you.'

The firemen had been working hard to reduce the fire that had blocked the roadway and the way was fairly clear. I turned the ambulance around carefully in the narrow street, put her into gear, let out the clutch, and pushed the accelerator. The Studebaker took us to Theobald's Road with the fire engine close behind.

'Are you all right in the back?' I said loudly, over my left shoulder.

'Tickety-boo,' said Celia.

The unmistakable sound of bricks crashing down competed with the noise of the flames. 'There she goes,' said Ed grimly.

What remained of the building that had sheltered them was now a pile of debris.

I turned into Southampton Row and headed for the hospital. Normally, the challenge for any ambulance driver in the Blitz was to get the casualties to hospital in the blackout, guided only by a beam of light the size of a shilling that shone through the masked headlights. Not tonight. Fires made all around us bright as daylight.

As we drove away a loud explosion tore apart the air and a cloud of dust rose over the burning rooftops.

'Dynamite, said Ed. 'Sometimes all we can do is try to stop the fire by destroying what's in its path. Seems a shame, though, for us to finish what Jerry started. Sort of like kicking an own goal.'

CHAPTER TWO

Friday 7 March 1941

When you are about to die, your past life is supposed to flash before your eyes. Only, when the car bore down on me I didn't think of my mother, or my childhood in the Sheffield slums, or my dancing career, or my months spent driving ambulances in the Blitz. Oddly enough, I wished I was wearing nicer lingerie for the trip to the mortuary. (It was clean, you understand, but much darned and rather shabby.) And I thought how stupid I was to die like this, in a road accident.

The incident was entirely my fault. I had rushed out on to Charing Cross Road without thinking, exhausted after a night when my rest had been measured in the short intervals between air raids. I knew perfectly well that road accidents in the blackout had caused thousands of deaths – I'd driven some of the injured in my ambulance – but all I had in my mind was the thought of a nice warm bed.

The squeal of brakes alerted me but there was no time to think of anything (other than my shabby underwear and my stupidity) before I was on the ground, gasping from the pain of a skinned knee and hand, and scarcely able to take in that I was alive. The car door opened and a man tumbled out to kneel beside me. He put an arm around my shoulder.

'You okay?' he said, in a clipped, anxious tone. 'Please tell me you're okay.'

I felt his sigh of relief when I shuddered and took another gasping breath.

'I'm fine,' I croaked. 'Really. Please help me to stand up.' He assisted me to my feet, keeping a firm arm around my shoulder. It was still too dark to see him clearly, but he was a couple of inches taller than me, slim, broad-shouldered and his arm was strong. As I was ridiculously shaky I leaned against him, feeling like a fool.

'Let me get you to a hospital,' he said.

'I'm fine. Really I am. The hospitals are busy enough without me pushing in with a skinned knee and hand.'

He blurted out, 'I couldn't avoid you. You appeared out of nowhere.' There was a fierce intensity in his voice. 'I tried to swerve, but there was no time.'

It was then I realised he was American.

'I'm entirely to blame,' I said, with a smile he couldn't see. 'And you didn't hit me. Actually, you must have remarkable reflexes *not* to have hit me. Well done. Jolly good. Just the ticket.' I was blathering, so I shut up and concentrated on the pain in my knee.

'I thought I hit you.'

'No, you swerved away in time. I fell down out of blind terror.' I gave a short laugh and said, 'Idiotic of me to dash out like that. Please accept my apologies.'

'You're very cool about it all. Is this an example of English phlegm?'

'I hate that word. Sounds like the symptom of a cold.'

'The Blitz spirit, then?'

I gave an unladylike snort, then smiled. 'Pure embarrassment. I was a fool to race out on to the road when it's so dark. It's this bl – I mean, stupid – blackout. I'm entirely to blame. Really, I'm fine.' I gently extracted myself from his arm and stood, still rather shaky, beside him.

'At least let me buy you breakfast. Or a cup of tea. You English always drink tea in a crisis, don't you? I've a flask of whisky in my pocket if it'd help. We could tip some hooch in the tea. You're too damned calm, actually, and I suspect you're in shock.'

Shock indeed! I know all about shock, thank you very much, Mr arrogant American, and I am not in shock. His cool assumption of authority annoyed me, but I did feel rather unsteady on my feet, and my hand and knee were burning where they'd been scraped. The thought of walking to the club without at least a short rest was daunting. So I smiled at his dark form and said, 'I'd love a cup of tea, thank you.'

In Soho there's always a tearoom or cafe open, even before eight in the morning. The little tearoom he found had just opened its doors, and he ushered me through the blackout curtain into a cheerful room filled with round tables covered by check tablecloths.

As he helped me to a chair I finally had a chance to look at him properly. Brown hair curled against the brim of his hat and his eyes were a pale icy blue. I thought he was probably in his late twenties, and also that he must have a few bob in the bank because his suit was hand-made, if I was any judge. He looked shrewd and intelligent, and attractive enough, but it seemed to me that his face was too sharp-featured to be considered really handsome – honestly, you could open an envelope with those cheekbones! Nice hands, though.

He ordered a pot of tea from the sleepy-eyed waitress, who delivered it in a brown pot and gave him a lovely smile along with it. No smile for me. As I poured, he pulled a slim flask out of his breast pocket and held it up enquiringly. I shook my head and took a sip of my tea, which was strong and reviving.

He tipped a jigger of whisky into his own cup. 'For *my* shock. And it's the only way this stuff's drinkable. I can't understand how you English quaff it like you do.'

I felt annoyed on behalf of all Britons. 'When in doubt, brew up' was getting us through this war. I couldn't survive without my tea, preferably well mashed (as we'd say in Sheffield). In other words, I preferred a very strong cup indeed. There was no point in showing my annoyance to the man. So I smiled and took another sip.

I smile a lot. Maybe I smile too much, but I got it from my mother. 'Smile,' she'd say. 'If it's bad, just smile. It'll soon be better if you don't dwell on it.' Mam died when I was sixteen, and I miss her every single day.

The American lifted his cup and saluted me. 'Here's looking at you, Miss . . ?'

'Halliday. Maisie Halliday. Thanks again for being such a good sport about this.'

'Michael Harker. And it's me who should be thanking you for being so forgiving.'

He smiled. He had a rather devastating smile. I looked down at my tea and wondered why Americans all seemed to have such good teeth. It was most unfair, really. Embarrassed, I said the first thing that came into my mind.

'We have the same initials. M. H.' I realised immediately what a stupid remark it was, and could only hope he'd put it down to shock.

He smiled again, but this time I was expecting it, and it didn't affect me in the slightest. 'What else do we have in common, do you suppose, Miss Halliday?' he said.

Now he was flirting, which annoyed me, so I replied, quite coolly, 'Nothing, I expect.' *Unless you drive ambulances and used to dance in a chorus line.* 'You're American, aren't you? Or Canadian?'

'I'm all American, Miss Halliday. Born in western Pennsylvania.'

Why did Americans always tell you what state they hailed from? Those I'd met on the French Riviera had been the same, telling me they were from Texas, or from Boston, or New York, as if it would matter to me. I'd never heard of Pennsylvania, let alone its west.

I nodded, as if I knew all about Pennsylvania, north, west, south and east. 'What brings you to wartime Britain?' I asked.

'This and that. I've been here a year now.'

'Through the Blitz?'

'Through it all.'

My grazed right hand and knee were throbbing painfully, although I was pleased that the bleeding seemed to have stopped. Both grazes needed washing and some iodine, and I needed to rest. I frowned down at my scraped knee, and at the torn and blood-stained rip in my trousers. The wounds were minor and would heal, but I only had two pairs of trousers to wear to work. Now, what had been the better pair would have a large darn right across the knee. More annoyingly, I couldn't afford to pay anyone to darn it for me. That meant I'd have to sew it up myself, and I was not a good seamstress.

'I really think that someone should look at your wounds,' he said, watching me. 'Will you let me take you to a doctor?'

'My wounds?' I laughed. 'A grazed knee and hand? Mr Harker, I'm an ambulance driver.' I pointed to my badge. 'I can take care of my very minor wounds once I get to my room.'

'An ambulance driver? Little thing like you? No wonder you're so calm about it all. How long have you been doing that? Have you been driving in the Blitz?'

He had to be flirting. No one in their right mind could call me little. I'm almost six feet tall.

'I joined the service in December thirty-nine. Yes, I've driven throughout this Blitz.' I finished my tea, and stood up, trying not to wince at the pain in my knee. 'And I really should get home or they'll worry. I apologise again for dashing out on to the road like that.'

'It's clear that you're a girl who can take care of herself,' he said, standing also and throwing some money on the table, 'but please, let me see you home safely and explain to your parents what happened.'

'It's just around the corner. And it's a boarding house.'

'Please, Miss Halliday,' he said, with another disarming smile. 'I knocked you down after all.'

'You didn't knock me down, I fell. It was my fault entirely. And I'm perfectly able to see myself home.'

I wondered why this man was making me behave so rudely, why I found him so disconcerting. Something was wrong about him, and I couldn't put my finger on what it was. Perhaps it was the half-smile that always seemed to hover over his mouth, by turns making him seem knowing, shy, rueful and ironic. Perhaps it was the annoyingly devastating full smile.

Or was it that he was American? The rich Americans on the Riviera had been like this, all chummy and egalitarian, until you realised that deep down they were just as class conscious as anyone else. As an exhibition dancer, a former chorus girl, I was never of the right class to be treated with real respect.

'Miss Halliday, my mother would tan my hide if she knew I had injured a girl and not made sure she got home safely.' This time his smile was rather calculated. 'I warn you, if you stride off on your own I'll follow you anyway.'

'I don't think I'll be striding.'

'All the more reason to let me drive you home. Please.'

I huffed out a breath. 'I'm just around the corner, not more than a hundred yards away. Driving me would be ridiculous.'

'Please, Miss Halliday, allow me to *walk* you safely home.'

He held out his arm in a mock courtly gesture. Mr Harker was clearly the sort of man who was used to getting his way. Accepting the inevitable, I put my hand on his arm.

CHAPTER THREE

We walked the little distance along Charing Cross Road towards Manette Street in the pre-dawn gloom. Foyles big bookstore still dominated the corner, although the long rows of bookshelves out the front had gone and the plate glass windows were covered with plyboard. A few small squares had been cut in them so customers could view the latest releases. In front of the shop, on Charing Cross Road, was the huge bomb crater from a raid in October. It hadn't been filled in, but a temporary bridge of metal plates had been laid across it.

'That's a big 'un,' he said, pointing at the crater. Michael Harker seemed to be in a very good mood, which I put down to knowing that I was only slightly injured and to my capitulation on the question of seeing me home.

'Everyone calls that Foyles Bridge now,' I said. 'Because of the bookshop.' A London bus bumped its way across as we watched, making the metal plates rumble and clatter.

Mr Harker nodded at Foyles as we turned into Manette Street.

'Do you like to read, Miss Halliday?' he asked.

'Yes.'

'Reading was all that kept me sane as a boy.' He didn't elaborate. 'It's a swell shop, Foyles. I'll have to visit it again soon.'

I said with a smile, 'They say that when Hitler was burning all those books in Berlin before the war, Foyles's owners wrote to him and asked him to *sell* the books to them instead.'

He laughed. 'I assume he didn't take advantage of the offer?'

'I don't think he gave them the courtesy of a reply.'

'Dashed bad manners,' he said, in a stage English accent.

I rolled my eyes. 'Apparently Foyles has stacked copies of Hitler's *Mein Kampf* in the roof instead of sandbags as protection against air raids. It's mad, of course, because the roof will go up like blazes if an incendiary gets in.'

'Sounds like a beat-up to me,' he said. 'Good publicity, though.'

'What a cynical American you are.' I smiled.

'Damn straight.' He smiled, too.

Dawn was close and a few ragged clouds drifted lazily above us. As the day lightened into a sky of clear, washed blue, Manette Street was revealed in all its shabby glory. We walked slowly, me leaning on his arm and limping slightly. The throbbing in my knee was worse, and all I wanted was to be in my room, although the thought of mounting three flights of stairs was a daunting one.

'This is a cute street,' he said.

'It's Manette Street. I'm told it's named after a character in one of Charles Dickens's novels.'

He smiled. 'Sure it is. Dr Manette in *A Tale of Two Cities*. Never thought I'd see the street he lived in.' He looked around. 'I wonder which house was his?'

'You do know he's a fictional character?'

'Dickens must have had a place in mind.' He shrugged, but I could see he was looking around with real interest. For a moment I saw the boy who had so loved to read.

We passed under the archway next to the Pillars of Hercules pub.

'Now that's a cute name for a pub,' he said. 'Old?'

'I suppose so. A couple of hundred years at least, probably. Most of the buildings around here are a few hundred years old.'

'I'm pretty sure the Pillars of Hercules is mentioned in *A Tale of Two Cities*. Have you read the book?'

'No.'

'You should. It's worth reading. All of Dickens is.'

Greek Street was its usual jumble of people and colour and noise, even so early in the morning. The colour came from the government posters that had been plastered on every available space: 'Dig for Victory', 'Beat Firebomb Fritz – Join the Fire Guard', 'Be like Dad, keep Mum – Careless Talk Costs Lives'. The scent of damp rot and bad drains provided an added piquancy to the scene.

'It's a funny place, Soho,' he said. 'Cosmopolitan. Reminds me a bit of New York.'

'I like it,' I said, looking around. Soho had many faces, from the sordid dance clubs, to the beautiful if tattered old buildings to the lush grass in Soho Square gardens. 'I lived here with my mother after we came up to London from Yorkshire, when I was twelve. It's a tolerant place. All sorts of people all get along here and I like that.'

'Isn't Yorkshire in the north?'

I nodded. 'Reyt oop north,' I said, in stage Yorkshire.

'So why do you come *up* to London from the north?'

'Because London's the centre of the world, don't you know,' I said with another smile. 'Centre of Britain, anyway. It's always *up* to London, whether you're coming from north, south, east or west Pennsylvania.'

He touched his forehead in a salute to acknowledge the hit.

My smile faded. 'It's why Hitler wants to obliterate the city.'

Directly across the road was the Theatre Girls' Club. My home. I waved towards the flat portico of the club, with its columns and curlicues.

'We're here,' I said. 'Thanks for the use of your arm, I'll leave you now.'

He was staring at the club, frowning. 'That's where you live?'

The long, rather austere building looked shabby, unkempt and uncared for. Like many of the old buildings in Greek Street, it had obviously once been rather grand, but no longer. Shrapnel and bombs had gouged out large chunks of the facade. The plaster, streaked with ash and dust, was in dire need of painting, and several windows that had shattered in a raid were covered by plyboard. Bars were set across the ground floor windows, which gave it rather a forbidding air.

'It's better inside than out,' I said.

'It'd have to be.'

'There's no need for that,' I said, annoyed. 'It's a famous London institution and, as I said, it's much nicer inside.'

'What's it called, this famous institution?' The teasing tone in his voice put my back up.

'The Theatre Girls' Club. It was set up in the twenties to help theatre girls survive among their own kind.'

'You're a theatre girl? I thought you were an ambulance driver.'

'In peacetime I'm a dancer,' I said.

'Ballet?'

We were a similar height, so I gazed straight into those icy blue eyes and smiled. 'Have you ever seen a ballet dancer who's five eleven? Before the war I was a chorus dancer. In Paris, mainly. The Folies Bergère. I was a Tiller Girl,' I added hastily, 'not a showgirl.'

I hoped he knew that the Tiller Girls had a reputation for prudishness and, unlike the showgirls, we never danced topless.

'Aren't you full of surprises. I've never met a chorus girl before.'

'Well, it's your lucky day then.'

'I'd not have picked you for one.'

'Oh, we look just like normal girls, only usually we're taller.'

'Just how old *are* you?'

'Nineteen. Nearly twenty.'

A crease appeared between his eyebrows. 'And you were dancing in France before the war?'

'Yes. I went there when I was sixteen.'

He began to say something, thought better of it, and gestured towards the club. 'Why are the windows barred? To keep men out or young theatre girls in?'

'Apparently they were put in last century, well before the club was even thought of.' My voice was huffy. I moderated my tone and smiled. 'Thank you again for seeing me home.'

'That's it?'

'What were you expecting?'

A rather odd expression flickered over his face, almost wistful. Then he grinned. 'Absolutely nothing. It's been nice meeting you, Maisie Halliday. I couldn't have knocked down a better girl.'

'You didn't—'

'And I sure hope I get to see you high-stepping in the chorus one day.'

With that he turned and walked away.

Later that day a parcel arrived from Foyles bookstore. A beautiful leather-bound edition of *A Tale of Two Cities*. On the fly leaf he'd inscribed, 'To the nicest chorus girl I've ever knocked over.' A card was tucked inside, with his name, Z. Michael Harker, and an address in Washington DC. No London address or telephone number. I wondered what the Z stood for, and looked at the card for a moment or two. Then I tore it up. It was no use to me. Mr Harker lived in America, and I was unlikely ever to see him again.

I went to the window. London was spread out before me, hazy and serene in the late afternoon light. The serenity would be fleeting; I knew that the night would bring ruin and devastation. Again my thoughts turned to Michael Harker, who had not thought I looked like a chorus girl, and whom I had found so annoying, although he'd done nothing but behave like a gentleman towards me.

It was then I realised why I was annoyed, and I laughed at myself. I expected men to behave in a certain way around me and he had not done so. Michael Harker had not flirted with me, not really. He had sent me a book, not flowers. He hadn't written the usual things on his card, begging me to see him again, telling me how lovely I was, suggesting dinner, as the men had done when I was dancing in Paris. If he had, I wouldn't have taken up his invitation – I never accepted those sort of invitations from chance-met admirers – but he had not behaved in the way I expected. If anything, Michael Harker had treated me like a younger sister, and it rankled.

I thought about it. He'd seen me in my ambulance outfit, which was filthy after a long shift, and did not make the most of my attributes. My face was pretty enough, nothing to write home about, but my 'vital statistics' were 36-22-35 and men usually took notice of *them*.

I stayed up late reading *A Tale of Two Cities*. I loved it. Which, perversely, made me all the more annoyed with Michael Harker.

CHAPTER FOUR

It was chilly with low clouds and some fog when I set out to walk to the ambulance station the following morning. Dark, too, so I had to watch where I put my feet on the cracked pavements. I moved a little gingerly, still slightly the worse for wear, but certainly not *hors de combat*. After six months of seeing how badly wounded a human being can be and still 'carry on', now I just carried on no matter how badly I felt.

I found myself thinking again about Michael Harker as I walked down Manette Street with only the light of my masked torch for company and I smiled to remember his boyish excitement at wondering which house was Dr Manette's. It was silly to think of him, I told myself, because I was unlikely ever to meet the man again. But how could I not think about an attractive man who had knocked me down and then sent me a book? Mr Z. Michael Harker was out of the ordinary, and that meant he was interesting. And not a man for me, I told myself firmly.

It was a good mile from Soho to the Bloomsbury Ambulance Station, and I walked the route six times a week. We'd moved to alternate twenty-four-hour shifts in the New Year so that under the present roster I worked from seven-thirty each Sunday, Tuesday, and Thursday morning until the same time the following day, with Saturdays off. That meant I had a very welcome weekend break from Friday morning until Sunday morning.

My route took me along Charing Cross Road (which I crossed with extra care), to Bedford Square, where the garden looked oddly naked without its railings. The massive shape of the British Museum soon loomed up on my right. So far the museum, with its treasures of objects and books, had escaped serious damage. The darkness that was Russell Square garden, also minus railings, soon took shape ahead of me. I marched around it to Woburn Place and down into the ambulance station.

Like most London County Council auxiliary ambulance stations in London, the Bloomsbury Auxiliary Ambulance Station (Station 11) was located in a garage. Ours was in the basement of a large block of flats, called Woburn Place. I'd been told that, before the war, the serviced apartments had housed mainly single young men who took advantage of the maid service and restaurant. Now, like so many other large buildings, the flats had been taken over by the government to house servicemen in London. We'd see the young men coming and going. They seemed to be mostly Polish, with some Czechs and Free French thrown in.

My grazed knee complained as I walked down into the garage. As I descended our vehicles came into sight, lined up in a row facing the ramp to the street so that we could be out on the road as quickly as possible in a call-out. One of the saloon cars was missing, which meant that the driver must be finishing a job. If you were on a job when your shift finished at seven-thirty, you just kept on going (and never expected overtime). The other saloon was there beside the three grey-painted ambulances.

The auxiliary ambulances could be anything from an old converted delivery van to a grey wooden box mounted on a saloon chassis. Inside each were racks for four stretchers. Grubby canvas curtains were the rear doors.

That morning, the drivers and attendants from the previous shift were buzzing around, working hard to make sure that their vehicles were left shipshape and Bristol fashion for the shift to come. I had just raised my hand to acknowledge a wave from one of them when I heard a soft toot. I turned to see a large Bentley saloon rolling down the ramp behind me. It was one of the two donated vehicles used to transport walking (or sitting) wounded. It was me or the car, so I pressed myself hard against the wall and its impressive bulk rolled past me into the garage. Sally Calder, who was driving, gave me a wave as she went by with only an inch to spare.

The garage exuded its usual smell of wet cement, petrol and oil. All of the vehicles lined up in front of me looked the worse for wear after six months of pummelling by shrapnel and bomb debris, but we'd had no major breakdowns, possibly because we were required to drive them no faster than sixteen miles per hour. This was infuriating when we had badly injured to get to hospital, but frustratingly necessary given the state of the roads, and heaven help the driver who came back with a puncture!

When I joined the station during the Phony War, some wag had dubbed us the 'Blinking Amateur Ambulance Station'. In those days, people used to laugh at us and call out insults when we practised bandaging and stretcher-bearing in the streets. It was true that most of us had to learn on the job, but no one could have called us amateurs after a couple of weeks of the Blitz. The insults stopped once the bombs began to fall.

Celia or I usually drove the reliable old Studebaker, which was a saloon car with a box van body welded to the back. It vied with one of the Fords (usually referred to as 'the monster') for most uncomfortable vehicle to ride in, but we were used to it now. At present, it was unattended, so I walked over to it and checked in the back. I was pleased to see that whoever had been the last attendant had cleaned it carefully and left it fully equipped with bandages and blankets. Reassured, I turned to see Celia free-wheeling down the ramp on her bicycle. I gave her a wave and climbed the stairs to the common room.

Our common room was just above the garage and it was where we relaxed while waiting for the call-out to an incident. In the centre of the room stood a large deal table and some upright chairs. More comfortable chairs were dotted around, along with low tables. Sandbags lined the wall closest to the street and partitioning at the far end formed the station leader's office and a store room. In the office was the all-important telephone, where the station leader took down the details of the incidents we had to attend. Our shift's station leader was Jack Moray, a dark-haired man in his late thirties with a wolfish smile. I liked Moray. He was sensible, practical and brave. Who could ask for more in a station leader?

On another wall of the common room hung a large map of London and a larger map of the West End; these were dotted with pins to show the location of incidents, detours, UXBs, and anything else we needed to know before setting off into bomb-altered London. A board hanging near the maps contained a list of the vehicles in the garage. Moray had chalked up beside these the names of those who had been allocated each machine for the shift. When I checked, as I'd expected, he'd chalked me up as attendant to Celia as driver, in the old Studebaker.

Over the past year and a half the common room had become more comfortable, but we didn't spend much of our time there. If there were no incidents to attend, Moray kept us busy. We were expected to make sure that the vehicles were in tip-top condition, and if they were, to spend time cleaning the station or keeping up to date with our first-aid skills. But we were often out of the station. There were always jobs to do in the daytime, even now that daylight bombing had almost ceased. Sometimes we were sent out to deliver supplies to hospitals, or collect road accident victims. Another task was picking up bodies or body parts from incidents and taking them to the nearest mortuary. That was a sombre, thankless task and one I hated.

I entered the common room to find my colleagues, George Squire, Stephen Armstrong, Sam Sadler and Myra Harris in there. They sang out greetings to me. There were supposed to be ten in our shift, including the station leader, but at the moment it was five men and four women, because Sally Calder had moved to another shift. Rupert Purvis and Doris Powell were absent and I assumed they had not arrived yet.

'Care for a cup of tea?' asked Harris.

'Yes, please.'

She poured me a cup from the large pot on the table in front of her. Harris was a volunteer, a grandmother in her fifties, who was brusquely efficient and knitted through the worst that Hitler threw at us. I doubt she ever dropped a stitch, no matter how intense the bombing. She could be gruff and managing, but she was also motherly and looked after the group in her own way.

I sat at the table and took a sip of tea. Through the sliding window into the office, I saw Jack Moray on the telephone. He looked up and nodded a greeting at me.

'Just how tall are you, Halliday?' asked Sadler. He gave me a cheeky smile. 'If you don't mind such an impertinent question.'

Sam Sadler was also a volunteer; he was in his mid-forties, a cockney spiv who was a band leader in a small nightclub in Soho. He was also the source of our black-market goods. I'd not liked him at all when I first came to the station, when he'd been very pally with a nasty little man called Fred Knaggs, who'd later been gaoled for looting. I'd heard that Moray had told Sadler if he didn't improve his attitude he'd be sent somewhere much worse than Bloomsbury. Since then Sadler seemed to have become less annoying, more a part of the team. When waiting for a call-out he played innumerable games of patience with a tatty old pack of cards he kept in his pocket, or tried to engage the others in what he called 'just a little wager between friends'.

'Not at all,' I said. 'Five eleven and a half.'

'You're sure it's not the full six foot?'

I shook my head. 'The half-inch makes all the difference. Why?'

'Had a little wager on it with the boys.'

I couldn't help a laugh. 'Who won?'

'Me,' said George Squire. 'It was just a friendly wager – in sixpences. I judged you at a smidge under eighteen hands. I knows me horseflesh, but I had to imagine you sideways.'

I wasn't sure how to take that. I opted for a smile because I liked Squire. He was a tough old former boxer who'd been bombed out of three houses and tended to spend raids humming songs under his breath, often Gilbert and Sullivan.

'Hey, Maisie,' said Stephen Armstrong, 'remember how you thought up a rhyme, after that big fire in the City in January?'

At seventeen, Armstrong was the baby of the Bloomsbury station and would be called up once he turned eighteen later in the year. The boy had found it hard to cope with the job at first, but hardened up as the Blitz went on, and I knew that Squire looked after him when he could.

'Yes. I made it up because they called it the Second Great Fire of London.'

'Well, here's one I've thought up.' He gave me a smile and began to sing to the tune of 'Oranges and Lemons':

Spitfires and Blenheims, say the bells of St Clements,
Cost more than five farthings, say the bells of St Martin's.
Keep'em flying, I pray ye, say the bells of Old Bailey,
All through London's Blitz, say the bells of Shoreditch.
Downhearted? Not we, say the bells of Stepney,
For we'll win, don't you know, says the great bell of Bow.

He finished with a deep bass, singing the last word in a note down near his ankles.

'That's the stuff,' I said, laughing. 'You should send it to the papers. They might give you something for it.'

'What about the last lines of that nursery rhyme?' said Sadler with a nasty smile. 'You know, the bit that goes, "here comes a candle to light you to bed and here comes the chopper to chop off yer head". My kids liked that bit best.' He made a chopping movement with his hand.

He was right, of course. That was always the best part of the game, running around trying to avoid the 'chopper' on your neck and screaming as it came down. But once you'd seen real decapitated heads – and we all had – it no longer seemed right to laugh about them.

Armstrong looked uncomfortable, but Sadler persisted, saying, 'This is a good one: *Here come a few flares to light you to bed, and here come's a parachute bomb to blast off yer head.'*

I saw Armstrong wince, and jumped in. 'Ugh,' I said. 'A bit too close to home, I think. This'll do: *Here comes a Warden to light you to bed, and into the shelter you go now, he said.'*

'That's much better,' said Harris, looking up from her knitting. Armstrong smiled at me, and blushed when I smiled back at him. He often blushed when Celia or I looked at him.

Sadler laughed at me. 'Yer an old softie, Halliday.'

'Good morning, everyone,' said Celia as she entered the room. She was greeted with smiles and nods.

Celia was an 'Honourable' former debutante, twenty-two and supremely self-assured. Also quite remarkably beautiful, with a mass of copper-beech red hair, dark blue eyes and an alabaster complexion. She was married to one of Britain's most notorious fascists, Cedric Ashwin, but they were estranged and I'd heard she wanted to divorce him.

When I first met Celia I'd had my doubts about her because I thought her stuck-up and rather cold. Everything had changed in the new year after she had been buried for hours in the cellar of a bombed house. Since then she had laughed more and was friendlier.

Newspapers loved to print feature articles about female Air Raid Precaution workers such as ambulance drivers, complete with pictures of the more glamorous ones. Celia and I had appeared in the *Evening Standard* last September. They made much of her posh upbringing and my dancing. In the photographs I had to show a bit of leg while she pretended to put on her lipstick. It was all for the war effort, so we didn't mind. Well, I didn't mind and Celia gritted her teeth and got on with it.

26

The article described us as 'latter-day Florence Nightingales' and said that we were only two of 'the lovely Bloomsbury Ambulance Girls'. That made me laugh, because at nineteen I was probably the only one of the women in my shift who could honestly be called a girl.

The door opened. Rupert Purvis and Doris Powell came into the room.

Rupert Purvis was a conscientious objector, an intellectual and also an artist who always seemed to have a sketchbook and pencil in his hand. He affected a Bohemian look. His hair was longer than was usual, he sported a beard and wore a cravat rather than a tie. He had a bit of a 'thing' for me, which I did not encourage.

Harris poured him a cup of tea and he thanked her with a smile.

Doris Powell was a housewife in her forties and a seemingly never-ending source of the most ridiculous gossip. She had a snub nose, a sweet expression and curly brown hair rapidly turning to grey. I liked Doris, whose snippets of Careless Talk usually made me laugh and were entirely harmless.

Doris Powell and Myra Harris were volunteers, but Celia Ashwin and I were employees and earned a weekly wage of £2 3s. It was little enough to live on, but I was used to making do on not much and I still managed to send a small sum to my grandparents in Sheffield each week.

I looked at the people around me and smiled. We had become a tight crew, tempered by the fire of the Blitz, but we were an extremely mixed bag indeed. We ranged in age from seventeen to sixty-four and came from all social classes: chorus girl, debutante, boxer, spiv, schoolboy, bank clerk, housewife, grandmother and artist. Despite that, we worked well together. I was happy to be a part of the team.

I plodded home after my shift early the following morning, looking forward to a long nap in my top-floor bedroom. As I had told Michael Harker, the Theatre Girls' Club was a boarding house in one of those enormous old buildings in Greek Street, Soho. It had been set up in the twenties for young dancers and actresses by a former chorus girl who married well.

That morning I was especially careful when I crossed Charing Cross Road, but there were no big black cars waiting to nearly run me down. My mild disappointment annoyed me and I strode on quickly until I reached the club. Once there I pushed hard on the doorbell and heard it echoing inside. A minute or so later, the door was opened by Millie, our maid, who was holding a grubby polishing rag. She was Irish, like most of the maids in London at the moment, because the Irish Republic was neutral and there was no fear of them being called up or volunteering to join one of the services.

'Good morning, Miss,' she said in her thick accent. 'Not so bad, last night, was it? Only one alert, and two hours in the practice room.' She grinned. 'Miss Lorna sang to us, and it was grand.'

The practice room, now heavily sandbagged, was in the basement and we used it as an air-raid shelter. It was quite a jolly place during a raid, as it had an upright piano and as Millie had said, we'd all try to sing through the noise of the planes and guns and bombs. *Barres* had been placed around the room for the dancers, but the long mirrors that had covered all the walls before the war had been removed in case they shattered in a raid.

Every day I wasn't on duty, I practised my dance steps and stretched in front of the only long mirror that remained. (It was laid face-down on the floor when there was a raid). I was determined to keep myself limber because I fully intended to return to France and the dancing life after the war was over.

'Lucky you,' I said, as she let me into the wide hallway. From the dining room came the smell of toast and bacon, and the noise of nineteen girls eating breakfast. The club's enormous kitchen was on the ground floor as was the dining room.

'Miss King thinks we're due for a big one any day now,' said Millie. There was excitement in her voice. Millie had come over from Cork only a couple of weeks before and air raids were still a novelty to her.

'Hope she's wrong,' I said, smiling, and I began the long trek upstairs to my room on the top floor.

Although the club was kept scrupulously clean, the corridors always smelled of overcooked cabbage, perhaps because overcooked cabbage seemed to be served at every meal. It was lucky for me that the Ambulance Service had put in a canteen at the Bloomsbury station once we went to twenty-four-hour shifts. I only had to eat at the club every second day. It was a glorious thing, not to be too dependent on the cooking of Mrs Mears.

The club was not palatial by any means, but it was clean and affordable. My weekly pound gave me the narrowest bed that could be called a bed, a thin mattress, much-darned sheets and two threadbare blankets in a room on the top floor, just under the roof garden and chapel. Although my room had three beds in it I didn't have a room-mate, because very few girls were willing to sleep so close to heaven (in every sense) during the Blitz.

I plodded up to the first floor. It contained the large drawing room, which was now our common room, along with the office and bedroom of the housekeeper, Miss Edith King.

I turned at the landing and dragged myself up another flight to the dormitory floor. This was where most of the girls slept, in cubicles divided off from one another by cretonne curtains. They called them their 'horse-boxes', but in reality they were very snug and good for gossipy companionship.

The stairs became narrower. They took me to the third floor and my bedroom. I loved my room. It was the first time I'd ever had a room to myself and I was able to spread out all my things and really relax in my time off. I even had a view, over Charing

Cross Road to the pretty spire of St Giles-in-the-Fields, the one they call the Poets' Church.

The only real disadvantage to living there was that the club's housekeeper, Miss King, was so terribly strict about keeping the rules of the club. The number one rule, and the one most stringently enforced, was NO MEN ABOVE THE FIRST FLOOR. Male friends could be entertained only in the common room, where they were in sight and earshot of everyone else in the club. If a girl was caught with a male upstairs then she was turfed out on her ear, presumably because such an infraction proved that she was a bad influence on the other girls. That rule wasn't the worry, because I'd sworn off men for the duration.

But another rule was that, unless Miss King had allowed you possession of the 'late key' – which she did only if you had a very good reason indeed – you had to be back by eleven each night. This meant that if a girl was away from the club when a raid started, she had to spend the night in a shelter, or wherever she could find a bed.

You'd think that the 'in by eleven' rule would be relaxed in the middle of a Blitz, but no. To Miss King, a rule was a rule. She personally locked the doors each night at eleven on the dot, and unless you could shimmy up a drainpipe – which some girls could, and did – or you had a friend waiting downstairs, hiding in the darkness and ready to unlock the door at a soft knock, then you were out for the night.

At last I reached my room. The blackout blinds were still up, so it was quite dark in there. The door clicked shut behind me and I sat on the bed, wondering if I really did need to wash and change into pyjamas or I could go to bed in my underwear, as I was.

Mam had always insisted that I wash before going to bed. 'I don't care how tired you are, Maisie,' she would say. 'At a pinch – but only at a pinch, mind you – a tired girl can skip washing her face. But if she doesn't brush her hair, wash her feet and wash *down there* before she goes to bed, then she has no self-respect.'

'Yes, Mam,' I murmured.

I got up, washed, changed into my pyjamas, brushed my long black hair and crawled into bed. Thoughts of the day grew dim, I closed my eyes and fell into velvety darkness.

CHAPTER FIVE

Saturday 9 March 1941

It was seven o'clock on a Saturday night and I was determined to go out. So I dressed, made up my face, fixed my hair and left my room. As I descended, the chatter and laughter of the other girls increased in volume with each step down. When it was busy, the club housed up to forty girls. At present there were only twenty of us, but twenty young women could make a lot of noise. It sounded like a flock of exotic birds had descended on the common room, and I suspected that it wouldn't be long before Miss King put a stop to the racket.

Sure enough, her strident voice rang out. 'Girls, please. You sound like a band of wild monkeys in the jungle. Quiet, please.' The volume of noise ceased suddenly, as if a radio had been turned down.

Miss King emerged from the common room with a triumphant expression as I reached the first floor. She had been in charge of the club for almost twenty years, and was a tall, spare woman in her early fifties. Her fair hair, now fading to grey, was regularly subjected to an expensive permanent wave that set it in rigid curls. As usual, she was beautifully dressed. That evening it was a dove grey suit over a cream silk blouse. She smiled when she saw me.

'Going out, Maisie?'

'I'm off to the cinema.'

Miss King shook her head and I watched, fascinated, as not one of the curls moved even slightly. 'You really should stay in,' she said. 'There'll be a raid tonight.'

'Oh, Hitler's too busy in the Balkans to bother with us.'

'We've clear skies and the moon's nearly full,' she said darkly. 'There hasn't been a really bad raid since January and we're due one. They'll be over, and bombs will fall.' Again she shook her head and again the curls obediently stayed put. 'You should know better, in your line of work, than to venture out on a night like this. If you're not careful you'll end up being carted off in one of your own ambulances.'

I said, in mock seriousness, 'Oh, no. The Soho station near Leicester Square picks up wounded from around here. My station's in Bloomsbury, remember, near Russell Square.'

'No need to be cheeky. You know what I mean.'

'I won't stay out long,' I replied, laughing. 'Promise.'

'Much better to stay in and listen to the wireless. If there's a raid you'll be nice and safe in the practice room.'

'It's Saturday night and I want to feel that the Luftwaffe doesn't rule my life. Anyway, the new John Wayne is on at the Odeon.'

'I saw it yesterday,' she said, 'and it's very enjoyable, even if that Marlene Dietrich is in it. I don't approve of her, not really. She's a German.'

Miss King tended towards the 'all Germans are bad, always' way of thinking.

'She's American, now,' I said. 'And has spoken up against Hitler.'

'Hmm. It's easy to say it. She could be a spy.' Miss King's face lightened. ' I like John Wayne, though. He's a *real* man.'

'Who is?' Lorna Gaskin burst out of the common room followed by a gust of laughter. Lorna was small and round with a halo of blonde curls and had the singing voice of an angel.

'John Wayne, apparently,' I said.

'Ooh, I like him,' she said. 'He's lovely. So manly.' She gave me an appraising look I knew all too well. I braced myself. 'Man like that'd be just the ticket for a girl like you. He's lovely and tall.'

'John Waynes are thin on the ground in London right now,' I said lightly, pushing thoughts of Michael Harker out of my head.

'You'll never know if you don't look,' said Lorna. 'London's full of men in uniforms from all over the world, all of them after a good time. Any girl with any sort of good looks can have the time of her life. And you've got the looks, Maisie.'

'Honestly,' I said, 'I'm not interested in a boyfriend, whether he's tall or short, American, English or – or Zulu. I really don't know why you lot are so obsessed with men, when all you do is complain about your blokes and how awfully they treat you.'

She grinned. 'And we keep coming back for more, don't we? If you do meet John Wayne, ask if he has a friend. I dote on Yanks. Not that I've met any, but they seem lovely in the movies.'

I shook my head in mock exasperation. 'Don't hold your breath. I work twenty-four-hour shifts, remember. Any men I meet tend to need bandaging.'

'What about that Mr Purvis from your station?' said Miss King. 'The one who took you dancing at the Trocadero. He seemed nice enough.'

I shook my head. 'We only went there to help out a friend. It wasn't a date. I don't like him like that. And anyway, Rupert's too old for me. He's thirty-five if he's a day.'

'That old?' said Lorna. 'Still—'

'There'll be time for romance when this is all over,' I broke in, but smiled at her persistence. 'I've seen too many girls left heart-broken when their fellow is killed. It's a mug's game, falling in love during a war. And I'm no mug.'

'Well, you must be the only girl in London who thinks that way,' said Miss King.

'Thinks what way?' Bobbie Davis had come upstairs from the practice room. A dancer like me, only six inches shorter, she was dressed in a leotard and ballet pumps and had a towel wrapped around her neck.

'That she doesn't need romance in her life,' said Lorna.

'No one really *needs* romance, but it's fun,' said Bobbie. 'So many men around now, so handsome in their uniforms.'

With infinite grace, she raised her arms in a stretch, then put her slippered leg straight up against the wall and leaned against it, ignoring Miss King's frown. I knew how good it felt to push into such a deep stretch after dance practice, when muscles were tired but loose, and I ached to join her.

'I'm off to dinner and dancing tonight with a dashing Free French Officer,' she said, as she swapped legs. 'The trick is not to take any of it too seriously.'

'Take your leg off the wall, Bobbie. Right now, if you please!' Miss King's tone was sharp.

In a leisurely fashion, Bobbie stood upright, then bent from the waist into another long and graceful stretch. 'You should find a fellow and join me and the Frog,' she said, from somewhere near the floor. 'It's just a night out, no need to be serious.'

'That's what I keep telling her,' said Lorna.

'Telling who what?' Jill Peterson – a slim brunette dancer with a cheeky grin – entered the hall from the common room. She was munching on an apple, so her voice was muffled.

'Telling Maisie to enjoy herself and not worry so much,' said Lorna.

Jill swallowed her mouthful of apple. She opened her eyes very wide and said earnestly, 'That's so true.'

'I'm going out tonight with a Dutch sailor,' said Lorna. 'He's a mechanic on a ship and ever so nice and tall with lovely blue eyes. Some of those Dutchmen are quite handsome, Maisie. I could phone him, see if he has a friend.'

I shook my head. 'Thanks, but no. I'm going to the movies.'

'Alone?' Her face was a picture of horrified surprise.

'Yes, alone. I like going alone.'

'I hate going alone to the movies. I'm sure that everyone is thinking I'm there because I couldn't find a man to take me.'

Bobbie laughed. 'Even dressed like that, no one would think that Maisie couldn't find a man to take her to the movies.'

I turned on her. 'What's the matter with how I'm dressed?'

She looked me up and down. 'Slacks, sweater, jacket, brogues. Not exactly glamorous.'

Ellie Kavanagh appeared. 'Well, *I'm* off to the Café de Paris with Raymond and his best friend and his best friend's new girlfriend,' she said, her eyes shining. 'I can't wait to see the place. It's supposed to be a dream.'

Ellie was a young dancer from Birmingham, who had been at the club for six months. Her boyfriend was a Canadian soldier.

'Lucky you,' I said.

The Café de Paris was a sumptuous subterranean haven, a nightclub and restaurant with crooners, cocktails, chorus dancers and swing bands. The clientele might not be quite as select as it had been before the war – uniforms were a great social leveller – but it was still the place where the smart set chose to go for a good night out, to dance till dawn and forget about the war.

'I love that place,' said Bobbie. 'I don't know how, but somehow, the men all seem extraordinarily handsome down there.'

'And the young women all so very beautiful?' I replied, tongue in cheek.

'Absolutely. Oh, the evening gowns the women wear in that place! And fur coats, too. They're simply to die for.'

Ellie smiled at me. 'Want me to see if there's a spare Canadian? You could come too?'

I shook my head.

'Are you sure?' she said, and smiled at Miss King. 'I have the night key, because it's such a special occasion.'

Lorna chimed in again. 'No one knows if they're going to be alive tomorrow, so why not take your fun whenever you can?'

'Fun? Who's having fun? Tell *all*.' Pru Hort came bounding up the stairs from the practice room, followed by Esther Jacob. Pru was an actress with ENSA, the Entertainments National Services Association, that put on shows for the troops. It was affectionately known as 'Every Night Something Awful'.

'What fun is Maisie taking, please?' asked Esther in her broken English. A Jewish refugee from Poland, Esther was a ballet dancer with huge dark eyes and a ravaged face that belied her cheerful disposition.

'None!' I said, laughing. 'This place is a madhouse. Goodbye all, I'm off to the flicks. Alone.' I fled down the stairs before anyone could reply.

Miss King's voice floated after me. 'Please be careful, Maisie dear, and be sure to go to a shelter when the raid starts. Leicester Square if you can. It's always safer underground, remember.'

'If there's a raid, I'll try to get there,' I shouted back. I knew that being underground was not necessarily safer in a raid – I'd helped with the injured after the Bank underground station disaster, when a bomb exploded on the concourse – but there was no point in mentioning it to her. Besides, Leicester Square station was probably safer than most places.

With the never-ending summer time the sun was still up when I stepped out on to Greek Street, even at seven o'clock in early March. Sunset was near, though. As daylight faded, the blueness above paled into a clear bleached brightness and a chalky circle was high in the sky. It would be a full moon tonight and I suspected that Miss King was right about the raid. German planes still came over London nearly every night to drop incendiaries and bombs, but the last really bad raid had been in January. We were due for a big one.

I walked slowly along Greek Street, dodging the crowds who were trying to get home or get to shelter before the blackout was in force. The street walkers were out, whispering suggestively to passing men, or calling out from windows and doorways or jangling keys to draw the attention of potential clients. Some were dressed to the nines in black-market finery – those were the affluent ones, who kept flats – but most who walked the streets rented rooms by the hour when they were needed or popped into a vacant shelter.

I had come to know most of the prostitutes on Greek Street by sight, and occasionally stopped for a chat with them if their business was slow, especially in the mornings when I was returning to the club after my shift. Apparently the blackout had been a boon to them.

'It's this Blitz,' one had told me last week. 'Gets the punters excited, not knowing if they'll be killed by a bomb tomorrow. And it's all secret doings in the blackout, you can get up to just about anything. Some of them shelters are real comfortable.'

A little further along Greek Street I heard a voice I recognised. Edna was trying her luck at her usual patch, just outside the old Prince of Wales Theatre. I liked Edna and I felt sorry for her. She'd been an actress once, and could tell a fine story or two about her time treading the boards in the Music Halls in the twenties. But gin and poverty had taken their toll and now she walked the Soho streets. Poor Edna, she'd developed a cough over winter and it was lingering.

'How about it, love?' Her voice was high and wheedling, and ended in a cough. 'For a fiver I could take you to heaven.'

Her man wasn't interested, and walked off quickly. I gave her a wave as I walked past.

'That you, Maisie love? I think we'll have a raid tonight – so you be sure to take cover.'

'I will,' I said, and walked on.

I had a firm suspicion that something about me said I was motherless, because older women always seemed to want to look out for me. Younger women often saw me as a potential rival, which was annoying.

Daylight faded quickly. I took my pencil torch out of my handbag but didn't switch it on right away because it was easy enough to navigate using the white stripes that had been painted on kerbs, fire hydrants, lamp-posts, steps, anything that could be stumbled over in the dark.

Londoners had been told to wear something white in the blackout to help prevent road accidents. People smarter than me had sewn white bands and patches on the sleeves, legs and shoulders of their coats, even on the brims of hats. Tonight my 'something white' was a pale pink scarf around my neck. I was not intending to be knocked over by an attractive American again.

The sandbagged entrance to the cinema was just off Piccadilly Circus. I paid my one and nine pence and the usherette led me to a seat. There I sat comfortably enough in the warm fug of cigarette smoke, human bodies and cheap perfume. After the cartoon the newsreel began. We were informed that the Italians were busy invading Albania, but they were being harassed by the Greek air force and by the RAF – loud cheers from the crowd at the sight of Spitfires and Hurricanes sending enemy planes crashing to earth. The scene shifted to Somaliland, where the Italians were frantically withdrawing. We had taken over nine thousand Italian prisoners and there were loud jeers and whistles at pictures of a few bored Tommies guarding long lines of Italian prisoners in the desert. Some of the Italians looked dejected, but others grinned at the camera.

'Bet they think they're well out of it,' a woman beside me whispered.

'I bet they do,' I whispered back. As I did so I pondered how things had changed since the Blitz began. People talked to strangers now, which had never happened in London before the war.

'Well, I hope all those I-tye prisoners stay in Africa,' said the man next to her. 'How can we feed them when there's hardly anything for ourselves?'

The Warning went, the awful warbling-like sound that reminded me of a howling wolf. A collective groan sounded, and the man sitting behind me said, 'Old Wailing Winnie sounds just like the wife when she can't find her teeth in the morning.' A few people laughed.

There was another groan when the usual sign flashed on the screen: 'An Air Raid Warning has just been sounded. If you wish to leave, walk, do not run, to the exits. Do not panic. Remember, you are British! Those who wish to remain may do so at their own risk. The film now continues.'

In six months of Blitz I had never known anyone to panic. The usual feeling seemed to be one of resigned annoyance.

'Bloody Hitler. Can't even let us watch a picture in peace.'

'I hope we're hitting Berlin just as hard.'

'He's a sheeny beggar, awright, that Hitler.' My heart beat a little faster, because that accent was one out of my childhood in the city built on seven hills. (I mean Sheffield, of course, not Rome.) 'He can't bide us hitting Berlin, so he keeps on at London.'

'Aye,' agreed her companion.

For the first time in a while I felt homesick. That brought thoughts of my mother. Tears gathered, but I blinked them away.

No one moved. Londoners had long since given up exiting on the Warning alone. Not until we knew that the raiders were directly overhead would we consider taking shelter. I decided to stay put. Eventually the siren ceased. The message on the screen disappeared and the newsreel began again, followed by a short Ministry of Information film about the need to check your home for salvageable rubbish, and a longer Crown Film Unit production about the dangers of Careless Talk. Finally the credits for the feature appeared. Around me people settled down in their seats to watch.

The cinema rocked like a boat on a stormy sea as bombs fell around us. John Wayne fell in love with a sexy cabaret singer on a South Sea island and risked both his naval career and his life for her. He was handsome, I thought. He looked nothing like Michael Harker.

Or only a little bit.

Not much at all, really.

CHAPTER SIX

Like everyone else, I stayed to see the National Anthem played to the end, and then pushed outside with the crowd.

The night sky was lit up with the criss-crossing beams of searchlights, but the sound of aeroplane engines had faded, and the crump of bombs was now faint and far away. Somewhere nearby a fire was raging, turning the darkness to pink and then blood red. The All Clear sounded.

What with the moonlight, searchlights and firelight I could clearly see the faces around me. There was still defiance in most eyes, but more and more I was seeing a dreary sort of resignation. Londoners accepted that they were on the front line in this war, but they didn't like it. I was beginning to worry that their bravado was wearing thin. But then, how could it endure month after month after month of constant bombardment?

Londoners had developed a devil-may-care sort of fatalism. 'If it's got my name on it, then I'm a gonner no matter what,' was often heard. Many people were no longer going to the shelters, trusting that in a city as big and populous as London, someone else would 'get it' instead of them.

The people who pushed past me tonight would tomorrow plod to work through streets strewn with broken glass. They'd hear the mournful thud of army engineers' demolition charges, as dangerously teetering structures were levelled. They would pass by what remained of ancient buildings that had withstood the last Great Fire in 1666, buildings that were now reduced to rubble by German high-explosive bombs, or burned to ashes in incendiary attacks or destroyed by our own engineers.

Perhaps they'd ponder how much London was changing before their eyes. Did it sadden them or anger them that so much of the city of their childhood was now gone? How would I would feel, I wondered, if I were to return to Sheffield after all this time and see a pile of broken bricks where the Marples Hotel – that grand landmark of my childhood – had stood in Fitzalan Square. I'd heard that it had been utterly destroyed in the Sheffield Blitz of the twelfth of December.

More important than buildings, though, were Londoners themselves. Familiar faces would be missing at bus stops tomorrow and there would be vacant chairs at workplaces. Every time you said goodbye to a friend or colleague you had to accept the possibility that it might be the last time you saw them. I remembered how the girls had teased me about my non-existent love life and gave a small, grim smile. It would be a mug's game indeed to fall in love in a time of such uncertainty.

Shaking off such morbid thoughts I continued along Coventry Street. Above me the sky was tremulous with the glow of fires. The footpath was much less crowded than when I had gone to the cinema, which was not surprising, but a fair number of people had emerged from shelters on to the streets.

As it was some time yet until the eleven o'clock lockout at the club, I thought I'd go to the Lyon's Corner House for a cup of tea and a treat. It was next to the Rialto Cinema and the entrance to the glittering Café de Paris nightclub, not more than a few minutes' walk away. I knew that Corner House well. It was where my mother had worked after we came to London. I think Mam had enjoyed working as a Nippy, or at least she had told me that it was a pleasant change from the steel factory in Sheffield. The Corner House had been bombed back in October, but it had opened again two weeks ago and I wanted to see how it was doing.

The street was strewn with the usual after-air-raid mess. I stepped across bits of barrage balloons and shrapnel and dodged the piles of sand that had sprung up like molehills all over the footpath and on the road. Under each pile was a smothered incendiary bomb. The sand had been taken from the sandbags that surrounded nearly every lamp-post. Not all fires had been successfully extinguished, because somewhere not far away, an inferno was raging. Firelight coloured the scene in flickering shades ranging from pink to blood red, and the light wind was bitter with the smell of burning.

I was about to enter the Corner House when I heard my name being called. I turned to find myself facing Ellie Kavanagh and two tall men in Canadian army uniform. One was Ellie's current boyfriend, Raymond Abbot. I didn't know the other. Ellie took my arm.

'Come with us to the Café de Paris,' she said, sounding light-hearted and more than a little tipsy. 'Cameron has been stood up and we need another girl or he'll be a third wheel. Do say you'll join us.'

I glanced down at my outfit: old raincoat, woollen slacks, cream pullover and tweed jacket, with sensible brogues on my feet. Ellie was wearing a rose-coloured evening gown under a white coat.

'I'm not dressed for a nightclub,' I said, brushing my slacks

'Oh, they'll put us in the balcony. They always put the ones who're not in evening dress in the balcony,' said Raymond.

'Do say you'll come,' said Ellie. She looked around and seemed to take in the fires and smell of smoke. 'Oh, come on, Maisie. It'll be safer in the Café de Paris than the Corner House. Everyone knows it's the safest place in town.'

She had a point. The Café de Paris was twenty feet below ground and its manager promoted it as 'the safest and gayest restaurant in town'. Going there with Ellie and two Canadians would be a lot more fun than sitting in the Corner House alone. And quite a bit safer.

His companion gave me a smile. 'I'm Cameron Martin, the one who's been stood up so shamefully. It'd be swell if

you could join us and turn my evening of misery into joy.'
I thought he was laying it on a bit thick, but he had a nice smile.

Raymond said, 'Yes, please do, Maisie.'

As I dithered, the Warning sounded again. More raiders were coming over. I took it as a sign.

'I'd love to,' I said.

Cameron took my arm and the four of us walked past the garish façade of the Rialto Cinema to the nondescript doorway that led into the Café de Paris. Cameron held back the long blackout curtain and I entered the nightclub. To the left, just off the entrance at ground level were the cloakrooms. Ellie and I retired to leave our coats and fix our make-up.

'I have no idea why I'm here,' I said, as we sat in front of a couple of long mirrors. I pulled out my pins, shook my long hair free before pulling my comb through it and re-pinning it into a chignon.

'You do that so easily,' said Ellie, obviously impressed.

'You get used to quick changes in the chorus line.'

She patted her own elaborate pin-curl creation, reached into her handbag and took out a lipstick and compact. 'You're here because Cameron Martin is nice-looking and eligible. And this is certainly a fabulous place. Did you see the furs hanging in the cloakroom?'

'I'm also here because it's a safe place in an air raid.' I looked at myself critically. 'Could I borrow your lipstick?'

'What's mine is yours,' she said, handing it over. 'Except Raymond. I think I'll keep him.' She smiled. 'I mean that. I really do think I'll keep him.'

I applied her lipstick, which was a bit too orange for my complexion, but would do. Ellie took it back, touched up her own lipstick and dabbed her nose with powder. We joined the men, and descended into a scene of hectic gaiety with champagne, bright lights and raucous dance music.

The Café de Paris was on three levels. A flight of stairs led down from the entrance at ground level, where the cloakroom was, to a wide semi-circular balcony set up with tables and a cocktail bar. The dance floor and main restaurant area were on the floor below that, and were reached from the balcony by a broad staircase that divided and curved in two gold and crimson arms to wrap around a small stage where the band played. In front of the stage was the dance floor and past that were rows of tables.

Ellie and I joined the men at a table on the balcony. As the others chatted I snuck a look at Raymond's menu and gasped. Caviar at 8s 6d, oysters at 10s a dozen, steaks at 4s 6d, grouse at 10s 6d or a full-length dinner beginning with iced melon, and continuing with sole, chicken and *peche melba* for 15s 6d. The top price for vintage champagne was 30s a bottle. The best cigars cost 3s 6d.

I earned £2 3s a week. I hoped that the Canadians were well paid or well heeled. Cameron answered my unuttered question, by telling the waiter, 'We'll start with two dozen oysters and a bottle of champagne.'

I looked up at the glittering ceiling, then down at the dance floor. It heaved with officers in uniform, dancing with women who were dressed in beautiful evening gowns or were also in uniform. I was pleased to see that, as was becoming more common, more than a few of the women wore day clothes, even slacks. So a dance or two with Cameron was on the cards. My spirits rose. It had been a while since I'd been out dancing with a handsome young man.

The music stopped and the dance floor emptied in anticipation of the floor show. The band leader raised his baton and a drum roll sounded. The saxophone's smooth notes were the signal for a troupe of twelve chorus girls to glide on to the small stage in a shimmy of long tanned legs under a fringe of gold lamé. They weren't bad, but two or three were out of time and my kicks were higher. They left the stage to rapturous applause.

'Gorgeous girls,' said Cameron.

'The bandleader's Snakehips Johnson,' said Raymond.

'Isn't he marvellous,' said Ellie.

Our oysters arrived and the champagne. We toasted each other and the oysters slipped down my throat like silk. I was beginning to feel fizzy, light as the champagne.

'Dance?' Cameron was looking at me.

I smiled. 'Love to.'

The saxophone sobbed over occasional flares of trumpet, the piano tinkled out the tune and the drums kept the rhythm. We seemed to glide around the dance floor.

'You're a wonderful dancer, Maisie,' said Cameron, who was holding me a little too close. 'Isn't this place merry and bright? It's as if there's no war on at all.'

The famed Café de Paris reminded me of a stage set of an opulent hotel, or photos I'd seen of one of those glorious transatlantic liners that took passengers to America before the war. Floor-to-ceiling mirrors covered the walls, reflecting images of luxury and fleeting gaiety. The music rose up to the glittering chandeliers and as Cameron whirled me around I let myself get carried away by the glamour.

We returned to the balcony for more champagne as the chorus kicked their way through another floor show, bare legs swinging and hips gyrating. Cameron couldn't keep his eyes off them. He was handsome and polite, but I thought him a little boring.

'Do you like Charles Dickens?' I asked.

He put his head on one side. 'I had to study him at school. Not much. You?'

'I've only read *A Tale of Two Cities*, but I loved that.'

'I liked Ronald Colman in the movie,' he said. I nodded.

Above us the planes droned on, their noise not quite drowned out by the band. I looked around at the glittering gaiety and thought it was rather like Dickens had written, this was the best of times and the worst of times. I tried to remember the rest. An age of wisdom and foolishness, of belief and incredulity, a season of light and of darkness. The spring of hope and the winter of despair.

The chorus girls shimmied off. Snakehips Johnson took the floor, and raised his baton to begin another tune. Raymond asked Ellie for a dance and they descended the staircase to join the milling crowd below.

Cameron downed his champagne and looked at me. 'Care to dance?'

I smiled assent. We walked together towards the elegant steps that led down to the dance floor, and had just reached them when I realised I'd left my handbag at the table. I was too canny to leave it unattended in a crowded place. 'Just a minute,' I said. 'I forgot my bag.' I dashed back to our table.

And then the world exploded.

My grandfather was a lay preacher at the Hill of Zion nonconformist chapel in Sheffield, and when I was living with my grandparents Granddad had often practised his fire and brimstone sermons on me. That meant I grew up with an intimate knowledge of the fiery pit of hell. Granddad described it in great detail: how destruction would come like a whirlwind and sinners would be swept away like the chaff of the summer threshing floor into the fiery pit. He was a rousing preacher, my granddad, and when I began to drive ambulances it seemed that his descriptions of the horror had anticipated the Blitz.

Not one of Granddad's sermons came close to what I saw that night in the Café de Paris, after the bomb exploded.

CHAPTER SEVEN

There was a rush of air and the lights went out. The floor rocked beneath me. I fell to my knees. A deafening roar was followed by cascading crashes. In the utter darkness a deathly silence descended on the nightclub. The smell of cordite was choking.

A woman began to scream.

'Shut up,' someone yelled, but the silence had been breached. More screams, shouts and moans floated up into the darkness from the floor below. I heard names, supplications to God, desperate entreaties for help. On the balcony was a murmur of movement. I coughed in the dusty air, wiped my moist hands on my slacks and ran my tongue over dry lips.

All around was black as coal and I felt disorientated, unable to think clearly. I needed light. My torch. It was in my handbag and that was by my chair. I crawled over to where I thought it was, groped and fumbled on the floor until I located it. I snapped it open and felt around until I found the torch and switched it on.

The air was thick with dust and smoke, but when I shone the thin beam of light around it was clear that the balcony itself was freakishly untouched by the explosion. Most of the chairs were upright. Glasses and bottles of champagne stood on tables, a testament to the jollity before the bomb hit. The mirrors behind the cocktail bar were cracked but the rows of bottles stood, still stacked neatly. Broken glass littered the floor, and part of the ceiling was hanging down, otherwise the damage was light.

People were walking across the balcony in a silent throng, feeling their way, heading for the stairway that led to the street.

All those who could walk, with or without assistance, were seeking an escape from the nightclub

I shone my torch upward. It revealed a jagged hole above the dance floor, from which I surmised that the glittering ceiling had collapsed, missing the balcony almost completely, but crashing to the floor below and undoubtedly causing havoc when it landed. The room downstairs had been lined with mirrors and I knew all too well how an explosion turned shards of flying glass into sharp, deadly bullets. Many of the people downstairs would have been terribly injured by blast and flying glass and the fallen ceiling.

I turned my torch on to the divided semi-circular staircase that wrapped around the stage. The left side, where Cameron had been standing, had fallen into a pile of rubble on the floor below.

The right side of the staircase was intact and it thrummed with survivors, nearly all blast-blackened and bloodied, with their clothes in tatters. There was no panic, but they moved as quickly as injuries and shock allowed, a grim cavalcade ascending from the horror below, stumbling across the balcony and heading for the stairway to the street. Wounded leaned on others for support; some men carried the injured. When my torch lit their faces, their eyes seemed dead, which I put down to shock.

One man staggered into my torchlight, bent under the weight of a bloodied young women in a tattered evening gown. He seemed familiar, and I realised it was Raymond with Ellie, unconscious in his arms. He was taking her up to safety. I knew I should be happy that they had survived, but my ears were ringing from the explosion and I felt numb.

I crawled to the railing and shone my torch over the balcony on to the floor below, looking for Cameron among the wreckage although I thought it unlikely he had survived the fall. My torchlight cut through the pall of smoke and dust to reveal a macabre vista of mangled corpses and debris, a horror worse than anything I'd been exposed to in six months of driving an ambulance in the Blitz.

I found out later that the bomb came in through a skylight in the roof. It bounced off the side of the balcony, taking out the left arm of the stairs, and crushing Cameron, who was standing there. Then it exploded on the stage. Those closest to the detonation were killed outright, including Snakehips Johnson and most of his musicians. The dance floor in front of the band had been thick with couples. Many of those dancing had been killed by the blast, and also some who were sitting at the coveted tables close to the dance floor. Others had been struck by bomb debris – bits of the stage, musical instruments, broken tables, bottles, glasses and cutlery. As I had suspected, the massive mirrors that had lined the walls spat out lethal shards of glass when they shattered under the force of the blast. Appalling injuries were also caused by the ceiling when it collapsed.

The numb feeling began to dissipate as I knelt by the balcony railing and looked down on the shattered restaurant floor. It seemed that no ambulances or rescue crews had arrived yet. I knew first aid. Perhaps I could help. One thing they drill into you in the Ambulance Service is that speed is of the utmost importance in treating the injured. The people downstairs would need all the help they could get. And right away!

My hands shook and my heart thumped wildly, but I pulled back my shoulders, raised my chin and took a deep breath. It was a mistake – the air was very dusty and smoky. When I'd finished coughing, I whispered into the darkness: 'I'm ready for anything.'

I stumbled down what remained of the grand staircase, following the slim beam of my torch and pushing past survivors who were staggering upwards. They were blast-blackened and bloody, their hair white with plaster dust. Beautiful dresses were in ribbons. Some were almost naked, as the blast had stripped off their clothes.

At last I reached the main restaurant area. Little lights hovered about in the darkness as others besides me searched for the living and wounded, using torches, cigarette lighters, matches, whatever would give light. The pitiable groans and shouts had increased in volume and seemed to be coming from all over the room.

I took a few breaths to steady my nerves and clambered over a pile of rubble, probably the fallen ceiling. Then I lurched across the littered floor following the will-o'-the-wisp of my bobbing torchlight.

Close to what had been the dance floor I came upon a table of four, two men in the uniform of Canadian officers and two women in evening gowns. A bottle of champagne stood upright on the table in front of them, untouched. They were sitting quite naturally, as if just about to eat, or talk, or smile. They were all dead. Blast does that. It's entirely unpredictable. Sometimes it explodes lungs and doesn't leave a mark on the corpse.

When I have nightmares about the bombing of the Café de Paris, it is that table of the dead that wakes me in fright. Those two handsome young officers and their lovely girls so beautifully dressed. Those four corpses watching each other with dead eyes across the bottle of champagne.

My mouth became very dry. I tried to swallow, but it was as if a lump of coal was in my throat. Nothing could have prepared me for this. My torchlight jerked up and down and the scene shattered and dissolved. I was confused until I realised my hand was shaking violently and tears had flooded my eyes. I started as someone touched my shoulder.

'You all right?' It was a woman's voice. I blinked the tears away and forced myself to become calm. I was down there to help, and help I would.

'I'm fine.' My voice was surprisingly even.

'You a nurse in mufti?'

'Ambulance officer in mufti.' I turned my torch around to see who it was and a woman in nurse's uniform was revealed. 'Maisie Halliday,' I said, 'from Bloomsbury Auxiliary Station.'

'I'm Sister Grant,' she replied, 'from Charing Cross Hospital.' Her low voice was calming. 'I was on duty in one of the shelters when I heard that something had happened at the Café de Paris. Never expected anything like this. Isn't it ghastly? I've used up nearly all my dressings already and I haven't any morphia. I've sent someone all the way to St Martin's Crypt to get bandages. Don't suppose you've got any?'

'No. I was upstairs in the balcony and came down when I realised what had happened.'

She sighed. 'Do what you can for the poor souls. Help's on its way.' She moved across to the table of the dead and picked up their bottle of champagne.

'What are you doing?' I squeaked.

Sister Grant gave a soft laugh and handed the bottle to me. 'We've been improvising. There's no water so we've been using champagne to clean the worst wounds. Matron would be horrified. Only, we're running out of champagne, too. Make it last. It's like holding back the tide. Surely help will arrive soon.' This last sentence was said like a prayer, as she moved away into the darkness.

I squared my shoulders and got to work, using champagne to wash out the wounds of a young woman with injuries caused by flying glass fragments. My pink scarf became her bandage.

She was shivering and whimpering in pain. 'Keep still,' I told her. 'Help will be here soon.'

What remained of the champagne went on the next poor soul, whose nearly naked body was a mass of cuts and abrasions. 'Help is coming,' I whispered to him.

I stumbled over an unopened bottle of champagne and grabbed it just as my torchlight picked out a human-sized shape in the darkness. Clutching the bottle firmly, I clambered over a pile of plaster to reach it. The man was unconscious and his left hand had been almost severed at the wrist. Blood was pooling on the ground and it was clear that he'd bleed out without a tourniquet. I had nothing left. My slacks were tough wool and anyway, I had no knife to cut them.

I shone my torch around in desperation. A few feet away a fair-haired woman in a long frock was kneeling by the unmoving body of a man in naval uniform, weeping uncontrollably. I felt a sharp jab of pity for her, but it was the silk sash around her waist that took my eye.

'Miss,' I yelled, shining my torch on to her face. It was blast-blackened and her tears had left it strangely patterned, almost like a horror mask. She appeared to be uninjured.

I tried again. 'Miss.' This time she looked up, blinking in the torchlight. I shone the torch on to the face of the man I was attending then flicked it back at her.

'I need something to make a tourniquet or this man will die. Could I use your sash?'

'What? Just a minute.' She lurched across the debris-strewn floor in a sliding, scissoring movement. As she did so she held her left hand up, away from her body.

'Are you hurt?' I asked.

'Lost a finger,' she said, and raised her hand. Torchlight revealed it was covered in a soiled and bloody handkerchief.

'Middle one's gone entirely,' she said, 'and most of my ring finger. Flying glass, I think. Otherwise I'm fine.' She glanced back towards the man she'd been weeping over and sucked in a shaky breath before stating, in an utterly expressionless voice, as if remarking on the weather, 'Robbie's dead. He's dead and we never ...'

She swallowed convulsively, her face working as if not to cry again. Then she turned back to me. 'How can I help this chap? My right hand works perfectly well, but this one's out of action.'

'I need your sash,' I said. 'Is it silk?'

A quick nod, and she murmured on a sigh, 'It was Robbie's favourite, this frock. He loved me to wear it.' Her voice became brisk. 'Of course you can have whatever will help.'

Together we managed to undo the knot on her sash and she handed it over. I wrapped it around my patient's arm as I'd been taught and pulled tight. The bleeding slowed, then ceased to a slow trickle. I quickly examined him. A nasty penetrating wound on his right shoulder needed further investigation, but it was difficult to see what I was dealing with. With shaky hands I tried to open the bottle of champagne that I'd found.

'Good heavens, whatever are you doing?' said the girl, in a shocked voice.

'It's to clean his wound.'

My hands were slippery and it was hard to get a good grip. I steadied it between my legs and used my thumbs. Finally the cork flew out of the bottle with a loud pop and a gush of liquid. As I poured it on to his wrist and shoulder wound the patient moaned and shifted fitfully, then subsided again into unconsciousness. I felt around in his shoulder for any large pieces of glass with my fingers and dribbled more champagne over him, then over my own hand, now sticky with blood. I remembered the handkerchief in my pocket. It was clean, so I used it to pack the wound, but I had nothing to bandage it in place with.

'You a nurse?' the woman asked. She had been watching me closely.

'Ambulance driver. Maisie Halliday.'

'I'm Lucy,' she said. 'Lucy Evans.' She gestured towards her frock. 'If we could tear this material into strips, it would make reasonable bandages. It's good quality silk.'

We exchanged quick smiles and I nodded. I used a shard of glass to tear the material and with Lucy helping the best she could, we tore off three good-sized strips. I wrapped one around the man's wrist and used another to bind his shoulder. He woke again as we were doing this, and cried out in pain.

'Hush,' said Lucy. 'You're alive. Be glad of that. The pain means you're alive.'

'Let me see your hand, Lucy,' I said.

She shook her head. 'Save your champagne. I'll have it seen to later. It can wait.'

Help was arriving at the nightclub. There were heavy steps on the stairs and in the darkness I heard a warden calling orders to his men. Powerful flashlights and arc lights were turning on, revealing the extent of the tragedy that the explosion had caused. I stifled a sigh. There were so many injured.

'Could you bear to stay with him?' I asked Lucy. 'Stretcher-bearers will be here very soon. Grab one for him. And do be sure to have your hand seen to.'

'Will do,' she said. 'Where are you going?'

'To see if I can help any others.'

CHAPTER EIGHT

I stumbled on until I was checked by an overturned table. Something soft lay beside it and my torchlight revealed a man who was bleeding from a head wound. Kneeling, I supported his head and dribbled champagne into the wound. The pain caused him to jerk against my hand and his eyes opened.

'What happened,' he muttered. His words were strangled, but his accent was American. 'There was a bomb and then ... Where's he gone?'

'Mr Harker?' I said, shocked. It looked like Michael Harker, but I couldn't be sure in the darkness. I looked again. It was Michael Harker.

He squinted up at me. After a second or so he said, 'Who is it?'

I turned the torch on to my face. 'Maisie Halliday. We met a couple of days ago. You bought me a book. Are you injured?'

His face lightened, almost into a smile. 'Bess,' he murmured. 'No. Maisie.'

He shook his head as if to clear it, as if he were confused. 'I remember, the chorus girl. What are you doing down here?'

'Trying to help. I know first aid.'

'Help me up, will you, kid?' I helped him to sit up. He touched the wound on his forehead. 'What did you wash it with? Booze?'

'Champagne. There's no water.'

He gave a quick laugh, and winced. 'I hope it was a good vintage. I'm fine. Just this bump on my head. Got any bandages?'

I held up the last strip of Lucy's dress. 'The women are tearing their evening gowns. If you have a handkerchief I'll fix you up, Mr Harker.'

He handed me a folded handkerchief. I mopped the wound with it and bound his forehead with the silk strip.

'So you're checking to see if anyone needs help?' he asked.

'That's the idea, but I've run out of bandages. Still got a little champers left.'

'I'm looking for a friend,' he said. 'He's somewhere in this mess. Mind if I tag along with you? I've got a torch.' As if to prove it, he turned it on. The stronger light illuminated, more clearly than my little torch, the extent of the devastation. 'And for pity's sake,' he said, 'call me Michael.'

He found another bottle of champagne, and after he had expertly opened it we followed the sound of groans to find a woman whose face was a mess of cuts from flying glass. Michael had a penknife and used it to cut strips from her long frock for bandages. I washed her bloodied face and he helped me to bind it with pieces of her silk dress.

The extra lights the rescue crews had brought helped us to negotiate the wreckage, but it was still quite dark in the area under the first-floor balcony where the arc lights couldn't reach.

Mr Harker's torchlight picked up an unconscious figure a few feet away.

'Better see how that guy's doing,' he said.

I scrambled across to the unconscious man, knelt down and put my fingers on his neck. His pulse was faint and unsteady. As I did so, his eyes opened and they widened when they saw me in the half light. He tried to speak, clutched at me, grabbing my arm in a hard, convulsive grip.

'What happened,' he muttered. His breath was catching in his throat and his words were strangled. His accent was American. 'There was a bomb and then—'

'He okay?' Michael knelt beside me.

The man's eyes widened. 'Harker?' He struggled, trying to rise. 'What the—'

I pushed him down gently. 'Try to relax,' I said. 'A bomb exploded in here. I'll check you over, see if I can help. What's your name?'

'Egan, Harry Egan. I feel so cold. Oh God, I'm dying. Am I dying?'

I used my fingertips and torchlight to examine him. His laboured breathing and the rattle in his chest gave me grave concerns. It probably meant blast lung, which was often fatal. The table of the dead was proof of that. The man needed oxygen and I could only hope that the stretcher-bearers arrived quickly.

He grabbed at me again, his hands scrabbling for my arm and grabbing the material of my slacks instead.

'Shhh. Lie still, Mr Egan,' I said. 'The stretcher-bearers will be here soon.'

He coughed wetly and the rattle in his breathing became more pronounced as he lapsed into unconsciousness.

'What's the problem with him?' asked Mr Harker.

'I think it's blast lung, although he may also have internal injuries. He's very unwell.'

'He going to die?'

'Perhaps. I can't tell.'

Behind me a woman moaned loudly. 'I can't do anything for him and I have to see to her now,' I said.

I crawled across to the woman. Her arm was at an unnatural angle, obviously broken. I set to work, first cleaning the wound with champagne. I needed a splint, so I felt around in the wreckage, looking for a likely piece of debris. A bit of broken wood came to hand, perhaps part of a chair leg. It would do. I placed it carefully on her arm and began to wrap it, when a movement caught my eye.

Michael Harker was rummaging around in Mr Egan's clothing. At first I couldn't believe what I was seeing, but then realised he was being very thorough. First he checked the front breast pockets, then the inside pockets of his jacket. He pulled out a wallet and a watch, which he pocketed. Then he felt in each trouser pocket. He even removed the man's shoes and shone his torch inside.

'Leave him alone,' I said, through gritted teeth.

'He's dead,' said Michael. 'Slipped away just now.'

'You can't—'

'I have to. It's not what it seems.'

Torchlight flashed in my face. I turned away from him to blink up into the light, tense and ready to defend this patient at least from any looters.

'Hello, ambulance girl,' said a female voice. She turned the torch on to her face and it was Sister Grant.

I looked towards Mr Egan. Michael Harker had disappeared.

'I've got some more bandages,' said Sister Grant, handing me a couple of rolls.

'Where did these come from?' I asked.

'Scots Guards have formed a cordon around the entrance. The nice men gave me their field dressings and I'm distributing them.'

'Good for you. Any more champagne? I've just run out.'

'Sorry, no. But I'm pleased to say that stretcher-bearers and rescue parties have arrived. With too few ambulances, but it's a start.' She hesitated. 'Be wary. There are men down here ransacking corpses for valuables. Soho thugs, probably, after easy pickings. The police are on to it, but it's too dark to see much. They think it's the Hoxton Mob.'

That was the biggest of the London crime gangs in Soho, with long tentacles that reached out into all parts of Soho life, especially black marketeering. Most of the girls on the street paid a proportion of their earnings to the Hoxton Mob as 'protection' from the other gangs.

The Café de Paris might be a swanky nightclub, but it was in Soho, and gangs were a part of life in the poorer areas of any city. Not only German bombs, but Soho gangs, had crashed into the privileged lives of these Café de Paris revellers. But why had Michael Harker dropped to their level? What was he looking for in the pockets of his supposed friend? He'd said he had to do it. Why?

Sister Grant reached out to pat my shoulder. 'You're doing a splendid job, my dear.'

The calm kindness in her voice made me feel teary, but I managed to hold myself together. Sister Grant disappeared into the darkness.

I placed my torch carefully on the floor beside me and began to unroll one of the bandages Sister Grant had given me. My patient's figure suddenly sharpened. Something was throwing more light into the room, revealing the restaurant floor to be a hive of busy people treating the injured, loading them on to stretchers and carrying them upstairs. Surprised, I looked up to see that rescue workers had set more and stronger arc lights along the balcony and on the stairs.

I finished splinting my unconscious patient's arm. When I'd tied off the bandage ends I lowered the arm gently on to her chest and turned my torchlight on my own upstretched arm to call a stretcher-bearer. Across the room, one nodded at me as he hoisted the stretcher he was dealing with, to indicate he'd seen my signal. Less than a minute later a couple of stretcher-bearers arrived, put my patient on a stretcher and carried her off.

Rescue workers, doctors, nurses were doing their jobs around me, and doing a better job than I could. I was no longer needed. So I stood and stretched weary muscles and imagined a warm, comfortable bed. I remembered to search the cloakroom on the way out to retrieve my raincoat. I shone my torch over a pile of very expensive fur coats that didn't tempt me at all, and sighed with relief when my own tatty raincoat was revealed.

I pulled it on over my filthy and bloodied clothes, pushed through the blackout curtain and emerged into a world of thick smoke and flickering red shadows. Monstrous fires lit the sky over to the north. Their light, allied to the moonlight, revealed the crowd that had gathered around the doorway to the restaurant and the ring of soldiers that kept them back.

I fought an almost overwhelming urge to rage at the crowd of sightseers, call them ghouls, take out my anger at what I'd seen on them. Instead, I thrust through the crowd in silence. When I was in relative solitude further along Coventry Street I sucked in a shaky breath and looked back at the onlookers. They huddled together, held back by the soldiers, calling out questions to anyone who emerged, muttering amongst themselves.

My anger receded. Some of them probably wanted to help, others were fascinated by the horror, or were relieved that it had happened to someone else. Some might feel a perverse pleasure in the knowledge that most of the victims were young and beautiful, the wealthy and privileged. A few, I now knew, were hoping to slip inside to steal wallets and jewellery, take easy pickings from the dead. The crowd was undoubtedly as diverse as London itself.

I sighed and turned away from them to walk towards Leicester Square. Ahead of me was a couple – a woman in a tattered evening gown and a man in uniform – locked in a passionate embrace. When they drew apart I saw, to my surprise and no small amusement, who they were. The woman was Celia Ashwin and the man was Dr Simon Levy, an army doctor stationed in London who often helped out in the Blitz. They were a surprising couple indeed. Dr Levy was Jewish, the brother of an ambulance officer from the Bloomsbury station who had died last year and whom I had liked very much.

Celia Ashwin and Simon Levy! I smiled as they walked away arm in arm. They had obviously been down in the Café de Paris and, knowing them both, they would have been helping the wounded. I'd been so sure that they disliked each other. As they rounded the corner I sent them a good-luck wish. Falling in love in wartime was definitely a mug's game, but it was also a vote of confidence in a future where lovers no longer needed to fear they would be torn apart by death.

And then I remembered Lucy in the wreckage of the Café de Paris, weeping over the body of her Robbie, who had liked her to wear the evening gown we had torn up for bandages. So many bodies were down there. How many tears would be shed for those who had died tonight? I grimaced at the moon.

'It's absolutely true, you know,' I said. 'Falling in love in wartime is a mug's game.'

And then I laughed at myself for talking to the moon. I had more important things to think about, such as Michael Harker looting the dead body of Mr Egan. He'd said he had to do it. Why? I couldn't work it out. Just who was Mr Michael Harker?

I pushed those thoughts aside to consider later. Right now I needed to decide where I would spend the rest of the night. My friends either lived with me in the club or were my colleagues in the ambulance service and lived too far away. It was long past the eleven o'clock lockout in the club and the late key had gone away with Ellie, presumably to hospital. Poor Ellie. I could only hope she was not badly injured.

After a minute of feverish thinking, I was on the point of resigning myself to wandering around Soho to find an early opening cafe, when I realised that the answer was obvious. It was only a few hours until my shift at the ambulance station began and bunks had been installed there when we moved to twenty-four-hour shifts. I'd sleep at the station.

Unfortunately, it was easily a half-hour walk away.

'Needs must,' I murmured. I squared my shoulders and set off briskly.

By the time I was halfway along Wardour Street my steps had slowed to a weary plod.

'Maisie,' a man called. 'Maisie, wait.'

An American accent. I didn't need three guesses as to who it was, and he was someone I really did not want to speak to, because I intended reporting Michael Harker to the police just as soon as I could. So I ignored him and continued walking. His steps were loud in the empty street as he came up quickly behind me. Then he grabbed my arm.

Stupid move, chum.

I swung around in an arc and thrust my elbow into his face, making sharp contact with his chin. He grunted, released my arm and took a step backwards. Then I linked my hands and swung around again to elbow him hard in the chest. He stepped back further, holding up his arms in a gesture of surrender.

'If you don't walk away immediately,' I said, 'I'll scream the place down.' My voice was clipped and angry, and I hoped he couldn't see how shaky I was. I curled my hands into fists and dug my nails into my palms. The pain focused me. 'I have a very loud scream, Mr Harker.'

He had become very still.

'I could ask you what this is about,' he said, 'but that would just rile you all the more, wouldn't it?' He sounded easy and friendly, but there was a hint of ruthlessness in that suave voice.

I stared at him. 'You looted Mr Egan's body.'

'I had a reason. A good one.'

'I'm sure you did.' My voice was sarcastic. 'Let me see. What could it have been? Was it that he had something you wanted?' I glared at him. 'A nice watch, perhaps? A wallet full of cash?'

Harker took a few breaths, as if trying to remain calm. My own breathing was fast and my heart was pounding. He'd looted a dead man's body, but I didn't think he was the sort of man to hurt a woman. So I turned my back on him and began to walk away.

He said, 'I know you think I'm a—'

'I think you're much worse than that,' I said, without turning around.

'Than what?' He was following me, but keeping his distance.

'Whatever you were about to say. I think you're the lowest of the low. Scum.'

'Maisie, I had a good reason to search Harry's body.'

'What reason?'

'I can't tell you.'

I kept walking.

He tried again. 'I had to get hold of something he was carrying. I can't tell you what it was, but believe me, I had to do it. That's all I can say. Please, Maisie, it was that important.'

'Go away. If you don't stop following me I *will* scream.'

The sound of his footsteps behind me ceased. I continued my walk to the station.

CHAPTER NINE

By the time I arrived I was stumbling with fatigue.

I marched down the ramp into the station to find that all the vehicles were out at incidents and the only person in the place was Beryl McIver, the station leader for that shift. McIver, a cheery Scotswoman, wore her iron grey hair in two long plaits wound around her head, which I always thought made her look like a much older version of Heidi. She gave me a warm welcome when I explained what had happened.

'Of course you can sleep here,' she said. 'But have a bite with me before you head off to bed. I've just made a fresh pot of tea.'

I followed her into the common room and almost collapsed into a chair. McIver poured me a strong cup of tea and pushed a plate of squashed-fly biscuits across the table. I munched a biscuit and sipped my tea, and felt a little better for it.

'So you were in the Café de Paris,' said McIver. 'I've heard it was pretty bad. Bathurst and Bydder were sent there on diversion once it was realised just how serious it was, but they haven't returned yet to tell me about it.'

'It was about as bad as it gets,' I admitted. 'I didn't see Bathurst or Bydder, but I think I saw Ashwin. And also Dr Levy.'

'It's just the sort of place Ashwin would go to. I hope she's not injured.'

I shook my head. 'Ashwin looked fine,' I said, 'although her frock was in tatters. Lots of the girls were tearing their dresses for bandages.'

'Dr Levy always seems to turn up where he's needed.' McIver smiled. 'Lovely man, just like his brother was.'

'Most people were wonderful down there,' I said. 'There was some looting, though.'

McIver shook her head. 'Soho gangs, no doubt. Easy pickings.'

'Apart from the Café de Paris, was it a bad raid last night?' I asked.

'The worst since January. Buckingham Palace was hit again. There were a fair few casualties at Garland's Hotel, and that's where our other vehicles were sent. The Café de Paris was much the worst, though.'

The room was beginning to swim and McIver gave me a sympathetic smile. 'You look exhausted, Halliday. Go and get cleaned up and then get some sleep. Moray's on duty in two hours. I'll tell him where you are and how you spent last night. I expect he'll not disturb you until mid-morning.'

I nodded, rose slowly and plodded along the corridor to the women's washroom. In the room were numerous pegs on the wall, each holding a black steel helmet with the letter 'A' painted in white at the front. The peg holding my helmet was over to the right and looking at it now I remembered the first time I'd worn it. How excited and happy I'd been to be able to help out in the war. How innocent that Maisie had been. I was still honoured to be a part of the London County Council Auxiliary Ambulance Service, but I had no illusions now about the horror of aerial warfare, the devastation it caused to lives and property. It was a dirty, bloody business, driving an ambulance in the Blitz. And there was nothing else I'd rather be doing.

McIver hailed me and I turned to see her enter the washroom carrying a kettle. 'Forgot to say, gas is off, so no hot water except what we can heat on the oil stove. Pour this into a basin and do what you can.'

She reached into her pocket and pulled out a small bar of soap. 'Courtesy of Sadler, so it's probably black market, but much better than any other soap at the station.'

I thanked her with a smile. It was kind of her to offer me her soap. Most wartime soap was such poor quality that it never formed a lather, no matter how hard you scrubbed, but this soap appeared to be good quality. When I gave it a sniff, it was scented with roses. Sam Sadler often had goods to sell that were probably of black-market origin. We all bought them, though.

McIver looked me up and down. Her forehead wrinkled and she asked, 'Do you have any clean clothes here?'

'No.' Unlike some of the others, I didn't keep any clothes at the station. I had only two sets of trousers for work – one now with a badly sewn patch across the left knee – two white shirts, one blue tie and one pullover. I relied on my raincoat to keep off most of the blood and mud because we had to launder our clothes ourselves.

'Ashwin keeps a spare set of clothes here.' She gave me a knowing smile. 'The shirts and trousers are tailor-made. Pre-war, of course.'

We exchanged looks that said how nice it must be to have money enough for oodles of tailor-made shirts and trousers.

'I'm sure she won't mind you borrowing some clothes,' said McIver.

I poured the hot water into a basin as McIver rooted around in one of the closets.

'Ah ha!' She said on a note of triumph. 'Thought so. She's also got a pair of pyjamas here. Just the ticket. And a spare pair of socks – you'll want them. Her clothes are hanging up in here.' She put a pair of folded flannel pyjamas and a roll of socks on the bench. 'You're both around the same size, I'd guess, although she'd be a couple of inches shorter.'

'You're sure she won't mind? I hate to borrow her things without asking.'

'Needs must. Wash it all before you bring it back, mind.'

'Of course.'

With a cheery grin, McIver left the washroom. I stripped off, flinging my dirty, bloodied clothes on to the floor. Shivering in the cold air, I wet a flannel in warm water, loaded it with soap and scrubbed at the dirt and grazes on my body until most of me was rose-scented. I finished with a cold water rinse that brought up goosebumps and made my skin tingle. It was invigorating to say the least, but not unpleasant.

The difficulties and privations of wartime had not been so much of a shock to me as they seemed to be to those who had been raised in greater comfort. I had grown up washing with a flannel, hard soap and cold water from a basin.

When I'd seen London's East End slums I'd thought they were no worse than where I had lived until the age of twelve, in one of Sheffield's notorious 'courts'. My grandparents' back-to-back house in Park Hill was one of a close-packed mass that clung precariously to the hillside. All around us was begrimed with smoke from the railway. We shared a cold water tap and the privies with the residents of the five other dwellings that clustered around our court.

There was no electricity or gas and we used oil for cooking and lighting. Our front door opened directly into 'the room'. In one corner was a door leading to the small coal cellar. In the other was a staircase that led to the bedroom where my grandparents slept. Above that was the leaky attic, reached by a pull-down ladder. Mam and I slept in the attic. It made me want to laugh out loud when Celia spoke of how cold her family pile was in Kent. She had no idea of what it meant to live through a Sheffield winter in that leaky attic.

My mother had refused to let poverty defeat her and insisted that I was always as clean and well turned out as she could make me. We'd wash every night, as I had just done, using a flannel and a pan of hot water with a cold water rinse. And every Friday we'd visit the public bathhouse, where hot water was available in scalding quantities and where, for a few pence, we could soak ourselves in gigantic bathtubs.

And yet, although we had been poor – very poor – in Park Hill, there was a sense of community in those grimy Sheffield streets that I had not found in London until the Blitz had winkled it out. It seemed to me that it was only when we all faced utter annihilation that Londoners were prepared to speak to each other in the street or on buses.

By now I was so weary that I felt ill and a little hysterical as memories of the night kept pushing into my mind. I needed sleep. I pulled on Celia's pyjamas, gathered everything up and stumbled to the women's bunk room. I climbed on to a narrow bunk and fell asleep as soon as my head hit the pillow.

When I opened my eyes it was nearly eleven o'clock. I rubbed sleep from my eyes and headed to the washroom. A quick splash of cold water on my face brought me fully awake and with some trepidation I put on Ashwin's clothes. The shirt was too tight in the bust, and the top three buttons strained dangerously, seemingly ready to pop. I undid those buttons and pulled the dark pullover over the gaping shirt. Celia's trousers were a good three inches too short and my ankles, covered in Celia's dark woollen socks, poked out. *Not* an attractive look. At least I had my own brogues to wear. They were caked with dust and blood, so I grabbed some paper from the ladies' toilet, wet it and rubbed them fairly clean. Only then did I head for the common room.

I'd timed it well. It was eleven o'clock. Everything had stopped for elevenses, our mid-morning tea. When I walked in, Sadler, Squire, Armstrong and Harris were in the room. Through the sliding window to his office I saw that Moray was on the telephone.

'New fashion,' asked Sam Sadler, nodding towards my too-short trousers.

I gave him a smile. 'I've borrowed a pair of Celia's.'

George Squire's big face was less jovial than usual. 'We hear you were at the Café de Paris last night.'

'Yes. I was there when the bomb exploded.'

'Bad?'

'As bad as it gets,' I said, sitting beside him in a canvas chair. 'Big bomb, confined space. Crowded, too.'

He gave me a sympathetic smile and reached over to pat my hand. 'Yeah. That'd be bad.' He paused, then said quickly, 'I'm worried about Ashwin. She's not turned up this morning. You don't know if she was ...'

'She was there,' I said. 'I saw her afterwards. She was with Dr Levy, actually. Don't worry. Celia wasn't injured so far as I could see. They'd been helping out.'

Squire's face relaxed and he gave me a smile. He was close to Celia, which some might think unusual, as he was a former boxer from Seven Dials and she was a blue-blood from Mayfair. Somehow, though, they seemed to understand each other and had become firm friends. Perhaps it was their shared love of Gilbert and Sullivan.

'Where are the others?' I asked him.

'Purvis and Powell are on a mortuary run.' He looked up as the door was pushed open. 'No, here they are now.'

They came in.

'Back already?' said Harris. 'Cup of tea?'

'Watch out if you're driving along Tottenham Court Road,' said Purvis as he dropped into a chair. 'That big crater – the one a bus fell into a few weeks ago – it's been reopened by another bomb. Gas and water mains are all in pieces again.' He looked at Harris. 'I'd love a cup of tea, please.'

She pushed it over to him.

'Thanks,' he said. 'I despair, sometimes. Too many people are accepting war as a normal condition of life now. They won't go into the Anderson shelters because they're damp and cold. Well, *of course* they are, but there's no point being comfortable just before you die.'

Powell also accepted a cup of tea. 'Thanks ever so. Are there any biscuits? Purvis is talking about a family of four we picked up just now. They had an Anderson shelter in the backyard, but had taken to sleeping on mattresses in the front room.'

'And that's where they found them,' said Purvis. 'All dead together in what remained of the room.'

'Lovely cup of tea,' said Doris Powell, who seemed to be blinking back tears.

'Blasé,' said Sadler. 'That's the word. They've become blasé about it all. Think it won't happen to them.'

'What people need are those new shelters,' said Armstrong, very earnestly. 'Morrison shelters, they're called, after Mr Morrison. A fellow in our street has one and I'm trying to get Mum to get one, and my sister as well. They're supposed to be for people without a back garden, but I think we should all have one.'

'They're the ones like a big dining room table?' asked Squire.

'Yeah. But specially reinforced.'

Sadler sneered. 'So you're stuck in them as the house comes down around you? Buried alive.'

Armstrong flushed.

I said, quickly, 'Until light and heavy rescue arrive to dig you out. I think they're a marvellous idea. Would have saved those people Powell and Purvis just picked up, I'll bet.'

The boy nodded vigorously. 'Would've, you know.'

Moray poked his head out of the door of his office.

'I've some news,' he said. 'Ashwin won't be in today. Like Halliday, she was at the Café de Paris last night helping with the casualties. She's fine, but her husband was also there. He was injured, and she's just received word that he died of his wounds.'

There was a moment of shocked silence. Celia's husband, Cedric Ashwin, was notorious in London as being a high-up member of the British fascists. He was not well liked, some said hated, but Celia was one of us. It was difficult to know how to take the news.

'Good riddance, I say,' said Sadler. 'That Ashwin, he were a Nazi. And who are we fighting? The Nazis, that's who.' He gave a short, mirthless laugh. 'Funny how it were one of his mate's planes what dropped the bomb what killed him.'

'His mate?' asked Armstrong.

'Hitler. Ashwin were a mate of Hitler's. Even went to Berlin to see him before the war.'

Armstrong's eyes went wide, and he looked very young.

'I'm not shedding any tears,' Sadler continued, in a low, bitter voice. 'Nor will Ashwin, I bet. She wanted to divorce him. They came to my club when I were playing there one night and you should have seen how he—'

'That's enough,' said Myra Harris sternly. 'The man's dead and he'll account for himself to a greater authority than you, Sam Sadler. If we can't have respect for the dead, no matter what they were when they were alive, then we're as bad as the Nazis.'

There was a short, embarrassed silence. Moray cleared his throat.

'I also have some happy news. We're finally getting a new officer, and it's someone we already know and like. Lily Brennan, or Lily Vassilikov, as she now is.'

That was very good news indeed. All the group knew Lily, who was a *très petite* Australian. She had worked with us until December, and was well liked.

'Vassy-Vissy-what?' said Sadler. 'I can't call out that name in an emergency. By the time it's out she'll have been run over by a lorry, or buried under a falling wall or something. Other stations use nicknames.'

'Her husband is often called Vassy, I believe.' Moray spoke slowly, and seemed uncertain. 'But Ambulance Service policy is to use surnames. I don't like nicknames.'

Harris spoke up. 'We can't call her Vassy, it's undignified. But I can't pronounce that awful Russian name either.'

I said, 'Let's just call her Lily, shall we?'

'Yeah,' said Squire. 'Good thinking, love. Better to just call her Lily.'

Moray threw up his arms. 'Do whatever you want. I'm just the station leader, following policy. Call her Digger if you like. Or Anzac. Why listen to me?'

We were democratic, however, and had a show of hands. Lily it was, by unanimous vote, with Moray abstaining.

CHAPTER TEN

At eight o'clock the following morning I arrived back at the club with the dawn, having crunched over broken glass most of the way home. I carried my dirty clothes in a string bag. Millie answered the doorbell and as I walked inside I heard someone – probably Lorna Gaskin – warming up in the practice room. As usual, she fluffed C sharp. There was a lot of noise in the dining room, but I had already breakfasted, so I climbed upstairs. On the first floor Bobbie Davis was using the bannisters as a *barre*.

It was all so normal, so peaceful. It was as if I'd not spent the night before last in hell.

'Morning, Bobbie,' I said, with an attempt at cheeriness. She leaned low over her leg, and made a bowing motion at me with her arm. I took it as a welcome.

Standing beside Bobbie, oblivious to everything around her, Pru Hort declaimed Shakespeare to a wall covered in framed theatrical posters. '*By all the vows that ever men have broke, In number more than ever women spoke, In that same place thou has appointed me, Tomorrow truly will I meet with thee.*' She stopped, and said piteously, 'Is it "I will meet with thee", or "will I meet with thee"? Oh, God, I can't remember *anything.*'

Pru had told me last week that ENSA were putting on a shortened version of *A Midsummer Night's Dream* for the shelterers in Aldgate. I suspected the audience would prefer something a little less worthy – George Formby had played there last week to rapturous applause at every twang of his ukulele – but the Authorities had declared that a bit of High Culture was

75

needed. The *Dream* was probably the best choice, I thought, with all its magic and fairies and dancing and outlandishness.

'Morning, Pru,' I said.

She turned a tormented face to me. 'What time is it? We're on tonight, and the final rehearsal is at eleven and I can't remember any of my lines.'

These girls had no idea of what I had had to face in the Café de Paris, and I was glad of it.

'You sound brilliant to me,' I said.

Ignoring her grimace, I opened the door to what once had been an elegant drawing room and was now the large, cheerful, messy common room. Whatever colour the threadbare carpet had been once, it had faded to an indeterminate pink. The walls were grey with age, but red lampshades lent everything a rosy glow. Stage magazines had been tossed on to the big gate-legged table by the window. The all-important *The Stage* shared space with *Theatre World, Dancing Times, Theatre Arts Monthly, Film Pictorial, Picturegoer* and even a few old *Photoplays* and *Variety*.

Our multi-coloured blackout blinds had been taken down. Pam Thatcher, an artistic type, had stencilled bright designs on them so that now they were a riot of English country flowers: bluebells, forget-me-nots, foxgloves, hollyhocks, roses, fritillaries and primroses. 'It's silly. bluebells are never out with roses,' Bobbie had remarked once they were up, and a few girls had uncharitably suggested that the blinds be positioned with the flowers facing the street, but I thought they added a bright cheerfulness to the common room.

Esther Jacob was sitting at the table, unpicking a pink fluffy jumper to re-use the wool. She looked up and gave me a brilliant smile. Next to her sat Jill Peterson, reading a book.

'Cheer up, Maisie,' said Jill, looking up and giving me a grin. 'You'll be dead soon enough. Might as well smile.'

So I gave her a weak smile. There was no point destroying her mood by telling her what I'd been doing.

'How's tricks, duck?' said Esther.

'What?' I replied, laughing. 'Wherever did you learn that?'

Esther's eyes became wide, and she seemed confused. 'I heard Mrs Mears say it. Is it not correct?'

Jill gave a trill of laughter. 'It's absolutely correct for a Cockney cook. Not so much for a *reefained* ballet dancer.'

'I do not understand,' said Esther. Her huge eyes had filled with tears. 'It is so difficult to speak correctly in English. Everyone speaks it differently.'

'Just copy us girls,' said Jill, 'and not Mrs Mears.' She became more sombre and lowered her voice, saying to me, 'You've heard about Ellie Kavanagh?'

I shook my head, and felt a wash of fear. Last time I had seen Ellie she had been carried out of the nightclub unconscious. 'What happened to her?'

'She was in the Café de Paris when it was bombed. She lost an eye, and a man she was with – not Raymond, but his best friend – was crushed to death.'

I said the right things to Jill, and quickly left the common room. Hearing about Ellie and Cameron had brought back to me the horror of the night in the Café de Paris, and my pity for the girl caused a physical ache in my chest.

I hurried past Bobbie and Pru, up the stairs to my room. Once inside I threw the bag of washing on the floor and fell on to my bed. I buried my head in the pillow and took comfort in a good, long cry. Thoughts of Ellie, Cameron, Mr Egan, Sister Grant, Lucy, Celia Ashwin and Dr Levy and all the heroes and villains of the night in the Café de Paris trooped through my head. And Michael Harker. I wept for them all, and eventually fell into a deep, dreamless sleep.

It was a good five hours later when I awoke, feeling disoriented and anxious. For a moment I thought that I'd slept through the day but I soon realised that my room was dark only because I had not removed the blackout blinds. I got up and took them down and looked out over London. A plume of smoke floated far up into the sky where a fire still burned, but that was some miles from Soho. The streets around the club were peaceful in the early afternoon haze.

I opened the window and breathed in the cool air. It smelled of brick dust and smoke, as it had done since the Blitz began. Unbidden came a memory of the fresh sea air of the French Riviera. That brought a sigh, because I had loved the beauty of the place and ease of my life there. I had been so certain that all I wanted to do when the war ended was return to exhibition dancing there.

Could I really return? I'd changed so much in the last year. Would the idle luxury of my life in the Riviera suit me now, after all I'd seen and experienced? But what other choices did I have? I still loved to dance and it was the only life I knew. My fear was that the war would last another ten years. No one would want to see a chorus girl of thirty.

A rumble in my stomach made me aware that it had been some hours since I had breakfasted at the station. I looked across the rooftops and checked the St Giles clock. One o'clock. Time for lunch. After that I'd need to launder my clothes as well as the ones I'd borrowed from Ashwin. As I pulled on an old tweed skirt and a sweater I told myself not to worry about my future until the war was over. If Germany won, I might not have a future to worry about!

After I'd finished my lunch I begged a bucket of hot water from Mrs Mears in the kitchen and took my bundle of laundry to the club's washroom. In there was a row of square basins and two dolly tubs. A hand mangle stood in the corner. Most of the club's laundry was done by a hefty Italian woman at a place down the street, but the girls tended to do their own laundry in a basin or in one of the two dolly tubs, using a peggy stick to agitate the clothes and a posser to pound them down.

I washed Celia's pyjamas and uniform, and put them through the mangle. So far, so easy. The clothes I'd worn in the Café de Paris were an entirely different prospect.

I upended the bag containing them on to the concrete floor. Socks, slacks, sweater and jacket emerged in a tangle. They were so filthy with ash and dust and blood and sweat that they all needed a rinse in cold water first. Then they'd go into a dolly tub along with soap and more hot water from Mrs Mears.

As I began to sort through the clothes I felt something hard in my slacks pocket. I reached in and pulled out a gold locket. I stared at it, thinking I had never seen it before and wondering how it had got into my pocket. Then I remembered the way that the dying man, Mr Egan, had scrabbled at my clothes. Had he given it to me? I stuffed it into my skirt pocket, thinking I'd worry about it later, and I got on with my laundry.

Once the clothes had been rinsed, soaped, agitated and pounded, and rinsed again, I put them through the mangle and took everything up four flights of stairs to the roof garden. We'd set up a washing line there. It was a sunny afternoon, though chilly, and I had hopes of a breeze later so I hung it all out to dry. My chores done I returned to my bedroom, closed the door and took out the locket.

Had it come from Mr Egan? If so, it was a worry, because Mr Egan was somehow mixed up with Michael Harker, and after seeing him loot the man's body I had no desire to ever see the man again. I knew I should tell the police about how he had ransacked Mr Egan's body, but I didn't want to do it.

I reached into my pocket and pulled out the locket. *Well, at least you didn't get this, Michael Harker.* I held it up examine it more closely.

It was a pretty thing, gold, about one and a half inches square. A star had been etched into the middle and it was set with a blue stone. It was so plain that I wondered if it were actually a man's watch fob rather than a locket. Before the Great War, when men wore pocket watches as a matter of course, they would attach an ornament – a fob – to the watch chain.

I pushed at the catch, and it opened. A photograph of a woman with the high collar and big hair of the early years of the century had been placed inside. She smiled at me, eternally young and beautiful, although I guessed she'd have to be well into her sixties by now. Mr Egan's mother? It might account for his determination to keep the locket safe. Perhaps he knew that Michael would search his pockets and he thought I was more honourable. Perhaps he had wanted me to return it to the right person.

I nibbled at my lip. Should I take it to the police straight away? I doubted the local bobby would know what to do with it and it might become lost in the system rather than returned to Mr Egan's family.

And I really wasn't sure if Mr Egan was the one who had slipped it into my pocket. I'd seen many injured people that night, and several had grabbed at me. Mr Egan did seem to be the most likely prospect, though. Could this little thing be what Michael was looking for? I discounted the idea at once. It wasn't a valuable object. Not worth risking gaol for.

Perhaps I should ask Moray what to do. I had a lot of respect for our station leader. I could speak to him about it tomorrow, when I was next on duty at the station. I'd ask him about the locket and also whether I should tell the police about Michael Harker's behaviour. I blew out a breath, annoyed that I could not decide for myself what to do about the man. Anyway, there was no urgency. The locket would be safe enough with my sweaters. I tucked it into the drawer and pushed it down among the woollen garments.

I glanced at my watch. Four o'clock, Teatime. Mrs Mears might be an average cook on the whole, but she excelled in making sweet things, whipping up treats even with rationing. I closed my door and headed for the stairs.

I was almost at the dining room door when Miss King hailed me.

'A man phoned for you yesterday, Maisie,' she said. 'A Mr Michael Harker. He said he was from the American Embassy.'

She handed me a piece of paper, with Michael's name clearly printed, the words 'American Embassy' and a telephone number.

'Ready for tea?' she asked. 'Mrs Mears has made a lovely carrot cake. Good for our eyesight in the blackout.'

I thanked her and took the paper. 'I'll be there in a minute. I've something to do first.'

Miss King walked into the dining room. I walked outside, tore the note into tiny pieces and let them drift away in the wind.

CHAPTER ELEVEN

Lily Vassilikov, nee Brennan, arrived at Bloomsbury station at seven-thirty the following morning and was given a rapturous welcome by us all. The Australian girl was around ten inches shorter than me and delicately built, with curly brown hair and a sweet face. At first sight she seemed far too frail to assist with the wounded, but Lily was one of the strongest people I had ever met, not so much physically as emotionally. She never hesitated to take on whatever was required of her. In November she had crawled into the cellar of a bombed house to rescue two trapped children.

'Oh, it's great to be back with you all,' said Lily. 'Berkeley had some wonderful people, but it was such a big station that I felt awfully insignificant.'

'You should all be aware that Lily is so insignificant she's been recommended for the George Medal,' drawled Celia, who was standing in the doorway.

Lily blushed. 'Oh, it's silly, really. I wish you hadn't brought it up, Celia. My Jim's DFC is much more impressive than any medal they give me. All I did was help a family out of a bombed building.'

Celia smiled at her and walked into the room. It was her first day back at work since the Café de Paris bombing and her husband's death but she greeted everyone cheerfully.

'Oh yes,' she said, smiling, 'it was nothing at all. A woman, her elderly mother and two children were huddled together on the roof of a seven-storey block of flats that had been badly bombed and was on fire. All Lily did was crawl up to the top floor with the place falling down around her and get all four of them safely to the ground. And she wasn't even on duty at the time.'

'I got a terrible scolding from Jim later,' said Lily with an abashed smile. 'But no one else was willing to go up to them. What else could I do?'

'Good on yer, love,' said Squire. He turned to Celia and said, in a formal and stiff manner, 'Please accept my sincere condolences.'

Her smile became fixed. 'Thank you. Cedric and I were estranged, but it was an awful way for him to die.' She looked at me. 'I hear you were there.'

I nodded. Some devil of mischief prompted my next comment. 'I saw you, on the street afterwards. Was that Dr Levy you were with?'

Celia wasn't in the least discomposed. She smiled and said, 'Yes. It was.'

As she chatted to Lily and Squire I realised that it was the first time I'd seen Celia look uncomplicatedly happy. It seemed she was not wasting any time mourning her husband. I gave a mental shrug. Simon Levy was a lovely man, much more so than her dead fascist husband. But I thought that she and Dr Levy were an odd match. I didn't believe in opposites attracting, or rather, I didn't believe in an attraction like that lasting the distance.

'Welcome back, Lily', said Moray, coming into the room from his office. 'It's been decided that your new surname is too difficult and we'll call you Lily.'

She smiled. 'Vassilikov is not so hard to pronounce once you get used to it.'

Sadler rolled his eyes. 'I'll stick with Lily, thank you very much.'

'It's good to hear your Aussie accent again,' said Purvis, giving her a grin. 'Have you heard that there's an RAF bomber station whose officers' mess includes a sign saying, "English spoken, Australian understood"?'

It was Lily's turn to roll her eyes. 'That's bonzer, mate,' she said, broadening her accent. Then she laughed. 'At Berkeley Square station there was no discrimination against Aussies. None whatsoever. We had two Rolls-Royce saloons that had been donated to the cause, and I was given one of them to drive.'

Squire stuck his nose in the air in comic fashion. 'How can you bear to slum it with us?'

Lily dimpled. 'I'll cope.'

Powell entered the common room and said, 'I just don't understand it.'

'Understand what?' asked Squire.

'The deal Mr Roosevelt made with us last week. Lend-Lease, they call it.'

'It's a bit over my head, too,' I said. 'I think he's trying to help us out without it looking like he's helping us.'

'We need more weapons and ships to fight the Germans,' explained Purvis, 'but we can't afford them just at the moment. The American people don't want to get involved in our European war. Roosevelt knows we've right on our side. So he's arranged to *lend* us the stuff we need – planes, battleships, weapons, that sort of thing – and we can keep it all until we've put Hitler in his place.'

'I know where I'd like to put Hitler,' said Sadler, 'but good manners prevent me from elaborating.'

We all laughed, but just then the telephone in Moray's office rang. The room became silent as he went into the office to answer it.

The worst part about a job like ours was the waiting. It was difficult ever to really relax because you might be sent out at any time. In many ways, waiting at the station was worse than being on the road, because at least then you were busy and had no time to think about what you might have to do at any moment.

After the silent beat of apprehension when Moray left to answer the telephone, we all worked hard at pretending nothing was wrong. Sadler dealt himself another hand of Patience. Harris picked up her knitting. Purvis began to sketch Lily, who poked her tongue out at him. Celia and Squire started humming a tune together in harmony, probably Gilbert and Sullivan. Armstrong tried, and failed, not to stare at Celia, who seemed to glow with happiness.

'Have you heard,' said Powell, 'the government has requisitioned all the farms in Norfolk and told them they have to grow carrots. Only carrots. Aunt Glad's friend, Mrs Morrison, has a daughter who's married to a postman up in the fens. He says that all the farms he delivers to are given over to carrots now. And guess who they're for.'

There was silence for a beat. We all knew that Careless Talk was strictly forbidden, but Powell's rumours were often amusing, and strangely compelling. Purvis was the first to give in.

'I give up,' he said. 'Who are they growing all those carrots for?'

'For the RAF,' she said, triumphantly. 'It's so that the pilots will be able to see in the dark.' She lowered her voice. 'Carrots are our secret weapon against the night raiders.'

'We already know that eating carrots help you to see in the dark,' ventured Lily. 'All those posters up around town tell you to eat more carrots to help you in the blackout.'

Powell nodded vigorously. 'But now they've found a way to put whatever it is in carrots that gives you night vision into a pill. One pill will have the same effect as eating a thousand carrots. They're already growing carrots in special fields, so they can be harvested early. You just wait. Our boys will soon be shooting down every night raider, no matter how dark the night.'

'Just *you* wait,' said Sadler scornfully. 'Wait until summer. Remember summer, when it's only dark for a few hours each night? The RAF won't need night vision, coz it'll be light when the bastards come over.'

Powell frowned and began to fussily clear the table. 'I'm only saying what I've heard. And there's no need for such language.'

The door to Moray's office opened and he stood in the doorway. 'Halliday, could you spare me a minute, please?' he said.

'What's the matter?' I asked, once I had sat down in front of his desk.

He closed the door behind me. 'The phone call was from Scotland Yard. A couple of detectives are coming here to see you. It's something about the Café de Paris apparently.'

'They want to talk to me?'

I was perplexed, until I remembered the locket. Then I stared at Moray, rigid with fear. It had to be about the locket. And because I hadn't handed it in I was going to be arrested for looting. *Why hadn't I mentioned it to Moray as soon as I arrived? Stupid, Maisie. Stupid.*

'Did they say what they wanted to see me about?' My voice was surprisingly level.

Moray shook his head. 'Just that it related to an incident at the Café de Paris. I confirmed that you were there.'

I nodded dumbly. No one would believe that I hadn't stolen the locket. There was only my word that it had turned up in my pocket without my knowledge. My mind lurched into a complicated fantasy of the police interrogation I was sure was to come:

I only found it on Monday. I had no idea it was in my pocket.

Why didn't you turn it over to the police immediately?

I wasn't sure what to do.

It's been days since the bombing, Miss Halliday.

Only two days.

The man's wife is distraught with grief at the loss of her husband and a valuable family heirloom.

'Halliday,' said Moray.

Jolted out of my daydream, I looked at him.

'Whatever is wrong? Afraid it will bring back bad memories?' His voice was kind.

'I had no idea it was in my pocket,' I said quickly. 'I only found it yesterday afternoon when I was doing my washing. And it's quite a cheap thing, not a valuable family heirloom.' I sighed. 'Although I suppose it could have great sentimental value.'

Moray's eyes widened. 'What? Found what?'

'It wasn't looting. I promise it wasn't. I'd never do that. You know I'd never do that.'

Moray was looking at me as if I'd gone doolally. 'Halliday, I have no idea what you're talking about.'

I took a breath and explained. 'Sorry. Yesterday I found a gold locket in the pocket of my slacks. I think it must have been given to me in the Café de Paris that night, but I don't remember it happening. More likely, it was slipped in my pocket when I was distracted.'

'Why didn't you hand it in to the police yesterday?'

'I was going to ask you today what to do, but I forgot.' I found that I was wringing my hands together nervously. I'd never been in trouble with the police before. 'I'm such an idiot.'

Moray shook his head. 'Well, don't worry too much about it. Of course you wouldn't steal from an injured person. I'll tell them that if they ask. But I don't think that's what they want to discuss with you.'

'What else would it be?' I said gloomily.

Detective Chief Inspector Wayland was a big man with an air of quiet authority. Detective Sergeant Norris was shorter, no higher than five foot four inches, with a wiry build and quick dark eyes and an expression that seemed to say he'd seen and heard it all.

I sat in Moray's office facing them.

'Miss Halliday,' said Wayland, 'you must be wondering why we've asked to see you.'

Moray had suggested that I remain calm, be cooperative, but keep quiet unless asked a specific question.

'Mr Moray said it was to do with the Café de Paris.'

'Do you remember a Sister Grant?'

'Of course I do. She was simply marvellous. Managed to get bandages for us.'

'It was because of her that we found you. She remembered you well, and spoke highly of you.'

'What's this about, please?'

'Sister Grant told us that you were caring for patients in the corner under the balcony. Is that correct?'

'Yes. I cared for an American with blast lung and a woman with facial injuries due to flying glass and a broken arm.'

'How do you know the man was an American?'

'Um, he had an American accent.'

'You spoke to him?'

'Briefly. He told me his name was Harry Egan.'

Wayland exchanged a look with Norris, who wrote something in the notebook. He turned back to me. 'Go on.'

'I examined him as best I could, but there was nothing I could do for him. So I left him to tend to the other patient, a woman. Um, then I saw someone searching Mr Egan's clothes. I called out, told him to stop, said that Mr Egan was badly wounded. He said that Mr Egan was dead. Then Sister Grant appeared and when I looked again, the looter had disappeared. Mr Egan was dead when I went to check on him.'

Wayland rubbed at his thick grey eyebrows. 'Could the looter have killed him?'

I drew in my breath with an audible gasp. I hadn't considered this before. Surely Michael wouldn't have... I tried to cast my thoughts back to that night, to remember exactly what I had seen.

'He searched Mr Egan thoroughly, but I never saw his hand over Mr Egan's mouth. That might have killed him, if he had stopped his breathing. Mr Egan was very weak.' I looked up at Wayland, bleakly unsure of what I had actually seen. 'I really think Mr Egan was already dying when I saw him. Blast lung is very hard to treat and often fatal.'

I knew I should tell them that I knew who the looter was. I knew that they needed to know it was Michael Harker. I stayed quiet.

Wayland nodded. 'Thank you, Miss Halliday. I should mention that the American Embassy has expressed concern about Mr Egan's death. They are especially concerned about the looting of his body. Is there anything more you can tell us? What did the looter look like?'

And then it all came tumbling out. 'Um, I should tell you I found a locket in my pocket. It may have come from Mr Egan, but I'm really not sure.'

Wayland broke into my hasty apology. 'A locket?'

'It looked like one ...'

'Why do you think it belonged to Mr Egan?'

'I'm not sure that it did. But he grabbed at me when I was checking his condition and he could have slipped it into my pocket then.'

'Where is it?'

'I've got it at home. I'll bring it to you. I didn't steal it, really I didn't. I didn't know I had it until I found it yesterday afternoon.'

'Why didn't you hand it in to the local police station yesterday?'

'I wasn't sure what to do about it, so I thought I'd ask Mr Moray this morning.'

Wayland frowned at me. 'I'm not saying the law would necessarily treat what you did as looting, Miss Halliday. But you should have handed it in as soon as you found the locket. The situation could be easily misconstrued as an intention to keep it. The American Embassy—'

'But I didn't—'

'Please bring the locket to me at Scotland Yard.'

'I'm off duty tomorrow. I'll bring it tomorrow afternoon.'

He ran his big hand over his face and looked at me with weary eyes. 'We'll need to inform the American Embassy all that you've told us. They're making quite a fuss about this.'

CHAPTER TWELVE

He found me in Manette Street.

I was walking back to the club at the end of my shift, in the early morning gloom under low clouds that threatened rain. My body was weary to the point of delirium and I seemed to hear dance rhythms in the echo of my footsteps.

I'd spent the night on the road with Lily, driving to incidents, picking up the wounded, finding my way through endless detours, past burning buildings and demolished houses. And all the while I was trying not to remember Michael Harker looting a dead man's body. Perhaps committing a murder. Trying to work out why I hadn't simply told the inspector his name.

He stepped out of the shadows to stand in front of me. The day was lightening quickly so that his features sharpened and became recognisable, showing the white bandage that covered the wound on his forehead, and the purple bruise on his chin. Had I caused that bruise? I hoped I had.

I flinched as he reached into his coat, but he pulled out only a packet of Player's. He offered it to me and I shook my head.

'Mind if I do?'

'Of course not.'

Slowly, deliberately, he shook out a cigarette and turned away to light it. I wondered briefly if I should take the opportunity to run, but dismissed the idea. He looked athletic. He'd just catch me and haul me back again. Better to find out what he wanted, and work out how not to give it to him.

'If you are trying to scare me,' I said, 'I should tell you now that I don't scare easily.'

He looked amused. 'You think I'm some gangster heavy from Chicago?'

'I'm sure gangster heavies come from all over the United States. Even western Pennsylvania.'

'Aw, you remembered. I'm touched.'

'And I'm leaving,' I snapped. I turned and began to walk towards Greek Street. He walked with me, but kept his distance. There was a dawn freshness to the air and it cooled my heated cheeks. It was easy, now, to see where I was walking and to avoid obstacles. I hoped that I could similarly avoid any traps set by Mr Michael Harker.

'What's going on?' I asked. 'Why are you here?' My voice was clipped and angry.

'It's not what it seems,' he said. 'And I'm not a gangster heavy from anywhere. Let me buy you breakfast, so we can talk about it in comfort. I need a cup of coffee, and I'm sure you could use a cup of tea.'

I considered his offer. Surely I'd be safe in a crowded place, and I did want some answers.

'All right.'

The Victory restaurant in Greek Street was open for breakfast and he ushered me in. It wasn't crowded so early in the day, but there were about six people sitting at tables inside. One of them was my streetwalker friend Edna, who nursed a cup of coffee at a table near the window. Her face was white and drawn, but she had reapplied her lipstick so that her red mouth stood out like a scarlet slash. I remembered her telling me that she'd often duck into a cafe around this time of the morning, to be out of the cold when there was little chance of picking up any trade.

She saw us walk in, looked Michael up and down, raised her cup in a mock toast and winked at me. Edna's attempt at insouciance always touched my heart, especially as she didn't look particularly well that morning.

I walked over to her, followed by Harker. 'Are you hungry?' I asked her. 'If so, I'm sure Mr Harker would love to buy you breakfast.'

'It would be my pleasure, ma'am,' he said to Edna, with one of his charming smiles.

Edna's answering smile revealed several broken teeth and those that were left were badly stained. 'Thanks, love. Bacon, eggs, toast – the works, please. Y'er a champion.' Her look became stern. 'But you be sure to look after our Maisie. She's a treasure, she is. And a real lady, so no mucking about, hear.'

'None whatsoever,' he replied, and I gave an unladylike snort.

We sat at a table in a corner, and Harker ordered a full breakfast for Edna, a cup of coffee for himself and, when I refused any food, a pot of tea for me.

'Friend of yours?' he asked, nodding towards Edna. He looked elegant and unruffled, and a smile played around his lips. The bandage that covered his forehead gave him a vulnerable air that I knew to be utterly false.

'I've lived in Soho for years, on and off,' I replied. 'You get to know people. Edna used to be on the stage, but fell on hard times.'

'And you thought, there but for the grace of God ...'

'No. I'd honestly rather die than have her life. But I'd never judge her for it. Ever been hungry, Mr Harker?'

He leaned forward to stub out his cigarette in the ashtray, then settled back in his chair and gave me a long, cool look. 'Yes, I've been hungry. I grew up in a poor family, Miss Halliday.'

I didn't believe him. At least, I didn't believe he had any idea of what it was like for Edna on the Soho streets, or had been for me in Sheffield's slums.

'What do you want?' I asked.

'I'm with the American Embassy.'

He handed over a card which announced he was Z. Michael Harker of the United States Embassy in Grosvenor Square, Mayfair. Again, I wondered what the 'Z' stood for.

'How can I possibly believe anything you say,' I said. 'Did you run me over on purpose last week?'

'Of course not. You jumped out in front of me. Coincidences do happen.'

'Why are you here? What do you want?'

'Harry Egan, the man who died in the Café de Paris bombing on Saturday night, was a colleague of mine at the embassy. Yesterday afternoon we received from Scotland Yard the notes of their interview with you that morning. So we know you are holding a watch fob – what you called a locket – that may have belonged to Harry Egan. I'd like to see it, see if it was Harry's.'

'Because you didn't have a chance to steal it on Saturday night?'

He said nothing, but a muscle twitched at the side of his mouth.

'I don't know that it belonged to Mr Egan,' I said. 'I found it in my pocket. Anyone could have put it there.'

'Let me see it and I'll tell you. He used to wear a fob attached to his watch chain. A square-shaped gold locket embossed with a star. A sapphire was in the centre of the star. If it was Harry's then his widow will want it back.'

I tried again. 'And that is what you were looking for when you searched his body?'

He paused, and stared down at the table, then said, quietly, 'Not necessarily. As I told you that night, I knew he was carrying something important and I wanted to retrieve it before his body was taken to the morgue and searched there.'

I glanced at the card he had given me. 'Anyone can have a card printed. It's a different card from the one you sent with the book.'

'Did you like the book?'

There was a boyish eagerness in the way he asked the question.

My cheeks became warm. I looked down at my tea, and murmured, 'Yes, I enjoyed it very much. Thank you.'

'Please look at this,' he said.

Michael reached into his breast pocket, pulled out a folder and passed it to me. The folder contained an identity paper from the US War Office. It identified 'Zebulon Michael Harker, born October 23, 1912. Eyes blue, hair brown, weight 160 lbs, height 6 foot 2 inches'. The photograph was a good likeness. The document even contained his fingerprints, neatly printed at the side. It had to be real. No one would make up a false identity with that name.

'Zebulon?' I asked.

'My grandpa's name. It's from the Bible, of course. The sixth son of Jacob and Leah.'

'I know that,' I said, a trifle smugly. After twelve years of listening to Granddad practise his sermons I had a fair knowledge of scripture. 'Zebulon dwells at the haven of the sea and shall be for a haven of ships. You should be in the navy, Zebulon Michael Harker.'

Michael shook his head slowly and gave a short laugh. 'You're full of surprises, Miss Halliday. Or may I call you Maisie?'

'By all means call me Maisie ... if I may I call you Zeb.'

'Michael will do.'

'Then so will Miss Halliday.'

He was no longer smiling. 'Very amusing. But I think we should be serious.'

I glared at him. 'So do I. You rifled Mr Egan's body. It was horrible.' I sucked in a shaky breath. 'Did you kill him? They asked me.'

Again he had become very still. 'I've seen your statement. You didn't mention I was there. I think it's because you know I didn't kill him.'

'I'm not sure why I didn't tell them about you.'

He pulled out his packet of cigarettes from his breast pocket and shook one out. He didn't light it, but rolled it around in his long fingers, back and forth, in and out.

'He died a minute or so after you left him,' he said, watching the cigarette as he rolled it through each finger, with no small amount of skill. 'Poor old Harry.'

'Did you touch him at all before he died?'

'No. I was talking to him, but he didn't seem to hear me. He took a gasping breath, and died.' He looked at me, fixing me with his ice blue gaze. 'We were friends, after a fashion. I didn't kill him. The German bomb did that. I'd gone to the Café de Paris to see him, though. He was going to meet someone, and I hoped to convince him not to go through with ... what he'd intended to do.'

'What did he intend to do?'

'Something dumb and dangerous.' Michael was still looking down at the cigarette he was rolling around in his fingers. 'In all the darkness and confusion I lost him.' He looked at me, imploring me to trust him. 'Maisie, I'm with the US government. I hated to search his body, but it was important. I needed to get hold of what he was carrying. You can trust me.'

'Well, I *don't* trust you, no matter what government you work for.' I frowned at him. 'You say you read Inspector Wayland's report. Then you must know I'm going to take the locket to the police in Scotland Yard today. Why not get it from the police once I've handed it over, or at least ask them to show it to you?'

'I'd like to get hold of it first. It may contain material that's potentially embarrassing to the US government.'

'How? In what way, embarrassing?'

He was silent. The waitress arrived with his coffee and my tea. She placed them carefully on the table, giving Michael a smile as she did so.

I poured myself a strong cup, took a sip and sat back in my chair, watching him and thinking furiously. So Zebulon Michael Harker worked for the War Office and was attached to the US Embassy in London. Everyone knew that if you worked for the War Office you worked in Intelligence. It looked awfully like Michael Harker was an American spy. So where did his allegiance lie?

A new American ambassador had arrived in London the week before to replace Joseph Kennedy, who had been known in London as

'Jittery Joe', because he'd moved out of the capital rather than face the Blitz. He had been no friend to Britain. Ambassador Kennedy's speeches had been widely reported in the newspapers and in them he had said that he thought that Britain was facing defeat at the hands of the Nazis. He also said that he was utterly opposed to any American aid being given to us to help us fight the Nazis. He wanted America to stay neutral, no matter what Hitler did in Europe.

I had no time for Michael Harker's former boss and I certainly didn't care if Jittery Joe Kennedy was embarrassed. On the other hand, I liked President Roosevelt, who seemed to be a friend to Britain.

Michael took a sip of coffee, grimaced and put the cup down. 'Maisie, what the locket may or may not contain does not concern you.'

'There's nothing in it,' I said brusquely.

'What?'

'I looked in the locket. It has a photograph of a woman from around 1900. Nothing else.'

'Then there's no harm in letting me look at it.'

'And no harm in me giving it to the British police and letting them decide whether to show to you.' I took a sip of tea and opened my eyes widely in what I hoped was an artless look.

His mouth tightened. Any hint of a smile had disappeared, and for the first time I could see that Michael Harker would be a dangerous enemy.

'If it has what I think it might have in it,' he said, 'and that falls into the wrong hands, then it would be embarrassing for my country, but potentially disastrous for yours.' He put his arms on the table, leaned forward and looked straight into my eyes. 'I'm being straight with you, Maisie. It's that important. For your country and for mine.'

I looked away, confused. The whole episode was bizarre, and I was tired after a long night on duty. I no longer wanted to engage in verbal sparring with Michael Harker, I just wanted to curl up in bed and forget all about him. And so I capitulated.

'You can look at it, see if it has what you want but not take it away with you. If it does, you can get it from Scotland Yard. I promised to give it to the police today and I will.'

'Thanks, Maisie. You're a champ.'

I had a feeling the word should be 'chump', so I added a rider. 'You can look at the locket,' I repeated, 'but only where I can keep an eye on you, because, well, to be frank, I don't trust you not to steal it.'

He gave me one of his devastating smiles. 'Where?'

'The Theatre Girls' Club. My boarding house.'

'The barred and gated harem? I'm sure looking forward to that,' he said.

Edna called out to Michael as we left the restaurant. 'Thanks, love. Any time I can do you a favour, just ask.' When she was rewarded with another of his dazzling smiles, she raised a hand to her forehead and pretended to swoon. 'He's a corker, love,' she called to me.

Not the word I'd have used.

CHAPTER THIRTEEN

We didn't speak, but I could feel his good humour as he walked beside me to the club. It worried me. From what I could tell, Zebulon Michael Harker was so sneaky that he made a fox seem dull-witted.

I rang the bell and we waited in the early morning sunshine for someone to open up.

'You don't have a key?' he asked.

'No. We can only come in between six in the morning, when the cook gets up, and eleven at night when the housekeeper goes to bed.'

'Sounds like the girls' dorms at my college,' he said. 'Very strict rules. But somehow they always found a way around them to have a good time.'

I shrugged. 'The restrictions at the club chafe a little, but it's a safe, clean and friendly place. That's all I need after a hard shift.'

He didn't reply. When I twisted around to look at him he was watching me. For once his face was open, unmasked and there was no smile. Again, I felt fixed in the pale blue of his eyes.

I was suddenly all too aware of how I must look. Hair tumbling out of the low chignon I swept it into when I was working. My filthy uniform partially covered by a tatty raincoat. Face only as clean as a quick wipe-over with the flannel at work could make it, because the hot water was off again that morning and I'd not been inclined to take a cold shower. I knew I looked tired, because I felt utterly exhausted.

'You're no older than those girls at my college were,' he said, reaching out to brush some hair away from my eyes. 'Only nineteen.'

My mouth had become dry. 'Nearly twenty.'

The corner of his mouth lifted. 'Nineteen. And not one of those college girls would ever have gone through anything like what you face, night after night. I saw you down there, in that nightclub, acting like a – a – like an angel of mercy.'

I swallowed, embarrassed, and blurted out, 'I'm not—'

'You're an example of everything that's good about this country.' He stared at me again for a long minute, reached his hand and ...

And Lorna Gaskin opened the door.

'Hello, Maisie,' she said in a sing-song voice. Then she caught sight of Michael and her eyes went wide. 'Oh, are you seeing Maisie home safely?' Her smile lit up her face. 'Maisie never – I mean, silly me. How do you do? I'm Lorna Gaskin.'

Michael smiled at her. I thought she'd keel over on the spot.

'Pleased to meet you, Miss Gaskin. I'm Michael Harker.'

'Oh – you're American.' She looked at me, wide-eyed. 'I thought you were joking about wanting to go out with John Wayne.'

I could feel Michael's amusement. It emanated from him in waves.

'I *was* joking,' I said, flushing. 'It's not like that—'

'Of course it's not like that,' he said smoothly. 'I make a point of never dating teenagers.' I had a feeling the comment was directed not at Lorna but at me, which was annoying.

'I'm twenty-two,' breathed Lorna.

I broke in, saying hurriedly, 'Mr Harker is here to see a piece of jewellery I found at an incident. It, er, it might belong to him.'

Her face became a mottled red. 'Oh, sorry. Please do come in. The common room's upstairs.' As he climbed up before us she whispered to me, 'So, is he married?'

'I have absolutely no idea,' I replied, and swept past her up to the common room as regally as I could.

Michael had already made himself comfortable in one of the armchairs. Very comfortable indeed. With six young women chattering and laughing around him, he brought to mind a sheik surrounded by his harem, which was just the word he'd used to describe the club. Lorna pushed me aside to join in the fun.

'It's simply marvellous to meet an American,' Bobbie was saying. 'And we do appreciate all that your country is doing for us.'

'I dote on Mr Roosevelt,' said Lorna, who had burrowed her way through to the front of the crowd.

'I'll get it, Mr Harker,' I called out from the doorway. 'Be back in a moment.'

He was barely visible through the gaggle of theatre girls, but I caught sight of his hand waving in reply.

I clumped up the stairs. *Was he married*? I had no idea, but it was clear that he saw me as a kid, a college aged girl. *I make a point of never dating teenagers*. I'd been looking after myself since I was sixteen, thank you very much, Mr Harker. And that meant I was really much, much older than those American college girls in their bobby socks and ponytails and good times. *An angel of mercy*. Hah! I did my job, that was all.

And who was Michael Harker anyway? A privileged American with great teeth and a college education. How I detested men who thought that they were entitled to take their pick of the girls because of their money and their upbringing and their good looks. Give me a man who knew what it was like to be cold and hungry, knew how it felt to see those you loved suffer, knew how tough the world could be. Not anyone in the slightest like Zebulon Michael Harker. *Ridiculous name, anyway.*

I found the locket buried under my blue sweater and pulled it out into the light to look closely at the photograph inside. Could this pretty woman in her old-fashioned clothes somehow be able to embarrass America and put my country in danger?

It made no sense. And then, as if a lever had clicked into place in my fuddled brain, I realised. Spies used miniature cameras. And miniature film.

I found my eyebrow tweezers and gently lifted the corner of the photograph in the locket. It came out with a bit of coaxing. Behind it was a small, neat, thin package that revealed itself to be four photographic negatives wrapped in rice paper.

Michael was sitting at his ease when I entered the common room, still surrounded by young women but now chatting to Miss King. From her smile it was clear that he had charmed her as well. I despaired of my sex.

He threw his devastating smile at me when I entered the room. I did not return it and held up the locket. The smile faded and he stood up as I walked across to hand it to him.

'Yes,' he said, holding up the locket to the light. 'That's it.' He opened it, gazed at the photograph inside and sighed.

'So it is yours?' said Bobbie. 'Is that your mother's photograph?'

'Sure is. Can you see the likeness?' The girls crowded around to look and my exclamation was lost in the general cooing. The consensus was that Michael was the image of Mom, and what a pretty woman she had been.

'It's my only memento of Mom as a young woman. She ...' He blinked a little faster than usual, to give the impression of holding back tears.

'I'm so sorry,' murmured Bobbie, usually the most hard-nosed of all of us. 'When did you lose her?'

'Two years ago. She was plain worn out from looking after us all, I guess. I'm from a family of eleven.'

'She sounds wonderful,' said Bobbie as I stared on in horrified amazement.

Bobbie, you're an actress, I wanted to shout to her. *Can't you tell he's acting? It's flimflam.* I wondered what other tales he had told the girls and Miss King in my absence. How easy I had made it for him with my stupid lie to Lorna. I had wanted to stop her questions, but it seemed that he'd used and embellished my story. *Sneakier than a blinking fox is Z. Michael Harker.*

The girls made the usual noises of sympathy to Michael, but as they did so they tossed back their hair, stuck out their chests and licked their lips. Zebulon Michael Harker was certainly a hit with the theatre girls. Even Miss King patted her curl helmet.

I'd never spoken about what had happened in the Café de Paris to anyone in the club. No one knew about my interview with the police yesterday, except for Michael. No wonder he had seemed so chirpy. How could I now tell the truth, say to the girls that the locket had belonged to a dead man and I had promised to give it to the police today? They would think I'd gone mad. I had a mad fantasy of snatching it from his grasp and running away, but he'd only catch me. I contented myself with glaring at him.

He chatted with the girls and Miss King for a few minutes longer, then rose and looked at me. I swear I saw him wink.

'Maisie,' he said, 'I can't thank you enough for returning this family treasure to me.' He slipped it into his breast pocket and stood up. 'And now, sadly, I have an appointment that can't wait.'

Unless they physically held him back, and it was clear that some of them itched to do so, the girls had to allow him to leave the room.

'Give it back,' I said flatly, as I walked with him down the stairs.

'Sorry, I can't do that.'

We had reached the front door. He was about to walk away with the locket and I couldn't think of a single thing I could do to stop him.

'What am I supposed to tell Inspector Wayland?'

He reached into his pocket. I had a moment of delirious hope that he would return the locket to me, but instead he pulled out a card. He held it against the door jamb while he scribbled something on the back. He handed it over.

It was the same card he'd shown me before, with his name and the US Embassy address. On the back he'd written a telephone number and, '*Not her fault. I tricked her and took it.*' He had signed his name.

'That should do it,' he said. 'They won't blame you.' He gave me a hard, straight look. 'What I told you earlier about what might be in the fob is secret. It's important to keep it secret.'

'But—'

'I'm sorry, Maisie. You're a good kid. I promise you it is important, or I wouldn't have pulled such a cheap trick.'

A wave of fury swept through me, but I kept my voice calm. 'It was a beastly trick. You are a sneaky, nasty rat.'

'If it makes you feel better, I'm going to make sure that Egan's widow gets this. Now you please get some rest, you look like you're about to keel over.'

And with those comforting remarks, he turned on his heel and set off along Greek Street without a backward look. Which meant that he didn't see me smile, or hear me whisper, 'Sorry, Michael. But I'm a Yorkshire lass, who won't stand for t'egg under t'cap.' Which meant I was not as gullible as Michael would like to believe.

In my room, in my underwear drawer, tucked safely into my empty powder compact, was a small packet of rice paper wrapped around four photographic negatives.

CHAPTER FOURTEEN

I felt much better after a few hours' sleep, although I faced a barrage of questions about Michael when I ventured downstairs. To all of them I replied that he worked for the US Embassy and I had no idea if he was married. Also that I was unlikely ever to meet him again.

Safely back in my room, I retrieved my powder compact and opened it to look at the little square parcel. Had I made a serious mistake in removing it? I had been so tired earlier that I'd found it hard to think straight. If Michael were to be believed, it could be devastating for Britain if this information fell into the wrong hands. But I really wasn't sure that his hands were the right ones.

I'd taken the negatives because he had lied to me, tricked me and treated me like a fool. Although he worked for the American Embassy, I wasn't sure where his loyalty lay. To Jittery Joe Kennedy, who was no friend of Britain's? Or did he support the brand new Ambassador Winant, who had made all the right noises about being on Britain's side in this war?

Should I give the negatives to the police? I liked Inspector Wayland, but he was a detective, not involved in espionage. It might be better to make sure that someone in the British Intelligence Service had them. Or simply to destroy them.

Lily's husband, Jim Vassilikov, had transferred to Air Force Intelligence after being too badly injured to keep flying. Should I speak to him about the negatives? Or perhaps I should tell Michael that I had what he wanted, but I would not hand them over until he gave me a clear explanation as to what they were.

The problem was that I wasn't at all sure I liked the idea of seeing Michael Harker again. He was too untrustworthy, and far too charming.

First of all, though, I had to go to Scotland Yard and explain what had happened to the locket. I was not looking forward to telling Inspector Wayland what a fool I'd been. I wasn't sure I could rely on Michael's card. I'd need some protection from the inspector's anger.

The gas had come back on an hour before and I was able to have a hot bath. Only then did I feel human. I put up my hair into a pompadour at the front and my usual chignon at the back. My face was brightened with my small supply of pre-war powder, mascara and lipstick. And then I dressed up in a showgirl's armour, clothes that made the most of my figure. I slipped on a white woollen sweater that fitted like a second skin. This went under a well-cut blue-and-white check suit that I'd bought in Paris before the war. It fitted snugly – very snugly – in all the right places. There were some advantages to my figure. We Tiller Girls used to call our bosoms and backsides and long legs our 'assets'. I knew how to use my assets to distract men who might be inclined to scold me or ask too many difficult questions.

I looked in the mirror. My stocking seams were straight, and my shoes high-heeled to make the most of my slim ankles. I placed a perky Paris hat carefully at just the right angle and pulled on some lacy white gloves. It wasn't a particularly cold day and it didn't look like rain, so I decided to forgo a raincoat in order to take full advantage of my outfit.

I must have looked all right as I had a couple of low whistles when I passed a heavy rescue unit in Charing Cross Road on my way to the bus stop. The number 24 arrived fairly quickly, not a red London bus, but a brown bus from goodness knows where. It was pot luck as to which route the non-London bus would take, as there were so many diversions, but it lurched off in the right general direction along the crater-strewn and potholed road.

The journey was slow and depressing. We were diverted down narrow side streets that allowed us to peer into the first-floor windows of houses and flats. I saw a man in pyjamas, yawning, probably a night-shift worker waking after his daytime sleep. In another house a family was sitting down to tea. Their little girl waved at the bus as it passed.

Eventually we reached Charing Cross Road. The National Gallery was looking sadly the worse for wear, pock-marked by shrapnel and bullets. In Trafalgar Square, red-brick air-raid shelters, windowless and intimidating, had replaced the fountains. Nelson still stood on his column. With his good eye he would see prodigious destruction down The Mall, and in every direction, north, south, east, west. I wondered if he turned his blind eye to the mess. The statue of King Charles I astride his horse was penned inside a wall of brick and timber. The stone lions were scarred by shrapnel and I could see only a few pigeons.

My mood lightened as I remembered one of Powell's rumours. She had gravely informed us last week that the best West End restaurants were paying people to shoot the Trafalgar Square pigeons, so they could pass the meat off as chicken. Perhaps it was true, although I could not understand how any sniper could take proper aim at pigeons in the blackout. I suspected that this, like most of Powell's rumours, was claptrap.

We passed the now common sight of shops whose windows had been blasted. In place of glass the owners had erected plyboard facings with small holes cut in the middle so customers were still able to see the window displays. All around the plyboard were painted vivid and exuberant depictions of the shop's wares.

From shop doorways the usual queues stretched out along the footpaths. In January the meat ration had been halved. This was not such a deprivation for me as it seemed to be to everyone else, because meat was available only as a special treat when I was a girl. But it wasn't just the lack of meat that was so dispiriting to Londoners; for the past couple of months our diet had been generally restricted and meagre. There were so few items available to choose from. We weren't starving so much as bored, and food seemed to have replaced the weather as the main topic for conversation. What was particularly annoying was that everyone knew it was much easier for the rich than the poor to find a good meal.

It seemed to me that war was a mixture of horror and tedium. The horror was in my job. Tedium was everywhere else. There were no street signs, so you never really knew where you were. Every spare bit of wall was covered in posters nagging you not to waste bread, use unnecessary fuel, make long telephone calls, take an unnecessary journey or talk carelessly. Every day there were fewer items on the shop shelves, not just food and clothing, but the little things that made life easier. I could no longer imagine an end to any of it, not to the bombing or to the queuing or the black-out or any of the petty inconveniences of war.

'It broke my heart.' The woman in the seat behind me was chatting to her friend. 'How could I feed the poor little blighter if I'm not even supposed to give him scraps? Had to put him down. I don't know as how I'll tell Stan. He doted on that dog.'

'My little Tiger more than earns her keep, what with all the rats and mice she kills,' said her companion. 'But she can't survive on that alone. I have to feed her. I don't care what they do to me.'

'Bloody stupid rule, us not being allowed to feed our dogs and cats. I say, let's starve a politician instead.'

'Bloody stupid rule,' echoed her friend.

They fell silent when the bus turned into Whitehall and the terrible destruction of the past few nights became clear. I had to blink away tears. Smoke was still rising from the new ruins, and the bus bumped over the twisted coils of fire hoses that snaked across the road and disappeared into the rubbish and the wreckage.

My stop was just beyond the Cenotaph, and as I walked back past it to Richmond Terrace I remembered an old woman I'd treated, early on in the Blitz. She'd only suffered mild abrasions but seemed unable to stop crying. I had put my arms around her to let her weep on my shoulder.

'I'm so sorry, Miss,' she had said, between sobs. 'But my only son was killed in the Great War, the one they said was to end all wars. What good was it, my boy dying like that, now that we're doing it all over again?'

New Scotland Yard was an imposing building, sitting in red and white striped splendour on the Embankment. I took a deep breath, marched in and asked to see Inspector Wayland. As I followed the constable down a series of narrow corridors, I unbuttoned my jacket.

His office was small. Files were piled high on the desk and had spilled over on to the floor. He apologised for meeting me there, but said that the interview rooms were all being used.

There was a commotion at the door and Sergeant Norris bustled in and sat beside me, pad and pencil ready.

'So, Miss Halliday—' Wayland began.

'I don't have Mr Egan's locket.' My hands were gripped tightly around my handbag, which rested on my lap. I sucked in a quick breath and huffed it out, then looked up into his eyes.

'A Mr Michael Harker, from the American Embassy, tricked me into letting him see it and he took it. Stole it from me.'

I reached into my handbag and pulled out his card. As I did so I brushed my powder compact, which was empty except for the negatives. I still had not decided what to do with them. Michael had said that they were secret.

'He told me to give you this.' I handed over the card.

Wayland read carefully, front and back, then gave it to Norris.

'Did he say why he wanted the locket?'

'He … he wanted to give it back to Mr Egan's widow.' Wayland's brow wrinkled and he exchanged looks with Norris.

'Did you look inside the locket?' Wayland asked.

Now was the tricky part. How to tell some, but not all of it. I crossed my legs slowly and sat back in the chair, arching my back slightly as I did so. The jacket fell away, and my assets were clearly outlined in the tight sweater. Neither man was now looking at my face.

'Yes, I did look inside,' I said. Wayland looked up and held my gaze. I shifted again in my seat and smoothed my skirt over my knees. It was quite a short skirt. He no longer looked me in the eye. 'There was a photograph of a woman inside. From the way she was dressed, it had been taken about forty years ago.'

'Yes,' said Wayland. 'Well. Thank you, Miss Halliday.' He seemed about to say something else, but just then I reached up to brush a small piece of lint off my chest. There was silence for a moment. I looked enquiringly at Wayland, who dragged his eyes up to meet mine.

'Yes,' he said again. 'Well. Thank you, Miss Halliday. I'll telephone this Mr Harker and see what he has to say.'

I stood. Both men jumped up. Norris ushered me out, and Wayland followed him to the door. As I walked slowly away along the corridor I knew they were watching. My skirt was tight and I made the most of the long walk.

Outside the building I breathed a sigh of relief and glanced at my watch. Five o'clock. I could return to the club straight away, but I felt jittery, anxious and wanted to walk it off. What I needed, I decided, was a nice cup of tea. I'd pop into an ABC for refreshment and think about what I should do.

I was walking along the Embankment when I heard a whistle. I was used to men whistling, so I ignored it. What I could not ignore was the nasty feeling that someone had come up close behind me. I twisted around, ready to face whoever it was. Michael Harker was standing behind me.

'What do you want, Mr Harker?' I instinctively clutched my handbag closer. 'I gave your card to the Inspector. He said he'd telephone you. There's no need to stalk me.'

'But it's so delightful to stalk you,' he said, looking me up and down. He seemed less amused than usual. His voice was cool, and there was no smile. 'I think it's the first time I've seen you cleaned up and, my word, don't you just look pretty as a peach. Or is that too wholesome an image?'

'What do you want?'

He sighed. 'If you've got it, you know already. If you haven't got it, then it'll just have to remain a mystery.' He gave me a quick sharp glance. 'Did you take it? Give it to the police?'

I turned away from him and continued my stroll. He caught up and walked beside me.

'Bet I can walk longer than you can in those skyscraper heels.'

I looked steadily at the river, continued walking and said nothing.

'You know,' he said, musingly, 'one of my colleagues – a female one – tells me that when she wants to avoid the hard questions she dresses up real pretty. Works a treat, she tells me, and she has nowhere near the, er, natural advantages that are clearly – very clearly – outlined by that little number you're wearing.'

I continued my stroll, pretending I wasn't listening. His accent had changed, become different, more of a drawl. I had the feeling that he was extremely angry indeed. I wouldn't look at him. He wasn't to know I had the negatives in my handbag. He'd never dream I'd be that stupid. If I said nothing then perhaps he'd go away and I could work out what I should do with them. Perhaps I'd even give them to him, but I needed time to think about it.

'So I have to ask myself,' he went on, 'why would the kid dress up like that for a simple police interview? All I can think of is that she wanted to avoid the hard questions.'

He put a hand on my arm, pulled me around to face him and took hold of my chin to force me to look directly into his eyes.

'Questions like, did you find anything in the watch fob, behind that picture? Did you take the negatives, Maisie?'

I managed to look into those icy blue eyes for only a few seconds before I felt myself reddening and I dropped my gaze. His hand fell away from my face and he let go of my arm. He pointed to a bench and said, abruptly, 'Sit down.'

I sat, staring at the ground in front of my feet. My hands clutched my handbag. Michael sat beside me.

'Kid, this is not a joke. It's not a movie or a book or some jolly game. It's deadly serious and it's dangerous. For you and for me and for others also. I need them, and quickly. Where did you put them?'

I stared at the concrete path near my feet. It was cracked and pitted from shrapnel and bullets. Red brick-dust had filled the cracks so that it looked like a crazy painting in the earth.

'Answer me, kid. Where did you put them?'

'I'm not a kid.'

'Inhabiting a woman's body doesn't mean you're grown up. Where did you put them?'

'Or what? You'll torture me?' I was still looking at the ground. I felt him shift uneasily beside me.

'My colleagues will decide what to do with you.'

'Now you're trying to scare me.' I looked at him. 'I'll run back to Scotland Yard. They'll protect me.'

He took hold of my arm again and his voice was low and very cold. 'I won't let you do that.'

I shuddered. 'And you wonder why I don't trust you.'

His hand fell away.

Across from us was a half-destroyed building. All around me was evidence of what had been happening in the past six months. My face flamed, but now it was with anger. *How dare he threaten me? Here, in London.*

'Now you listen to me, Mr Michael Harker.' My voice was low and bitter. 'You told me that I'm mixed up in a very serious business. You said I'm in danger. What of it? I'm living through a Blitz. I'm in danger every bloody night. Don't you dare to talk to me about danger.'

I took a breath and tried to moderate my voice, but I was furious and I didn't care if he knew it.

'Britain is at war. London is under constant attack. Thousands of civilians have died already and more will die before the end. And I've been out there, night after night. I've watched them die. Our men are dying on battlefields and in the air and at sea. This country – my country – is fighting for its very existence as a free nation. Don't you *dare* talk to me about danger.'

He opened his mouth to speak, but I pressed on.

'How can I know that giving the – this thing – to you will help Britain? President Roosevelt seems to want to help us, but many prominent Americans are isolationist.'

I raised my eyes, and this time I held that blue gaze, forced him to look at me.

'Your Ambassador Kennedy has made it clear he wants to keep America neutral, stop *any* help coming to Britain. It's almost as if he would be happy for Germany to – to annihilate us.'

Michael shifted uneasily on the bench, then his mouth firmed. He said, 'There's a new ambassador now, who thinks differently about it.'

'And he's been in Britain, what? – a week? How do I know that you aren't in sympathy with Ambassador Kennedy's views?'

'I'm not.' His voice was low, urgent. 'Believe me, kid, I'm not. Of course I want to help this country. I've seen what it's going through, seen the everyday bravery and it's been an eye-opener for me. I *do* want to help you.'

I shook my head. 'Even if you sympathise with us, how do I know that your superiors – the ones who want this thing so desperately – how do I know they feel the same? What if they don't?'

I stopped my tirade and glared at him. This time his gaze fell first, which gave me a quite unreasonable feeling of elation.

'So I have to convince you that what you've got will be used for Britain's benefit?' he said slowly.

'At the very least, that it won't be used against us.'

'Hungry?' he asked.

'What?'

'Let's talk over dinner.'

CHAPTER FIFTEEN

I decided to accept his offer, mainly because I still had no idea
what to do with the negatives. I could have screamed, made
a fuss, insisted on returning to Scotland Yard, but how would
I explain what I had done? I wasn't at all sure that Inspector
Wayland would not have insisted that I immediately return
the negatives to the American Embassy, if they could prove
that the locket belonged to Mr Egan. A thought struck me like
a shard of ice. *Was it theft to remove the negatives? Had I
committed a crime?* And if I hadn't actually lied to the police,
I'd come very close. *Was it a lie to withhold information? Was
that a crime, too?*

'It's too early for dinner,' I said. 'What I'd really like is a cup
of tea.'

Apparently I'm what the Americans call 'a cheap date'. Or
so Michael said, after we alighted from the bus at Charing
Cross Road and I passed by the more exclusive teahouses.
Instead I chose an ABC. Michael ordered a pot of tea for
me and quaffed two cups of coffee himself as we talked
disinterestedly about the weather and what was likely to
go under the ration next, and anything but what was on our
minds. It was a relief to sit quietly drinking tea and let my
thoughts settle.

'I take it this is designed to make me trust you?' I said, as
I finished my second cup. 'It might work. I was becoming
desperate.'

Michael's eyes widened as I poured myself a third cup from
the dregs in the pot.

'That'll tan your insides,' he said, looking at the dark brown liquid that emerged from the teapot.

'It's certainly well mashed, as we say in Sheffield,' I said. 'No point in an insipid cup of tea, it's an abomination.'

'You're from Sheffield? That's where they make the steel, isn't it?'

I felt my cheeks become heated. 'Yes. Not many people know where I'm from. I usually keep my background to myself.'

'Why? Ashamed of it, or something?'

I took a sip of tea, which was strong even by my standards, and very bitter.

'Not ashamed.' I paused, considering how to answer. 'It's a wonderful city, and the people there – my people – are wonderful. Tough, no-nonsense and hard-working. They take nothing from no one but they'll always stick up for those around them. I'm proud to be of that stock. But I'm from a poor working-class background and that counts against you in this country.'

He raised the corner of his mouth in a slight sneer. 'Your English class system? That why you speak like you do? To fool people you're from a better class?'

I sighed. 'As I said, it counts in this country.'

Michael sat back in his chair, looked at me, but said nothing. I had a strong, almost irresistible, urge to talk to him about my childhood, and checked it with another sip of the almost undrinkable tea.

Then I told him anyway. 'I had a hard childhood. We were terribly poor. I was earning money for the family dancing in pantomimes from the time I was eight.'

'What about your dad?'

I stiffened and unwisely took another sip of tea.

'He, um, left when I was very young. We lived with my grandparents, who were ... difficult.'

'But you got yourself out of that poverty with your dancing. That's admirable. Why hide it?'

'You're American. In your country it's a badge of honour to have been born poor and overcome hardship to be rich.'

'Log cabin to president, you mean?'

I shrugged. 'I suppose so, although I'm not sure what that means. I mean that in America you're not judged by where you were born and who your parents were, and you're not put into a box because of that and never allowed to really break out of it.'

He started to speak, but I carried on. 'It's subtle, our class system. It's how you speak, and how you dress and how you hold your cutlery and where you went to school, and there are a thousand traps to catch those who pretend to be a higher class. But if you don't pretend then you're trapped, put into a box. Working class. Lower class. Common.'

How I hated the word 'common'. I'd heard it when I moved to London. *That Maisie Halliday, she's such a common girl. Common as muck. And a bastard to boot.*

'I love Sheffield,' I went on. 'In many ways I miss it terribly. But my dancing took me out of Sheffield to a dance academy in London. There it was made perfectly clear that my accent had to go. I'm not sorry about that, because even in the chorus line, if I spoke the way I was brought up to speak, I'd be treated entirely differently.'

He leaned back and looked at me. 'So, how were you brought up to speak?'

I laughed. 'Ge'ore.'

He smiled.

'Nah then, chuff, da shunt ask a lass aboot sech ma'ers. Tha bes'nt't dood at.'

Michael laughed. 'I got only two words in all of that.'

I laughed, too. 'It's a grand place, Sheffield. If you went, you'd probably only hear the constant thud of the drop hammers and see the black walls and the soot – all the walls are black and there's always soot and smoke in the air – but it's so much more than that.'

'Have you been back often?'

'Not since I left when I was twelve.'

'Not even to see your grandparents.'

I hesitated. 'To tell you the truth, I didn't get on with them. I send them money regularly, but I'm happy not to see them.'

'Treat you badly?'

'My grandmother isn't well and my granddad is a very religious man. They didn't really appreciate having me or my mother around.' I looked up and gave him a hard stare. 'And I'm not saying anything more about it.'

Another sip of bitter tea made my stomach lurch.

'Do you think this class stuff will change after the war?' he asked. 'You're all pulling together now against the Germans.'

'I think this Blitz is breaking down class barriers at the moment, but as to whether it will last …' I shrugged. 'Who knows. It runs pretty deep in this country. I hope so.'

'I think it's screwy.' He finished his cup of coffee. 'Look, it's too early to eat, so what about checking the news for an hour or so and then grabbing a bite?'

I accepted this offer, too. I wanted to get to know Michael Harker better, to understand more about the negatives and why he wanted them. That was what I told myself, anyway.

The news cinema was almost full. It was common for people to pop in after work, to check what was happening in the war.

We saw film of fierce fighting by the Greek army on the Yugoslavian frontier. Then our own British army which, despite heavy enemy attacks, was steadily making headway to Keren, in Ethiopia.

'My knowledge of geography has certainly improved with this war,' I whispered to Michael. He breathed a laugh.

The next item was the widespread, but as yet unconfirmed, reports that the Japanese planned to send a hundred thousand troops to Thailand, from where they would head towards British Malaya or turn north-east, towards the Burma border.

'Japan is the great unknown in this war,' Michael whispered to me. 'You Brits think that Singapore is impregnable, but I have my doubts. The Japanese army is a tough, well-trained opponent, one that you continually underestimate. I think America does, too.'

The final story was the American Lend-Lease Bill, which had been just signed into law by President Roosevelt.

'What does the Lend-Lease Bill mean?' boomed the announcer. 'Is it a financial transaction? Is it purely a declaration of warm friendship between Great Britain and the United States? Actually, it enables weapons and munitions to be handed over in various ways – by transfer, exchange, selling, leasing and lending.'

The magnitude of the Lend-Lease plan was staggering. America was to begin filling British orders for war supplies worth £750,000,000, including fifty thousand planes, nine thousand tanks, nearly four hundred warships and vast quantities of munitions.

'See,' said Michael, as we left the cinema, 'America is trying to help you as much as it can.'

I was sceptical. 'Your munitions factory owners are making a lot of money while you're doing it.'

'The important thing is that you don't have to pay for it right now. Lend-Lease gives you what you need, even though you can't afford it.'

'We'll have to pay for it all eventually, though.'

'Everyone has to pay for everything eventually, kid.'

'The way I see it is that Britain will have a huge national debt at the end of the war. I just hope your so-called American generosity doesn't bankrupt us.' My voice became higher. 'I wonder if Roosevelt is really on our side with this Lend-Lease scheme, or just lining the pockets of his wealthy industrialist friends.'

I'd been brought up in the Steel City, and such talk came easily to me. 'Never trust a wealthy factory owner' had been taken in with my mother's milk. So I wasn't prepared for Michael's response.

He took my arm in a tight grip, pulled us closer to a sandbagged shop front and swung me around to face him. Our sudden stop meant that a few people bumped into us, gave us puzzled looks, then walked on hurriedly, their faces turned away. Michael ignored them. The sun had set, but in the twilight I still could make out his tight mouth and the deep crease between his eyebrows.

'You criticise my president without any understanding of what he's up against.' I flinched at the bitter edge to his voice. 'You have no idea – absolutely no idea – how much Roosevelt is putting himself on the line for your country. He's risking almost everything to try to help you Brits.'

After a beat or two he dropped my arm. He reached into his jacket, took out a packet of Player's and shook out a cigarette. He didn't light it. Instead he played with it the way he had before, running it through his fingers in the way a magician played with a card before he made it disappear. I watched him, worried about his sudden angry mood. Then he looked at me and smiled. It was somewhat forced, but a smile.

'We can talk about it over dinner,' he said.

I agreed, telling myself yet again that I wanted to know more about this Michael Harker, and more about what I was holding. But I think I knew he wouldn't let me leave unless I agreed to hand over what I'd found in the watch fob. Like the Japanese Empire, Michael Harker was a tough opponent, and one I dared not underestimate.

He laughed when I suggested that we go to a British Restaurant, and vetoed the suggestion immediately.

'Why?' I demanded. 'Are you a snob? The food is filling and good quality. You can get a three-course meal for 9d.'

'That's not the problem. It's too well lit. And you're wearing ...'

'A woollen suit.'

'That's been sprayed on to you.'

I ran my hands down the side of my jacket to my waist and swept him a look through my eyelashes. 'This old thing?'

He rolled his eyes. 'That doesn't work with me, kid. But I'm worried you'll start a riot if we go anywhere that men other than me can get a good look at you. Haven't you been noticing the looks you're getting, even in the blackout.'

I gave a gurgle of laughter. 'No, I most certainly haven't. I do think you're exaggerating.'

As I spoke a man twisted around to look at me by moonlight and banged into the corner of a brick surface shelter that jutted out on to the footpath.'

'See. You're a war hazard, a danger to the men of London.'

I shrugged, in the French manner, but dispensed with the pout. 'I suppose I'm used to it. The Tiller Girls always caused a lot of interest in Paris. Men would follow us down the street, calling things out. We learned to ignore it. It was only a problem when the men thought they had a chance and made a nuisance of themselves. We learned how to deal with that, too.'

'And they didn't have a chance?'

I laughed. 'You have no idea how strictly chaperoned we were in Paris. Miss Barbara scrutinised every girl's potential boyfriend. And if she didn't approve, he was out.'

'And what did she think of your potential boyfriends? Rejected all of them, I hope. You would have been, what? Sixteen?'

'I'd put my age up. They thought I was eighteen when I arrived.'

He shook his head. 'I can't believe your mother let you head off to France alone when you were only sixteen.'

'Mam didn't know. She ... died suddenly. And then I decided to go to Paris.' My voice faded, and I swallowed. 'It was her heart, they think.'

His voice was gentle. 'I'm sorry. It's tough to lose your mom so young.'

I swallowed, blinked a few times, then managed another shrug. 'If you won't take me to a British Restaurant,' I said briskly, 'then where?'

'I know a place in Soho, close to your Theatre Girls' Club. Nice and dark with good food.' He looked around. 'We'll never get a taxi, so it's the bus.' He shrugged off his raincoat. 'Put this on, will you? I'm tired of the attention you attract. It'll come to blows soon.'

'My hero,' I said, in a mocking voice. But I shrugged on the raincoat he was holding out to me. It was warm and subtly scented with his cologne. An Englishmen wouldn't be caught dead wearing cologne, but Americans were different. I liked the spicy, rather oriental, scent.

The bus that stopped for us was smartly coloured, in cream with wide blue stripes.

'What's up?' said Michael. 'Your eyes are wide as saucers.'

We climbed on board and, sure enough, a sunken aisle was down one side with the seats up a little step. I brushed away a tear.

'What is it?' repeated Michael.

I pulled out my hankie and blew my nose when we'd sat down. 'It's silly really. This is a Sheffield bus. London buses are red all over, but they're running out of them because of war damage, so they've begun importing buses from all over the country. I was on a Manchester bus the other day, but this is my first Sheffield one.' I waved at the advertisement for Stone's Bitter. 'No Londoner would have heard of that.' I blinked away more tears, and tried to laugh. 'You must think I'm such a chuff – I mean a fool – for becoming sentimental over a beer advertisement.'

Michael smiled and shook his head. 'I don't think anyone's a fool, or even a chuff, because they feel homesick once in a while.'

We got off in Soho and walked down Dean Street, past the York Minster pub, that locals now called the French House. Loud laughter and some singing floated out from behind the blacked out windows, and I deduced that, as usual, it was overrun with Free French soldiers. About halfway down the street Michael found a discreet doorway and ushered me inside.

I pushed through the blackout curtain to find he'd brought me to a little French bistro that reminded me achingly of Paris, especially as the only language I could hear being spoken was French. Like the French House, it was obviously a Free French haunt.

The patron, whom Michael addressed as Leon, assured him that he could find Monsieur 'Arker a table in a quiet corner.

'Leave the raincoat *on,*' hissed Michael, as I began to take it off.

Leon winked at him, said something in French and deftly peeled the raincoat off my shoulders. He hung it on the coat stand by the door and turned back to me, gazing appreciatively, in the way that only a Frenchman can manage. It's somehow a compliment, a leer, a question and a promise, all at once. Michael grimaced, grabbed my arm and hauled me through the crowded restaurant to our table.

As it was full of Free French soldiers, I was ogled extensively and came in for lascivious looks, whistles, wordless cries and a few pithy remarks. Michael's scowl was truly fearsome, which made me feel like giggling. So I smiled, and the comments, whistles and shouts increased in volume.

'I pity the man you end up with,' he said, when we finally made it to our table.

'They're just being French. It's a game with them.'

'You're used to that sort of thing?' He sounded incredulous. 'It was like feeding time at the zoo.'

'You learn to ignore it. They think it a compliment. Englishmen, and perhaps Americans also, are mainly interested in a woman's face. French men look at the whole picture. They appreciate a woman's figure, and also how she walks, carries her clothes – her style. You may not like my suit, but it flatters my figure and I look stylish in it. The men were telling me that. I appreciate why they do it, but I don't particularly enjoy it.'

'I don't think they were whistling at your style.' His eyes narrowed. 'And you *were* enjoying it. I saw your smile.'

123

'Look,' I said, on a huff of exasperation, 'chorus girls are just like any other girls. We do a job. Part of that job is to be a fantasy, and so we smile. But that's not necessarily who we are. The reason I don't have much of a social life is because men assume ... well, you can guess what they assume. And, to be frank, I'm not that sort of girl.'

He leaned back in his chair and gave me a straight look. 'What sort of girl are you, Maisie Halliday? The sort that steals important information? Maybe you're the sort that wants money to give it back?'

CHAPTER SIXTEEN

I couldn't breathe: it was as if my entire body had been doused in icy water. Goosebumps tingled on my arms. Then thought returned.

How dare he? How dare this man, who had been so friendly, laughing with me, so protective and so – so nice that I had revealed private things to him, how dare he insinuate that I was a cheap little money-grubbing ... *How dare he*?

I swallowed, took a breath, and sat up straight. Then I looked him straight in the eye. 'I'll leave you now,' I said, very quietly. 'I'd rather take my chances with a pack of rowdy Frenchmen than spend a minute longer—'

He grabbed my arm in a hard, uncompromising grip. 'No. You stay right here, Maisie. You can leave after we've finished our chat. I've upset you? I'm not sorry for that. Often it's the way to be sure about somebody. I'm now pretty sure that the thought of payment had never entered your head.'

'It didn't.'

'Does it now? I'm authorised to offer a substantial amount of money to you for the safe return of the, er, object.'

My eyes widened. I stared at him, then found myself laughing. His hand dropped away and he sat back, watching me through narrowed eyes.

'No, Mr Harker, it doesn't. I'll give it to you if I think it's the right thing to do. Don't mention money again, please.'

'Then what? What *should* I mention? What would it take to get you to give it back?'

'Tell me about the dead man?' I asked. 'Why did he have the, er, thing?'

'His name was Harold Egan. He was American and a clerk at the embassy. That's all I can tell you. What Egan had, why he had it, is not your business. It belongs to the American government, Maisie. That's all you need to know.'

'Then we're at a stalemate.'

Michael stared at me for a few beats, frowning furiously. He sucked in a deep breath, picked up the menu and spent some time glaring at it. Then there was a swift glance up at me.

'Says they have chicken in their stew. Want to risk it? Might be pigeon.' His voice was pleasant, a polite enquiry.

The change in his manner disconcerted me. It was as if our previous conversation had never occurred.

'I'll risk it.'

As Michael ordered our meal, I thought about what had happened. The way he had behaved reminded me of men who wanted to get me into bed. Just like Michael Harker they had only one goal, and to get it they were prepared to lie, cajole, flatter, feign interest in me as a person. Michael's single goal was to obtain the negatives. How could I trust him? I didn't trust him.

I felt dizzy, unsure of what my next step should be. Michael said I'd stolen the negatives. Inspector Wayland would probably agree, and that worried me. I was not a thief. But who did they really belong to? Why did Mr Egan take them to the Café de Paris? Who was he meeting there? Why was Michael so determined to get them? I had thought I could sum up a man's character well, but Michael Harker stumped me.

His voice broke into my thoughts. 'I'm going to order some wine. What's the drinking age here?'

'Eighteen.'

He ordered a carafe of wine. It arrived quickly and he poured me a glass of ruby red liquid. I resolved to drink it slowly. I'd need all my wits about me in dealing with Michael Harker.

I took a sip of wine. It was deceptively smooth, far too easy to drink, so I put the glass back on the table. I didn't trust him, and getting a girl drunk was the oldest trick in the book.

'I repeat,' he said in an easy voice, 'what would it take to get you to give it back?' His expression sharpened. 'Have you told anyone about what you took?'

'Not *told*, not exactly,' I said. I hoped that the answer was vague enough to be worrying. If he thought others knew about the little package then perhaps I'd be safer.

'What do you mean?' His voice was sharp, worried.

I was saved from replying by the arrival of our food. We were quiet for a while as we ate. I enjoyed the rich stew and didn't give a fig if it was pigeon or chicken.

Eventually I looked up. 'What about you? Tell me about yourself,' I asked.

'Why?'

'I want to know who I'm dealing with.'

He stared down at his wine, seemingly fascinated by its ruby depths, then raised his head to look at me almost defiantly.

'Not much to tell. I'm from a small town in western Pennsylvania. My dad was a miner, and his family from way back, and my mom's family. Mom's mom is from Ukrainian stock, which is where I get these –' he pointed to his eyes '– and these.' He touched his cheekbones.

'You said you were poor.'

'We were. It's a tough life in the coal towns. Especially in the Depression. The company owns everything, your town, the shop where you spend the money you earn in the mine, your house where you raise another generation to work in the mine. Eventually the company owns your soul. After a few holiday stints down the mines I decided that I never wanted to end up a miner.'

'How did you escape?'

He gave a wry smile. 'I used to be mighty good at American football. What they call a quarterback. My family made sure

I stayed on at high school and then I got myself a football scholarship to college – the University of Pennsylvania – where I majored in English literature.'

'Charles Dickens?'

'Among others.'

'And now you work for the American Embassy in London.'

He put his fork down and leaned back in his chair. 'I work for the United States War Office, not the embassy.'

'So it's the War Office, and not the embassy, that wants … what I might have?'

'What you have is dynamite. Be careful not to blow yourself up. And yes, it's the War Office that wants it. The embassy wants it too, but I'd prefer that it didn't get it.' He took another sip of wine. 'What I don't get is why you took it in the first place.'

'Because I suspected that you'd try to steal the locket and make a fool of me. I wanted to beat you at your own game. That's the only reason.'

He shook his head and gave a quick laugh, then bowed as if to concede the point. 'You got me good. I never thought you'd do that.' His voice changed. 'Now give it back. Those negatives don't belong to you and you're heading for a mess of trouble if you keep them. I'm nice; others won't be.'

'More threats?' My lips tightened. 'They're becoming tiresome.'

Before he could reply the Warning began its shrieking wail, sounding like a tormented animal. Leon announced that he had no air-raid shelter in the restaurant. There were public shelters nearby, he informed us. The ugly symphony of AA guns began firing, and then a noise that was unmistakable, a distant uneven drone that might have come from some far-off factory.

Michael and I exchanged looks. 'Want to find a shelter?' he asked.

'I'd rather return to the club.'

He shook his head. 'No, you're staying with me until we work out what to do about this.'

'Then let's find a shelter. I often don't bother, but the skies are clear tonight and they've been stepping up their attacks lately.'

When we emerged into Dean Street, the night air was filled with light and sound. The drone of planes was loud overhead and the AA guns were firing at a terrific rate. Around us was the clink of falling shrapnel. Red and green lights from tracer bullets soared towards the darkness; comet-like AA shells trailed plumes of fire and lit the sky when they burst. On the street dozens of incendiaries were bursting into fizzing balls of fire.

A sudden sharp cracking sound pierced the air, and Michael dived down, pulling me with him.

'Rifle shot,' he said.

'Rifle? Nonsense,' I replied. 'This is London.'

Another crack sounded, then another. I suddenly realised what it was.

'It's the slate roofs,' I said with a laugh. 'When the shrapnel falls on them it sounds like a rifle shot.'

'Oh,' Michael said, and got up. He put his hand down to me. I took it and was hauled to my feet. 'We're not staying out in this. Where's the public shelter Leon told us about?'

I pointed to where a bobby was standing on the corner, waving his masked torch in the direction of a narrow alleyway. He was a giant of a man, broad-shouldered but not hulking. The fitful gleam of the moon shone on his steel hat, illuminating the large white 'P' that had been painted on the front. His cape gave him the outline of a stage villain from the pantomimes I used to dance in as a child.

'Shelter's that way,' he was telling the passing parade. 'Now be sensible, won't you, and take cover.'

The noise had increased to include the tinkling crash of shattered glass, the shrieking whine of bombs and the shuddering crump when they landed.

We followed a small group to where an illuminated 'S' for shelter offered safety about halfway down the alley. Michael pushed open the door and we descended a dozen or so steps into a square room fitted with slatted benches. It had a slight odour of mould and urine overlaid with Jeyes fluid, but was as comfortable as any shelter I'd been in. I thought it was a cellar or even a former crypt because the ceiling was arched and, from what I could tell, it was made of the small bricks that I'd been told dated from Tudor times.

Michael and I sat near an elderly lady who seemed remarkably chipper, given the circumstances.

'Oh, I quite enjoy a raid,' she said. 'Enjoy the company, anyways. This is a friendly shelter.' She gave me a cheery smile. 'Aren't you pretty. You from round here? I'm sure I've seen your face before.'

'I live in Greek Street. The Theatre Girls' Club.'

She eyed me with the interest I usually got from non-theatrical types. 'I should have guessed. You've a lovely figure, deary. And so tall.' She leaned towards me and whispered, 'You're not a Windmill girl, are you?'

I felt Michael's amusement, but managed a smile. The Windmill show featured tableaux of completely naked women, who weren't allowed to move a muscle. According to the law, if naked women were still it was art but if they moved, it was obscene.

'No,' I whispered back. 'I make a point of keeping on at least some clothes during a show. I was a chorus dancer, here and in France, until the war started. A Tiller Girl. Now I drive ambulances.'

'A Tiller Girl and now an ambulance girl,' she said, and picked up a mass of khaki wool. 'Well, good for you, love.'

Soon she was knitting. The clicking of her needles was a comforting sound, but we had barely settled ourselves when the anti-aircraft guns started up again. The succession of bangs became ever louder and more violent. Then, as the sound of aircraft reverberated in the confined space, we heard the crash and rumble of exploding bombs coming ever closer.

Michael had begun a conversation with another elderly woman on his left.

'You sleep through the raids?' he said, raising his voice to be heard over the thunder outside. He sounded incredulous. 'How do you manage that?'

She grinned at him. 'Well, I comes in, I sits down and reads me book, then I says me prayers. "To hell with Hitler", I says. And I goes to sleep.'

I caught Michael's eye and we shared a smile.

The shelter rocked as a stick of three bombs screamed downwards and landed with three shuddering crumps somewhere not far away.

You never get used to the bombing. Well, I never did. It wasn't long after the Blitz began that I realised I was a beastly coward. But I took pride in not showing how I felt, and I soon discovered that most people were exactly like me, afraid and not showing it.

The shriek of falling bombs became louder, the thumps more intense. A crack appeared in the ceiling and brick dust floated down. The one globe that illuminated us flickered, went dead and flickered back into life.

I tried not to dwell on the stories I'd heard about shelters suffering direct hits, and although I managed to compose my face into a semblance of serenity, my hands were held in tight fists. Michael put his arm around me and pulled my head down to rest on his shoulder. I had a vague feeling that I should protest, but it felt good – right – to be so close to another human being. The entire room juddered as a bomb crashed down nearby. Michael's arm tightened around me.

'Anyone sing?' asked a man with a guitar. 'We could have a sing-song.'

No one volunteered, so he led us through all the old favourites. Most joined in with 'There'll Always be an England', 'Tomorrow is a Lovely Day', 'Pack Up Your Troubles', 'Franklyn D. Roosevelt Jones', and of course, 'One Man Went to Mow'. Eventually he ran out of steam. The singing became softer, and eventually faded.

Michael reached out his hand towards the man holding the guitar, and it was handed to him. He held it as if he was practised in playing. The corner of his mouth raised in his usual half smile as he began to strum gently. Then he plucked out a sweet, sad tune and began to sing in a pure baritone. It sounded like an English folk tune, but I didn't recognise the words, sung in his American accent. The song spoke of love and loss, and death made poetic.

I knew that death was not poetic at all, not the deaths I'd seen anyway. But somehow the old words and the sweet tune brought to mind bravery and passion and sadness that had no connection to the hideous destruction going on around us.

When the last notes died away the knitting woman said, 'That was a sweet song, mister. Do you know any more?'

He sang us three more. A travelling song about wayfaring strangers, doomed to wander. A jaunty reel about a roving sailor. A mountain song about lost love and memories blown away in the wind.

Michael had begun to sing about working in the coal mines, when we heard a banging at the door. Heads came up. The music stopped, and the banging came again. It was a sinister sound, as if Death had come knocking. Fear showed in the faces around me, a pinched desperation that caused a lack of charity. No one moved.

I glanced at the old woman next to me, whose eyes were wide. She shook her head. 'There's no room,' she whispered.

'We have to let them in,' I said, looking at Michael.

He put down the guitar and stood up. 'This is nuts,' he said, marching across to the door. 'It's life and death out there.'

When he hauled it open we all gasped because for a moment it really was as if Death had pushed through the blackout curtain. An apparition, huge, and caped, filled the doorway like anybody's worst nightmare. Michael stepped back into the light and it entered, diminished and became the bobby who'd directed us into the shelter. Another man followed him in, a fair-haired man, aged around forty in a civilian suit.

'Thanks,' said the bobby. 'It's a bad raid.'

'Is there room at the inn?' asked the fair-haired man. His smile was tremulous; in fact, his whole body was shaking. He had a clipped accent that reminded me of the way Celia spoke.

We all nodded vigorously.

'Harker,' he said, turning to Michael.

Michael stalked back to where I was sitting, followed by the man, who sat beside me, swallowed and took a few deep breaths. His hair was fair and thinning, his moustache sharply delineated, and his expression toffee-nosed. '*So well-bred, don't you know, what*?' I murmured under my breath. Once he had regained his composure he looked quizzically at the guitar, then glanced at me and gave Michael an ironic smile.

'Well met by moonlight,' he said, and shuddered. 'It's mayhem out there.'

Michael handed back the guitar to its owner. 'How are you, Denbeigh?' he said.

'Fine, fine,' murmured Denbeigh, who was looking me up and down in a slow, considered manner, just short of insulting. 'Haven't seen you in months, Harker. Are you well?'

'I'm okay,' said Michael.

Denbeigh smiled at me. I smiled back, but guardedly.

He turned again to Michael, and said in a light, chatty voice, 'And how is your charming wife? Vivian, isn't it.'

Michael's reply to Denbeigh was low, and curt to the point of rudeness.

'Yes. Vivian.'

CHAPTER SEVENTEEN

My first feeling was shock. The next, annoyance at my shock. Michael had said he was immune to my so-called charms. Well, of course he was. He had a charming wife. Why should it surprise me? Michael Harker was a twenty-eight-year-old man, presentable-looking – some might say good-looking – and charming himself when he wanted to be. For goodness' sake, he could even sing! Of course he was married. But he could have damn well told me he was.

It changed nothing. I still had to decide what to do with the negatives. I sat back, rested my back against the wall, closed my eyes and tried to escape into memories of the chorus line at the Folies. I imagined I was one of twenty-five tall girls all beautifully dressed, standing in a row. First a little jump with our feet together and then up comes the right leg, nice and straight until toes are at eye level: the 'eye-high kick'. Repeat. Repeat. Repeat. We were the *danseurs anglaise,* the Tiller Girls at the Folies Bergère, who could do thirty-two-and-a-half high kicks a minute. Our show would have knocked the socks off even the oh-so-charming and married Michael Harker.

'And who is this lovely young lady?' asked Denbeigh. I opened my eyes.

'Another refugee from the raid,' Michael replied curtly. Denbeigh blinked at him, then turned to me.

'She's a dancer,' put in the knitting woman. 'Chorus line, mind, not the Windmill. A Tiller Girl.'

The major's eyes became wide. 'Well, I call it serendipity. A Tiller Girl. Marvellous. My dear, you'd be a shoe-in. Just what we need.'

'What you need?' I said. 'What *do* you need?'

'Girls like you. Young lady, you should be in the movies. Allow me to ...' He fumbled in his pockets and extracted a card.

I smiled and took it, mainly because I thought it might annoy Michael. It did. I could tell from his tightly compressed lips.

The card announced the stranger to be 'Peregrine Denbeigh, Ministry of Information. Crown Film Unit'.

'And I'll tell you now without any exaggeration at all,' he went on, 'that we need girls just like you. Yes, just like you.'

'How do you do, Mr Denbeigh,' I said, with one eye on Michael's scowling face. 'I'm Maisie Halliday. But I don't act, or sing. I only dance.' Another glance at Michael. 'I do know how to stand, though.'

I stood up and took off Michael's raincoat, unbuttoned my jacket and slipped it off, as well. Tight sweater, tight skirt. I stood in my showgirl pose, chest out, chin up, arms by my sides, right leg slightly extended. There was scattered applause from the others in the shelter.

'Capital,' said Denbeigh, in a strangled voice. 'Just a dancer, what? Capital. Perfect. No need for you to act at all.'

'You're a corker, love,' a man called out.

'She'll up the morale of the troops,' said another man.

'Up something of theirs, anyway,' said the first, sniggering. The other joined in. Michael jumped to his feet and glared at them, holding his hands in tight fists.

'We'll have none of that,' said the policeman, addressing the man who had spoken. He walked over to Michael and put a hand on his arm. Michael shook it off, still eyeing the sniggering men angrily.

'Sit down, miss,' said the bobby to me. 'There's a good girl. I'm sure you'd be lovely in films, but this is an air-raid shelter. I really don't want any fuss.'

He was quite right. I was being silly, and I wasn't sure why. Flushing, I slipped the jacket back on, then the raincoat, and sat down.

'Sorry, Mr Denbeigh,' I said, 'but I work for the London Auxiliary Ambulance Service. I can't up and leave them to join your unit.'

'Oh, that's no problem at all. Easily fixed. It's important work we do. Morale, you know. Wins wars. They'll give you time off if we ask.'

'No, really. I like my work. It's important. And anyway, I don't want to be in films.'

Denbeigh seemed shocked. He opened then closed his mouth, checked his nails and turned to Michael. 'Can't you speak to her? It's a marvellous opportunity I'm offering the girl. And completely *on the level*, as you Americans say.'

Michael was sitting down, slumped against the wall. 'As if Miss Halliday would ever listen to a word I said. If I told her not to do it, she would, just to spite me.'

He looked up, caught my eye and said, in a level, disinterested tone, 'Hey, Maisie. Don't do it.'

'That's unfair,' I said, incensed. 'And if I want to, I will.'

At that, Michael began to laugh. 'Sure you will.'

I realised just how silly I was being, and I laughed, too.

'Listen,' said the knitting woman. 'No planes. No bombs.'

The room became silent. Sure enough, the bombing had ceased. The guns barked a few times, and the hum of the planes was faint and becoming fainter. The All Clear began its long, single note of hope. People around us began packing up their belongings. And all at once I realised just how tired I was.

'That's more like it,' said a woman. 'I hate all-nighters.'

'If I'm home quick I'll get a nap in before work,' said another.

'I just hope I've a home to get back to. I've already been bombed out once.'

'Take care moving around in the blackout up there,' said the policeman. 'Might be best to stay here until dawn.'

'This one's here for the night, anyway,' said Michael. He nodded towards my right. When I looked, the woman whose prayers consigned Hitler to hell was stretched out, fast asleep under a tattered blanket. Michael and I shared another smile.

'She really meant it about sleeping anywhere,' I said.

'C'mon kid, I'll take you home,' said Michael.

'No point,' I replied. 'The doors will be locked. I'm on duty in ...' I looked at my watch, 'five hours. If I go to the ambulance station now, I can take a quick kip before I start my shift.'

'I assume that means sleep. I'll walk you to the ambulance station, then.'

There was no point arguing with him. Besides, I'd appreciate the company.

'Thanks.' I stood and picked up my handbag.

Major Denbeigh also stood. 'I say, Miss Halliday, I meant it, you know. About being in films. You'd not have to act, just look good.'

I smiled at him. 'Thank you ever so much for the offer, but I'm really not interested. Perhaps if the Blitz ends and I'm not needed on the ambulances any more.' I shrugged.

He seemed genuinely disappointed. 'Well, if you change your mind, you have my card. I have an eye for these things and I really think the camera would – as they say – love you.'

A thought seemed to strike him. 'Are the other girls in your ambulance station who are like you? Young, I mean? And pretty?'

'Two of them are in their twenties. They're both pretty, but I doubt they'd be interested.'

'Miss Halliday, are you absolutely sure?'

I turned to Michael with a pleading look.

'She's stubborn,' said Michael. 'Let her make up her mind in her own time. Right now that dog won't hunt.'

Major Denbeigh and I both stared at him.

'Nagging won't cut it,' said Michael.

The major smiled at me. 'I get few refusals,' he said. 'And I am truly sorry to see you walk away. Are you absolutely sure?'

'Yes.'

When Michael and I emerged from the shelter, it was into a pitch-black world. The bright moonlight of the early evening had disappeared, hidden behind clouds. The air was smoky, and seemed thinner somehow. It always did, after a raid, as if all joy and life had been sucked away, leaving behind a whiff of fear and the stink of misery. As always, though, I caught a top note of defiance.

'I hope you know the way,' said Michael, 'because I'm not familiar with this part of London.'

I laughed. 'I'd know it blindfolded, but luckily I've got cat's eyes and can see in the dark because I eats me carrots. I warn you, it's a twenty-minute walk. And that's without bomb debris holding us up.'

'I'm up for it,' he said. 'Lay on, Macduff.'

We began our journey as one always did when there was no moonlight, by relying on our thin torchlight and the white bands painted around trees and on kerbs. I let the masked light of my slim torch shine on the ground by our feet, assisted by Michael's torchlight. When we rounded the corner, the glow of a fire somewhere over to the north-west gave us enough light to walk without turning an ankle on the inevitable detritus left by a raid.

Rescue workers had closed off Dean Street all the way to Oxford Street because of an unexploded bomb. So, arm in arm, Michael and I advanced tentatively towards the deeper shadow that was Soho Square.

'We haven't resolved our dilemma,' said Michael, holding me firmly as I slipped on some rubble in my 'skyscraper' shoes.

'I'm still thinking about it,' I said.

It was very quiet in the square itself, but the sounds of fire engines, ambulances and rescue trucks echoed in the streets nearby. We emerged from Soho Street on to Oxford Street, and turned into a small thoroughfare, more like an alley, which was, I knew, a shortcut to Tottenham Court Road.

'What the hell ...' said Michael, and pulled me to a stop.

A break in the clouds had revealed a scene of devastation. The house in front of us had suffered a direct hit. Nothing was left but a neat pile of wreckage, which in the moonlight had an unreality about it, as if it were one of the follies they used to build in fancy estates to add a gothic air. A water pipe had split open, so a fountain gushed into the sky, adding to the unreality of the scene.

'Why is no one here?' asked Michael. 'No rescue crews?'

'Perhaps they know it was an empty house. Or they're busy somewhere else and haven't got to this one yet. Or it's not been reported yet. This is a secluded little street.'

It was the dog that alerted us. Michael heard the whining first, and squeezed my arm.

'Is that a dog, or a child?'

I listened. It was a sad little whimpering sound.

'Dog, I think,' I said.

Michael released my arm and moved carefully over the wreckage, sliding a little because it was unstable, towards the pitiful noise.

'It's a dog,' he called out. He shone his torchlight on a small brown dog of uncertain lineage. It was whimpering and scrabbling in the debris, trying to wriggle itself into the mess of broken beams and plaster towards the back of what had been the house.

'Do you think someone's trapped in there?' he called out.

'It looks like it. Should I run for a rescue crew? There must be one in Dean Street near the UXB.'

'They'll be here soon enough. I'll see what I can do in the meantime.' He took off his jacket and tie and rolled up his sleeves. 'All I have is a pocket-knife,' he said. 'You got anything better?'

'Just a torch.'

'Better bring it here. Shine it where I'm working.'

Gingerly, in my high heels, I walked across the mess to him and held the torch as he pulled away larger bits of wreckage, broken beams, bricks and plaster. Every so often he would call out, 'Hello? Anyone in there?'

We listened. We heard nothing.

'Journey's end,' said Michael suddenly. In front of him was a tiled wall. 'Looks like a bathroom wall. I think the place was empty. Or they didn't survive the bombing. I can't get further in. Don't have the tools.'

We turned to leave, and had taken a step when we heard it. Faintly, very faintly, from somewhere beyond the wall in front of us, a man's voice was calling, 'Help. Help us please.'

CHAPTER EIGHTEEN

Michael stiffened and swore softly under his breath. 'I've got nothing, Maisie. Nothing. If I had a pickaxe, or a mallet … but there's nothing I can use.'

'I'll run for help.'

'Where to? You can't go dashing off alone into the dark streets.'

'Why not?' I said, bitterly, because I felt so helpless. 'Because you might lose your precious negatives?'

Michael turned and grabbed my arms, then shook me. There was real fury in his voice. 'Because that man might be dying and I can't help him by myself. And because dashing off all alone into the dark wearing shoes like that is a real stupid plan. I thought you were smarter than that. Now shut up and let me think.'

He asked me to shine the torch over the debris that was beyond the tiled wall. It looked like the entire house had fallen in. Michael tried to climb up and over the jumbled pile of rubble, wood, bricks and plaster that lay above the tiled wall, but it was too unstable. He picked up a piece of wood from the wreckage and tried to smash the tiles. They held, but the pile of debris on top of and behind it shifted worryingly.

'I guess there's some sort of cavity behind this,' he said, 'or another room, but I can't smash my way into it without a pickaxe. Even if I had a pickaxe I'd be worried about causing a further collapse. It looks pretty unstable up there and I don't want to bury the man further, maybe kill him.'

Michael put his back against the tiled wall and slid down so that he was sitting on the pile of rubble. 'I have to think, but there's no time to think it through properly.' He reached into his pocket and pulled out a small penknife, about six inches long. 'So I'll need to be smart, and very, very patient.'

He opened the knife and looked at the small blade, sighed and stood up.

'What will you do?' I asked.

'Use this to hack at the grouting around the tiles. It won't disturb the junk on top. I suppose there's lath and plaster underneath. I'm hoping to get through that into some sort of cavity or room that leads to whoever is trapped. Keep that torch on me, will you. I need to see what I'm doing.'

He used the blade like a small pickaxe, chopping at the grouting around the tile until the grouting splintered. Then he hacked into the strips of wood and plaster beneath. Hack, hack, hack went the little blade, a quick, neat movement that did little on its own but with constant repetition wore away the wall.

'Gotcha,' he said. He looked around and picked up a piece of wood. One sharp thrust with this and the tile fell through into a cavity beyond. He shone his torch into the darkness and called, 'You still there, buddy?'

Faintly the voice came back. 'We're still here. My wife was hurt when the house fell in. She's in pain. I'm all right, but we're both very thirsty.'

'Where are you ?'

'In the coal cellar, off the kitchen.'

'I'm at a bathroom wall.'

'That's next to the kitchen.'

'I'm doing all I can. Hang on.' Michael turned to me. 'Looks like we're settling in for the night. Call for room service, won't you?'

'Of course,' I replied, in the same light tone. 'Champagne? Caviar?'

'I'd prefer a strong cuppa Joe, but your taste is obviously on a higher plane than mine.' He dropped the light tone and said, 'I'm going to have to cut a hole through this wall, but I'd prefer to keep the wall itself as intact as possible. Frankly, I'm not sure about the structural integrity of what remains of the house. The last thing we need is more of it coming down on the couple in there. So I'll need to work on one tile at a time. When I've made a hole big enough I'll crawl through and figure out the best way of getting to them.'

'What can I do?'

'Your job, kid, is to keep the light shining where I'm working so I can see what I'm doing.'

It was a long, tedious and thankless task. The little dog ran around our feet, whimpering and crying, until Michael huffed out an angry breath.

'Will you please tie up that damn dog.'

'Using what?'

He ignored me, continuing his hacking at the tile grouting. I had an idea. 'Oh, I know, I'll use the belt of my raincoat. I mean your raincoat.'

Michael grunted, and I pulled out the belt, tied it around the dog's neck and then attached the other end to a piece of wreckage. The animal continued to whimper piteously, but at least it was out of our way.

One by one, painfully slowly, Michael's chopping loosened tiles and he used the piece of wood to push them in.

'I wish I could help.'

'Talk to me, kid,' he said. 'That'll help.'

I shone the torch on his face. It was dirty and sweaty and he was frowning at the tile he was attacking, looking grimly handsome and completely focused on the task at hand. Deep inside me it was as if something twisted, causing a sharp pain.

'Keep the light on the tile,' he said sharply. I moved the light down and he began to hack away at another tile.

'What do you want me to talk about?'

'Tell me about yourself. About Sheffield. Dancing? Anything that gets my mind off this. You said you grew up poor. Poor like those East End slums? Or poor like only one servant?' His little blade rasped on the cement as he hacked away, and the dog began to howl.

'Why are you interested?' I asked.

'I'm interested in you. You're interesting.'

'If you must know, poor like the East End slums.' I blew out a breath and the torchlight wavered. 'Do you know what a back-to-back house is?'

'Yes, I do.'

'We lived in one. No running water, often no money for food or proper clothes. Mam had been a dancer, but after I was born she returned to the steel mill where my grandfather worked. We had enough money to survive, but often nothing left over. My grandmother was very ill.'

'Tough. How was she ill?'

I sucked in a breath and let it out slowly 'Lead poisoning. She'd been a file cutter, and they call it the file cutters' disease. Her muscles and joints were always painful, she was often ill and her arms were weak. And ...' My voice fell away.

'And?'

'She'd fall into awful rages without any warning. When she did she'd blame me for ... everything really.'

I paused, remembering the terror of Nannan's rages. I grew up in a house that was ruled by her moods. Without any warning, and in a matter of seconds, she would go from quite nice to a screaming harpy, and I was usually the butt of her anger.

'Keep talking, kid,' said Michael, after a few minutes of silence, broken only by the faint sound of fire engines and ambulance bells and the tap tap of Michael's little blade on the cement around the tiles. 'It's mighty boring, this job.'

'Sorry. It wasn't her fault, you must understand. Lead poisoning is terrible, Michael. And – and she lost four babies, three to scarlet fever and one to diphtheria. Only Mam survived her childhood. Granddad said that it changed her. She didn't know what she doing when she hit me. I know that now. I forgave her years ago, but that doesn't mean I want to see her.'

Again there was silence for a few beats. Hack, hack, hack. Michael seemed to have a second wind, as he now hacked at the wall fiercely, almost angrily.

'What about your grandpa?'

I thought of Granddad, big, strong Granddad and his hellfire sermons. I smiled. 'He was kind when he could be. But if he made a fuss of me it made Nannan worse. She made life hell for Mam, too,' I said. 'So Mam and I were happy to leave Sheffield to go to London.'

'They your only family?'

'Yes.'

'You've been dancing since you were young?' he said, after a while.

'Since I was four.' I smiled into the darkness. 'I fell in love with it when Mam took me to *Cinderella* at the Theatre Royal.'

My life changed forever when I saw the fairies dancing before a gauze curtain all lit up with twinkling lights. I'd gasped and clutched the railing with one small hand and my mother with the other, half-afraid and half-hoping I would fall over the balcony and drift down to where the enchanting creatures flitted across the stage. I can still hear my determined little voice, whispering to my mother as we sat up in 'the Gods', telling her I wanted to learn to dance like a fairy.

'Poor Mam,' I said. 'I pestered her shamelessly to pay for lessons she couldn't afford.'

'How did she manage it?' asked Michael. Hack, hack, hack.

'I helped,' I said, with a note of real triumph. 'Mam hauled me down to the Gwen Wilken School of Dancing, For Correct Training in all Branches of the Art –'

Michael gave a soft snort of derision.

'– and demanded that Miss Wilken audition me. Miss Wilken saw my potential and agreed to give me the lessons for half-price.'

I remembered it vividly. Miss Wilken had told me to pretend to be an autumn leaf. She said to me, 'At first you will be happily drifting slowly down to earth, the way leaves do. Then the wind will catch you and make you whirl around. Finally you will fall to the ground, a dry brown leaf, shrivelled and dead. Can you do that?'

When the music began, I had lifted my arms and let the music take me. I became a floating leaf on its journey earthwards. And when I was at last lying on the ground, all shrivelled up and dry, I had tears in my eyes. *Poor little leaf*, I thought. *It didn't fly for very long*.

'And you were ...?' said Michael. Hack, hack, hack.

'Five.'

'How did your mom afford even the half-price fees?' Michael wiped his forehead with the back of his hand and began hacking at the next tile.

'She took on extra shifts at the factory. Most of the other girls at the classes came from far more privileged backgrounds than me. They wanted to learn ballet to become more graceful, but I knew from the beginning that dancing was to be my future.'

I reached into my handbag, took out my handkerchief and used it to wipe his forehead.

'Thanks.'

'It was a good investment, because it wasn't long before I began to earn money in the children's ballet troupe of pantomimes and shows.'

'Why'd you go to London? For work?'

'I was dancing in pantomime one Christmas, when I was nearly twelve, and I was seen by Italia Conti, who runs a very prestigious theatre academy in London. She offered to train me at a discounted rate. It was too good an opportunity to miss, so Mam and I moved to London. Miss Conti thought I was a good enough ballerina to try out for the Vic-Wells Ballet company. Classical ballet is my great love. Oh, Michael, you just can't imagine what a wonderful sensation it is to dance *en pointe*; it's as if you are about to fly away.'

He smiled, and continued to hack at the tiles.

146

'Why the chorus line, then?' Another tile was pushed through with a thwack.

I heard the touch of bitterness in my laugh. 'Because I grew like a beanstalk and began to pop out in all directions. No professional ballerina is five foot eleven with a bust like mine.'

'Tough,' he said, but I saw him smile as he wielded the knife blade.

'So I accepted the inevitable, left school at fourteen, and made a reasonable living out of dancing in the chorus lines of shows in London and the provinces.'

Another tile pushed through. Then another. Michael coughed a little in the dusty air, then sighed. 'I'd kill for a cup of Joe.'

'What is that? You keep mentioning it.'

'Coffee,' he said with a smile. 'Plain old glorious coffee.' He raised the penknife and hack, hack, hack. Another tile was pushed through. The hole he had made was about two feet square. He shone the torch into the void. 'Dammit.'

'What?'

'It's filled with debris. I'm going to have to tunnel in, using my hands.'

'Tunnel with your bare hands? You can't.'

'No choice, kid. I'll need to shore up the walls as I tunnel it.' He began on the next tile.

'But, Michael, you can't—'

'Then what happened?'

'What?'

'Then what happened in the life story of Maisie Halliday? C'mon, I need something to take my mind off this.' He began hacking at the tiles again. They came out more easily now, it seemed to me.

'Oh, there's not much to tell, really. Mam died and I became a Tiller Girl. '

'What about your time in Paris?'

I shrugged. 'It sounds glamorous, but it was a hard life in many ways. We'd finish the second show of the night at one fifteen in the morning, catch a few hours of sleep and begin rehearsals. Those went on throughout the day until the first show began at eleven fifteen at night.'

'And you were sixteen?' Hack, hack, hack.

'Mmm. I danced there for two years, living on my nerves and my wits. Honestly, Michael, as long as I could dance I was happy. And in those days I was dancing all the time. If ever I felt tired I would say to myself, "I am being paid to do something that I'd do for free". But after a couple of years I thought I'd like to try something different.'

'What?'

'I got offered a job as an exhibition dancer in a very smart hotel on the French Riviera.'

'Exhibition dancer?' He pushed two tiles through at once. The hole was now double the size, and very nearly big enough for Michael to squeeze through and begin the even more difficult task of finding a way into the wreckage to find the trapped couple.

A faint, wavering voice floated in from the darkness beyond. 'Are you still there?'

Michael yelled back, in an encouraging way. 'Still here. We'll be with you soon. Hang on.'

CHAPTER NINETEEN

'Tell me about exhibition dancing,' he said, chipping again at the tiles.

'Now that was fun!' I said, in a tone of forced light-heartedness. 'Are you sure I can't help? Let me push the tiles through.'

'It's a hard shove. You just keep talking. It helps.'

'Um, I loved the Riviera climate, the beaches and the easy life there. All I had to do was put on four exhibition dances each evening and then dance with any guests who asked me.'

'Who'd you put these exhibitions on with?'

'My partner was an Argentinian, Tito Moreau. He was tall, dark, very handsome, and—'

'Yes?' said Michael. 'And?'

I gave a gurgle of laughter. 'And not at all interested in girls. Tito and I got on well and we danced together beautifully.'

Michael paused to pass his hand across his forehead, then went back to the infinite tedium of cutting around each tile and pushing it through.

'You were, what, seventeen then?'

'Almost eighteen. I went there in March thirty-nine. Tito was such a dramatic man. If he misplaced a cufflink it was the end of the world. And his hair was always a bit too well oiled.' I gave a soft laugh. 'You smell of spice and cedar, and he always smelled of violets.'

'Spice and cedar?' There was amusement in his tone.

'Your raincoat. I'm still wearing it, remember.'

'Glad you approve.'

Michael paused to wipe his hand over his eyes and roll his shoulders into a stretch. When he returned to the task, hacking at the tiles I felt a wash of some strong emotion, and I didn't want to lie to him any more.

'I lied to you, when I told you about my father,' I said. 'The truth is, I was born illegitimate. That's one of the reasons why I hide my background.'

Immediately I regretted telling him. I wasn't sure why I had felt such a strong need to share such a personal thing with him. Illegitimacy was such a stigma that I had found that people treated me differently once they knew, dismissed me as one of society's dregs.

Michael kept tapping at the tiles. 'Did your father not hang around, or was it something else?'

'Mam never told me anything about him. I think he was married.'

'You look like him?'

I shrugged. 'Probably. I certainly don't look like my mother.'

On the night of my mother's death I had gazed at my reflection for what seemed like hours, trying to see my mother in my face. Possibly something in the way I held my head, perhaps. Something in my smile? But my dark eyes were nothing like my mother's soft blue and her hair had been a soft brown, not black like mine, with its blue sheen like a raven's wing.

I had gazed at myself in utter misery that night, until I realised that it didn't matter. So what if I didn't look like my mother if I had inherited her firm common sense, her easy laughter and her hatred of cruelty? I was my mother's daughter and that was enough.

'How old was your mom when you were born?' he asked.

'Nineteen.' The age I was now.

He paused in his task for a moment. 'Handsome man, young girl,' he said. 'Sad story, and all too common. Nowadays, just as much as then. You stay smart. Wait for the ring on your finger.'

'It's none of your business, Granddad.' I gave him a cheeky smile that he couldn't see. 'You sound like my mother. She made me promise ...'

The scene was clearly fixed in my mind. It was just before I left London for my first grown-up chorus job in the provinces. 'Don't make my mistake, Maisie,' she had told me. 'Men can be persuasive, but they're not the ones who are left with the consequences. I love you dearly, but it's been difficult for me, rearing a child without a father, and difficult for you also, through no fault of your own. Be sensible, love. *Please* wait for marriage. Promise me.' I had given her that promise.

'What did she make you promise,' said Michael, wiping his hand across his eyes again.

'Never you mind,' I said. 'Anyway, there's plenty of time to find the right man.'

Michael laughed. 'Sure there is, kid. I'm nearly done here. When did you come home to England from the Riviera?'

'I came back home *toute suite*, as they say in France, once war was declared. When your country is at war you want to be among your own people.'

'They're good people, your people,' said Michael. 'They impress me.'

'Most of them impress me, too.' I breathed a laugh. 'I thought I could easily get a job dancing in London, but when I arrived without a brass farthing in my pocket, I discovered that the government had closed all the theatres. So I was a skint chorus girl in a town without any theatres.'

'Tough.'

'I'd learned to drive in France, I'm not afraid of blood or hard work and I wanted to stay in London. Ambulance work seemed just the ticket.'

Michael gave a short laugh. 'Sure. Just the ticket.'

'I've never been sorry I chose it,' I said, a trifle defensively. 'Not even when the theatres reopened and dancers were in work again. Not even when the Blitz began. *Especially* when the Blitz began.'

'That's it!' The hole he'd made loomed in front of him.

'Can you fit inside?' I asked.

He eased his slim body through the narrow opening and shone his torch into the darkness beyond.

'It's a mess in here,' he said.

I shone my own torch inside. It picked out Michael and beyond him a tangled mass of wreckage. There was no obvious way through.

Another faint cry for help came from deep inside.

'We're coming,' Michael shouted. 'As soon as we can.'

'What will you do?' I asked.

Michael took a deep breath and let it out on a sigh. 'Use my hands.'

'You can't,' I said.

He ignored me. 'Maisie, I'd like you to look around and find me some planks of wood, say two feet long. Or anything else I can use to shore up the sides of the passage I'm going to make.'

I ran around on the bomb site, picking up likely pieces of wood. When I returned, only Michael's feet were visible. The rest of him was in a hole he had made, by lying on his back and pushing aside bricks and plaster and other debris with his bare hands.

'I'm back,' I called.

He eased himself out and lay there, looking up at me. 'Got anything?'

I showed him my finds and he grunted. 'I'll need more.'

He took what I had brought and, using his elbows and feet, wriggled backwards into the hole.

I went out to find more planks. When I came back, his feet had disappeared. I wriggled in after him, using my elbows and feet as Michael had, but on my front. By the time I reached him my knees were burning and my stockings were a tattered ruin. I refused to think of the state of my best suit and best shoes. There was a strong smell of rotten cabbages in the air and Michael was coughing.

'Gas,' he said on a gasp. 'Where's your handkerchief?'

'I put it back in my bag.' I wriggled out in a panic, ignoring my grazed knees, pushed through the hole and searched for my handbag. I reached in and as I did so I brushed the compact.

The negatives. They were the reason Michael was still with me, the reason we had come across this disaster. If he managed to save these people, was it somehow because of my stubbornness? I shook my head to clear it. *Don't be silly, Maisie.*

I pulled out my hankie, wet it in the gushing water pipe and wrung it out. Then I shuffled down the tunnel on my stomach. Michael had used the wood I brought him to prop up the unstable sides of the makeshift tunnel. I hoped it was enough to prevent the entire mess of bombed house from falling in and crushing him and the people he was trying to save.

The sides seemed to push in on me. The rotten cabbage smell of gas was heavy in the air and it seemed a long time before my torchlight made out the soles of his feet. He was still wriggling forwards, lying on his back and pushing aside debris as he did so. Working like a madman.

'I wet it, but it's not very big,' I said.

'It'll have to do.' His reply finished on a cough. 'Now I remember why I vowed never to go down a mine again.' He raised his voice and shouted, 'Keep calling out, man. I need to locate you.' He took the wet handkerchief and put it over his nose and mouth.

'We're here,' came the reply, out of the darkness ahead. It seemed closer.

I shone my torch on to Michael's hands. They were all over blood. The smell of gas was stronger. Saliva poured into my mouth and I gagged. The rotten cabbage fumes filled my nostrils, crept into my brain so that my head began to swim. It now seemed blindingly obvious that it was not living bomb victims who waited ahead of us, but we were following the voice of a ghost. Like a marsh light, it was drawing us on to be

153

smothered by gas or crushed by collapsing debris. I shook my head to clear away the fantasy.

'No good both of us being overcome by gas,' said Michael. 'You get out. Try to find some help. I'm not sure I can manage this by myself.'

I shook my head again and spoke with a semblance of briskness, trying to sound reasonable. 'I'm not leaving you alone in here.'

'I can't turn around.' He sounded annoyed, fed up. '*Get out*, Maisie. If you don't go now I swear I'll kick you. I'll feel a lot better if I know you're safe.'

It was a voice of command and it cut through the fog in my brain. I obeyed without further argument, shuffling backwards on my burning knees and elbows. At last I pushed through the hole in the tiles to suck in fresh if smoke-tainted London air. The night was dark, and in the distance were ambulance and fire engine bells.

After three deep breaths I felt somewhat better. The dog was still tied up near the entrance, still whimpering. I patted the creature.

'I know,' I said. 'Oh, God, please don't let him die. I don't know what I'd do if he died.'

I took another deep breath, let it out, and set about trying to find more wood to take back to Michael, to shore up the death trap he was digging for himself. The moon was down now, and I could see little, even by torchlight.

How could I get help? I had no idea where to go. Annoyed, I tore off the paper that was masking my torch. The beam strengthened. I ran it over the ground around me, on to the road, to work out where I should go.

A harsh voice cut through the distant wail of fire engines and ambulance bells. 'Put that perishing light out.'

The shock of it made me gasp. I swung my torch around and it flashed on a white helmet. ARP was printed on the front.

'Put the light out,' he barked. '*Now*, I tell you. You might try to realise that there's a war on.'

'Not bad, for a Yank,' had been the general consensus of the heavy rescue workers who arrived soon after. 'Doing our job for us. We owe you a pint, mate.'

After we'd seen the man and his injured wife hauled to safety through the tunnel that Michael had dug with his bare hands, the crew gave us a lift back to the Bloomsbury Ambulance Station in their van. There was talk of recommending Michael for a medal. He'd dismissed such talk angrily.

The van drove away. Michael and I stood quietly together by the entrance to the ambulance station and watched an ambulance from the previous day's shift roll slowly down the ramp. Michael's face was indistinct in the pre-dawn light but his slumped posture showed just how weary he was.

'You drive one of those things?' he asked, nodding at the ambulance.

'I do. They're monsters. You need to double de-clutch and there's no suspension to speak of. But they keep on going, no matter what we do to them.'

'Like their drivers,' he said, with a jaw-cracking yawn. 'You did good tonight, kid. But now you need some sleep. Go inside and get some, what did you call it, kip?'

'What about you? I'm sure they'd find you a bunk if I told them what you'd—'

'Don't worry about me. I'll grab a cab, or the underground will be running in a little while.' He looked down and laughed. 'I doubt a cab would pick me up. I'm filthy. I'll take the Tube.'

I flashed my torch on his hands. They were still bleeding; blood had painted the bandages that the first aid team had wrapped around them. He smiled. 'Don't worry about me,' he repeated. 'How're you doing?'

First Aid had bandaged my grazed knees, but they hurt. I shrugged. 'I'm fine. Sad about the ruined stockings, though. My last silk pair.'

We were silent for a space, standing together in the cool, early morning air. It was tinged with brick dust, but the light breeze seemed also to bring the scent of spring. Spring was supposed to bring hope, wasn't it?

'Do you think Hitler will end the Blitz before summer?' I asked.

'Maybe. I think he's beginning to realise that London's not about to curl up and play dead dog because his bombers drop their big stuff.'

It was something to hope for, anyway. We so badly needed something to hope for. Again there was silence.

I shrugged off his raincoat and held it out to him. 'You'll need to find another belt. It went off with the dog.'

He took the raincoat and put it on.

'Your pretty suit is just about ruined,' he said.

'I thought you hated this suit.'

He breathed a laugh. 'If you think that then you're far too naive to be wearing it.'

'What's all this about, Michael? I think I deserve to know something about it.'

He stared at me, and I held his gaze until he gave me his quirky half-smile.

'I don't know for certain,' he said, 'But I'm pretty sure that they're photographs of correspondence between the president and your prime minister, discussing how he can get around the US Neutrality Acts to give help to Britain. Politically embarrassing for Roosevelt, maybe even grounds for impeachment. Roosevelt's your best friend in America. You really don't want him out of office.'

No wonder Michael wanted it back.

'What was Mr Egan doing with it?'

'He wanted America to stay right out of the European war. I think he was going to give the microfilm to someone who would use it against Roosevelt.'

156

I nibbled at my lip. 'What should I do, Michael?'

'Give me the negatives. Or destroy them.'

And all of a sudden, I knew what to do. The answer was there, standing in front of me, utterly exhausted after risking his life to save two people he had never met, who had been injured in a war that wasn't his. I reached into my handbag and pulled out my compact, removed the little package and held it out to him.

'You had them with you all this time?' He gave a short laugh and took it from me, slipping it into his pocket almost as if it meant nothing at all to him.

'Thanks, kid,' he said. 'Now you get some sleep.'

He hesitated, then leaned across to kiss my cheek. His lips were dry and soft on my skin. 'You're one hell of a gal, Maisie Halliday.'

'You'd better go straight home to your wife, Michael,' I said. 'She must be worried.'

He began to walk towards Russell Square. Without bothering to turn around he raised his hand in a lazy sort of wave and disappeared into the early morning fog.

CHAPTER TWENTY

I stumbled into the station like a sleepwalker. McIver took one look at me and asked, 'Another night out on the town? You'll soon have no clothes left.' She glanced down at my bandaged knees. 'What happened?'

'A couple were trapped in a bombed house. I assisted a little.'

She shook her head. 'I don't suppose you've magically conjured a spare set of clothes?'

I shook my head.

'Och, use Ashwin's again. She told me that you could use her spare clothes any time you wanted. And her pyjamas. But if you intend making a habit of this you'd best keep some of your own here. You're a mite taller than Ashwin.' She glanced down. 'You'll need some shoes. Lord only knows how you walk in those heels. Ashwin has a spare pair of brogues and I'll put them out for you. I hope they're your size.'

I washed, pulled on Ashwin's pyjamas and crawled into a bunk. I was exhausted, but too wound up to sleep and always in my mind was Michael's face as he grimly tried to tunnel through to the trapped couple. This became a dream of him tumbling with me through bomb debris, buffeted by bricks and household items and wooden beams. Then Michael disappeared and I somehow knew that he had been rescued by his wife, leaving me to face the tempest alone. I was toppling headlong into the abyss, struck and jostled and shoved to and fro until I was sufficiently awake enough to realise that someone was saying my name. I opened bleary eyes to see Moray standing over me. He had hold of my shoulder and was shaking me.

'Sorry, Halliday,' he said. 'It's noon. I know you didn't get to sleep until after seven, but there are some men here who want to speak to you urgently.'

I sat up, clutching the blanket with one hand and rubbing my eyes with the other. 'What men?'

'From the American Embassy. The say it's urgent. I told them you were sleeping but they insisted.'

All at once I was wide awake. 'Is one of them called Michael Harker?'

Moray shook his head. 'No. Their names are Lowell and Casey.'

Once Moray had left I dressed quickly. I covered Celia's straining blouse with her spare pullover. Her shoes were a little small, but nothing to worry about, although I sighed again at the sight of my ankles under the hem of her too-short trousers. I looked ridiculous. I put a hand to my head and felt the matted mass of my hair. In desperation I ducked into the washroom, and was pulled up short by the sight of myself in the mirror. Heavy and sleep-crusted eyes, flushed face and bird's nest hair.

Mr Lowell and Mr Casey could just wait while I made myself presentable, I decided. So I took my time to properly wash my face and comb my hair into a smooth chignon. One more glance in the mirror and I entered the common room. Only Celia, Purvis and Harris were there.

I checked the big board on the wall first, noting that I'd been chalked up as attending Celia, who would be driving.

'Where are the others,' I asked.

Celia looked up from the book she was reading. 'Lily is delivering supplies to Middlesex with Squire. Armstrong and Sadler are on a mortuary run and Powell is doing maintenance on her vehicle. Moray wants to see you.'

'I know.'

I knocked on the office door and entered. Two strangers were in the room. One was a toughly built man with a quite terrifyingly short blond haircut and a bullish face. The other was younger, suave and well-groomed with a muscular physique. His dark blond hair was slick with oil and crisply parted at the side. Grey-green eyes and an air of brusque efficiency allied to self-satisfaction completed the picture. He was attractive enough, but he had a knowing air that I found off-putting.

The men stood, including Moray, who walked around his desk heading for the door.

'I'll leave you to it,' Moray said to the bullish one. He nodded at me and closed the door behind him as he left the room.

The bigger man introduced himself as John Casey, his companion as Dan Lowell. They handed me cards similar to the one Michael had shown me, but which said they were Special Agents of the US Department of State. I wondered what the difference was between that department and the War Office, where Michael worked.

We all sat down. I was wide awake now, and told myself that these men might be colleagues of Michael's from the American Embassy, but I didn't have to trust them. He hadn't wanted the negatives to go to the embassy, so I thought I'd tread carefully. They were not British police, so I didn't have to tell them the truth, either.

'Miss Halliday,' began Mr Casey, 'I'll get straight to the point. We have been charged with investigating the looting of the body of our former associate, Mr Harold Egan, after the bombing at the Café de Paris nightclub last Saturday night. We understand that he gave you his watch fob. We want to know why he would do that.'

'He was dying,' I said. 'People do strange things when they're dying.'

'We understand that you spoke to Harry Egan before he died on March eight. Is that correct?'

'Yes. But he was very ill. He didn't say much at all.'

'What did he say?'

'He asked if he was dying. That's all. He never told me that he was going to give me the locket.'

'You knew Mr Egan?'

'No. I'd never seen him before.'

'And he removed his watch fob from the watch chain and gave it to you?'

Put like that it did sound ludicrous. Even I wouldn't have believed my story.

'It's the truth, Mr Casey,' I said coldly.

'You say you didn't know you had the fob until Monday?'

'As I told Inspector Wayland when he interviewed me, I found it in my pocket on Monday afternoon, when I was about to do my washing. The inspector and I agreed that I would bring it to Scotland Yard yesterday, when I was off duty. Only your Mr Harker took it from me before I had a chance to take it to Scotland Yard.'

Mr Lowell inserted himself into the interrogation – because that is what it was – with a smooth fluidity.

'Miss Halliday,' he said, 'let me put it this way. When we took possession of the body, certain other personal items that Mr Egan was known to carry were not found, such as his wallet and a pocket watch. These other items have not been located. You told the inspector from Scotland Yard that you saw his body being looted. We understand that other bodies were looted that night. But somehow Mr Egan's watch fob ended up with you. You must admit it's peculiar.'

I became very cold. They thought I'd stolen the locket and the other items, the ones that Michael had taken. All at once I realised just how bad it all looked for me. Only I had seen Egan's body being looted and I had ended up with his watch fob. It did look shady. I took a breath and tried to calm myself down.

'I honestly don't know how I ended up with the watch fob,' I said, pleased at how level my voice sounded. 'All I can think is that Mr Egan must have slipped it in my pocket when I was distracted.'

'You must see our dilemma. Why would Egan give it to you?'

'As I said, dying people do odd things.' I stared at Mr Lowell blandly. 'Maybe it was very valuable to him, and he was scared that someone would take it. Maybe he thought I was trustworthy.'

Mr Casey gave a snort of derision. Mr Lowell's expression was politely disbelieving.

Annoyed, I said with some heat, 'I told the police that I had it. I didn't try to hide it. I was going to hand it in to them.'

'You didn't tell anyone you had it until the police asked you about it,' said Mr Casey brusquely. 'You're spinning a pretty story, little lady.'

I glared at him, although what he had said about the police was absolutely true. Again, I forced myself to calm down.

'I wanted to talk to Mr Moray, our station leader, first. Find out what he thought I should do to make sure the locket was returned to its rightful owner.'

Casey's lip lifted in a sneer. 'You think we're fools?'

I turned to Lowell who looked down at a sheaf of papers in his hands. 'You say that Mr Harker took the fob from you before you could give it to the police?'

'Yes. He used a nasty trick. Ask him about it.'

'Mr Harker handed in Egan's watch fob yesterday. When he did so, he told us that he tricked you in order to get it.' Lowell looked up, into my eyes. 'He was not authorised to do that, and we apologise on behalf of the US government. He will be severely reprimanded.'

'So he should be,' I said, with as much righteous indignity as I could muster.

'Mr Harker told us that he wanted to get the fob back quickly to give it to Egan's widow.'

'Has it been given to her?'

'Yes.'

I managed a sunny smile. 'Oh, I am glad to hear that. Mr Harker said he would give it to her, but I didn't really believe him.'

Mr Lowell leaned forward and looked at me again. 'We are interested in finding the man you saw looting Mr Egan's body. Did you get a good look at him?'

'No. It was very dark.'

Lowell stared at me, pinned me with his gaze, much as Michael had done only the afternoon before. I had given myself away to Michael, but I didn't seem to be able to keep things from him. Mr Dan Lowell was an entirely different prospect.

Mr Lowell stared at me a moment longer, then leaned back in his chair. 'Are you sure?'

'Yes.'

For the first time, a smile touched the corner of Lowell's mouth.

I continued to stare into his eyes, and when I spoke, it was the truth.

'I had never met Mr Egan until that night,' I said earnestly. 'I had no idea he had slipped the watch fob into my pocket. I'm telling the truth. I swear it.'

Of course, I hadn't mentioned a few things, but as I didn't like either of them, why should that count?

Lowell kept my gaze for what seemed like a long time, then flicked a glance at Casey, who shook his head. Both men stood.

Casey said, gruffly, 'I'm not going to thank you, Miss Halliday, because I think you've been playing us for fools. If I find you stole anything else from Harry Egan, I'll make sure you're properly dealt with. You can bet on that, little lady.' He pulled the door open and stomped out of the room.

Mr Lowell held out his hand and I shook it. 'Thanks for your time. Sorry about John's rudeness. Mr Egan was a friend of his. More importantly, Harry Egan was an American citizen and his widow is most upset that his body was looted. We take such matters very seriously. Please feel free to telephone me if you think of anything else.' His smile was easy, very appealing, and I smiled back reflexively. 'It's been a real pleasure to meet you, Miss Halliday.'

He left the office. As they crossed the common room I saw Lowell peel off from Casey and walk over to Celia, who must have returned from her errand. He greeted her cordially, and then his expression became solemn. I assumed that he was offering condolences to her about Cedric Ashwin's death. They chatted for a minute or so, and he followed Casey out of the room.

I looked down at Lowell's card. Like Michael's, it gave his name – Daniel Lowell – and the address of the US Embassy in Grosvenor Square. I wondered what Special Agents of the US Department of State actually did at the embassy. Michael had not wanted the negatives to go to the embassy, by which he must have meant Casey and Lowell. If Michael Harker did not trust those men, then I decided I would not trust them either.

Later that day I accompanied Celia on a transfer of patients from one hospital to another. As we drove back to the station I decided to play spy myself.

'Um, you seemed to know Mr Lowell,' I said, as she turned into Euston Road. Heavy Rescue was hard at work, demolishing a teetering building. As we passed by, they bulldozed a wall into a heap of bricks and plaster. Dust whirled around the ambulance.

'Dan Lowell?' she said, driving unperturbed through the cloud of dust. 'Yes, he was a friend of Cedric's before the war. Came across to offer his condolences.'

'A friend of your husband's?' It seemed fishy to me that Lowell would be friends with a high-ranking British fascist.

'Yes. He's some sort of security bod at the American Embassy, or so Cedric told me. All very hush-hush.'

I laughed. 'And yet you're telling me?'

'Dan was a friend of Cedric's, so I don't care for his politics. Why should I keep his secrets?'

'What do you mean, don't care for his politics?'

'The group who gathered around Cedric before the war were fascists. They might not all have declared themselves to be so, but they were. They admired Hitler and they wanted to avoid war with Germany.'

'Like Ambassador Kennedy.'

'Yes. Like Joe Kennedy, Dan is a committed isolationist. If he had his way, the US would keep right out of the European war. Why did he want to see you?'

'Oh, it was about an American who died in the Café de Paris. His name was Harry Egan. Did you know him?'

She thought about it.

'Name rings a bell, but I can't place him. I met so many at those embassy soirées before the war.'

Celia swung the ambulance into Upper Woburn Place, past St Pancras Church with its six elegant columns.

'I'll tell you this,' she said. 'Dan's a charmer, but I doubt he's any friend to Britain.'

'What about John Casey?'

She thought for a moment. 'Bullish looking creature with ridiculously short hair?'

'Yes.'

'Ill-mannered and boorish. I tried to avoid his company.'

It was a busy night and I had no time to consider what Celia had said. As I walked home early the next morning, crunching over broken glass, I ran over it in my mind. I trusted Michael Harker, who had assured me that he supported Britain's interests in this war. Michael said that the microfilm could be embarrassing to America but disastrous for Britain. If President Roosevelt was forced to resign, and the new president was an isolationist, then it would be a disaster for Britain, because we couldn't withstand the Nazis without the American goods and weapons and war items that came across in the Atlantic convoys.

Somehow I'd become involved in difficult and dangerous dealings. I sighed. And it was not just the microfilm. I had let myself get far too fond of Michael Harker, who was married, and American, and a spy. *Madness, Maisie. Forget the man.*

I sighed again as I turned into Manette Street. Michael Harker was not there waiting for me. Had it really only been two days ago that he had found me here and had taken the locket? Was it only the night before last that he had tunnelled into debris to save the couple? Only yesterday morning that I had seen him walk away from me?

Time seemed to be playing tricks. Shakespeare would have said that it was out of joint. I wondered what was next in store for me.

CHAPTER TWENTY-ONE

March comes in like a lion and out like a lamb. Or so the saying goes.

Hitler must not have heard of it, because he stepped up the air raids through March and into April. Every night came the Warning, followed by the drone of planes, the clatter of incendiaries, the screech of falling bombs, the dull crash of explosions and the inevitable smell of cordite mixed with smoke.

The bombs the Germans began to use in April seemed to be particularly heavy, so that when they fell they echoed along London's streets like the roar of a dynamite charge in a deep mine. Daylight always revealed more devastated and burned-out shops and houses, more glassless windows and smashed walls. And on the streets lay hosepipes that stretched out in wild loops, like gigantic snakes ready to lunge.

Londoners carried on, scarcely remembering a time without raiders every night and new destruction every morning. At Bloomsbury Ambulance Station we faced mercy dashes in darkness, under a rain of incendiaries and a hail of bombs. In daylight we undertook mortuary runs, the sombre task of collecting the remains of what had been a human being the day before.

I was so busy there was no time to think about Z. Michael Harker.

Not much time, anyway.

'It's cold in here,' grumbled Squire as I entered the common room to begin my shift on a rainy morning in early April. He crossed his thick arms across his chest and hugged himself.

'It's always cold in here,' said Celia. 'Don't be a baby, Squire. My parents' place in Kent was colder than this.'

'Ah, the trials and tribulations of a grand country house,' said Lily, as she came through the door carrying a tray. On it she had placed a big brown teapot, a chipped china milk jug patterned with red roses and a green glass sugar pot. Next to them was a tin of biscuits.

'Shall I be mother?' said Squire, in a mincing voice. It did not match his somewhat beefy exterior. 'I'm parched.'

'Please,' said Lily, unloading the tray on to the common room table.

Squire picked up the jug, which looked tiny in his enormous hands and carefully added milk to each cup.

'When did the family heirloom get chipped?' Celia asked Lily as Squire poured the tea.

'Last night, apparently. McIver told me this morning that when the bomb took out the place down the street – you know, the one next to the hospital – it rocked the station so hard that the old jug danced off the table. Was it valuable?'

'God, I don't know. It was part of a set we got for a wedding present. To tell the truth, I always hated it, but as it alone managed to escape the bombing of the Mayfair house I felt it deserved respect as an orphan of the war. That's why I brought it here.' She sighed. 'And now it's joined its brothers and sisters as crockery bomb victims.'

'It's a flesh wound only,' said Lily.

Lily passed me a cup of tea and pushed the tin of biscuits into the centre of the table. 'A present from Jim's godmother. Fortnum and Mason.'

I smiled at her, reached across and took one. 'Yum.'

'Do you sometimes wonder,' Lily asked, musingly, 'if one day, when this is all over, people will think that driving an ambulance in the Blitz was a glamorous job?'

Purvis laughed. 'If they see the newspaper photos of Halliday and Ashwin, the ones where they're laughing together, showing some leg and putting on lipstick, no one would think it's anything *but* jolly good fun.'

'Ugh,' said Celia. 'I loathed that photographic session.' She eyed me. 'You seemed to enjoy it.'

I bit into my biscuit, which crunched delightfully. 'I did enjoy it. And to answer Lily's question, they probably will think it's glamorous.'

Lily nodded. 'My Jim thinks that when it is all over, Londoners will look back on the Blitz with affection. Remember it as something big and meaningful.'

'I, for one, think that would be a good thing,' said Doris Powell. 'Keep fond memories of the comradeship, and forget the rest. No point dwelling on the horrors once they're over.'

Armstrong seemed unconvinced. 'But we need to make sure that things are better afterwards. We don't want to have gone through all of this for nothing.'

'I watched the Jarrow hunger marchers come into London,' said Harris, 'and I can never forget the looks on their faces. After the war we need to make sure that there's a proper fair share for everyone.'

Purvis nodded. 'Less privilege through possession of capital.'

'I'd like to see the government accepting that it owes a decent life to all of us, the poor as well as the rich,' I said.

'No more slums,' said Squire. 'That's what I want. No more half-starved kids, no more unemployed. A real national health service.'

Armstrong chimed in again. 'We have to get rid of the class system. It's wrong that people get things or don't get them because of what class they were born into.' He glanced at Celia, and ducked his head, as if worried how she would take his comments.

Celia smiled at him and pretended to clap. 'Bravo, ducky,' she said. 'I'm on your side. And so is Dr Levy, by the way. He says after the war he'll work hard for a comprehensive hospital service that's available to everyone who needs it, rich or poor.'

'Bloody communists, the lot of you,' said Sadler, but without any malice.

Later that morning Moray sent me and Celia to what he said had been a serious incident at a block of flats near Tottenham Court Road. We were to pick up the bodies and take them to the nearest mortuary.

'You may need a couple of trips,' he said.

Celia and I shared a grimace, nodded, and went to get ready.

The usual diversions delayed our arrival at the incident. Bombs had ripped open gas lines, sewers and water mains. Broken tram lines trailed forlornly, while dangling electricity wires sparked dangerously. In desperation, I turned down a narrow street that was more of an alley and rounded a corner to find I was heading straight for a familiar notice: 'Danger – Unexploded Bomb'.

I put my foot down hard on the brakes and the ambulance stopped dead with a screech.

'Not much room to turn around,' said Celia.

'Needs must,' I replied, wrenching the wheel to turn towards the grimy brick wall on my right, pushing hard on the clutch, shoving the stick into reverse, moving a few inches back and repeating the manoeuvre.

'It'll be a ten-point turn,' I said with a grim smile.

I had reached a point diagonally across the road, with only a couple of inches between the front of ambulance and a grimy brick wall, and not much more space between the back of the ambulance and another grimy brick wall, when Celia gave a shriek.

'Watch out.'

A lorry was hurtling in our direction. I braced for impact.

The lorry screeched to a halt, skidded on the damp road and ended up a foot or so away from my door. The driver, a fair-haired young man, gave me a wave and slammed the lorry into reverse. Slowly, with a series of metallic shrieks, it backed up, until it was out of the alley and waiting at the crossroad.

Four young men, an officer, a corporal and two privates emerged to stand beside it, taking time for a cigarette break. Celia jumped out of the ambulance and walked over to them.

In a seemingly interminable series of forward and backward turns, I got my ambulance around and trundled back towards the lorry. I stopped, and Celia climbed back in.

'There's a time bomb down there,' I said to the driver.

'Don't worry about us,' he said with a smile, 'we're the ones who've come to take it away.'

And then the world exploded.

How can I possibly describe the loudness of an exploding bomb? It is all the claps of thunder you have ever heard rolled into one roaring crescendo. The ambulance rocked and juddered. When the smoke cleared a little, the alleyway I'd been in a minute before was a mass of tumbled bricks and steel girders. Bricks had smashed the ambulance's windscreen and Celia's window. She was tumbled against the door and her face was bloody.

'Celia,' I shrieked, 'Celia.' I pulled her towards me.

Her eyes blinked open and she managed a smile. A thin trickle of blood was still running down her face, from a cut above her eyebrow.

'Still here,' she said, and wiped her hand across her forehead. 'My head is bloody but unbowed, as they say.'

'We'd better see to the bomb squad,' I said.

Celia's door had been crushed by falling bricks and she couldn't push it open. My side was relatively undamaged. I pushed open the door, jumped down and ran over to the truck to find three of the men, like Celia, bloodied but unbowed. The only casualty was the fair-haired driver, whose radius had fractured after being struck by a flying brick.

He grinned at me, despite his pain. 'We owe you. If you'd not got your machine stuck in that alley we'd have been down there when it went off. Must have been on a timer. You're our lucky star, Ambulance Girl.'

Their lorry was scratched but otherwise undamaged, and they drove off laughing to take their injured comrade to a first-aid depot. As they left, one leaned out of the window and said, 'Try Maple Street – left then right then right. I think it's clear.'

Celia and I plucked the bricks off our machine, and used rags to clear the seats of glass. I pushed the starter. The engine chugged into life after a few revs.

'No windscreen, but the back's undamaged,' I said. 'Should we do the pick-up?'

'I don't mind a windy ride,' said Celia. 'The deceased won't mind either, if you don't.'

'Oh, I like a bit of fresh air.'

We headed off, bumping over bricks, turned left then right then right and ended up where we wanted to be. As we rattled along with the wind in our hair, Celia spat on her hankie and scrubbed at the blood on her face.

Twelve pitiful sacks lay outside what had been a large group of flats. The smell of death hung over them. Smaller sacks and a few ash cans held smaller remains. The mortuary workers would face the daunting task of trying to identify the human flotsam with only a list of names of missing people and a brief description.

We took two trips. As we hauled the last sack into the back of the ambulance, Celia stretched and leaned her back against the vehicle.

'I need a cigarette,' she said.

Her attempts at cleaning her face had been a compete failure. No one but Celia could have managed to look so lovely despite the dried blood and dirt that caked her white skin and the brick dust in her hair.

'These poor souls won't worry if we're a bit slow in taking them to the morgue,' I said, and stood beside her, also leaning on the ambulance. 'I thought you were giving up smoking.'

'Simon wants me to give up. He says it stinks and it's bad for my health.' She laughed. 'I'm sure it is both, but on days like this I need it. A time bomb *and* a mortuary run. Ugh.'

She lit a cigarette, took a deep breath in and exhaled with a smile.

'You and Simon Levy ...' I wasn't sure what to say; her husband had died only six weeks before.

'That's right, you saw us outside the Café de Paris' she said, turning to me with a mischievous look in her eyes. 'Were we, er, locked together in passionate embrace?'

'Um, yes.'

'First time we'd kissed, actually. I adore him. We'll be married in September, six months after Cedric ... Well, you understand?'

'Of course. Are you going to, um, convert?'

'No. But the children will be raised Jewish. It's slightly complicated, in a good way.'

I said, tentatively, 'You and Dr Levy, you seem very different.'

'Him Jewish, me gentile, you mean?' She sucked in another lungful of smoke, and blew it out with a huff.

'No, not that ... I don't know really.'

'Actually, we're very alike in the way we see the world, our sense of humour, our hopes for the future – all the things that count.'

'And you were both born into wealthy families, of course.'

'That, too.' She smiled. 'But the other things are more important. He's my opposite in one way, though. People like him – he's so easy to like. I'm not.'

I began to remonstrate, but she laughed.

'You know it's true. Shall we say, then, I'm harder to get to know. I think Simon and I complement each other in that aspect.'

Celia was in a rare, chatty mood, so I thought I'd venture down the rabbit hole again. *Michael Harker.*

'You used to go to a lot of American Embassy parties, didn't you? Before the war I mean.'

'When Cedric was still *persona grata*? Yes, we did. He and Ambassador Kennedy had a bit of a mutual admiration thing going. Both wanted peace with Germany at any cost, and both rather admired Hitler. I told you we met Dan Lowell and John Casey at those dreary dos. Why?'

'Um, did you meet a man called Michael Harker? He has a wife called Vivian. Did you meet her?'

Celia thought about it. 'I remember Vivian Harker better than I do her husband. Her father's a congressman, wealthy family, socially well connected. Very pretty little thing, one of those china doll blondes. A bit milk-and-water for my liking. Pleasant enough, you understand, but vapid. Had no opinions of her own.' She laughed. 'Mind you, I would have been called vapid in those days, too. All of that social whirl ceased when war was declared, and Cedric was imprisoned. No one wanted to know us then.'

She took another deep drag at the cigarette, threw the butt on the ground and stamped it out. Then she stood still, as if thinking.

'I heard something about Vivian Harker. Last year, it was. Can't for the life of me recall what, though. Something sad.'

'What do you mean, sad?'

She shook her head. 'Don't remember. Something about children? ... No. It's gone.'

As we drove to the mortuary she asked me how I knew Michael and Vivian Harker.

'Oh, um, I met Mr Harker after the Café de Paris bombing.'

She gave me a sideways glance. 'Handsome man. Should I become all big sister and remind you he's married?'

'Oh, it's nothing like that,' I said hastily.

CHAPTER TWENTY-TWO

We drove down the ramp into the garage and parked the ambulance with a squeak of brakes. Celia's door was still jammed shut, so she slid across and jumped down to the concrete floor after me.

Armstrong was standing by the Ford with his arms full of blankets, replenishing its supplies.

'What happened?' he asked. 'Your vehicle's a right mess. Moray won't be happy.' Then he saw Celia and gave a start. 'You all right?'

'Had a tussle with a time bomb,' said Celia. She turned to me. 'Think I'll wash my face. Mustn't frighten the animals.'

When I entered the common room, Harris was sitting in the Lloyd Loom chair, the most comfortable in the room, knitting something in khaki. Sadler was playing patience. Purvis was deep in a newspaper, but looked up when I entered. He smiled at me and turned the page.

'The newspapers are shrinking every week,' he said.

'As you well know, the government wants all the paper it can lay its hands on for the war effort,' said Harris calmly. She nodded towards Moray's office. 'Moray wants to see you,' she said.

Through the window I could see Moray talking to a man in a suit. As his guest's back was to the window, his face was hidden, but I could see it wasn't Michael. Moray looked up and saw me and motioned me to come into the office. It was when I pushed open the door that I saw it was none other than Mr Peregrine Denbeigh, from the air-raid shelter in March. The man from the film unit.

I greeted him with cordial suspicion. He responded with a brilliant smile, revealing small, white teeth. Moray's demeanour was one of polite annoyance.

'Mr Denbeigh tells me that he met you in an air-raid shelter,' said Moray.

'Yes, last month,' I replied.

'And he asked you to take part in a short propaganda film.'

'I refused.'

Denbeigh leaned forward in his chair and radiated good humour, with an underlying sense of authority. 'As soon as I clapped eyes on Miss Halliday I knew. I saw it all in my mind. A film about the wonderful girls who drive our ambulances.'

I said, through a tight jaw, 'Mr Denbeigh, I can't act.'

He was all joviality. 'No need. No need at all. We're using Billie Prescott. She'll have nearly all the lines – you may have a few words but that won't matter. The important thing is that we can say we used real ambulance girls in the film. We're on the look-out for others.' His smile was dazzling. 'Marvellous. Simply marvellous.'

I was about to protest when Denbeigh's attention was diverted. He was now gazing through the window in a state of what seemed to be rapture. Moray rolled his eyes, and I turned to see that Celia and Lily had entered and were chatting together. Celia's face was clean, her hair brushed and she was the very picture of an English rose. Lily was smiling, and with her dimples she looked like Shirley Temple's older sister.

Denbeigh turned to Moray. 'And they're also ambulance girls?'

Moray nodded. 'They're part of this shift.'

'This is serendipitous indeed. I'll want all three.'

'I'm not—' I began.

Moray interrupted me. 'Mr Denbeigh has the full cooperation of the London County Council and of the Ministry of Information. You –' he glanced at Celia and Lily, through the window '– and perhaps the others, are obliged to attend at a screen test. If you pass it then you'll attend the film studio during filming. I am assured that your part in the filming will last no longer than two days. A film like this is seen as an excellent way to inform the public about the work we do here in the Auxiliary Ambulance Service. Your participation is to be seen as part of your duties.' His voice was even, measured, but somehow I knew that he was absolutely furious.

I stared at him. 'I have no say in it?'

Denbeigh smiled. 'It will be entirely painless, I assure you.' He looked up at the ceiling as if seeing there a finished film, and murmured, '*Ambulance Girls At War*. That's what we'll call it. And it must be entertaining. We've been informed in no uncertain terms that for a film to be good propaganda, it must also be entertaining. This film will be entertaining. It'll have girls with plenty of oomph and the right sort of message.'

I shared a look with Moray. Mine was tormented, his now amused.

Lily and Celia were a picture of opposites when Moray emerged with Mr Denbeigh and informed them that they were to help provide the oomph in an entertaining and propagandistic production entitled *Ambulance Girls At War*. Lily looked intrigued; Celia affronted.

'You do know who I am?' she asked Mr Denbeigh.

'Mr Moray explained,' he replied. 'Not a problem. Use your maiden name. Ah, what is it?'

'Palmer-Thomas, but—'

'No one holds grudges,' he said quickly. 'Your – well, he is dead, after all.'

'Tactful, isn't he?' murmured Moray to me. 'And shockingly single-minded. I think even Celia's met her match.'

Moray was right. Any other protests Celia made Mr Denbeigh simply waved away.

'Screen test on Friday?' asked Lily. 'That soon? What about a script? Can we at least see the script before we start?'

'Oh, it's being worked on now,' was Denbeigh's airy reply. 'Have it to you by Friday morning. Your job will be to look lovely, brave and utterly committed to the war effort. Most of the lines will be said by Miss Billie Prescott.'

Lily's eyes widened. 'Oh, she's a favourite of mine. I'll be in a film with Billie Prescott. Gosh.'

'Australian?' he asked.

'Yes. From Perth, in Western Australia.'

Denbeigh frowned. 'I think we'll make it Sydney,' he said.

Lily attempted a protest, but Mr Denbeigh's riposte was, 'Everyone's heard of Sydney. Convicts, etc. And Perth's in Scotland.'

Celia's face seemed to have become moulded of stone. A particularly fine alabaster. Even Moray quailed when she turned blazing blue eyes on him; Denbeigh seemed to shrink into his tailored suit.

'I won't do it,' she stated, in her most regal tone. Celia had a particularly regal tone. 'I hate making an exhibition of myself and I simply won't do it, I tell you.'

Mr Denbeigh dithered his way out of the common room, muttering to Moray, whom he dragged along with him.

When Moray returned he raised an eyebrow. 'Can't be helped, Ashwin. You're in the movies. If you pass the screen test. That's on Friday afternoon at Ealing Studios.' He raised his hands. 'I have to give you the time off, which is annoying for the rest of us. If you pass the screen test, then you'll have two days off work next week. Only during the day, mind. You'll be expected to come back to the station for the night shift'

'What's going on?' Powell and Squire entered the common room. They were told all about our foray into film-making.

'Ashwin, love, you'll look gorgeous up there on the screen. Show off your lovely face.' Squire's placating tone did not move Celia.

She pursed her lips and looked mutinous. 'If I have to, I'll stand there like a wooden dummy, but they can't make me act. I'd like to see them try to.'

'Well, I'm looking forward to it,' said Lily. 'It's in a good cause. And we get to meet Billie Prescott. She's the star.'

'Ooh,' said Powell. 'I like her ever so much.'

Harris said, with some dignity, 'It's part of the war effort, Ashwin. Letting the public know what we do. You should be pleased to take part.'

'As if people don't know what we've been doing,' said Celia scornfully. 'We don't need propaganda to show them what ambulance drivers do.'

'It's not that,' said Lily. 'I think it's more to emphasise how we're all mucking in together. You know, how the ARP services are a great leveller. They'll probably put in a few cockneys, someone from t'North, and us. I'll have to say a line in Aussie, to show that the Empire is right behind Britain in her finest hour.' She giggled. 'I bet they'll make Celia the posh girl slumming it, who comes to realise the worth of the great unwashed who drive ambulances with her.'

'Whatever do you mean, the great unwashed?' said Powell, affronted.

'Yeah,' said Purvis, making a comical expression. 'Wotcha mean? I washed me 'ands and feet before I come, I did.'

Purvis sometimes threw in odd remarks like that. They were humorous only to himself and I suspected it was to show his learning. He'd been to university, after all.

Lily gave a peal of laughter. 'It's an expression, not a reflection on your hygiene. "The great unwashed" means ordinary people.'

'It sounds like it's a reflection on our hygiene,' Powell muttered, her face flushed and annoyed. 'It's hard to keep clean with all the regulations and the water being off all the time. And when it's on there's no gas to heat it. How *can* we keep as clean as we'd like?'

When she saw that Powell was really quite upset, Lily went over to her and patted her shoulder. 'Of course I didn't mean it like that. It's just a silly expression.'

'It's not a nice one.'

'It's condescending,' said Purvis. 'Even if you mean it ironically, it's condescending.'

Lily looked abashed. 'I'm sorry,' she mumbled. 'I didn't think.'

'To tell the truth,' I said, smiling, 'we're all the great unwashed at the moment. As Powell says, there's never any hot water, and when the gas is on it's five inches only in the bathtub. I dream of a long hot bath with lovely scented soap.'

'Now, Maisie, you know perfectly well that running water wastes fuel,' said Squire, with a wink.

'And if you're up to your neck in it—' said Purvis, smiling.

'Oh, I know this one,' said Lily, excitedly. 'If you're up to your neck in it, that's a waste line.'

'Your waist line is the high water mark,' finished Powell, smiling at last.

We all knew the lines from the shorts at the cinema off by heart.

'Speaking of baths,' put in Sadler, ever on the look-out to sell his dodgy wares. 'Care to take a butcher's at my latest selection?' He reached down into a hessian bag near his feet and pulled out a half-dozen or so small cakes of soap, wrapped in bright paper. We all came over to look, except Celia, whose expression remained mutinous.

'I'll not say a word,' she said. 'I don't care what they do. They can't make me. People hate my accent. *I* hate my accent. I do not want it recorded for posterity.'

'Don't worry, Ashwin,' said Squire. He was examining a cake of soap wrapped in paper on which was a garish sprig of lavender. 'I'll take this one, mate. The missus'll be pleased.' Transaction completed, he looked at Celia. 'No one actually watches them propaganda films. They put them on in the intermission, or at the end, when we're all leaving.'

'I hate them things,' said Sadler as he gave Harris some change for a shilling. He raised his voice to imitate a middle-class accent. 'What have we here, in this here cupboard? Why, there's enough old wallpaper here to make simply thousands of cartridge wads. Salvage *is* important. Chri – I mean gawd, I hate that bloke's voice.'

'They can't make me do it,' repeated Celia. 'I won't.'

The script arrived on Friday morning, three copies, one each for me, Celia and Lily. We went to the ladies' washroom to read them together in peace.

I was 'Mary (middle-class girl)', Celia was 'Linda (upper-class girl)' and Lily was 'Sheila (Australian girl)'. The famous film star, Billie Prescott, was 'Rose'. There was another woman called 'Poppy (working-class girl)', who was also a real ambulance driver. She had one line about the sort of world she wanted when the war was over. The other actors in the cast were 'Bert (Cockney)' and 'Henry (Yorkshireman)' and 'Avis (shop girl)'. Like Miss Prescott, they were professional actors, and they had most of the lines.

The story was simple. The team is at the ambulance station, chatting and being friendly, getting on with their daily routine. A raid commences, and they all go out to collect the injured. It's a bad raid with lots of falling buildings and fire. The team are shown working together to get the wounded to hospital. Bert is overcome with fear and can't go on. Rose gives him a pep talk. Rose and shop girl Avis run into a burning building to save a trapped man. Great tension when everyone thinks they've been killed. They emerge victorious with their patient on a stretcher. Henry and Bert remark on what a great job the ambulance girls – indeed all British women – are doing in this war, and how they're often braver than the men.

My one line was, 'My word, Jerry's coming over thick and fast tonight.'

Celia was supposed to say, 'My parents didn't want me to take this job. They don't understand how glad I am to be here in this station with you all and doing my bit. Being a small part of something so big.'

Lily's lines were: 'Sometimes I dream I'm back home in Sydney, but once I'm awake I know there's nowhere I'd rather be than here in London, right now.' And later on, 'My convict ancestor would laugh to think I was over here defending the old country, the one that sent him out to Botany Bay. But, somehow, I think he'd approve.'

Lily read out her lines in a flat voice and looked up from the script in horror. 'This is simply ghastly. All of it, even the lines given to Billie Prescott, they're all appalling.'

She turned a few pages, and said in a tone of amused disgust, 'Good heavens. Look at this. Just turn to page ten.'

I flicked through the pages and found page ten.

INTERIOR: AMBULANCE STATION

Outside a raid is on. Sounds of gunfire and bombs falling. BERT and ROSE sit at a shaking table, drinking tea from tin mugs.

BERT (shakes head slowly): I can't do it. I can't go out there again.

ROSE: Bert, we must go out there. No matter what it's like, no matter how bad it gets. It's our job, you see. Our job. They're depending on us.

BERT: I sees all right. I sees you little scraps of things driving out into the heart of the Blitz, picking up the injured through bombs and bullets. Aren't you ever scared, love?

ROSE: Oh, Bert, don't ever think I'm not afraid. When the bombs are falling my heart pounds like a drum, but I can never forget that these people, our people, need us. And that it's our job to help them. We're all on the front line in this war, remember. Men or women, town or country, no matter what our background, we're all in it together. (Stands) So let's get back in that ambulance and drive to where we're needed.

BERT and ROSE exit the room.

*

Celia's expression as she read this was as if there was a particularly bad smell in the air. Lily pretended to vomit.

I said, encouragingly, 'I'm sure it all sounds better when said out loud by a proper actor and actress.'

Lily threw back her head and laughed. 'Oh, Maisie, how can it? It's putrid.' She said, in a mincing voice, 'It's our job, you see. Our *job*!'

Celia shrugged and threw her copy of the script down on to the table. 'Well, I'm not saying a damn thing. Just let them try and make me.'

We were picked up a few hours later by an ATS girl driving the film unit's big saloon. She deposited us at the entrance to Ealing Studios in west London, telling us to wait for 'Harry'.

I felt a tremor of excitement. I'd had acting lessons at Italia Conti, but I'd never been a great success. Maybe I'd be different this time. I fell into a daydream of being 'discovered', ending up as a famous film actress and receiving a fan letter from Michael Harker.

Lily chatted to the uniformed guard, who was an elderly man with a little moustache. 'How big is the studio?' she asked.

'Very big indeed,' he said, and continued in a well-rehearsed manner. 'Four sound stages giving us in total almost twenty-eight thousand feet of film space.'

Lily made a sound indicating amazement.

'Ealing Studios,' he went on in a smug voice, 'is the oldest film studio in the world and has been the centre of the British Film Industry since 1902.'

'Gosh,' said Lily, looking suitably impressed.

A thin older woman in slacks and a baggy cardigan emerged from the building.

'I'm Harry,' she said, and checked our names off on the clipboard she was carrying. 'Follow me.' She led us along a maze of corridors until we ended up at a small set somewhere in the rear of the building. It had a big table in it, in front of a plywood back with a painted window. The table had been set up with tin cups and a telephone. Cameras and lights in front of the table glared at it ominously. Harry pointed to a line of chairs against the wall and told us to, 'Sit there'.

Celia set her mouth mutinously at that and I feared trouble. She said, in her regal manner, 'A simple "please" wouldn't go astray.'

Celia's accent was the sort that ruled empires; it was, on the whole, loathed by all except those with a similar accent. The woman gave her a venomous glare.

'Dear ladies,' she said, through gritted teeth, 'please *do* sit down.'

We sat.

'What now?' asked Lily.

'You wait,' said Harry. 'There's an awful lot of waiting when you make a film. You'll need to get used to it.'

'This is only a screen test,' said Lily, but the woman had wandered off.

Mr Denbeigh turned up ten minutes later with a man he introduced as Les, the cameraman.

'Know your lines?' asked Denbeigh, smiling. 'Capital. Say them with plenty of oomph.'

We sat around the table and drank water from the tin cups as if it were tea and said our lines.

Lily was a natural, giving a performance with just the right degree of loneliness mixed with defiance. It turned out that she could even cry on cue.

'Perfect,' said Mr Denbeigh. He turned to the camera man. 'Be sure to get a close up of her in the action scenes. We'll make her face dirty and film the tears tracking through the dirt on her cheeks.'

I was wooden, and soon realised I was there only because of my assets.

'Could you arch your back a little,' said Mr Denbeigh. My shirt strained when I did so. I heard him mutter to the cameraman, 'Marvellous. We'll put her in a tight shirt and a short skirt.'

When Celia's turn came she stood in front of the camera as if she was carved of alabaster. She said her lines as if she were reading a train timetable, in an accent so clipped and county that her lovely lips barely moved.

Denbeigh stood behind the camera, seeing how the camera viewed her. He smiled.

'Marvellous,' he said, encouragingly. 'The camera loves you. Would you mind awfully if we cut your lines? You'd look simply wonderful in the background. No need for you to talk at all.'

Celia's face relaxed into a smug expression. 'No,' she said. 'I don't mind at all.'

Denbeigh looked up from the camera. 'All three of you are marvellous. Just marvellous. Pop along with Harry now to be fitted for your costumes and I'll see you bright and early on Monday morning.' Denbeigh walked away.

We followed Harry along the maze-like set of corridors to a large room filled with racks of clothes. Harry explained the needs to the wardrobe mistress, who referred to a sheet of paper she'd already been given.

'Pop your clothes off, dearies,' said the wardrobe mistress. 'Down to your undergarments, please. I'll take your measurements.'

'One change,' said Harry. 'Director wants Miss Halliday in a skirt. Make the most of her figure. Tight shirt, short skirt, that sort of thing.' She checked her clipboard. 'Silk stockings.'

I raised my eyebrow at the wardrobe mistress.

'Pre-war stock,' she said. 'Hen's teeth nowadays, of course. So, for God's sake, don't ladder them.' She frowned. 'I'll put you in lisle for the outdoor shots; no one will see the difference.'

CHAPTER TWENTY-THREE

Film-making is all rather a muddle. Lots of people wander all around the place and it takes a great deal of time to get anything done.

As soon as we arrived 'on set' on Monday morning, we were met by Anne Tait, a tall girl with clear grey eyes and a calm demeanour, who informed us that she was the assistant to the first assistant director. She carried a clipboard and seemed to be at ease with the controlled chaos that surrounded her. She said we were to present ourselves at Wardrobe.

'They've prepared your costumes,' she said as she led us to the costume room.

The uniforms they'd prepared were lovely. Tan slacks for Celia and Lily, tight skirt for me that came to the middle of my knees. Shirts, ties and fitted jackets. I was given a pair of lovely silk stockings. My shirt was a size too small. I looked at the wardrobe mistress.

'He wanted oomph, love,' she said. 'You've got plenty. Try not to pop a button, there's a good girl. I've put in some darts to make the most of your figure, and please use this brassiere – it's specially designed for girls with oomph.'

Once we'd dressed we preened in front of the mirror.

Lily gave me a whistle. 'Oomph galore,' she said. 'You'll knock their socks off.'

'Now to make-up,' Anne told us, again checking her clipboard. 'Stick with me.'

We stuck like glue. As we followed her along a narrow corridor I wondered how different it would be to be made up for a camera, rather than the stage.

The make-up room had mirrors along the wall with a seat in front of each, and an older man with a bright cheery attitude. I'd met many such in my days treading the boards. He must have been at least sixty but his face was determinedly young-looking, and I assumed that he used his products on himself.

'These are the ambulance girls,' said Anne.

'Good morning, lovely ladies,' he said. 'I'm Hal. Sit down, please. Who's going first?'

'I will,' I said.

Hal sat me in a chair and covered me with a sheet up to my neck.

'You an actress, darling?' he asked. 'You seem awfully at ease.'

'Before the war I was a Tiller Girl,' I said proudly.

'I can always tell a theatrical,' he said, with a brisk nod. 'I started out in the music hall circuit, and I simply adored the chorus girls.' He stared at my face, made a 'hmmm' sound and turned to rummage around in his box of tricks. 'They did their own faces, of course, but they were always so sweet to little old me.'

I thought I knew why. So many men backstage were predators, all too ready to poke, or pinch or push against you as you waited to go on, or came offstage. Someone like Hal, who seemed sweet, polite and obviously not interested in that sort of thing, would be a tonic.

'I think I'll give you the make-up I gave Googie Withers. Your features remind me of her.' He preened a little. 'I did her make-up in *Trouble Brewing* with Mr George Formby. Did you see it?'

'I did. I love Mr Formby.'

'Such a gentleman. But, my dear, his wife!' He shuddered.

Hal dotted pale greasepaint all over my face and blended it in with a ruthless efficiency. He followed up with a medium shade then a darker one. I'm quite olive-skinned, so a fair bit of the dark shade was used.

'You look awfully orange, Maisie,' said Lily.

I met Hal's eye in the mirror. 'It's for the lights,' I said.

Carmine was added to my cheeks to add some colour.

'Why the red?' asked Celia. 'It's a black and white film, surely.'

Hal and I had another silent communication in the mirror.

'It's so the shadows will look natural, under the lights,' I said.

Blue eyeshadow next, a touch of kohl eyeliner and mascara.

'They want a little dirt,' said Hal, and proceeded to artfully apply a few smudges.

This time I caught Celia's eye in the mirror and choked back a giggle at her horrified expression. I noticed, however, that Hal added less 'dirt' to Celia than me or Lily.

Faces made up and dirty, we were led to the sound stage, which was like a huge warehouse, with equipment and cables in jumbled heaps around the floor. We all sat down to a cup of tea and soggy biscuits, served from a cart by another woman in a grey overall.

I saw Mr Denbeigh chatting to a woman I recognised as Billie Prescott, the famous movie star. She was very pretty, with large grey eyes and chestnut hair, but was older than I'd realised.

'Is Mr Denbeigh the director?' I asked.

'Yes.'

'So he tells us what to do?' asked Lily.

'No, the first assistant director will do that.'

'Who's he?'

'Over there,' said Anne, pointing to a small, rotund man with a worried expression. 'Hubert Morris.'

'What does the director do, then?' asked Lily.

'He has a vision of the entire film, and will make sure that it ends up the way he wants.'

Celia seemed sceptical. 'This is a twenty-minute quasi-documentary,' she said. 'What vision is needed?'

Anne was obviously affronted. 'Every film we make is important, and every one of them has to fulfil the needs of the War Office and the Ministry of Information. This film will tell the public what ambulance drivers do in a raid, show how you women muck in and get the job done. It will give the audience a front row seat into your nights during the Blitz.'

'The script's awful,' said Lily. 'A dog's breakfast.'

Anne's mouth quirked up. 'The version you got isn't the final one. Don't worry, they're still working on it. And changes are often made during filming.'

As if on cue, a small girl in a long cardigan and baggy slacks approached us. 'You lot the real ambulance girls?' she asked briskly.

When we nodded she handed out some papers. 'Revised script.'

I leafed through my copy. My one line remained: 'My word, Jerry's coming over thick and fast tonight.'

Lily's lines were shortened:

INTERIOR: AMBULANCE STATION
LILY: Sometimes I dream I'm back home in Sydney.
BERT: Wish you was back there?
LILY (smiles): When I'm having the time of my life here in London? Not a chance.

'That's better,' said Lily, grudgingly, 'but still pretty dire.'

'It'll probably go through some more changes before it hits the screen,' said Anne. 'A lot is done on the run.'

The appalling page ten had been rewritten and was a little better. Celia's lines had been cut out entirely.

We waited.

'Get used to it, said Anne. 'Making a film consists of waiting, some frenzied action, and then more waiting.'

'Well I'm bored and tired,' said Celia. She shook out a blanket she'd found somewhere, wrapped it around herself and went to sleep in her chair.

'Want to join her?' asked Lily.

'I'm too wound up. I wish something would happen,' I said.

A young woman wandered across to us. 'I'm Diana Beauchamp,' she said, in a posh sort of voice. She glanced at Celia's sleeping form and lowered her voice. 'I'm from Station 39.'

'You must be Poppy,' said Lily, 'the one who talks about the need for a more equal Britain after the war. Are you going to put on an East End accent?'

'No. Poppy is over there.' Diana pointed to a small girl with dark curls who was talking to the cameraman. 'Molly Pike from our station. I'm a posh girl called Lady Harriet. Haven't a clue why they chose me for this, but I think it's my voice. They called me in at the last minute, but I'm not too worried. I've done some acting before.'

I looked at her, confused. 'But there's no Lady Harriet in our script. We got a new script at eight o'clock.'

Molly wandered over. 'I'm Cockney Poppy,' she said. 'And a right lump of school she is, too.'

'A what?' said Lily.

'A fool,' said Molly, laughing. 'In't the script awful? The audience'll think we're mental.'

'I think you have a different script to us,' said Lily, looking worried. 'Lady Harriet isn't in ours.'

Molly held up some papers. 'They gave this one to me and Beechy at nine.'

Lily went to Anne in a fever of anxiety, and Anne ran off to find the latest version. When we were handed the new script, our lines hadn't changed, but Diana/Lady Harriet had the lines previously given to Celia/Linda, although slightly improved.

We waited.

190

'Is this normal?' asked Celia, who had woken up and been introduced to Diana.

'Is what normal?' asked Diana.

'For everything to take an age?'

'Quite normal.'

The sound stage was full of people scurrying around not doing much. People frowned and moved cameras and lights to new positions then frowned again and moved them back to where they had originally been. Sounds of hammering came from somewhere over to our left.

'Watch that screen,' someone yelled.

'Over here,' yelled another. 'Not there!'

'Watch it!'

A loud crash made me jump, and then I shared a smile with Lily at the swearing that came soon afterwards.

At eleven-thirty we were all called to the set, an *ersatz* ambulance common room that looked much less comfortable than ours in Bloomsbury. There were many similarities, the big table, the sandbags, the map of London on the wall. There were also differences. The telephone sat on the table, rather than in the station leader's office, and two government posters decorated one wall: 'Be Like Dad and Keep Mum' and 'Dig for Victory' had prominent spots. In the re-rewritten script there was reference to victory gardens and to the dangers of Careless Talk. I supposed they'd decided to kill a few birds with one film.

Three of the four professional actors wandered over to us and introduced themselves.

'Arthur Hendry,' said a short, nuggety man with a long, mobile mouth. 'I'm a cheery Cockney chappy.' He made a comical face. Then he looked at me and Celia and sidled up to Lily. 'Blimey, I'll keep close to you, princess. More my size.'

'Henry' the Yorkshireman, was a tall, elegant man with the perfectly rounded vowels of a Shakespearean actor. His name was Aubrey St George.

'So you put on the accent?' I asked. 'Are you really from Yorkshire?'

He grinned and placed a finger at the side of his nose. 'Liverpool, originally, but I do a perfectly respectable Yorkshire accent. Please don't rumble me.'

'Shop girl Avis' was played by a dark-haired girl with an intense expression. She was Una Norman, and was polite but not friendly. Una whispered to me that Billie Prescott was a menace at grabbing shots. I had no idea what she meant, but I nodded sympathetically.

The famous Billie Prescott arrived a good twenty minutes after everybody else, took one look at Celia and dragged away Mr Morris to whisper feverishly in his ear. He returned looking shaken, but pulled himself together and addressed me, Lily, Celia, Molly Pike and Diana Beauchamp very cordially.

'Now I know that, apart from Diana who's playing Lady Harriet, you haven't done anything like this before, but just do your best. We'll be filming scene one first, which has all of your lines.' He hesitated, then said to Celia, 'I understand that your lines have been cut. They're now being said by Diana, who is playing Harriet? Is that correct, Miss Palmer-Thomas?'

'Absolutely correct,' said Celia.

Mr Morris darted a look at Billie Prescott and gave a quick nod. She smiled.

'The first scene is an establishing scene,' he went on, 'where we meet you all and it's clear that you're a tight team. We'll do your outside shots the day after tomorrow. They won't actually be outside, of course, because we'll be filming entirely on the bigger sound stage. You'll be hauling wounded into the ambulances and running around in the smoke. A dark filter will make it seem like night in the finished film, so you'll be filming under lights. Sound effects will be added later and film of a real air raid will be spliced in. The scenes you don't appear in will be filmed in your absence. Got that?'

We all nodded.

'So, in the first scene you're all sitting together at your ambulance station, relaxing. Rose, Henry and Bert have a discussion about victory gardens and careless talk – have you been given the final script with that dialogue?'

We nodded.

'The Warning sounds, the raid begins. Mary says her line, and it goes from there. You know all your lines?'

Lily, Diana, Molly and I nodded again. Celia looked beautiful and bored. Billie Prescott pretended not to be shooting looks of loathing at her. The immediate and fierce aversion she'd taken to Celia might be because she recognised Celia as the widow of the infamous fascist, Cedric Ashwin, but I thought it more likely that Billie Prescott was well aware of the danger that Celia would draw the viewer's eye whenever she appeared.

Mr Morris put us into our places in the fake ambulance station. Lily and I were near the front of the table. I was positioned so that my silk clad legs were in shot. He told me to put my jacket over the back of my chair, cross my legs and arch my back a little. This meant that my already tight shirt seemed about to pop a button or two. It appeared that Denbeigh had told him to take full advantage of my assets.

Lily sat next to me. I thought that Celia would be sitting next to her, but the director told her to sit in a far corner of the room.

'Mary,' he barked, 'pick up the newspaper and read it. When it's your cue, put it down and then say your line.'

Lily nudged me. I remembered I was Mary, and picked up the newspaper.

'Sheila, pick up that book, will you?' Lily did so.

He looked over at Celia, glanced at Billie Prescott and bit his lip. Turning, he motioned to Anne Tait. She came across to him and they had a whispered conversation. Anne left the set, returning a minute later with a half-finished jumper, some wool and knitting needles. These were handed to Celia, who looked at them in astonishment.

'What am I supposed to do with this?' she asked, her clear voice cutting through the noise around us.

'Knit,' said Billie Prescott, with a simper.

Mr Morris seemed abashed. 'I'm told that there's always someone knitting in these places. You'll be the knitter.'

'Can't knit,' said Celia, putting the mess of wool on the floor beside her.

'My dear,' said Billie sweetly, 'Actresses pretend. Can't you pretend, just a teensy bit? For the sake of the film.'

'I thought you wanted a slice of reality.' Celia addressed Mr Morris. 'If I'm filmed fumbling around with these things, all reality flies out the door.'

'I can knit a little,' said Lily helpfully. 'I could knit and Celia – I mean Linda – could read the book.'

From the look on Billie Prescott's face I could guess what she thought of the idea of a Celia in the back of the scene looking down at a book and drawing the viewer's eye to a slim neck and beautifully moulded features. Miss Prescott was very lovely, but Celia was a good ten years younger and, I thought, lovelier.

'I'm perfectly happy to be out of the film altogether,' said Celia, her chin rising toward the ceiling.

'Not a chance,' Cockney Bert whispered to me. 'Apparently the director insists that she's seen on screen, even if she has no lines. I can see why. She's a looker, all right, but awfully stuck up.'

'She doesn't want to be here,' I said. 'Celia's a good sort when you get to know her.'

Mr Morris dragged Anne away for another whispered consultation. The upshot was that Molly/Poppy was put next to Celia with a skein of wool wrapped around her hands. Celia was instructed to wind it into a ball.

Someone called out, 'Rehearsal's up', and we had three practice goes at scene one. By the end, Mr Morris was nodding in approval.

'What happens now?' I whispered to Cockney Bert.

'They'll go for a take. That means they'll really be filming. Before they start, they need to let everyone know that it's about to happen, so they'll shout out something like "picture's up" or "film's up". It lets the actors settle in and gets everyone ready so there'll be no interruptions later on.'

The make-up girl dashed over to pat our noses with powder, then drifted off along with the others who had been standing around us. A whistle blew, startling me.

'Quiet, please,' Mr Morris shouted. 'This will be a take. *Ambulance Girls At War*, scene one.'

All movement and sound on the set ceased. Voices called out words in what was obviously a standard sequence.

'Picture's up,' said Mr Morris.

'Picture's up' was repeated by several voices.

'Roll sound.'

'Rolling.'

'Speeds?'

'Sound speeds.'

'Camera speed?'

'Yes.'

A boy with a clapper board said 'One alpha. Take one. A mark.' He put the clapper board in front of the camera and snapped it shut.

'Set.'

'And, *action*,' said the First Assistant Director.

I read my newspaper industriously as Rose and Henry and Bert debated the war, throwing in a line or two about Henry's victory garden and a snippet of gossip that Rose derided as Careless Talk. The noise of planes increased.

'Cut,' yelled Mr Morris, making me start. 'Mary, you missed your cue.'

Mary? I was Mary. I looked up at him in horror. 'Oh, I'm awfully sorry. I forgot.'

He glared at me. 'Quiet on set. We'll try again.'

The clapper-board boy clapped the board. There was a sound of engines. I stared at my newspaper and listened to Rose and Henry and Bert. The victory garden was mentioned. Careless Talk. The planes increased in volume.

'My word, Jerry's coming over sick and sound tonight,' I squeaked and clapped my hand over my mouth in embarrassment.

After another three goes we broke for lunch. At the side of the soundstage a table had been set up with sandwiches and a tea urn.

'I'm so sorry,' I said to Lily and Celia. 'I don't know why I can't do it. It's absolutely perfect in my head, and then I speak and I get it wrong or it sounds awful.'

'You'll do it next time,' said Lily encouragingly and peered at the plates of sandwiches. 'Oh, God, fish paste and Bovril. Ugh.'

'Not together?' I asked, astonished.

Lily gave a shout of laughter. 'Some are fish paste, some Bovril. A few spam.'

'I'll have the spam,' I said. Celia raised an eyebrow, and I remembered that that was what they called bad actors. Hams. I bit into my sandwich defiantly.

Mr Denbeigh came over to speak to us. 'How are you all, girls? Looking marvellous. Just marvellous. I know it'll be a wonderful film. Help to draw people together. Common purpose, what? Show that everybody has a role to play in this war.'

I began to apologise for my lack of acting ability, but he brushed it aside. 'Difficult if it's all new. You look marvellous and that's the important thing. Lots of oomph. Just the ticket.'

'Thanks,' I said weakly.

'Seen Harker lately?' he asked.

'No. No, I haven't.' Celia looked at me and raised an eyebrow. Mr Denbeigh blundered on.

'So sorry about my *faux pas* that night. My wife tore strips off me when I told her I'd asked after his wife.'

'Oh?'

'I hadn't known of course.'

'Known what?'

Mr Denbeigh was obviously discomforted 'Didn't you know either? Poor Vivian volunteered to be a children's escort on the *City of Benares*. Wasn't one of the survivors.'

I stared at him, horrified. Seven months before, in September, the evacuee ship *City of Benares* had been torpedoed by a German submarine. It was carrying ninety children to Canada as refugees. Less than half those on board survived, and only a handful of the children. After that the authorities stopped sending children overseas.

'Oh, how very sad,' said Celia. 'I met her a few times and she seemed to be a lovely woman.'

Mr Denbeigh wandered off, leaving me in a state of utter confusion. I tried to remember what I'd said to Michael about his wife. Had I been sarcastic? I couldn't remember.

'I thought you barely knew Michael Harker,' said Celia.

Lily piped up. 'Is he nice? That's awful about his wife.'

'I only met him a couple of times,' said Celia. 'Spent more time with his wife than with him. She was very pleasant, and he seemed nice enough.' She gave me a sharp look. 'Apparently Maisie knows him better than she's let on.'

'Not really.' My gaze faltered under her clear stare. 'Actually, he's the one who saved the couple who'd been trapped in the rubble. I helped a little but he was awfully brave, digging into the wreckage with his bare hands, despite coal gas and the risk of being buried at any moment.'

To my relief, Anne came over and collected us. I was so distracted by the news about Michael's wife that I was able to lose my self-consciousness. For the first time I said the line correctly on my first go and said it well.

'Cut!' said Mr Morris. 'It's no good. A microphone slipped into the shot. Get that blasted microphone up and keep it there. We'll have to do it again. Let's make this a one-take, everyone. Silence on set.'

I pushed thoughts of Michael Harker from my mind and concentrated on listening for my cue. Rose and Henry and Bert chatted about victory gardens and Careless Talk. The roar of aircraft became loud. Louder.

'My word, Jerry's coming over thick and fast tonight,' I said, arching my back a little to make the buttons on my shirt strain, just as I'd been instructed, presumably to add 'oomph'.

'Looks like we'll be busy,' said Henry, in a creditable Yorkshire accent.

'My Nance's gone to the shelter wiv the kids. I 'ope they're all right down there,' said Bert, our cheery Cockney chappie, looking less cheery.

'They'll be fine, Bert. Don't worry 'bout them,' said shop girl Avis. 'We're the ones running around dodging bombs and shrapnel.'

Celia wound wool.

'Sometimes I dream I'm back home in Sydney,' said Sheila/Lily, sounding wistful.

'Wish you was back 'ome now?' asked Bert.

Sheila/Lily smiled. 'When I'm having the time of my life in London? Not a chance.'

Diana/Lady Harriet spoke about her parents and their opposition to her driving an ambulance, and how it felt right that she should be mucking in with everyone else.

Molly/Poppy talked of the kind of world she wanted after the war, one where class made no difference and there was a fair share for all.

The telephone rang. We looked at it expectantly, with a hint of trepidation, as instructed. Rose picked up the receiver, listened intently then scribbled on the pad beside it. She hung up, tore off the sheet and looked around the room. Her lovely face showed courage and resolution.

'They've hit the docks again,' she said. 'I'm afraid we're in for a bad night.'

'Better get going, then,' said Henry, his face grim and determined.

We began to rise, our faces showing our willingness to follow Rose into the breach, no matter how dangerous or difficult it was. We were all of England in one small room. We were the nation's finest and we would do our duty, no matter what dangers we faced.

'Oh, God,' muttered Celia in her clear, upper-class voice. 'I've dropped the bloody wool.'

'Cut,' said the First Assistant Director.

CHAPTER TWENTY-FOUR

The twenty-first of April was my twentieth birthday, and somehow word got out two weeks before.

'If it's your birthday,' said Lily, 'then we need to celebrate. There's no two ways about it. Please let Jim and me take you out. We'll make a party of it. What about the Hungaria?'

'The Hungaria? That's a bi—'

'It is, a bit,' admitted Lily, 'but the food's great and the company will be superb.'

I gave a laugh. 'Who's coming?'

'I'm not sure. You, of course, as guest of honour. Me, Jim, Celia, Simon. Is there a special someone in your life? You never talk about—'

'No special someone.'

'Anyone you'd like to invite from the station? Rupy Purvis seems quite taken with you.'

'Um, I think if we invited one we'd have to invite everyone. Celia's different because she's so often my driver and vice versa.'

'What about girls from that club of yours?'

'Could I invite Ellie Kavanagh and her Canadian boyfriend? She lost an eye in the Café de Paris bombing and it would be a special treat.' Ellie had been discharged from hospital a few days before. Her injured eye was still covered by a bandage. She was otherwise well, but I hadn't seen her smile since the night of the bombing. Perhaps a night out would cheer her up.

Lily smiled. 'Of course.' She hesitated, then said quickly, 'I'm just asking, and please feel free to say no, but do you want us to invite a spare male? Jim knows some awfully nice—'

'*No*!' I tempered this with a smile. 'Thanks but no thanks.'

'Fair enough,' said Lily. 'You picked a good day to be born. It's not only Princess Elizabeth's birthday, it's the week after Easter. That means we're through Great Lent and can really let our hair down.'

'Great Lent?'

'Russian Orthodox Lent. It's awfully strict. No meat, poultry, eggs or dairy products for forty-six days. Forty-six days! We're surviving on black tea, vegetable stew and fish when I can get it. But from this Sunday – Easter Sunday – Jim and I can eat and drink what we want.' She smiled. 'Within reason, given the rationing.'

'How's your conversion going?' Lily was undergoing conversion to the Russian Orthodox Church. Her new husband, Jim Vassilikov, was a Russian aristocrat by birth, although he was entirely English by upbringing, except for his religion.

'Slowly. Lots to learn.' She nodded purposefully. 'All set then. Dinner at the Hungaria on Monday the twenty-first of April.'

Celia said, as we drove out of the station later that day, 'Thank goodness your birthday is the twenty-first. Well done.'

I turned into Tottenham Court Road and the ambulance juddered over potholes. 'My mother has to take some of the credit. Why is it a good day?'

'The week of Passover finishes on the nineteenth, so no guilt for Simon in eating and drinking what he wants. He says that he intends to enjoy himself.'

'Glad to hear it,' I said.

Ellie flushed when I asked if she and Raymond wanted to celebrate with me.

'I hear that the Hungaria is very elegant,' she said. 'And underground, just like …' Her voice faded.

'It's very elegant indeed,' I said, although I'd never actually been there. 'It'll be fun. Please, do come. You'll like Lily and Jim, and Celia and Simon.'

She took a breath and let it out slowly, with a weak smile. 'Perhaps I will. Your birthday is well timed, because I'll have my glass eye by then. It'll be my first night out with two eyes.'

I saw tears in the other eye, but pretended not to notice.

'I'm so glad.'

'No more pirate Ellie,' she said, with another half-hearted smile. 'It's been an experience. I went to see an eye painter, who spent a long time making sure to match the colour to my other eye. The eyes he paints are wonderfully realistic.'

'I'm sure you'll look splendid.'

'I just hope to look normal, although I'm worried that I won't be able to continue my dancing career if I can't see clearly on my right side.' She shrugged. 'It doesn't really matter because Raymond wants to marry me.' This time her smile was real, although tremulous. 'I don't need two eyes to be his wife.' The smile faltered. 'Raymond took Cameron's death badly. We need something to cheer him up, so thanks for the invitation, Maisie.'

'You're very welcome.'

The door to the common room was pushed open. Jill Peterson entered and greeted us both warmly.

'When is your film going to be shown, Maisie? I'm longing to see you up there on the big screen.'

I smiled. 'It's only twenty minutes long, and I'm in it for about two of those. Just one line at the start and then glimpses of me among the mayhem being brave. The story is really about Rose and Avis, two plucky ambulance girls who dash into a burning building to rescue an old man. My friends and I are window-dressing. They're still finishing it, but said they'd let us know when it's going to be in the cinemas.'

'In time for your birthday?'

'I doubt it.'

'Shame. It would have made it extra special.'

*

The week before my birthday was extra special, but for all the wrong reasons. It was the week of 'the Wednesday' and 'the Saturday'.

On the nights of Wednesday the sixteenth of April and Saturday the nineteenth of April, German raiders came over in force and inflicted two of the heaviest attacks on London since the war began. By my birthday the lives of more than two thousand Londoners had been lost.

At nine o'clock on the Wednesday, six hundred bombers came over in waves and did not depart until just before dawn. The first wave dropped parachute flares to illuminate the streets. The next wave dropped hundreds of 'bread-baskets', cannisters filled with incendiary bombs. They were designed to split open as they fell so that each of them scattered dozens of magnesium-filled incendiaries that ignited on impact.

Each plane held as many as seven hundred bread-baskets, so thousands of incendiaries fell that night. The fires they started raged so furiously that at the height of the firestorm an orange glow lit the sky over London and that guided new waves of bombers. Some carried high-explosive bombs. Others dropped the dreaded parachute bombs, land mines attached to parachutes that drifted silently down to detonate upon contact, or on a timer. When they exploded they destroyed entire city blocks.

That is what happened at Pancras Square, a large four-storey block of flats near St Pancras Station. It was destroyed when a parachute bomb landed in the courtyard between a surface shelter and the flats.

My shift at Bloomsbury station was sent to Pancras Square to collect the wounded. We worked without ceasing, all night and into the day, ferrying to hospital dozens of seriously injured patients. Many more had been killed; we carried our stretchers past the rows of pitiful sacks that contained their remains.

The Pancras Square incident kept us busy all night, but it was only one incident in a night of horrors. More than a thousand Londoners lost their lives on the Wednesday. Thousands of buildings were hit, homes, offices, businesses. Almost every window in St Paul's Cathedral shattered. The Houses of Parliament, the Admiralty, the Law Courts and the National Gallery all suffered direct hits, and Selfridges on Oxford Street was completely burned out. It was the worst raid of the war so far.

I was off duty on the Saturday night. I spent it in the practice room at the club, huddled with the rest of the girls, trying to sing through the worst of it as more than seven hundred raiders swept up the Thames Estuary to London. Before they returned to their bases in France at dawn, the explosives, incendiaries and mines they dropped left a devastating trail of devastation, injury and death, worse than that of the Wednesday. Thirteen firemen lost their lives that night, the worse single loss the Fire Brigade had ever sustained. And in Hornchurch, an entire family of nine, including seven children under eleven, was wiped out when their shelter sustained a direct hit.

Despite it all, life went on. Milkmen still delivered, even though they had to pick their way through bomb debris. Mail was collected and distributed. People still grumbled about the meat rations, the butter rations, the government, Hitler and the air raids, but no one spoke of giving up. The food we ate might have been boring, but there was enough of it, thanks to the Land Army and the convoys from America. Those convoys were now escorted by US battleships as far as Iceland, because President Roosevelt had extended the Pan-American Security Zone. I wondered how long President Roosevelt would be able to act so obviously contrary to America's supposed state of neutrality in order to help Britain.

Our hopes of an end to the Blitz were raised when the RAF night fighters began to bring down more and more enemy planes. The story, just as Powell had said, was that our pilots had been given extra rations of carrots and this had improved their night sight. I was sceptical. Whatever it was, though, it seemed to be working, and the bombers did not always get through.

After seven months of bombardment, spring was coming to London at last. Green shoots appeared in bomb-site rubble. Primroses and daffodils and crocuses painted the parks with colour. I attended Easter services at St Giles-in-the-Fields and when I sang with the rest of the congregation:

> *Alleluia, alleluia, alleluia!*
> *The strife is o'er the battle done,*
> *The victory of life is won,*
> *The song of triumph has begun,*
> *Alleluia!*

I prayed my hardest that it would soon be true of this war.

And then it was my birthday.

CHAPTER TWENTY-FIVE

The Hungaria was crowded with men and women in uniform and evening dress. We followed the waiter to our table and as we settled into our seats I glanced around. The restaurant was a bustle of waiters serving tables and couples wheeling around on the dance floor. Flowery murals on the wall added a splash of colour. A gypsy orchestra was playing as we entered and the restaurant was very merry and bright.

Celia looked svelte in emerald green, and Lily was demure in a blue dress. Ellie wore a pretty frock of apricot silk. I wore a dress I'd borrowed from Bobbie, red chiffon with sequinned shoulder straps. On her it was floor length, on me, mid-calf, but it displayed my assets to full advantage. I thought I looked good, and was a little sorry that I hadn't agreed to let Lily ask one of Jim's friends to come along.

According to the sign outside, the Hungaria restaurant in Lower Regent Street, Piccadilly, was 'bomb-proof, splinter-proof, blast-proof, gas-proof and boredom-proof'. After the raids of the past week, this was more important than its reputation for good food. Yet I couldn't help but remember that the Café de Paris had enjoyed the same reputation for safety.

'Care to dance, birthday girl?' asked Jim Vassilikov, Lily's tall blond husband.

I smiled, took his hand and we entered the fray. I'd met Jim a few times before and I liked him. He was in RAF Intelligence and I sometimes wondered if I should have told him about the microfilm. It was too late now; I'd made my decision and I refused to regret it. I hadn't seen Michael Harker since the morning in March when I'd handed over the microfilm, but I'd thought about him far too much. A week after he had rescued the couple a package had arrived for me. It contained two pairs of silk stockings, but no note. I wondered how he had managed to find them, and could only assume that Americans had access to supplies that we British didn't.

'It's nice to look up to a dance partner,' I said, smiling. Jim laughed.

'Lily's been told by more than one woman that she acted most unfairly by marrying me, because at five foot one she had her pick of men, whereas tall girls need men my height.'

He whirled me around expertly and I settled in for an enjoyable waltz. We'd taken only a few steps, however, when a man tapped him on the shoulder and said, in an American-accented voice, 'May I cut in? Your pretty wife looks awful lonesome back there.'

Before I knew what had happened, Jim had surrendered me to Michael Harker and returned to Lily. Michael took hold of my hand, pulled me towards him, and into the dance.

'Neatly done,' I said, heart thumping embarrassingly fast. 'What are you doing here?'

He smiled. 'Celia Ashwin rang me at the embassy and suggested I might enjoy a night out. Said she'd be here with her new man celebrating a friend's birthday, and I'd know some of the party, including Jim and the birthday girl.'

'I'm the birthday girl,' I said.

'Sure you are, kid.'

'Not kid, I'm no longer a teenager.' I looked up at him through my lashes.

He smiled. 'Yep. You're almost grown up.'

'Almost?'

'Maisie, I like you more than any other girl I know, but I don't date minors. You're too young for me, honey.' He whirled me around and kept my hand in a tight grip as I tried to pull away from him. 'I'd be sad if we can't be friends, though. And I'd sure like to help you celebrate your birthday. Won't you let me do that?'

He swung me around until I was dizzy. I stared at his chin and surrendered to the music. Storming off because a man wasn't interested in you would be the height of stupidity. He didn't want me like that. I could wear the prettiest frock I owned, I could show my assets to their greatest advantage and he still wouldn't want me like that. He wanted to be friends.

I raised my eyes to his. He was looking at me with a worried expression, and the crease had appeared between his eyebrows.

'Can't we be friends, Maisie?'

He had lost his wife tragically only seven months before. *Try not to be so ridiculously self-centred, Maisie.*

I managed a real smile. 'Of course we can. We are already.'

His answering smile was quite devastatingly heart-breaking. I examined his chin again. He pulled me closer and we danced together like a dream.

'Thank you for the stockings,' I said.

'How are your knees?'

'All better. No scars.'

'That's good to hear, especially now you're a movie star,' he said teasingly. 'When is the masterpiece to be shown?'

'I'm not sure. In June, I think.'

'Can't wait.'

When the music stopped he led me back to the table. The first course was served. It was delicious, as was the wine. Between the courses I was given presents, which I hadn't expected. French perfume from Lily and Jim. A mysterious package from Celia and Simon, which she told me to open later, when I was alone. Scented soap from Ellie and Cameron. From Michael a small packet. He also said it was to be opened later.

When Michael and I were having our second dance I mentioned my interrogation by Casey and Lowell.

'Yeah, I heard about that,' he said. 'Sounds like you held your own with them. Thanks for not mentioning my name. It would have been difficult for me if you had.'

'I was tempted to throw you to the wolves. I think they suspect *me* of looting his body.'

He frowned. 'I doubt that Casey or Lowell will bother you again. If they do, let me know.'

'Um, I was really sorry to hear about your wife.'

His grip on my hand tightened, but he was quiet for a beat or two. 'Thanks,' he said. 'I try not to think about it. She loved life and it was a ... bad way to go.'

I felt like a fool to have brought up such a painful subject while we were dancing. For a while we were silent, moving to the beat of the music, his body guiding mine in movements so familiar I had no need to think. He was a good dancer, lightly leading me through the usual hazards of bunched groups and clumsy dancers, into the gaps that appeared without warning and gave us clear air.

After a while he smiled. 'You sure are provocative, kid. Wearing that dress in public. You're a menace.'

I laughed and glanced down. My assets were most definitely on show.

'It's borrowed,' I said, 'and bit small for me, really. But it's almost impossible to find nice dresses nowadays unless you're a good seamstress or you know one, or you've hoarded pre-war outfits.'

'I was kidding. It's a lovely dress. You look gorgeous. I'll have to introduce you to some nice American boys at the embassy who are more your own age.'

I shrugged. 'It's a mug's game to fall in love in wartime.'

'Sure it is, kid. But sometimes it just happens.'

He was absolutely right. Sometimes it just happened.

When I returned to the club later that evening I opened my two mysterious presents. Celia's gift was an exquisite set of silk lingerie. She'd put a note in with it saying that it had been part of her trousseau and had never been worn. I held the filmy stuff against my body and sighed. Perhaps I'd never wear it either.

Michael's present was smaller, a neat little box. Inside was a gold locket, oval, on a gold chain. It was engraved with my initials, M.H., surrounded by pretty flowers. They were his initials, too, of course. I pushed the catch and it opened to reveal space for a photograph, but it was empty.

It was a romantic gift, but his card said simply, 'I thought it was a fair swap. Thanks again, and happy birthday, chorus girl.'

CHAPTER TWENTY-SIX

A few days after my birthday I returned to the club after my shift to find that the previous day a note had arrived from Dan Lowell of the American Embassy. He asked me to do him the honour of lunching with him on any day that I was free. His handwriting was small and neat, not like Michael's more open scrawl. I stared at his note for a while, wondering what to do. Michael had told me to let him know if either Casey or Lowell contacted me, but I was trying awfully hard to forget about Michael Harker.

Lowell's note made it seem that he was flatteringly anxious for my company. It wasn't beyond the bounds of reason that he might have taken a fancy to me when we met, but I had a feeling that he still thought I knew something about the contents of Egan's watch fob, or he wanted information about Michael. The timing of his invitation was fishy, only a few days after I'd seen Michael.

I decided to accept the invitation and wrote that I would be free on Saturday, the third of May. His reply expressed delight and said that he would pick me up outside the club at one o'clock.

As Saturday drew closer I began to worry that I hadn't told Michael about it. Several times I went down three flights of stairs to the club's telephone, only to stare at it for a few minutes and return to my room. The thought of hearing his voice was too exciting. I wanted to see him far too much, and it worried me.

The Thursday before I was due to meet Lowell I decided to tell Michael. Only by then I was at the station and the only phone was in Moray's office. When I requested permission to use the telephone for a personal call Moray was not happy.

'You know it's against policy,' he said.

'I've never asked before. Please, it is important.'

He grudgingly agreed, saying, 'No more than three minutes.'

But when I rang the American Embassy, Michael Harker was away.

'No, I don't know when he's likely to return,' said the receptionist in a flat, bored voice. 'Do you wish to leave a message?'

Casey and Lowell both worked at the embassy. Would they see any message I left? *Think, Maisie.*

'No. Yes. Please tell him that, um, that Miss Tiller called. Tell him that I'm meeting our old friend, um, Miss Hyam, on Saturday, so I have to cancel our lunch appointment.'

The bored receptionist repeated the message and hung up.

I put down the receiver and smiled to myself. The message informed Michael of the facts; all he had to do was use his brain.

He was waiting for me in Manette Street, early on Friday morning as I walked home after my shift. The spring sunshine gave him no concealing gloom, and perhaps that's why I saw him immediately, lurking in a doorway.

'Good morning, Michael,' I called.

He stepped out, looking abashed.

'And to think I've been trained to be inconspicuous,' he said, walking over to me. 'What gave me away?'

I smiled and didn't answer.

'I got your message,' he said. 'Very cryptic, it was.'

'You worked it out, though?'

'I think so. You're meeting Lowell for lunch tomorrow. When did he invite you?'

'Last week.'

He frowned. 'I thought we'd agreed that you'd tell me if Casey or Lowell contacted you.'

'And I did tell you.'

'What's it about? Did he say?'

'He sent me a note. I've got it here.' I pulled it out of my pocket and handed it to him. Michael pulled it out of the envelope and read aloud:

My dear Miss Halliday,

I hope you won't take this amiss, but I have been feeling bad about the rough time we gave you the other day and I'd really like to try to make it up to you.

Would you do me the honour of lunching with me one day, when you are next free? I'd sure like to get to know you better.

Yours truly, Dan Lowell

Michael handed it back to me. 'Why'd you say yes?'

'Because it's poppycock. It wasn't the other day that they questioned me, it was more than six weeks ago. Why'd he wait so long if he wanted to ask me out? It makes no sense, so I wanted to know more. Do they still think I'm the person who stole poor Mr Egan's things?'

He frowned 'I'm pretty sure they don't.'

'Do you think they know you came to my birthday party?'

'Maybe. Lowell and Casey aren't my biggest fans. But why would that make Lowell ask you out?' He gave a short laugh. 'Unless he wants to cut me out of the picture. It might amuse him to steal my girl.'

'I'm not your girl.'

'He might think otherwise. Be sure to let him know how things stand between us.'

'That you think I'm an annoying child and I think you're sneaky, mysterious and often intensely irritating?'

He gave me his heart-stopping smile. 'I don't think you're annoying.'

I rolled my eyes. 'And you wonder why I find you irritating.'

'Nope. I've never wondered about that.' He flicked my cheek with a long finger. 'Want to meet me for dinner Saturday night, to tell me about your lunch with Lowell?'

'All right.'

His face became shadowed. 'Try not to give too much away, kid.'

'I'm not a kid.'

'Sure.'

We agreed that he'd come to the club to collect me and we'd go to the little French place in Dean Street, where he had taken me to before.

Dan Lowell called for me on Saturday morning in a big black saloon that looked expensive and powerful and emitted a low, thrumming sound. I got in and it swept me along Soho's narrow streets, dealing easily with potholes and bomb debris. Driving in London's bomb blasted thoroughfares took some skill, as I well knew, so I didn't distract him by talking. Instead I enjoyed the soft leather seat and the pervasive scent of luxury.

I stole a look at Lowell. He looked trustworthy, in a clean, American sort of way. Like Michael his teeth were perfect, his hands well kept and his blond hair neat. Undeniably an attractive man. I tried to find something to dislike and settled on his tie, which was garish, a vivid red-and-blue tartan.

Perhaps he felt me looking, because he flicked me a glance and smiled. I smiled back, feeling relief that his smile, although very attractive, did not make my heart thump painfully. I looked away, out of the car, and made some random remark about the bomb damage.

He drove well, taking the maze of closed roads and diversions in his stride, until he reached the outskirts of London. We crested a hill and a landscape of patched green velvet stretched out in front of us, little fields bisected by hedges with scattered clumps of trees. Far into the distance I caught sight of a larger wood, and beyond that a ring of low hills.

'Where are you taking me?' I asked.

'I thought you'd appreciate a chance to escape London. Forget about the war for a while.'

'So where are we going?'

'A pretty little pub I know in Surrey.'

I settled back into the soft leather. 'Sounds divine.'

It was one of those chocolate box cover English country pubs that Americans love so much. He parked outside and ushered me in. I asked for a sherry, and he had a beer. While we waited for our lunch we sat in a wooden snug that had been polished by the rears of unnumbered patrons through the centuries.

I sipped my sherry and wondered when Lowell would tell me why he had brought me all the way out there. Instead, he asked me about myself and I told him the official version. Widowed mother, trained in dance at Italia Conti Academy in London, left school to begin a dancing career. Became a Tiller Girl and danced in London, then in Paris at the Folies Bergère. Returned to England when war broke out and joined the Auxiliary Ambulance Service.

'Tiller Girl,' he said musingly. 'They're the high-steppers, not the topless ones?'

I gave him a look. 'No, we are not the topless ones. Fully, if sometimes scantily, clothed at all times.'

He smiled. 'I'd sure give anything to see you dance.'

'I won't be dancing again until we win the war.'

'You sound pretty sure of victory.'

'I am.'

He took a long swallow of beer, and I waited.

'Thanks for coming out with me,' he said, with a winning smile. 'As soon as I saw you that day I thought, that's a fine young woman and I'd like to know her better.'

I smiled, but inside I was confused. Surely he wasn't courting me?

He looked up as the barmaid approached to tell us that lunch would be served in the little parlour. We followed her in to a small, panelled room set up with five tables. She showed us to a table by a casement window of diamond-paned leaded glass that allowed a fractured view of the empty beer garden outside.

As we settled in to a lunch of leek and potato soup ('From the Victory Garden'), followed by chicken casserole ('An old boiler, just killed this morning') and apple pie with real cream ('From our Daisy; she's marvellous for milk'), we talked about the weather, the delights of the countryside and – a perennial favourite – what would go under the ration next.

By the time the coffee was served the room had emptied of diners and we were alone. I looked at Lowell over the rim of my cup. He leaned back, pulled out a cigarette case of etched steel, opened it and offered it to me. I shook my head.

'Mind if I do?' he asked.

'Of course not.'

Slowly, deliberately, he lit the cigarette, took a deep breath and blew a stream of smoke away from me.

'Maisie, I wanted to get you alone to warn you off Mike Harker.'

'I don't understand.' My heart began to thump.

'We know that you've been seeing him and—'

'You've been spying on me?'

'Not at all. We've been keeping an eye on Harker. Ever since his wife died he's become a lone wolf. Blames the Germans for it all, I guess.'

'Well they did torpedo the ship his wife was on,' I said drily. 'A ship that was carrying a cargo of children.'

'Yes, it was a terrible thing,' he said, attempting a placating tone, 'but it was always on the cards. I liked Vivian Harker a lot, but she knew the risks when she got on board that boat.'

I stared at him. 'It was a war crime.'

He slowly shook his head. 'How could that U-boat commander have known it was a boatload of children? It was a British ship on the open sea, and a fair target.'

I bit back any reply. He had a point, but it was such a shocking tragedy that emotion trumped such reasoning. I supposed that Michael felt the same way I did.

'Your country is at war with Germany,' Lowell went on. 'Mine isn't. America has to tread very carefully as far as Germany is concerned. At present we're a neutral country, and most Americans want it to stay that way.'

'What has Mr Harker to do with all this?'

'He's not treading carefully. He's blundering around, making my job more difficult. His mistakes could have an impact on America's involvement in this war, and not in a good way for Britain.'

'I don't understand.'

'We know that Harker was with you at the Café de Paris that night. We suspect that Harker murdered Egan to steal what he was carrying.'

I couldn't help a gasp at that and an unthinking, 'No. He told me—'

'He told you he didn't touch Egan? We think that Harker either smothered him on purpose or stopped his mouth to keep him quiet while he searched him. Either way, we think Harker caused Egan's death.'

'Mr Egan was already dying,' I said, through stiff lips. 'Michael didn't touch him until after he was already dead.'

My mind was racing, jumping to conclusions, then discounting them. Had Michael lied to me? I had seen him bending over Egan. Had his hand been over the man's mouth? He'd told me that Egan was already dead, but how did I know that was true? Michael had been willing to loot his body, after all. What did I really know about Michael Harker other than that he was unscrupulous, willing to trick me to get the locket. He had charmed me, called me 'kid', lulled me into thinking he was harmless. Making me fall for his ...

I remembered his feverish attempt to save the people trapped in the bombed house. Michael was a good man. He had to be.

I couldn't believe that he'd murder a colleague. I couldn't have misjudged him so badly. I couldn't feel so much for a man who was a villain.

Lowell was still talking. 'We know that you and Harker are more than friends, Maisie. I saw you together at the Hungaria.'

I gave him a look. 'That's simply not true. Mr Harker did come to my birthday party, but I didn't invite him, Celia Ashwin did. This is a silly conversation.'

He leaned across the table and looked straight into my eyes. 'Do you want to know what we think? We think that Harker spun you some yarn and you believed him.'

'Who is "we"? You keep saying "we".'

'Me and John Casey. We're responsible for security at the embassy. We have real doubts about Michael Harker's bona fides. As I said, he's become a lone wolf, doesn't trust anyone any more. And that makes him dangerous. You're very young, Maisie. Michael Harker is highly trained and knows how to deal with women. I've seen them fall for his tricks on many occasions. He's charming. You're not the first girl to be taken in by him.'

I swallowed, looked down, felt ill. Then I became indignant.

'I'm not sure I even believe you. Celia Ashwin told me that you were one of her husband's good friends before the war. One of the fascists who hung around him. Why should I believe a fascist?'

Lowell's face closed up as completely as if a shutter had fallen across it. 'I was instructed to befriend Ashwin,' he said. 'The only side I'm on is America's. I support whatever policy my government supports. At present, Roosevelt is helping you all he can, within the bounds of our Neutrality Acts. And that means I am, too.'

'And you don't think that's the case with Michael Harker?'

'Harker is carrying out a personal vendetta, and it'll blow up in all our faces if he's not stopped. If he carries on it could affect

British–American relations, which would be a disaster for this country.'

'A vendetta?'

'He knew that Egan was a fifth columnist. So did we. We'd been watching Egan for a while.'

'You and Casey?'

He nodded.

'Mr Egan was an American fifth columnist? But America's neutral.'

'We do have them. Mainly people who are sympathetic to Russia, communists who want to destroy America. Lately, though, the Germans have been getting in on the act. White Russians, too.'

My mind was spinning. How had we got from Michael at my birthday party to American fifth columnists? Lily's husband, Jim, was a White Russian. What Lowell was telling me sounded like a plot from one of the *Saint* novels.

'I don't understand,' I said. That was an understatement.

'Harker wanted to confront Egan. We think he did, and he killed him.'

I realised that I was gripping my hands together tightly, and that my palms were moist. I wiped them surreptitiously on my skirt.

Lowell went on. 'The way Harker's going, he'll ruin his career and he could do some real damage to your war effort into the bargain.'

'But what do you want from me?'

'Fill in some details about what happened in the Café de Paris that night. When Harker searched Egan's body, did he take everything? We know Egan gave you the fob, although we can't work out why, but Egan's wallet, document folder, diary and watch are all missing. We know Harker took the wallet and watch, but we need to know if he took the rest as well.' He looked straight into my eyes. 'Maisie, it's in Harker's interests for us to know all of it. He's looking at suspension at the very least. Do this for him.'

He seemed to know most of it already, and I thought there would be no harm in letting him know the whole.

'Michael Harker did not kill Mr Egan,' I said. 'I'm absolutely sure of that. And I told the absolute truth when I said that I didn't know that Mr Egan had given me the fob before he died. Mr Harker only took his wallet and a watch. I never saw any document folder or diary.'

In my defence, I was only twenty and I'd never been involved in anything like that before.

Everyone makes mistakes at twenty.

CHAPTER TWENTY-SEVEN

Lowell dropped me outside the club at four o'clock that afternoon. I had a great deal to think about and I was due to meet Michael for dinner that evening. As I climbed the stairs to my room I considered what Lowell had told me. He thought that Michael was behaving like a hothead, trying to avenge the death of his wife. Michael had never struck me as a hothead. Even when he began his rescue of the trapped couple, he thought it through and worked out the best way to get to them. He'd been irritated at me when I refused to hand over the watch fob and wouldn't leave the dangerous tunnel, but I'd not yet seen him really lose his temper.

On the other hand, Celia thought that Dan Lowell had been a close friend of Cedric Ashwin. Her husband had definitely been a fascist sympathiser who had admired Hitler. Had Lowell spent time with Ashwin's group only because he had been instructed to do so, or had it been his own inclination?

I wished I had someone to talk it over with. Someone who knew both men. *Celia*. She lived in Gray's Inn Road, up near Clerkenwell. I glanced at my watch. Ten past four. Michael was due to pick me up at eight. I had time.

So I ran downstairs. Celia obviously wasn't on the phone because her number was in the book as her flats, St Andrew's Court. I put a coin into the slot and dialled. The Irish doorman answered, said he would go upstairs to fetch her. A few minutes later and she was on the line.

'Hello? Is that you, Maisie? Whatever is wrong?'

Now I had no idea what to say to her. 'Um, I was wondering if you were free to have a word with me. Not on the phone, in your flat.'

'Simon's here. Is that a problem?'

'No-o, I don't think so. It's important.'

'Come over then.'

I took the Tube and was there in half an hour.

I'd not spent a lot of time with Dr Simon Levy before, although I had known his brother, David, quite well. Simon wasn't as handsome as David had been, but he had a pleasant, likeable face and an easy manner. Celia asked me to sit down. I sat in her big, comfortable armchair and wondered what I should say.

'Um, you must be wondering why I was so secretive on the phone just now. I'm afraid I'll have to remain secretive, but you're the only person I know who knows both Michael Harker and Dan Lowell.'

'I know neither of them well,' said Celia. 'What are you after?'

I sighed. 'They both work for US Intelligence. Michael for the War Office and Dan Lowell for the Department of State. I'm not sure what that difference means.'

Simon answered. 'The State Department advises the president and represents the US in international affairs and foreign policy issues. It also runs the embassy.'

'So Lowell may well be responsible for security matters to do with the embassy. He said he was, together with John Casey.'

Simon nodded. 'I'd say it's likely.'

'What about the War Office?'

'If Michael Harker is in the War Office then it's odds on that he's in a position similar to an agent in our Secret Intelligence Service.'

'What do they do?'

Simon shrugged and gave me a smile. 'It's top secret, obviously. I think it's generally accepted that they gather intelligence about foreign powers.'

'Spies?'

'Spies,' he agreed.

'So who should I should believe?' I wailed. 'Lowell spun me some yarn about Michael being a wild card, who's dangerous. Michael says he doesn't trust Lowell and he is looking after Britain's interests.' I looked at Simon. 'I – I can't tell you any more.'

Celia handed me a brandy and I took a gulp. It burned like fire all the way down, but felt wonderful.

She was drinking sherry, and took a sip. 'I didn't know him well, but I liked Michael Harker,' she said, and shrugged. 'I was never too fond of Dan Lowell, and I detested John Casey.'

I pressed on. 'Lowell told me that he'd been instructed to get close to your – to Cedric Ashwin – and he didn't believe any of what he was saying to him.'

Celia shrugged. 'He gave a good impression of believing every word that came out of Cedric's mouth. And I'm sure he told Cedric that he was part-German.'

'Lowell isn't a German name.'

Simon shrugged. 'Names can be changed. Lots of Germans changed their names in the first war. Lots of British Jews are changing their names in this one, in case of German invasion.'

'But not you?'

His expression firmed. 'I'll live and die as Simon Levy,' he said.

'Lowell might have been ordered to tell Cedric that,' I argued. 'To help him to infiltrate the British fascists.'

'Maybe,' said Celia. 'But why would the Americans want to infiltrate the British fascists?' She took another sip of sherry and looked up at the ceiling. 'Dan Lowell was always pleasant enough to me, but …' She gave a delicate shrug. 'As I said before, he seemed to be a committed American isolationist and an admirer of Hitler.'

'But you liked Michael Harker.'

'Yes. Again, pure instinct and probably completely unreliable, because I scarcely know the man. I met him a few times at embassy parties. He never came to our house, although Vivian came once on her own to a party we held.' She took another sip. 'Poor Vivian. What a horrible end.'

'Lowell said that Michael was on a vendetta, trying to get revenge for Vivian's death on the *City of Benares*.'

Celia considered this. 'Well, it's possible, I suppose. But, honestly, they never seemed like lovebirds to me. You can usually tell when people are happy together.' She glanced at Simon, and they shared a smile. 'Vivian Harker was rather disparaging about her husband on at least one occasion. I thought it poor form, and wandered off. Perhaps all the passion was on his side. It happens. Or maybe he feels guilty for not being the husband she wanted and he's trying to make it up to her somehow, now she's gone.'

Simon dropped me back at the club in his tiny Hillman, which was a far cry from the luxurious beast driven by Dan Lowell. I rushed upstairs to bathe and prepare for the dinner. I chose a pretty pale green jersey dress from Paris before the war. It was a day dress, but fine for the Soho restaurant. Nowadays everyone seemed to wear day dresses when they went out, sometimes even slacks, in case they were trapped all night in a shelter.

I checked myself in the dressing table mirror. It was rather a clingy dress and quite low cut. I wondered if Michael would like it.

I'd wasted my efforts. When I joined him on the doorstep, he scarcely glanced at me. I had wondered what it would be like to see Michael Harker angry, and it seemed very clear that I was about to find out.

CHAPTER TWENTY-EIGHT

Michael's face was all stone and jagged edges. He took my arm and practically dragged me along the street until we came to the restaurant doorway. A knock and we were through the blackout curtain and inside. It was again full of Frenchmen, who again whistled and called out to me. Michael ignored them, too.

Our table was in a corner, and we had relative privacy.

'Why did you do it, Maisie?' were his first words.

I stared at him, wide-eyed. 'Do what?'

'Turn me in to Lowell and Casey. They've strung me up good and proper. I've spent the last couple hours trying to defend myself.'

'What?' I stared at him, aghast.

'Now I'm under suspension – I'll be sent away in disgrace.' All the anger drained away from his face, and it softened to blank misery in his eyes. 'I hate to leave Britain when things are still so bad. And I sure don't trust Lowell or Casey to do anything to help this country.'

'What? What do you mean? What did I do?'

He laughed, somewhat bitterly. 'If you don't know then I guess he played you, honey.' He looked up, into my eyes. 'What'd he tell you? That I killed Harry Egan?'

'Yes, but I didn't believe him.'

'You believed something. You told him what he wanted – that I was at the Café de Paris that night, and that I searched Harry's body, took his wallet and watch. That was all he needed to know.'

'He already knew it. I just ...'

My voice trailed away as I realised Michael was right. I'd been played for a fool. Lowell hadn't known for sure that Michael was there that night. He'd said it and I'd confirmed it.

'I'm so sorry. He said—'

Michael pulled out a packet of cigarettes, shook one out and lit it. He sucked in the smoke as if it was a lifesaver. 'He said he just wanted you to confirm a few details. Is that what he said?'

'Yes. But it was more than that. He—'

'What?'

'He also said you were on a vendetta. That you were a – a lone wolf. You blamed the Germans for your wife's death and were blundering around and making mistakes that could hurt America and Britain. He said that they knew about Egan. He said that you went there to confront Egan and kill him, and that your actions could ...'

Michael was shaking his head, and a slight, bitter smile hovered around his lips. I stared at him. 'I'm so sorry. I should never have believed him.'

'He's good at what he does.' Michael breathed a laugh. 'So he said I was on a vendetta because of poor Vivi's death.' He shook his head. 'Her death was a tragedy, but this is war. The German U-boat commander didn't know it was a ship full of kids. It was bound to happen one day, the way they kept sending children overseas. I told Vivian not to go, but she wouldn't listen. She wanted to get away from England and she wanted to get away from me.'

'What do you mean?'

'She was leaving me, Maisie. The marriage had been over for a while. When the bombing began Vivian decided that there was no point in staying here and pretending any more. She was going to get a divorce in the States.'

'Will you lose your job?' I asked, trying to gather my thoughts together.

'Nah. Lowell is trying to say I killed poor Harry, but he can't prove anything, because I didn't. The lone wolf story is one he's spinning at the embassy, too. It's obvious now that Egan was a fifth columnist, and everyone's ducking for cover. If Lowell or Casey convinces the Ambassador that I'm too hot to handle, they'll send me somewhere else.' He sighed. 'It'd sure be a shame. I've gotten fond of old Blighty and I was willing to go out on a limb to protect it.'

'Like turning up at the Café de Paris that evening?'

'Yes.'

I didn't know what to say. I'd made a stupid mistake. Michael might be sent away, probably somewhere dangerous. Perhaps he'd be killed. It was all my fault.

'Michael, I—'

'Forget it, kid.' He stubbed out his cigarette. 'Let's eat, drink some wine and forget it. It was worse thinking that you'd been willing to betray me.'

'It's better to know that I'm a gullible fool?'

'You're certainly no fool.'

'But I'm gullible,' I said bitterly.

He smiled. 'You're young and you trust people.'

'I trust you, Michael.' My voice broke.

He held my gaze for a while, then breathed a laugh. 'It hurt to think that you didn't.'

I blurted out, 'Is there anything—'

'Nothing, but thanks.' He looked down, readjusted the cutlery with a long finger. 'In my job there are always ups and downs. I'll miss England.' Michael looked up and smiled at me. 'And I'll miss you, chorus girl.'

At his smile I felt again that sharp pain somewhere deep inside me. I looked down at the table, and found that I was clutching my napkin in a tight, twisted grip.

He sighed. 'I'm sorry I was so angry. I should have realised that Lowell had gotten around you. I forget sometimes what a baby you are.'

At that I looked up, indignant. 'I'm a twenty-year-old woman, thank you very much.'

'You're a baby when it comes to men like Lowell.' His expression sharpened. 'Did he make a pass at you?'

'No. He flattered me, but no pass.'

'Shame.'

'What!'

'Then I'd have an excuse to slug him.'

'I can look after myself, I'll have you know, Mr Michael Harker. I'm not your property to be defended.'

He smiled. 'Sure, kid.' His gaze shifted downwards to my chest. 'So you like the locket I bought you.'

'I love it,' I said, touching it with my fingers. The frock was low cut, and when Michael dragged his gaze back up to my face I saw with some satisfaction that his cheeks were tinged with red. He seemed to collect himself and called the waiter over to order the meal.

'Do you really come from a family of eleven?' I said, teasingly, once the waiter had left. 'That's what you told the girls at the club.'

He laughed. 'No. And Mom's in blooming health, in case you were worried. I'm one of six kids. Four boys, two girls. I'm the youngest, the spoiled baby. Which is why I got to go to college while the others had to work as soon as they turned fourteen. I'm the first and only member of the family with a college education.'

'They didn't mind?'

'They insisted. The whole family kicked in to make sure I stayed at school and then found enough between them to buy what I needed to start college. The scholarship paid for most, but not all and I worked my way through.'

'And went down the mine in the holidays?' He looked surprised, so I said, 'You told me that when you were digging through the bomb-site rubble.'

Michael smiled. 'Yeah. When I was fourteen I got a bee in my bonnet about not contributing to the family. You know how boys are at that age. I wanted to be independent. Then Dad arranged it

228

so I could work in the mines over the holidays. Told me I could see how I liked it.'

'And you hated it.'

'It's a rotten job. Smelly, dirty, tough work. I liked the men I worked with, but not the job. And it's a trap. You end up bound to the mine-owner for life because you never seem to make enough money to get out. I worked there every holiday until I graduated. It was a great incentive to do well at college.'

'That's how I felt about factory work,' I said. 'I was determined to make a career of dancing. My mother had been a dancer before I was born, so I suppose it's in the blood.' I sighed. 'Having me put paid to her career. She couldn't go away dancing with a baby, so she moved back with her parents and became a steel factory worker.' I paused, then said, 'Mam was my grandparents' only living child – of five children, the only one living – but they were shamed by my birth and never really forgave her for it.'

'Your grandparents didn't ever thaw towards you?'

I toyed with my napkin. 'Not really. Granddad could be kind sometimes, when Nannan wasn't looking.' I smiled at the table. 'He was a lay preacher and used to practise his sermons on me. I loved it when he did, although what he said was often terrifying.' I looked up at Michael. 'Hellfire and brimstone, that sort of nonsense.'

'And your grandmother?'

'She was never ... kind.'

'You told me she used to hit you.'

'Did I? Only when she could catch me.' I gave him a cheeky smile that quickly faded. 'When I was a little girl, I'd be left with Nannan all day when Mam and Granddad were at the steelworks.' I toyed with my cutlery. 'She disliked me when she was sane, and hated me when she wasn't. I learned very young to get out of the house when her eyes turned darker. We had lovely neighbours, who understood and would take me in until she calmed down. It was a close-knit community.' I gave him another smile. 'At heart, I'm still more a Yorkshire lass than a Londoner.'

'You and your mom came to London. How did your grandparents take your leaving?'

'Granddad was hateful. He was really mean to Mam, ranting and raving and saying we'd both go straight to Hell. It was horrible. I'll never forgive him for it.'

His red, angry face had terrified me. And so had his declaration that we were destined for Hell, because I knew how he felt about the place from his sermons. It still upset me to think about the day we left Sheffield.

'Honey, you were only twelve. You'd have seen things in a childish way. Do you think he might simply have been hurt that you were both leaving? His only daughter and grandchild were going away and leaving him alone with a wife who was …' He shrugged.

'I suppose you may be right,' I said, huffily. Michael had no idea how terrifying it had been to see Granddad like that.

'And you've never been back to see them.'

'Mam visited them once, when I was on tour. Then she – she died. I was so angry when they didn't come to London for her funeral that I haven't wanted to see them.'

Michael seemed to be searching for the right words. 'It was a long time ago. Don't you think you should reach out to them, now you're back in England? You're all they have.'

'I send them money,' I said, defensively. 'Even when I can scarcely afford it.'

'When your mom was in trouble – pregnant and unmarried – they took her in. They looked after you both. Some parents wouldn't have.'

I stared at him. How could I explain it to this man, with his loving, happy family who had all made sacrifices so that he could stay on at school, go to university? He had no idea how awful my childhood had been with Nannan's rages, and the grinding, relentless poverty. And then, when I had a chance to escape, Granddad had said such spiteful things to Mam. She had cried all the way to London. I could never forgive him for doing that to her.

'But your ma forgave them, kept in touch with them?' he said.

'She wrote every week from London. When she – she died, I telegraphed Granddad to tell him, but I had no reply. I wrote after the funeral, and I got a short letter back from Granddad saying he hadn't been able to come to London.'

I glared at Michael. 'Then he asked if I had a job, because Mam had been sending them money each week, and they needed it. So I wrote that I'd send them what I could. And I have done, every week except when I wasn't in work.'

'You should at least write to them.'

'Why should I?' My tone was angry. It hurt that he should take their side. 'I've never told them my address because I don't want to have anything to do with them.'

'You're all they have, and they're all you have.'

'They don't love me, Michael,' I said angrily. 'They never did. I was an embarrassment to them, and they thought I'd ruined my mother's life. You know nothing about it, so keep out of it.'

'Okay, I'll keep out of it,' he said. 'It's your life, kid, but it cuts me up to think that you're all alone in the world.'

Our meal arrived then, and I busied myself with eating. Michael was just trying to be nice, to look after me. As usual, he was treating me like a younger sister. The trouble was, I didn't want him to think of me like that.

'When are they likely to send you away?' I asked a short while later, although the thought of him leaving caused a real pain, deep in my chest.

He shrugged. 'Next week, maybe the week after.'

We'd got to the coffee before I remembered. I reached out and grabbed his arm. 'Michael, Celia says that Dan Lowell was often at her house before the war, being pally with her husband. Cedric Ashwin, the fascist leader.'

'Lowell might have been ordered to keep an eye on Ashwin.'

'That's what he told me when I asked him about it. Only, Celia is fairly sure that Lowell told Ashwin that he was part-German.'

Michael frowned at the table. 'There are lots of Germans in America, Maisie. Even if he is, it means nothing.' He looked up at me. 'I've never liked him, though.'

Neither had Celia. If she and Michael both had the same reaction to him, it was good enough for me. And he had tricked me to get Michael away from England.

Michael sipped his coffee and said nothing for a while.

'You need to flush him out,' I said. 'How can I help? What should I do?'

'Nothing. I'm trained for this sort of thing and you're not.'

I gazed over his shoulder, hoping that I wasn't giving myself away. 'Is it dangerous, what you're trained for?'

'Sometimes. But so is what you do.' His voice changed, became harsher. 'I hate that you're out there in the raids. I hate that you might be injured, or killed, like those firemen in April.'

I looked at him then. He was staring at me fixedly, and with an intensity I'd not seen before in his eyes. My heart began to thump. *Perhaps it's not all on my side. Perhaps he does want me like that.* He broke eye contact to look at the table top.

'Maisie,' he said, still looking down, 'I'm sorry, but I can't . . .'

'It's all right,' I said. 'Why don't you walk me home.'

We walked along the dark, silent streets to the club. The slender light of our torches lit the fractured footpath in front of us, meeting, mingling and falling apart. At the door to the club I turned to him.

'I want to help you expose Lowell.'

'We don't know he's done anything. Honey, leave it to me.'

'But—'

I stopped talking because he was leaning in towards me. My heart was thumping so hard in my chest I wondered if he could hear it.

He turned his head at the last moment and touched my cheek with dry, cool lips. 'You're a good kid, Maisie Halliday,' he whispered. 'The best.'

'I'm not a kid,' I said.

'I know.' He kissed my cheek again, then turned and walked away.

CHAPTER TWENTY-NINE

At the station the next morning Moray told me I'd be going with Celia to deliver supplies to Middlesex Hospital.

'What are we carrying?' I asked.

'Bandages and iodine,' said Moray. 'And if Celia promises not to cover it in bricks and smash the windscreen, she can drive the new ambulance. The Studebaker will be M.I.A. for a while yet.'

'Can't make that promise in the Blitz,' said Celia. 'I'll do my best, though.'

'Honestly, Moray,' I said, annoyed. 'It was a time bomb. How was I supposed to protect the Studebaker?'

'I should have thought that was obvious.'

'What? How?'

'Keep away from time bombs.'

I made a face at him, and he laughed.

'Is it really a new ambulance?' I asked hopefully.

Moray grinned. 'No, it's a modified 1935 Humber 16/60 saloon. But it should be a smoother ride than the Studebaker.'

'I, for one, am extremely jealous,' said Lily, looking up from her knitting. 'I'm stuck with the Monster for eternity, it appears.' On her return to Bloomsbury station Lily had been given the same 1937 Ford V8 she had driven before she left.

'There's a reason for that,' said Moray. 'Only you have the knack of taming the beast.'

'Wish I could tame this dratted wool,' she said, gazing wistfully at Harris. 'I've dropped another stitch. How do I fix it up again?'

Celia and I went down to the garage to see our new machine. We circled it warily.

'Yet another chimera,' said Celia.

'I have no idea what that word means,' I replied.

'Greek mythology. A monster with a lion's head, a goat's body and a serpent's tail. I mean that the Hummer, like the Studebaker, is several things joined together.'

I could see her point. There was an elegant Hummer front, but a square box had been riveted on to the back. I checked, and the previous shift had left it properly supplied with bandages and blankets. The first-aid box was all in order, too.

'Moray's right,' said Celia, once we were on the road, 'It's much smoother to drive than the Studebaker.'

'I'll find out on the Wednesday shift,' I said. 'Moray had better let me drive it then, or else. Turnabout is fair play.'

'The old Studebaker was a good girl, though,' said Celia. 'Absolutely reliable.'

'And incredibly uncomfortable.'

Celia smiled and shook her head. 'She got us through the fire and she saved us from the time bomb. It was worth a little discomfort.'

We picked up five big crates from a warehouse near Euston and headed off along the potholed streets towards Fitzrovia.

'By the way,' said Celia, as she turned into the Euston Road, 'I had a thought about your dilemma.' She raised her voice to be heard over the sound of the engine. 'You should speak to Jim Vassilikov, Lily's husband. He's in RAF Intelligence. If the Yanks are playing games, he should know about it.'

'I can't. I shouldn't have told you as much as I did.'

She smiled. 'Oh, Simon and I are safe as houses. But I do think it's wise to tell Jim. I could mention it for you.'

'No,' I said firmly. Then, less firmly, 'I don't know, Celia. I'm not sure what to do.'

'Think about it, anyway.'

I did think about it, all that week, especially after Michael telephoned on Wednesday and asked me to dinner on Saturday evening.

I hoped it wasn't a goodbye dinner, because the thought of Michael going away made me feel utterly miserable. Especially as it was all my fault because I had let Lowell trick me so easily.

I'd looked after myself since I was sixteen and thought I knew all the tricks men could play. But Lowell – and Michael – were different from any men I'd met before. Perhaps it was their training, or because they were American, or it was their personalities. All I really knew was that I loved one and loathed the other and the one I loved was leaving, perhaps forever.

I walked back to the club on Friday morning after my shift through a chilly mist that matched my gloomy thoughts. By the time I reached Manette Street, hazy sunlight was valiantly trying to pierce the gloom and I tried to be optimistic. Perhaps they wouldn't send Michael away after all.

A man stepped out of a doorway and hailed me.

I stopped dead and peered at him through the mist. Jim Vassilikov was standing there, tall, fair-haired, dressed in RAF blue. Moisture had settled on the wool of his greatcoat like tiny drops of mercury, and his face was damp.

'Did Celia tell you to speak to me?' I asked, annoyed.

'Not Celia, Simon Levy. He was worried about you. Said you might want to talk.'

'There's a cafe nearby. Let's go there.'

The Victory Restaurant was almost empty. Edna was out on the streets somewhere, trying to scratch a living from men's desires. I wished she had been there, as I would have asked Jim to buy her breakfast. She would never allow me to buy her so much as a cup of tea.

We settled into a table near the back and Jim ordered a pot of tea.

'What did Simon Levy tell you?' I asked.

'That you're mixed up in something that concerns the US Department of State and the US War Office. Spy business. And that it's worrying you.'

I took a sip of tea. It revived me and banished some of the chill that the morning had put into my bones. I took another sip and felt able to face Jim's questions.

'What if a British citizen knows a secret that concerns both the American and British governments? Is she obliged to tell someone like you? What if the Americans have said that it should be kept secret?'

Jim toyed with his cup, twisting it around in its saucer. He looked up into my eyes. 'Secrets are best kept secret. Unless they've already been divulged. Then it's best to work out how to minimise any damage that comes from that.'

'Do you know Michael Harker?' I asked.

'Yes.'

'Talk to him about it. I can't tell you anything.'

'I had a chat with Jim Vassilikov this afternoon,' said Michael, as he ushered me into the Victory Restaurant on Saturday evening. It looked much as it had done the previous morning when I had been there with Jim: brightly lit, clean and utilitarian. Not in the least romantic.

'Are you annoyed?' I peered at his face, trying to read his emotions. 'Simon Levy called him in, not me.'

Michael glanced at me. 'He told me that. Don't worry. I think it was the best thing to do. Only, don't tell anyone else about Lowell or about me. Please.'

'I promise. What happened?'

'Jim took me to see someone and we talked.'

'And it's all going to be sorted out?'

He seemed to consider the question. 'Maybe. It won't be easy, though.'

'Are you still going away?'

'Yes. Heading out tomorrow.'

'Oh. That soon.' My eyes flew up to meet his. 'You can't say where, I suppose?'

'Sorry, kid, I can't.'

I was quiet for a beat or two. 'So this is a goodbye dinner.'

He smiled. 'And such a glamorous location, isn't it? I thought it would be easier to say goodbye here, a place close to your home and well lit.'

'Well lit?'

'So I'm not tempted to become mushy.'

'Mushy? You sound like a kid yourself. Are you tempted to pull my pigtails?'

'Yes. And to ask to hold your hand and carry your books. You have that effect on me.'

'Do I?' My heart was thudding and I felt the heat flood into my cheeks.

He leaned across to brush my cheek with a finger. 'Why do you think I call you kid?'

'To be irritating, obviously.'

His mouth quirked up. 'To remind myself how damned young you are. You're a baby, despite that spectacular showgirl's body. It's hard to remember sometimes, when you're near.'

'I'm not a baby! I'm twenty.'

'Some twenty-year-olds are going on thirty. You're a complete innocent.'

'I'm not! Why do you say that? I've been looking after myself since I was sixteen and I—'

His smile became knowing. 'It's obvious. Look, honey, it's a good thing I'm leaving because I ...' He paused, and looked away, over my shoulder. 'Because I like you too much to take this any further. I'm in a line of work which, in wartime especially, makes my future pretty unpredictable. The last thing you need is me hanging around just long enough to break your heart, or make you hate me, or both. You find a nice English boy and settle down with him.'

'But I—' I stopped short and bit my lip as the waitress approached our table and stood ready to take our order.

I let Michael order for me. Whatever I ate would taste like sawdust anyway. He *did* want me like that, but he was leaving. And even if he wasn't leaving, he wasn't going to take it any further.

When the waitress had left, I looked across at Michael. 'May I write to you?'

'Better not.'

I looked down, traced a line on the tablecloth. 'Why not?'

'Maisie.' I glanced up, our eyes met and locked. 'It's best just to forget you ever met me.'

'How am I supposed to do that?'

He stubbed out the cigarette, leaned across and took my hand. 'Honey, I met Vivian when we were both at college. She was eighteen, I was a year older. She was everything I'd ever dreamed of. Beautiful, cultured, lively and charming. Her family were well connected and they were willing to take in a miner's son and treat him with affection. We married when she was twenty and I'd just turned twenty-one.'

'So what went wrong?'

'She was too young. Vivian changed. People do. They grow up and become different people. When she was twenty, Vivian thought I was perfect: the star quarterback from the other side of the tracks. By the time she was twenty-seven she was bored and miserable. She wanted a different man, but I sure as hell couldn't change who I was. I tried. I really tried.' He began to toy with the cutlery. 'You're only twenty, Maisie. The same age as Vivi was when we were married. You'll change, grow tired of me. I can't go through that again, watch love slowly fade to misery.'

'Not everyone changes. And I don't think you're perfect. In fact, I *know* you're not.'

'Aw shucks, you say the nicest things.'

I gave him an irritated look. 'I don't care that you're not perfect.'

'I do. You deserve it.'

My face was flaming, and I sent a silent apology to my mother as I stammered out, 'We have tonight. We could—'

'Maisie, with you it's marriage or nothing. I accept that, but I'm not marrying a twenty-year-old again.'

'We can—'

'Wait? No. Not when I have no idea where they're sending me, or when I can get back to England.'

Anger washed through me and I pulled my hand away. 'So you like me enough to consider marrying me, but won't court me because I'm too young. That's ridiculous. I'm not Vivian.'

He looked at me with eyes that were quietly intelligent, and utterly forlorn. 'I know you're not.'

'Celia says that the really important things are the same outlook on life, sense of humour and hopes for the future. Don't we have all that?'

He looked over my shoulder again, avoiding my eyes. 'Maybe we do, but I'm heading off tomorrow. I'm not going to trap you into a situation where you don't find a better guy because you think you owe something to me.'

'But—'

'Look, it's my last night in London. Let's just enjoy our evening and then wish each other luck and say goodbye.'

I looked up at him, saw the misery in his face, and nodded. 'All right.'

Our soup arrived and as we ate we had a stilted conversation about nothing much. When we got to what was likely to go under the ration next I began to laugh.

'This is ridiculous,' I said. 'Let's pretend that you're not going away tomorrow, that we didn't have that little talk, and just enjoy our last evening together.'

Michael smiled his sudden, devastatingly attractive smile. 'Suits me.'

'You won't be able to see my movie. It's being shown in early June.'

'Shame about that. What's it called?'

'*Ambulance Girls At War.*'

'Great title.' He smiled. 'Perry Denbeigh thought the camera would love you.'

I rolled my eyes. 'I'm much better at dancing than acting. And I love it, although it has ruined my feet.'

He glanced down at my ankles, which were clad in the silk stockings he had given me. I was wearing my best shoes.

'They look very pretty to me,' he said.

'The shoes hide it, but they're both misshapen from dancing *en pointe.*'

Michael laughed. 'I'll swap your misshapen feet for the jagged scar on my left thigh. I got it when I broke my leg in my second year of college. The result of an altercation with a linebacker. Like you, the thing I loved to do most – play football – was rough on my body.'

I gave a dismissive wave and a smile. 'Oh, a scar like that would make you look tough and masculine. It's different for women. And I have scars, too, you know. From my dancing, on both my big toes.'

He raised an eyebrow. 'I'll meet your puny toe scars with my smashed collarbone. It wasn't set properly and left me with a bony knob sticking out. Here.' He pointed to the left of his collarbone. 'Had to miss the final game because of that one.'

'Another altercation with a – um, linebacker?'

'Nope. That would be a run-in with a safety.'

'You know that those words mean nothing whatsoever to me?'

'It's a beautiful game, kid,' he said with another smile. 'I'll explain it to you one day.'

'I can't wait. Um, Michael?'

He put down his fork and leaned back. 'What?'

'Celia thinks Dan Lowell's a committed isolationist, determined to keep America out of the war.'

'Lots of people in the States hold that view. Some of them very high up in government. It's our policy. Roosevelt may have pushed through Lend-Lease, but under the Neutrality Acts we still can't send our ships into war zones. If Lowell wants to keep us out of the war, he's got a lot of support behind him. John Casey, for one.'

'I loathed Mr Casey when I met him. Do you think it was him who handed over what was in the locket, to Mr Egan?'

'Dunno. What was in the fob was dynamite, handing it over was the act of a traitor. Casey is isolationist, but I don't think he's a traitor.'

'Dan Lowell? Do you think Mr Egan was going to the Café de Paris to meet Lowell? He made a lot of asking me if Mr Egan had said who he was to meet that night.'

'I doubt it. I think it was a British fifth columnist he was meeting. Like I said, what he had was explosive stuff.'

'The letters between Churchill and Roosevelt?'

'Mmm.'

'Is that what the British are looking into? Who Mr Egan might have been meeting?'

He shrugged.

I tried again. 'Don't you think it's strange that Dan Lowell hates you so much? Enough to trick me to get you fired.'

'I put a few noses out of joint when I turned up at the embassy last year. I suspect he just dislikes me.'

'And there's nothing I can do to help?'

'Not a thing.'

He walked me the short distance back to the club before the eleven o'clock lockout. It was a clear night; the almost full moon was extraordinarily bright and moonlight etched his face with shadows, highlighting the angle of his chin, the hollows under his cheeks. We stood for a while outside the door, holding hands and saying nothing.

The Warning went.

'That's my cue to leave,' said Michael. 'Stay out of trouble, will you?'

'And don't you do anything fat-headed,' I said, and looked up at the brilliant moon. 'I'm worried about tonight. I think they'll be over in force.'

'Because of April's full-moon raids?'

'Yes. I think it'll be bad tonight. Please promise me you'll take cover.'

'Sure, kid.'

'Goodbye, then.' My voice was creditably even.

'Goodbye, Maisie.'

We stared at each other. My heart beat a tattoo against my ribs.

His mouth suddenly twisted and he seemed to shudder.

'I really shouldn't do this,' he said, and seemed to hesitate. So I met him halfway by launching myself at him. His lean body was pressed hard against mine when I lifted my face to him, and then he kissed me.

CHAPTER THIRTY

When we could think again and drew apart slightly, I realised that the raiders were already over London. The drone of their engines was like the loud hum of a factory floor and the AA guns were firing. Not intermittently, as they usually did, but all at once. The thunder of that continuous barrage pounded against my ears and thumped in my chest. It could only mean that hundreds of raiders had been sighted.

We both flinched as little cylinders fell around us with a tinny tinkle, to explode into balls of flickering blue-white light. The red flaring of oil bombs already lit the middle distance and further away high-explosive bombs were whistling down to earth, each explosion making a 'crump' sound. The raiders were upon us.

'Better get inside, kid,' said Michael. His face was tense and anxious.

'Not until I know you're safe. There's a public shelter in Soho Square gardens, just over there. It's under the pretty hut in the centre. Go there now. *Please*, Michael.'

He pulled me hard against his chest as a raider roared low overhead. It released a bomb that shrieked as it plummeted down. We threw ourselves flat on to the footpath, covering our ears. The ground shook and a deafening crash sounded as it landed no more than five hundred yards away. I lifted my head to see a huge cloud of dust rise up from somewhere beyond Charing Cross Road. It rose in a pure white and compact curtain, like a solid mass, and it blotted out the moon.

The wind blew it towards us as we staggered to our feet. Greek Street was soon enveloped by a thick dust fog that made us both cough and my eyes water. It was now impossible to see more than a foot in front of us. Above us, the roar of massed planes had increased to a maddening and constant noise. Incendiaries continued to rain down, landing with thuds on the footpath and bursting into balls of flame.

'Come *on*,' I said, pulling at Michael's arm. 'We need to get to a shelter. *Now*.'

'How? I can't see a thing.'

'I know my way around Soho.'

I took the lead and we ran together down Greek Street, holding hands like children, dodging shrapnel and incendiaries, heading for Soho Square. Fires had started. The smell of smoke competed with the choking dust, and the white fog that surrounded us began to flicker red.

As we got closer to Soho Square the dust cloud diminished. I pulled Michael across the road and we had reached the edge of the garden when all around – Michael, the street, the garden and the fairy-tale structure in black and white at the centre – lit up with a brilliant white light. Above us, three chandelier flares descended slowly, dripping stars.

As if in a nightmare, I was rooted to the spot, transfixed. I felt terribly cold and would have fallen had not Michael's arm been like a steel rod, crushing me against his body, holding me steady. The light grew brighter and still brighter, until Michael's face was as clear as if we stood in daylight. Streams of red and green tracer bullets rose up in colourful arcs towards the flares, and two were suddenly extinguished.

'Thank God,' muttered Michael, but the next wave of planes was already overhead, dropping high-explosive bombs that screamed as they fell and shook the ground when they landed. One was falling towards us and again we threw ourselves down. Michael covered me with his body and I tasted damp earth and grass as I again covered my ears. The screaming ended in a dull thud, as if an old enamel bowl with something in it had been dumped on the ground. There was a tremendous bang, a flash, a deep rumbling sound and, finally, silence. Michael got to his feet, hauling me with him. A solid white cloud of dust hovered over Dean Street, its edges pink with reflected firelight.

'That was too close,' I said, in a voice I scarcely recognised.

Michael didn't answer. He began to run, pulling me along in his wake, heading for the mock-Tudor structure in the centre of the garden. We reached its rough wooden pillars as another bomb began a screaming descent.

'Where's the damned entrance to this thing,' he shouted, pushing at the doors in front of him.

'Other side.'

His grip on my hand was hard, uncompromising. He dragged me around to the shelter's entrance, hauled the door open and practically threw me inside. We stumbled down a dozen steep steps and pushed open the doors at the bottom. A single electric light in the concrete ceiling revealed a large crowd of people sitting on rows of benches in a brick-lined room with bunks around the walls. They looked up at us in dull surprise.

The shelter shook as the bomb hit the ground nearby.

'Welcome, strangers of the night,' said a man with a plummy voice.

'Thanks,' said Michael. 'We're glad to be here.'

A portly gentleman in a shabby raincoat rose to greet us. 'I'm the shelter warden,' he said, in the same plummy voice. 'I recognise you, miss. You're from the Theatre Girls' Club. And you, sir, are American, if I hear your accent correctly. Please, sit anywhere. I fear we're in for a long night. All the bunks are spoken for, but we have some spare mattresses if you don't mind the floor.'

'Halliday,' called out a voice I knew. I looked towards it, and Moray was sitting on a bunk near the entrance, with a newspaper propped against his knees. He was reading it by torchlight.

I walked over to him and introduced Michael.

'Don't you wish you were on duty tonight?' said Moray. 'I know I do. It's easier to be busy than to wait these things out down here.'

I knew what he meant. Somehow, no matter how dangerous it was, when you were out in the ambulance you could push away your fear. You were just too busy. Sitting in a shelter was much harder on the nerves.

Michael and I sat together on a wooden bench. He put his arm around me and I rested my head on his shoulder. Around us I heard bits and pieces of muted conversations, but the thunder of the guns and crash of falling bombs penetrated even the thick walls and concrete that protected us. The shelter quaked with each near explosion. And always the faint, sinister and unceasing roar of the bombers was above us.

'Comfortable?' said Michael, pulling me even closer.

'Mmm.'

'I guess I was being a damn fool in that restaurant. But I'm trying to protect you, Maisie. I don't want you to end up like—'

'Vivian? I'm able to protect myself. And I'm not Vivian.'

'No,' he murmured into my hair, 'you're not. I love you so much, kid.'

My heart gave a lurch. 'No one has loved me since my mother died,' I whispered, and his arm tightened around me.

'I just want you to be happy, Maisie,' he murmured.

I said, slowly, 'I really think we've a much better chance of being happy together than apart. And I love you, too, by the way.'

He breathed a laugh. 'You win. I'll find a way to come back to you, I promise. And then we'll see if we can make this work.'

I might have been sitting in a smelly public shelter, experiencing the worst raid of the entire Blitz, but I was with Michael and we were in love. I felt a surge of pure happiness.

The raid continued without the usual lulls. Instead, not long after midnight, we were shocked to realise that the roar of bombers had increased. As had the frequency of explosions.

I could feel the fear in the people around me. It pressed down and deadened the atmosphere.

At the beginning of the Blitz it had been a matter of pride to keep up the pretence of bravery. In nightclubs, even when bombs fell close enough to rattle the glasses, bands would up the ante and everyone would sing, shout, yell out the words to cheery songs until the siren, the guns, the bombs were all drowned out. But we'd been suffering through the Blitz now for eight months; defiance fades when one has to keep on being defiant, night after night after night. We all sat glumly and tried not to flinch as more bombs fell around us.

'Must be hundreds of them up there,' a man called out. 'Mebbe a thousand.'

'My God, poor old London,' said another.

The night of the tenth and eleventh of May 1941, came to be called 'London's Longest Night' because, to those of us who lived through it, those seven hours of continuous bombing seemed never-ending. Pray God, London never endures anything like it again. Wave after wave of bombers came, hour upon hour, dropping devastation upon an already devastated city. At around three in the morning I became convinced that I would die that night. I knew, somehow, that the shelter would suffer a direct hit. Michael and I and everyone in there would die. I hoped it would be quick.

I whispered my fears to Michael, and he murmured, 'Won't happen. I won't let it happen.' And, strangely enough, I felt heartened.

Hours dragged by and still the raiders were above London. Their bombs were now falling so close together that there was no respite. We seemed to be in the middle of one enormous, never-ending explosion that juddered and rocked the shelter unceasingly. There was no singing, no sense of community spirit. We were a crowd of cowed people sitting silently in a box of concrete and brick, as the world outside was being blown apart.

And then, after the longest night I have ever experienced, came what seemed like a miracle. There were intervals without the dread roar of engines. The noise of the planes grew fainter and eventually faded into the distance. The guns fell silent.

The long, glorious note of the All Clear sounded. I checked my watch. It was six o'clock on Sunday morning.

'We made it, kid,' he said. 'Told you we would.'

Smiling, I lifted my face to him and he kissed me.

People around us smiled. Some cheered, others wept. A man thumped his neighbour on the back.

'We're still here, mate,' he shouted. 'Still here.'

I caught Moray's eye and he gave me a thumbs-up.

Michael and I climbed out of the shelter into Soho Square gardens to find it was a beautiful May morning, with clear skies and bright sunshine. Around us was a mess of charred wood from burned trees and shrapnel. Trees were uprooted and branches were down. The air was thick with dust and smoke and bits of charred paper and the smell of cordite.

'Look,' I said to Michael. 'The king survived.'

King Charles II still stood in the garden, hand on hip, surveying the wreckage with an elegant aloofness. The statue was not even chipped.

'Kings usually do,' he said. 'Want me to walk you to the ambulance station? You're due on duty in an hour or so, and you'd be able to grab a nap there.'

'Could we look around first? See just how bad the damage is.'

Michael shrugged. 'Why not? It's your town.'

Soho was a shambles. It was hard going on foot. Cascades of broken glass still tinkled down from all the shattered windows. Shops were burnt out in Tottenham Court Road, a good part of both Charlotte Street and Old Compton Street had been completely destroyed by fire. The entire block between Dean Street and Wardour Street was a pile of rubble. Fires, or smouldering ashes, were everywhere we looked. It seemed that if high-explosive bombs had missed a building, it had been claimed by incendiaries or oil bombs. On all sides columns of smoke whirled up from fires and tongues of flame gushed from craters in the roads.

'And we haven't seen the City yet,' I said, my eyes swimming with tears. 'This is the worst raid we've had.' I looked at Michael and said, my voice cracking, 'London can't take much more of this, you know. We can be as defiant as we like, but God knows how many died last night. And look at the damage!'

'London will survive it,' he said, taking my shoulders and giving me a little shake. 'Yes, it's bad, but London will survive. You Londoners kept going between September and December when there were raids every single night. You are able to face whatever is to come.'

My worst shock came as we walked to the ambulance station. Much of Bloomsbury had been hit, including Russell Square and Bedford Square. The ambulance station was located in Woburn Place, which was undamaged, but the buildings directly behind the station in Herbrand Street were now a pile of debris. The high-explosive bomb that destroyed them had missed the block of flats above the station by a mere fifteen yards or so.

I've always cried too easily. Tears fell then, running down my cheeks, no doubt etching channels in my dusty face, the way Mr Denbeigh had wanted Lily to be filmed. Michael cupped my cheeks with his hands and wiped away my tears with his thumbs.

'Promise me you won't take any silly risks when you're out there in the bombing,' he said fiercely. '*Promise me*.' He leant forward to kiss me, hard and possessively.

'I suppose I can't ask for the same promise from you,' I said, gasping a little when he released me.

'Nope. Sorry, honey. It comes with my job.'

'It does with mine, sometimes.'

'I know. That's why I said silly risks.'

'Promise me the same, then.'

He laughed. 'I promise not to take silly risks. I promise to come back to England as soon as I can, and to court Maisie Halliday properly when I do. And I promise to marry her when she's twenty-one, if she still wants me to.'

It was a lot of promises. I wiped away the last of my tears with shaky hands, and smiled. 'She'll want you to,' I said. 'She's not an idiot.'

'You'll get no argument from me on that.'

He left me standing there. A hug, a frantic kiss, and he was gone, striding down Herbrand Street past hoses and rubble, heading for Russell Square Underground Station. I stumbled into the ambulance station like a sleepwalker. It was close to the end of the shift and McIver was still on duty.

She took one look at me, and said, 'Don't tell me. You were caught in the raid and spent the night in a public shelter.'

'How can you tell?'

'The heavy eyes, filthy face and slept-in-clothes appearance.'

I smiled and brushed hair out of my eyes.

'The shelter in Soho Square,' I said. 'Moray was there too. It was a bad raid.'

'The worst yet in this Blitz. They bombed all over London – every one of the boroughs got hit. The British Museum is well alight around the corner. They took out most of what was left of Red Lion Square after the parachute bomb last month, and all of Red Lion Passage, much of Theobald's Road, too. I hear that what remained of the City is pretty much gone, although St Paul's is still standing. Westminster Abbey was hit and the Palace of Westminster – we've lost the House of Commons entirely. Holborn is in ruins, Finsbury, Romford and Hornchurch as well. They're telling me there's over a thousand dead, perhaps closer to fifteen hundred. Many more thousands injured.'

I swallowed convulsively. 'It's even worse than I'd thought.'

'My God, Halliday,' said McIver, and her face crumpled. 'Hundreds and hundreds of planes came over last night – more than five hundred, I'm told. They'd drop their bombs, go back to France, refuel and come back with more bombs, and they did it again and again and again. There were bombs coming down every two minutes. One plane let eight bombs go, one after the other. I counted them as they hit, just like you'd count Big Ben's chimes, only it was bombs hitting London. How can there be anything that hasn't been hit? You saw the incident in Herbrand Street? I can't believe we survived.'

I watched her, appalled. McIver was usually so stolid, so dependably cool, no matter what the crisis. I knew that last night she would have taken it all in her stride. It was the shock of surviving that had undone her. She took a breath, visibly pulled herself together, and gave me a smile. 'But we did survive. Lord be praised.'

'Are all the vehicles out?' I asked.

'All out. All frantically busy. You get yourself cleaned up and go to bed for a nap. You'll be needed soon enough when last night's shift returns from duty. And you'll find Harris in one of the bunks. She was bombed out and arrived here an hour ago.'

'How terrible.' I shut up when I realised how trite that sounded, given what had happened last night. Harris was alive. So many others were not.

'I'll bring the kettle into the washroom,' said McIver. 'There's no hot water, or any water. I filled every basin and bucket we had when the raid began because I thought it might be a big one. At least your shift will have water for tea and to wash your hands.'

I turned to leave, and she added, 'Ashwin's spare clothes are ready and waiting for you.'

As I washed in the meagre supply of hot water I thought how sensible I had been to choose the ambulance service as my job when I returned to London. I couldn't imagine working anywhere else.

CHAPTER THIRTY-ONE

Lily shook me awake at eleven o'clock that morning.

'I know you didn't get to sleep until after seven,' she said, 'but you're needed. Armstrong hasn't come in at all and we're very worried because Moray can't raise him on the telephone. You heard about Harris?'

'Bombed out,' I said, as I threw on Ashwin's spare clothes.

'Powell has offered her a bed, but she's got grown daughters who will take her in. Poor thing's worried about her old cat, thinks that this might all be too much for it. She says that she can't lose Tibby on top of everything else and who can blame her for that? I've never seen Harris so close to breaking, I mean—'

Lily was chattering almost frantically.

'What's the matter?' I asked, putting my hand on her arm.

Lily stopped walking and raised the back of her hands up to her cheeks, as if to cool them.

'Oh, am I being silly? I'm a bit jittery today.'

'Why?'

'It's just that we were bombed out, too. It's Jim's second time, but my first. Oh, Maisie, it's such a strange and horrible feeling. We came up from the shelter and found that our home – the entire block of flats – is now a pile of dust.' She gulped in a breath, and gave a faint smile. 'Well, not just dust, of course. There was lots of debris, but you know what I mean.'

'Where will you live?'

'Jim has a few friends who have moved out for the duration and left their flats empty. He's ringing around. We'll be fine, but there's nothing left. No clothes, or crockery or – or anything.'

She began to shake, and put her hands over her eyes. 'Oh, I'm sorry to be such a mess. But it was so awful last night. All through the night, bomb after bomb, all falling so close to where we were. And you know how every bomb within five hundred feet seems to be falling on top of you. I knew perfectly well that the odds were against us being killed unless we suffered a direct hit, but I've seen direct hits on shelters.'

She turned a tear-stained face to me. Lily, who was brave as a lion and rushed into danger without a second thought. Lily, who was to be awarded a medal for her bravery in rescuing a trapped family from a bombed building.

'I thought we'd die, Maisie. I really thought it last night. It was the first time I've thought that, but the raid was so bad. I clung to Jim and prayed that if it had to happen, please make it quick and if Jim goes, take me too.'

I put my arms around Lily and let her cry herself out. She pushed away from me, wiped her tears, took a deep breath and said, 'Sorry. I was bound to begin blubbering some time. I'm glad it happened when I was with you. I'm sure Celia would think I was a frightful fool. Would have told me to pull myself together.'

'No. She'd understand,' I said. 'And I do, too. I was in a public shelter last night, and I thought we would all die. It was the worst raid I've ever been in.'

'So many people did die,' said Lily. 'We're lucky. People all over London are making arrangements to go the mortuary to identify bodies.'

'Yes,' I agreed. 'We're the lucky ones.'

When I entered the common room Moray was in the office on the telephone. He saw me and waved as he replaced the receiver. He came to the office door.

'Halliday. Good, you're up. They're still digging people alive out of the ruins in Theobald's Road – Purvis and Powell have taken an ambulance load to hospital already, and Ashwin and

Squire are there now. Harris took the saloon, but the warden has asked for another ambulance.'

He held up a chit and I walked across to collect it from him.

'Here's the address,' he said. 'Get over there with Lily in the Studebaker right away.'

'Any news of Armstrong?' I asked.

He shook his head. 'I can't raise him. I'll keep trying.'

Lily and I exchanged looks. We were both worried for Stephen Armstrong, the 'baby' of the station.

'Where does he live?' I asked.

'Finsbury. It took quite a battering last night.'

As we were leaving he called out, 'Eight hospitals were hit. We've been told to take our wounded to Middlesex.'

Lily and I drove past Russell Square with its uprooted, scorched and blackened trees, some half-buried by piles of bricks. On the footpath, in the rubble of a ruined house, was a battered tin hat. I hoped the owner had made it out alive. In Southampton Row the damage became more poignant. A perambulator lay on its side, smashed and flattened, with a headless doll beside it.

A little further on and the entire front of a house had been ripped off, revealing three layers of flats, each with different wallpaper. In the top flat a bedroom was on show, with two chairs still neatly place on either side of a double bed where a towel had been laid out, ready for morning ablutions that would never be taken; one floor down revealed a dressing table and wardrobe with a dressing gown still hanging neatly on the back of the door; in the next flat down the floor tilted dangerously. On it was a kitchen dresser pitched at a sharp angle, but the crockery it held was still in place, cups neatly on hooks. The table was set for breakfast that would not be eaten. It was like a crazy, life-sized doll's house.

We arrived at the incident to find piles of bricks, rubble, splintered wood and plaster that swarmed with rescue workers. Little was left of the houses that had been there. Just the external walls, with nothing between them but slats of wood from the ceilings. I flinched as a nearby building collapsed in a deafening roar. As it shuffled downwards it released a cloud of choking dust that mingled with the smoky air and caused me to cough almost uncontrollably. Through streaming eyes I saw the Warden approaching us.

'How many more do they think are in there?' I asked him.

'We're not sure. Can you wait a bit?'

'Of course.'

As we waited my mind flitted between themes: the wonderful job the rescue teams were doing, the knocking sound I'd heard in the engine as we drove to the incident, whether Dan Lowell was a German sympathiser, my longing for a cup of tea and food; but the recurring thought was of Michael, who was going away today to goodness knew where. I had no idea when I was likely to see him again. He had told me he loved me; I was loved. The last person who had loved me was my mother, and I was sure she would have approved of Michael.

I looked up at a scream of 'Silence!'

A rescue worker was stretched flat out with an ear to the wreckage. One, two, three seconds passed. Then he began tearing at the rubble as if possessed. Others joined him, and the hole they made became larger. A man was lowered into the cavity. Five long minutes went by. The rope was hauled up and he appeared carrying a girl of fifteen or so, who was clutching a small dog to her chest.

It was the dog that had saved her, I found out later. They were trapped together in the cellar, with gas wafting around them. The terrified dog began to whine, and so she picked it up and, in an attempt to calm her pet, sang songs to it. The rescue worker heard her singing.

As Lily dealt with the girl's cut arms and legs, another shout came from the site. Three men appeared, carrying an elderly man in their arms. He held a towel over his bloodied face and seemed dazed. We loaded both of our wounded into the back of the ambulance and Lily covered each of them with a blanket.

My job now was to get them to Middlesex Hospital as fast as I could. As I pulled out, Squire and Harris came back to the site in the Ford ambulance. They pulled up close to rescue workers who dug frantically into rubble, near where the old man had been extracted.

I drove steadily west at sixteen mph, but was diverted south into various little streets where torn blinds and curtains fluttered from empty, shattered windows and I drove over layers of shattered glass, dodging the contents of shop windows now scattered across the road. The area beyond was a wasteland. Two parachute bombs had landed and at least eight high-explosive bombs also. High Holborn was open, but had taken another hit. I drove along New Oxford Street, which was again partly in ruins, but found Bloomsbury Street was impassable, cordoned off because the British Museum was still on fire, so I continued on to Tottenham Court Road. Not far along, and it was also blocked. I turned into the narrow side-streets and drove all around the houses until I finally arrived at the red-brick Middlesex Hospital.

Lily helped to unload the wounded. As she disappeared into the hospital I called out, 'Be sure we get our two blankets back.'

Blankets were scarce and we would need them for the next patients.

We did. It was a very long day.

Lily and I arrived back at the station after our fourth pick-up at around five o'clock. Apart from a quick cup of tea and a piece of cake I'd grabbed at a tea van in Theobald's Road, I'd not eaten all day.

We rolled into the garage and I almost fell out of the ambulance.

'We need to eat,' said Lily. 'And have a cup of tea. Moray can't send us out again until we do.'

But when we arrived in the common room Moray told us that there were no more pick-ups at the moment. 'Squire and Ashwin are standing by at an incident in Holborn, just in case someone comes up alive, but they've told us to rest here until they've dug out some more survivors to be transported. It'll be mortuary runs all day for tomorrow's shift, poor sods.'

A plate of sandwiches was on the table and a freshly brewed pot of tea. Harris poured me a cup as I wolfed down a couple of sandwiches.

'I heard about you being bombed out,' I said to her. 'I'm so sorry.'

She patted my hand. 'Thank you, Halliday dear. I think it was bound to happen some time, but it was the house I'd moved to with my late husband when we were married and I did love it so. My eldest daughter wants me to come to her until things are more settled.'

'Where does she live?'

Harris grimaced. 'That's the problem. Right out in East Finchley. I may have to ask for a transfer to a closer ambulance station, though I hate to think of leaving you all.'

I was sad to think we'd lose Harris, who mothered us all while keeping us as firmly in line as did Moray.

'Is there any news about Armstrong?'

She shook her head. Moray appeared in his office doorway with chits in his hand. 'I need two ambulances to go to Regent Square. They're finding survivors. Powell and Purvis, you go now. Lily and Halliday, eat something first, then get going.'

By eight that evening we had all returned to the station and were sitting around the big table finishing our dinner when the door opened and Armstrong entered. Squire jumped up and went over to the boy. There was a dead look in his eyes that I associated with shock.

Squire led Armstrong to the table and sat him down. He gestured to Harris, who poured him a strong cup of tea and put in a couple of spoonfuls of our precious sugar.

Armstrong gulped the tea, then sat back in his chair, eyes fixed on the table.

'What happened?' asked Sadler, in a surprisingly gentle voice.

Armstrong looked up at him. There was a quiet dignity to the boy, but nothing could mask the horror in his eyes.

'Direct hit on the shelter behind my sister's house. Lost my sister, her baby – it was a little girl, Lois – and the twins, George and Penny. They'd just turned three.'

The room was silent. No one could think of a thing to say that would fit such a list of horrors.

'Joy's husband's a sailor and he's away at sea. Dad's in Liverpool on war work. There's only me and Joy, and I wanted to spare Mum the pain of having to identify the bodies, so I did it.' His voice was a monotone, as if by showing no emotion at all he could deal with what he was telling us. 'The people at the morgue had done their best, but ...' He looked up at Squire with haunted eyes. 'You know the worst bit?'

Squire shook his head.

'I told them it wasn't Joy's body, because Joy had a scar on her hand where the kettle had scalded her when she was a kid.' He swallowed. 'I said it looked like Joy, but it couldn't be my sister because that woman's hand had no scar.' His voice dropped and we could scarcely hear him say, 'They said that it was someone else's body under the sheet. They do that quite often, they told me, to make the person think that their loved one is – is intact.'

Still the boy didn't cry. He finished his tea, put the cup carefully on the saucer, and sat up straight. 'Aunty May's looking after Mum, so I thought I should come in, because you'll all be really busy tonight if there's another big raid.'

'That was thoughtful of you,' said Moray quietly. 'We'll need all the help we can get if they come over again. You're with Squire, in the Ford.'

He looked at Squire, who nodded and put his hand on the boy's shoulder.

'Come on, mate,' said Squire, 'let's check the vehicle.'

They walked out together, the tough old former boxer from Seven Dials and the boy who'd lost most of his family in one night, but thought he should come in to help.

CHAPTER THIRTY-TWO

There was no follow-up raid that night, or the next night, or the night following, or the night after that. Occasionally there were sirens, which made my heart race, but there were no raids.

One week, two weeks, and no repeat of the raid of tenth/eleventh May. Our nerves were stretched almost to breaking point as we waited for another big raid. We sat in the common room to discuss it on Sunday morning, exactly two weeks after living through the Longest Night.

'It's the weather,' said Harris. She had decided to move in with her younger daughter, who lived closer to Bloomsbury, saying she'd become too used to us all to leave the station. Today she was knitting socks in navy blue.

'I heard they don't want to bomb us in case they kill Rudolf Hess,' said Powell, 'because Hitler flew him over secretly to negotiate peace.'

One of our biggest shocks after the big raid was to find out that, while London was being bombed to pieces, Hitler's deputy, Rudolf Hess, had parachuted into Scotland. Germany reported that he was mentally ill, had stolen a plane and Hitler had not authorised his departure.

'Nah,' said Sadler. 'That Hess, he's mum and dad.' At Lily's puzzled look, he elaborated. 'Barking mad. Negotiate peace, my foot.'

'I think it's because they're too busy bombarding our troops in Crete to bother with us at the moment,' said Purvis.

'Maybe the Blitz is really over,' whispered Armstrong.

'Shhhh,' said Squire, as if the Germans might hear him and be provoked into another attack. Sadler knocked on the wooden table. Moray fingered the lucky gold sovereign I knew he kept in his pocket.

'They're still attacking the other cities,' I said. 'Provincial cities are still being hit, just not London.'

'Which means the Blitz is like a good West End show,' said Purvis, with a weak smile. 'After a long run in London, it's touring the provinces.'

'That joke is in bad taste,' said Harris, looking up from her knitting. 'Personally, I think it's psychological. They'll hold off for a while, convince us that the Blitz is over, then destroy all our hopes with a really big raid.'

'I think you're right,' said Lily, usually one of the more optimistic of us. 'They're giving us a break to destroy our morale for good.'

'Well, I wouldn't be surprised if there's a good old Blitz on London next Saturday,' said Squire.

'Then we'll see the rest of Westminster Abbey go,' said Lily bitterly. 'And St Paul's probably. And maybe Big Ben, too.'

'Nah,' said Sadler, 'they'll wait until autumn, then blast London to smithereens and invade.'

Powell nodded. 'Apparently one of our leading astrologers – who is almost always right – has predicted that the next raid we have on London will be the worst ever in the history of the world.'

'Well, it hasn't happened yet,' said Celia, in a bracing voice, 'so buck up everyone. Who wants a cup of tea?'

'I'll help,' I said, and followed her into the kitchen, desperate to escape the never-ending talk about when the next raid would come.

'A whole fortnight without a raid,' said Celia, as we were preparing tea. 'I can't think why they don't try and finish us off.'

Living without raids, not knowing when the bombers would next come over, was more taxing on the nerves than living through the worst of the Blitz.

When I arrived at the station early the following week, Moray announced that the Home Guard were conducting 'invasion exercises' in the ruins of the City, and they'd asked for ambulances from various stations to be on hand.

'What's an invasion exercise?' I asked.

'Hundreds of men will run around pretending the invasion has come and we need to fight them on the beaches, etc. Any volunteers?'

'I'll go,' said Lily. 'I've not seen the City since the big raid.'

'And me,' I said.

We set out in the Monster. Lily drove past devastated Russell Square, along Southampton Row with its shattered windows. There was only an enormous pile of rubble as we turned into Kingsway, where Heavy Rescue had finished dynamiting what remained of a large bank. The rubble from the explosion was being shovelled into large lorries. I'd heard that London's rubble was used to make airfields, from which, no doubt, our bombers took off to wreak the same sort of havoc on German cities, in an insane and never-ending cycle of hate and devastation.

Lily drove up the Strand, along Fleet Street, through Ludgate Circus and up Ludgate Hill. New paving had been laid over the yawning craters, but we couldn't miss the glimpses of ruination in the little side streets, where buildings were down like teeth torn at random from a jaw. Office blocks were shattered, little shops burned out, everywhere boards where there had been glass.

The Home Guard exercises were to take place in the area of worst devastation, a wasteland nearly three-quarters of a mile square around St Paul's. The cathedral still stood proud on its hill, but around it scarcely a structure remained intact, and many had been obliterated. The dynamite squads had tidied it up, so that what remained had a more peaceful look, as if a great wind had destroyed all in its path.

'That was the centre of the publishing trade,' said Lily, gesturing at stunted ruins, where fire-seared walls surrounded shells of what had been great blocks of warehouses. 'Seven million books went up in flames on the night of the big fire raid at the end of December.'

Lily parked the Monster behind the other five ambulances that were lined up in the street.

'Here to watch the fun?' asked a chubby young woman with a pretty smile as we joined drivers and attendants from other stations at the mobile refreshments van. 'I'm Violet.'

'Maisie. Can't wait.' I reached up to take the cup of tea passed to me by the girl in the van.

'Did you hear?' said Violet. 'We shot down thirty bombers last week as they crossed the coast. The RAF is becoming a dab hand at getting the blighters at night.'

'Do you really think it's carrots?' asked the woman in the van. 'I've taken to eating them at every meal, but I can't see any better in the blackout.'

'Maybe it takes a while to start working,' said Violet, 'and that's why it's taken eight months before our boys have been able to hit Jerry at night. I reckon that's why they've stopped coming to London. Too many losses.'

As I sipped my tea, I looked around at the destruction that had been wrought by eight months of bombing. Were the attacks on London really over? There had been planes that dropped a few bombs, but no major raids on the capital since the big one in mid-May. The provincial towns and cities were still being hit, though not as badly as before. Like many Londoners, I suspected the Germans were simply waiting for autumn and the longer nights to resume the attacks on London. And yet, I couldn't help wondering if Violet was right and it really was due to our improved night fighting techniques. Thirty 'kills' last week was an amazing result.

'No troops ever had such a realistic place to train in,' said a gaunt-looking man, as he surveyed the devastated City. 'It's a dream.'

'It's a nightmare,' said Lily.

Home Guardsmen acting as ground defenders sat at machine-gun posts amid the debris. Riflemen poked their weapons through shattered, first-storey windows in the occasional remaining building. Their 'attackers' were steel-helmeted Scouts, who advanced down the blasted streets of the City.

As the main attack developed, the Home Guardsmen worked forwards, moving slowly, clambering over remnants of City offices. They were forced to scramble through shattered glass, relics of filing cabinets and typewriters, rusty radiators and fire-blistered safes. The men crawled around the edges of bomb craters, now choked with avalanches of rubbish, and gathered to draw breath within the shelter of the blackened walls of a burnt-out church.

It was a lot of fun to watch, but had a dark purpose. These were the men who would protect us if Germany launched a ground assault on London. They were grimly efficient, but many were old, many very young. There was an air of controlled chaos about it all, and I wondered how long London would survive if these men faced the sort of action our troops had faced on Crete. We'd just heard that after twelve days of what had been described as the 'fiercest fighting of this war' and sustaining 'severe losses', it had been decided to withdraw our forces from Crete.

Of course, there were casualties in the Home Guard exercises also. A man in his sixties collapsed with what was thought to be a heart attack. There were ten sprained ankles, one broken wrist and numerous cuts and grazes caused by the many glass shards that littered the site.

When the manoeuvres were finished, the Scouts and Home Guardsmen settled in for well-earned cups of tea and biscuits.

One nuggety cockney standing near me congratulated his mate on his handling of the exercise.

'I reckon we'd show Jerry a tough time if he invades,' he said.

His mate, a tall lanky man with a thin moustache, took a long swallow of tea and then waved his mug at the wasteland around us.

'These blighters just wasted their bombs,' he said, in all seriousness. 'Imagine if they had done this to something that really mattered.'

The following Friday was the premiere of *Ambulance Girls At War*. It wasn't a fancy Hollywood premiere, but we'd been told that it would be shown then for the first time before the main feature. Lily, Celia and I decided to make a night of it, and turn up at the Odeon, along Jim and Simon and some from the station, to watch it together.

Clothes rationing had been introduced the week before, but hats weren't included. So I decided to spend Friday afternoon in bomb-damaged Selfridges, looking for a new hat to celebrate the occasion. I'd loved the grand department store since I was a girl. If Mam was working at the Corner House, my first port of call was Selfridges in Oxford Street. I would gaze at the ball gowns on the first floor and imagine myself in them. Sometimes I'd ride the lift to the terraced gardens on the roof, and watch the fashionable ladies and their well-dressed partners promenading around. There were cafes up there, a mini golf course and a women's gun club. The Selfridges roof gardens were the height of sophistication to a girl from the Sheffield slums. Now the shop was a fire-blasted shell of its former glory.

It was as I was walking through the Soho Square gardens on my way to Oxford Street that he stepped out in front of me. A thick-set man, some inches shorter than me who had very short blond hair. I thought he rather resembled photographs I had seen of Nazi storm troopers and I remembered Simon's remarks about Germans changing their names in the last war.

'Good afternoon, Mr Casey,' I said, politely, but without any enthusiasm.

'I'd like to talk to you, little lady.' His tone was curt, almost rude.

Given the tone, I felt no compunction in refusing.

'I'd rather not,' I said. 'I'm frightfully busy right now.'

As I stepped around him he took hold of my wrist. I twisted my hand towards his thumb and pulled my hand free.

'Where'd you learn that trick?' he said, looking impressed.

'You'd be surprised what we learn in the chorus.'

'You learned how to lie, for one thing.'

I stared at him. 'I beg your pardon?'

'You lied to Dan Lowell and me. You knew all along it was Harker who looted Egan's body in that nightclub.'

'I don't want to talk about it.' I began to walk away from him.

'You're in a hell of a lot of trouble,' he said. 'You lied to your police. I'm looking at making a formal complaint about you to that Detective Wayland.'

I stopped walking, but did not turn around. He was right. Casey could prove that I had lied to the police.

'You give it over,' said Casey. 'Give it to me and I won't speak to Wayland. There'll be no questions asked if you just give it to me.'

I decided to bluff and turned around to face him. 'I have no idea what you mean. Give what to you?'

'What Harry Egan was carrying that night.'

I looked into his muddy blue eyes. 'Mr Harker took the locket. You told me it had been given to his widow.'

He gave a derisive smile. 'Yeah. Like I said, you learned how to lie real well in that chorus line. You're a regular lying champion, Miss Halliday.'

'And you're a obnoxious boor. I don't care who you talk to.'

'Another lie,' he said with an obvious sneer. 'You care, all right. Look, I don't want to make trouble for you. Just hand it over.'

'Go away, Mr Casey.'

He gave me the approximation of a smile. 'So I have to get it back myself, do I? Let me tell you this, li—'

'Don't call me that! I'm not little, and it's obvious you don't think I'm a lady.'

His jaw clenched, and he said, 'You'd better watch it, Miss Halliday. The US government is a bad enemy, but I'm a worse one.'

He turned on his heel and walked quickly away. I stared after him until he disappeared down Greek Street. So Casey thought I had the microfilm. I hoped he wasn't going to be a nuisance. I wasn't frightened of him, but he might be able to make my life difficult, especially if he reported me to Inspector Wayland.

I blew out a breath. Jim Vassilikov would be at the cinema that night. I decided I'd try to speak to him alone and ask him for advice.

CHAPTER THIRTY-THREE

Friday 6 June 1941

Lily, Jim and I stood outside the Odeon on Friday night, for the first screening of *Ambulance Girls At War*. We were expecting a small crowd from Bloomsbury Ambulance Station, and sure enough, we were soon joined by Celia and Simon, and then Squire and his wife, Joan. Armstrong brought a young girl with curly red hair and freckles who he described as 'my girl, Rose'. Even Purvis brought a date, a slim artist he introduced as 'Nancy Mair, a watercolourist'. Then, to my surprise, Sadler and his wife Mavis arrived. Harris and Powell had promised to watch the film at their local cinemas and tell us what they thought at the next shift on Sunday.

I felt sad that Michael wasn't there. He'd hand-delivered a note, a cheque and a book to the club the day after the big raid. The note told me that he loved me, he'd be back as soon as he could, and I should spend the money on pretty things. The cheque was for £20, which was a very generous amount indeed. And he had added a cryptic postscript: 'Watch for me by moonlight.' I knew that was from the poem *The Highwayman*, but couldn't work out what he meant by it. The book was *David Copperfield* by Charles Dickens, which had made me smile. Michael seemed determined to make me appreciate his idol.

Since then I'd heard nothing. Almost four weeks. It seemed like a lifetime.

As the others chatted, Purvis whispered to me that he wouldn't have brought Nancy if he'd known I'd be alone. I murmured a non-committal reply and he wandered back to Nancy.

We were in line for our tickets when Moray arrived, alone. He always kept his cards close to his chest, and although he'd mentioned a wife and children who had evacuated to the country, he had given us no other details. Moray was a dark horse, one I had never really been able to make out. I suspected that his political views were very far to the right, almost fascist. Also that he was anti-Semitic because he had sometimes treated David Levy, Simon's brother, with contempt. I tried not to judge him because, since we had gone over to twenty-four-hour shifts, he had been an excellent station leader, very cool and practical, but sympathetic also.

'I'm the lucky one,' he said. 'What an honour to partner Halliday.'

When we were seated in the dark cinema he whispered, 'Where's your dashing American?'

'Away,' I replied, and we sat back to watch the screen.

The newsreel gave us no rousing victories to celebrate. When the cartoon came on I began to feel nervous. My heart started to thump during the short film telling us to eat more potatoes. When *Ambulance Girls At War* began my stomach roiled with nausea. I thought then that it was a good thing that Michael wasn't there to see me make a fool of myself.

It seemed to take forever to get to the actual film. I sat through the certification that the movie had been passed by the British Board of Film Censors, some stirring music, and the title, in big letters. Next came: 'Produced by Crown Film Unit, with the full cooperation of the London Auxiliary Ambulance Service.' Our names came up, for all the world to see, followed by: 'on loan from London Auxiliary Ambulance Stations 11 and 39'.

Words scrolled down the screen: 'This is a story of the London Blitz – and of those who drive their ambulances into the teeth of the storm to ferry the injured to hospital. Many parts are played by the ambulance girls themselves. This film is dedicated to them and to their sisters – to the Ambulance Girls of the London Auxiliary Ambulance Service.'

And it began.

Magic had taken place since we had filmed it. The ambulance common room looked authentic. There I was, shirt buttons straining, silk-clad legs a mile long, reading a newspaper. I looked quite fetching, I thought. Lily looked adorable, reading her book. Celia rolled her wool, the picture of a serene English beauty.

'Cor,' said a male voice behind me. 'I like the little one.'

'How about the legs on that one at the front,' whispered his neighbour, then said something quite vulgar about my straining shirt buttons.

'Want me to take him out the back?' whispered Moray.

I laughed and shook my head.

'I'll have the one that's winding the wool,' said a third man. 'What a beauty. I've been waiting all my life for you, me darling.'

Celia was sitting next to me and I felt her stiffen. Simon put his arm around her and when he whispered something, she laughed.

On the screen, Rose, Henry and Bert spoke of Careless Talk and Victory Gardens. The noise of the planes increased and I said, in a sweet and crystal-clear voice: 'My word, Jerry is coming over thick and fast tonight.'

It really didn't sound like my voice and I wondered how they had done it. As the scene went on it dawned on my befuddled mind that it hadn't sounded like me because it wasn't my voice. It was a nice voice, but it wasn't mine.

Lily/Sheila spoke in her own voice, and Diana/Lady Harriet spoke in hers. Why hadn't they kept my voice?

In the background, Celia industriously wound her wool. They cut to the group, then back to Celia, who dropped the ball of wool. As she did so she laughed in surprise, and her face suddenly came alive. 'Oh gosh,' she said, 'I've dropped the blinking wool.' It sounded like Celia's voice, but they'd changed two words. The telephone rang and the mood darkened. We departed to face who knew what dangers.

The movie continued. We dashed in and out of the smoke during a raid. I was clearly visible in a couple of shots, looking grimly efficient. The shot of Lily's face, filthy and marked by the tracks of her tears, was deeply moving. There was humour and then real tension when Rose and shop girl Avis were inside the burning building. The audience cheered when they emerged out of the smoke carrying their patient. The film ended in a voiceover saying that we owed much to the selfless bravery of London's ambulance girls. The audience clapped and whistled and cheered.

It wasn't a bad film, not wonderful, but not bad.

We all had a whispered conversation during the short interval. Lily, Jim, Celia, Simon, Moray and I decided to leave before the feature film. The rest stayed on to watch it.

Lily was in a good mood as we stood together in the foyer. 'I think that went very well indeed,' she said. 'Let's go to a Corner House for supper. I was too anxious to eat anything before we came.'

'You were fabulous,' said Jim, giving her a kiss. 'Knew you would be.'

'As far as I'm concerned, Celia stole the show,' said Simon. 'Especially when she dropped the blinking wool.'

Celia rolled her eyes. 'They moved things around. I actually dropped it at the end of the scene. And they changed my bloody to a blinking.'

'Quite right, too,' said Moray. 'It's a family show.' He turned at me. 'How did you manage to make your voice sound so different? It didn't sound like you at all.'

I gave him a look. 'That's because it wasn't my voice. It was someone else's voice. A professional actress probably.'

Lily nodded. 'I thought they must have done that.' She smiled and said, sympathetically, 'You've a much nicer voice than the one they dubbed over yours.'

'Obviously Mr Denbeigh didn't agree,' I said.

'Don't worry about it, Maisie,' said Simon. 'You looked gorgeous.'

I smiled and made some reply, but inside I was fuming. What was the matter with my voice? By the last few takes I thought I'd done very well indeed. They should have told me what they were going to do, not let me find out in a cinema surrounded by my friends.

Someone called out my name and I turned. Dan Lowell was striding towards us. I felt physically ill to see him. The rotter had tricked me and he was the reason that Michael had been forced to leave Britain. I had no desire to speak to him.

'Maisie,' he said, with a brilliant smile, as if we were good friends. 'You were spectacular.' He looked at Celia. 'You, too. What a show! You must both be over the moon. I saw you creeping away and had to come out to offer my congratulations.'

Celia made the introductions, but I saw her frown at Lowell's slight hesitation before shaking hands with Simon Levy. Jim was his usual reserved self, and you'd never dream from his demeanour that he'd ever heard the name Dan Lowell.

By the time the introductions were complete I had control of my emotions and could greet Lowell reasonably cordially, if without any enthusiasm. He didn't seem to notice my reticence, and asked me about making the movie.

'Oh, it was an experience,' I said. 'I'm not intending to do it again.'

'I hope you do. You're quite the actress. Every word was crystal clear. I liked your stage voice.'

I gave him a weak smile.

'Well, I'd better be going,' he said.

Jim spoke up. 'We're off to the Corner House for a bite to eat. Care to join us?' I gave him a startled look, which he ignored.

'That would be swell,' said Lowell, smiling.

As we stumbled through the dark streets towards Piccadilly and the Corner House I thought about why Jim had invited

Lowell to join us. Michael had told me that Jim's people were looking into the man. I decided that Jim saw this as a good opportunity to get to know Lowell better.

It was a pleasant dinner. Lowell was entertaining, if a bit too self-possessed and self-regarding. He sat next to me and kept up a flow of animated conversation, mainly about himself, and the people he knew.

'What do you fly?' he asked Jim, who was in his RAF uniform.

'Used to fly Hurricanes, but I was shot down last year and at the moment I'm a ground wallah.'

'Say what?'

'RAF officer who doesn't fly.'

'Your boys sure have been doing well against the Luftwaffe lately.' He grinned. 'You can't tell me it's all down to carrots. I eat a lot of carrots, but I can't see in the dark.'

Jim shrugged.

'Say, Jim, your last name sounds Russian' he said.

'I was born in Russia,' said Jim. 'Before the Revolution.'

'Not a commie?'

'Quite the opposite.'

'So you're one of those White Russians.'

'Yes.'

'Hate the commies?'

'Yes. Of course. With a passion. What about you?'

'So do I. You know, I think Communist Russia is as much a threat to this country, and to America, as the Nazis are. Maybe more.'

'You may be right,' said Moray, to my surprise.

Simon said, in his quiet voice, 'It's not the Russians who are bombing London. I think we'll all agree that Nazi Germany is the greater threat right now.'

'Well, of course,' said Moray. 'But Mr Lowell has a point. In many ways it's a shame that we ever got pulled into war with Germany. Together, Germany and Britain could have defeated Stalin.'

Simon turned to him, frowning. He opened his mouth to speak, thought better of it and stood up. 'I've an early shift at the hospital tomorrow,' he said, 'so I'll leave you all now. It was great to see you up on screen, ambulance girls.'

Celia stood, too. 'I'll join you. Goodbye everyone.'

They left.

I saw Moray and Lowell exchange amused looks. Seething, I stood and murmured something about powdering my nose. Lily joined me in the ladies' room.

'He's a pig,' I said. 'An utter pig. And Moray's no better.'

Lily stopped putting on her lipstick and stared at me in the mirror. 'Jim's been goading him, letting him talk. There's a reason.'

'But what about Moray?'

'He probably has his reasons, too.'

As we were about to leave at the end of the evening, Lowell smiled at me. 'I was going to phone you, Maisie,' he said. 'Ask you for a repeat of our lunch. I really enjoyed seeing you that day. I hope my company wasn't tiresome. Please say you'll meet me again.'

I was about to make a polite excuse when I caught Jim's eye. He gave me a slight nod, as if he wanted me to accept the invitation. I hesitated, then smiled and murmured that I'd be delighted. Lowell beamed at me.

'Are you free tomorrow?' Lowell asked. 'We could go back to the pub in Surrey.'

A slight shake of the head from Jim.

'I'm sorry,' I said, 'but I'm busy tomorrow.'

'Next Saturday?'

'That would be lovely.'

'That's swell. I'll pick you up at noon.' He strolled off with a jaunty air.

As we walked along Piccadilly looking for a taxi (they were hailed by shining your torch at your feet), Jim deftly managed to arrange it so that he and I fell a little behind Lily and Moray.

'Well done,' he said.

'What was that all about?'

'Look, I'd like to talk about it with you before your date with Lowell. Would you meet me tomorrow?'

'How can I refuse when it's all so mysterious?' I paused. 'Um, John Casey confronted me this afternoon. He thinks I've got . . . what I gave to Michael Harker. He threatened me.'

Jim frowned. 'We'll discuss it tomorrow. I'll pick you up at one o'clock. Outside the Theatre Girls' Club.'

CHAPTER THIRTY-FOUR

The following afternoon Jim arrived in large black saloon driven by a pretty ATS girl.

'Where are we going?' I asked him, once we were seated together in the back.

'Pimlico.'

I don't know what answer I was expecting, but Pimlico wasn't it. He said nothing further, so I sat back and watched the wounded face of London go by as the driver wound through the usual diversions. Eventually we arrived at a quiet stretch of road by the side of the Thames and pulled up outside the entrance to a modern and expensive-looking block of red-brick flats. 'Dolphin Square' was in letters over the centre of three archways leading into the complex.

I'd heard of it, of course. Dolphin Square was a massive group of flats that had been built at great cost in 1936. It was quite the address. Oswald and Diana Mosley had lived there before Oswald Mosley's arrest last year. I'd heard the place was full of aristocrats, and also politicians, who enjoyed its proximity to the Houses of Parliament. I suspected that most of the residents had scurried back to their country houses and electorates when the bombs began to fall.

As we entered through a massive portico, the development seemed to me to rather resemble a posh prison. The sixteen (I counted them) blocks of flats were connected to each other and arranged around a central quadrangle. This was planted with grass and trees and criss-crossed by paths, like an exclusive exercise yard.

Despite its important residents, the Blitz had not missed Dolphin Square. Two blocks of flats were in ruins and a massive bomb crater destroyed the symmetry of the gardens. I felt a twinge of satisfaction to think that, in this war, luxury and wealth were no guarantee of safety. Then I felt terribly guilty and hoped that no one had been killed or injured in the raid.

Jim led me to the third block on the eastern side. The lobby was clean and modern with a very shiny floor and wave decorations in the plaster of the walls. Behind a porter's desk to the side sat an elderly gentleman in a uniform who sported a natty moustache. I gave him a smile and he smiled back. Jim gave our names and said we were there to see Mr Temple. The porter assumed a solemn expression, picked up the telephone receiver on his desk and dialled a number.

'Flight Lieutenant Vassy – vassykoff and Miss Halliday are here,' he said in the sort of earnestly solemn tone reserved for the terrifyingly important. 'Yes. I'll do that.'

I began to wonder if I should be apprehensive about meeting this Mr Temple. On reflection, I decided not. I was doing a favour for these people by going out with the poisonous Dan Lowell. It was up to Jim and Mr Temple to flatter and cajole me into doing what they wanted. And if I didn't want to do it, then I jolly well wouldn't.

The porter walked with us across the shiny lobby to the lift, which gave us a smooth, almost silent ride to the sixth floor. I followed Jim as we both trod noiselessly along the carpeted corridor. He stopped outside a door marked '608'. The dignified silence of Dolphin Square made me feel nervous, and despite my intentions to be cool and relaxed, my heart began to thump. I wondered if Jim would use a special knock, as the spies always did at the flicks, but it was tap, tap, tap, just as normal people knocked, only quieter.

An efficient-looking young woman in a neat suit stood in the doorway, and said, quietly, 'Flight Lieutenant, Miss Halliday. Do come in.'

I could only assume that even her crisp efficiency quailed at pronouncing Jim's surname without practice. The thought gave me heart.

She led us down an oblong hall that had been laid with cork, Our shoes made no sound as we followed her to the lounge.

The room had been set up as an office. Antique-looking furniture gave a it an air of solid respectability, but all I could think of was how much it resembled a stage set. *Act one, scene one: In the spymaster's study*.

A man with thick dark hair and a long face sat behind an ornate desk in front of a large window. He was probably in his early forties, and was wearing tweeds, like a country gentleman. His watchful light-coloured eyes were not quite green, not quite blue. A pipe jutted from the side of his mouth and the room was scented with the aroma of tobacco. I thought him rather ordinary-looking, but then supposed that spymasters would need to be inconspicuous. In front of him were a telephone and a typewriter and one file, closed, from which I deduced that the spymaster had a neat mind. He stood and came out from behind the desk to greet us.

'How d'ye do?' he said to Jim. 'I hear you've been busy.' His voice was soft and slightly breathy.

Then he turned to me. 'Miss Halliday. I'm delighted to meet you. You may call me Captain Temple.'

I wondered if Temple was his real name and if he was actually a captain. I murmured a greeting.

'Please, do sit down,' he said. 'Would you care for anything. A drink, cup of tea?'

I was longing for a cup of tea but, taking Jim's lead, I declined the offer. Captain Temple waved me towards the sofa, where I perched uncomfortably while he and Jim took an armchair each. Miss Quiet and Efficient left the room, closing the door behind her and it wasn't long before the muffled sound of a typewriter drifted in.

Temple turned to me and smiled. 'You must be wondering why I asked Jim to bring you here, Miss Halliday.'

'I think it's to do with Mr Lowell of the American Embassy,' I said, looking straight into his pale eyes. They reminded me of a bird's eyes, sharp and watchful. 'Jim seemed to want me to accept Mr Lowell's invitation to lunch next Saturday. But you should also know that Mr Casey threatened me yesterday.'

'You're a woman who comes straight to the point, I see. Capital. Yes. We want to speak to you about Mr Lowell and Mr Casey. Also Mr Harker and Mr Egan.'

I couldn't help giving a slight jump when he mentioned Michael's name. He drew on his pipe. A thin stream of smoke soon escaped from his lips and as the musty scent of his tobacco wafted over to me I pictured him in a deerstalker saying, 'Ah ha, Watson, the game's afoot.'

'Before we get to the purpose of your visit here today, I have to make a few things clear,' he said.

'Yes?'

'What we are about to discuss is top secret. Do you understand what I mean by that?' As before, his soft voice had a breathy quality that made it seem almost as if he was whispering.

'I understand,' I said.

I did understand. I'd seen the posters: 'Careless talk costs lives'; Keep it under your hat'; 'Keep Mum, she's not so dumb'; 'Be like Dad and keep Mum'. Just the other week I'd watched a propaganda film in which a tiny bit of gossip in the pub had caused the deaths of hundreds of British sailors. I understood very well what top secret meant.

'What it means,' he went on, as if I'd not spoken, 'is that our discussions today relate to the security of this country. What it means, Miss Halliday, is that if you divulge a word of what we speak about this afternoon, you will be liable to ten years' gaol with hard labour.'

My heart gave a thump. I hadn't known that.

'Nor must you reveal anything of the matters which led to me asking you to come here today. You spoke about them to Mrs Ashwin and Dr Levy. Don't do so again. Anything that relates to the death of Harry Egan, what he carried and what happened to it must be kept absolutely secret. Do you understand that, Miss Halliday?'

'Yes,' I said, looking straight into his eyes. 'I understand. I won't say a word to anyone about any of it.' What he had said had shocked me into an appreciation of just what I was involved with. It was deadly serious and as dangerous as Michael had told me.

'Good.' His smile was charming, good-humoured and avuncular. It terrified me. He puffed on his pipe and said, 'It is frequently alleged that women are less discreet than men, because that they are ruled by their emotions and not by their brains. My own experience has been very much to the contrary. I have investigated a large number – possibly hundreds – of cases of loose talk and have found that in most instances by far the greater proportion of the offenders were men, usually trying to build themselves up to other men or impress a woman.'

All the time he was talking he subjected me to that sharp, birdlike gaze. I felt like a small, furry creature faced with a swooping owl, transfixed not so much by terror as by awe.

'I can be discreet when I need to be,' I said. 'I can keep secrets.'

He nodded as if he knew that already and I wondered if my background had been investigated already by this frighteningly gentle and soft-spoken man.

'You must be wondering who I am, what I do,' said Temple. 'My job is a simple one. It involves keeping an eye, and often two, on any undesirables who may be in this country. Sometimes this means lifting up a log in order to expose the things that lurk in the dark underneath it. Sometimes it means investigating in places that should be above reproach, such as the American Embassy.'

I nodded, imagining Dan Lowell and John Casey as cockroaches, scurrying around under a log.

'What exactly did Mr Harker tell you about what Mr Egan was carrying when he died?' asked Temple.

'I know it was a little package of microfilm. I found it behind the photograph in Mr Egan's watch fob. Mr Harker told me it contained photographs of damaging correspondence between Mr Churchill and Mr Roosevelt.'

Jim and Temple exchanged looks, and I had a moment of doubt. Surely I was right to trust Michael. He couldn't be one of the nasty creatures crawling around under Temple's rock. I couldn't have misjudged him so badly.

'That's what Mr Harker told me,' I said, now feeling uncertain.

'He thought it did contain such correspondence when he went to the Café de Paris that night,' said Temple, in his soft, whispery voice. 'He assumed it was similar to a case last year, when an American cypher clerk called Tyler Kent at the American embassy had been secretly copying correspondence between Winston Churchill and President Roosevelt for a far-right group in London. The American clerk was prosecuted in secret, along with others, and is currently serving time in a British prison.'

I was puzzled. 'If he worked for the embassy wasn't he immune from prosecution?'

'Ambassador Kennedy revoked his diplomatic immunity when the situation was explained to him,' said Jim.

'I should mention that the Americans were not at all pleased to learn that we'd had one of their employees under surveillance,' said Temple. 'Not pleased at all. So we need to tread very cautiously in this case.'

'Michael Harker was posted to London to prevent such incidents occurring again,' said Jim.

'So Michael Harker is a spy?' I said.

He's an investigator,' said Jim. 'What they call a Special Agent. He works for the War Department, on secondment from the US Federal Bureau of Investigation.'

My eyes grew wider. I'd heard of the FBI, who investigated spies and gangsters in the United States. They were called G-Men. I knew that because I'd seen the James Cagney movie.

'Then why were the people at the embassy so angry that Michael had searched Egan's body? Surely it was his job.'

'Harker has no formal embassy position,' said Jim. 'He must defer to officers from the Department of State, who are responsible for embassy security and who see him as treading on their toes. He is in a difficult position. He was unwilling to tell them that he has seen the microfilm. All he could say was that he was suspicious about Egan's integrity and motives for going to the nightclub, and that is why he searched his body and obtained the watch fob from you. Not surprisingly, his explanation was not well received.'

'Michael hasn't told anyone at the embassy that Egan had microfilm and he found it?'

'No,' said Temple.

'Why not?'

'Once he had a look at it he knew that someone else at the embassy had to be involved in the matter. Egan didn't have the security clearance to allow him even to see what was on the microfilm, let alone the opportunity to photograph it.'

'Which means whoever gave it to Egan will be desperate to get it back, in case it can incriminate them,' said Jim.

'So it's not just correspondence?' I said.

'It's much more important than that,' said Temple. 'If the information it contained fell into German hands, it could cost us the war.'

I stared at him, wide-eyed. *Was this real?* I'd carried the microfilm in my handbag for over a day.

Temple puffed on his pipe again, and seemed to be thinking. 'Miss Halliday, what I am about to tell you is about as secret as it gets, but I believe in letting my agents know the truth.'

My heart began to pound. *His agents?*

'What did the microfilm contain?' My voice was surprisingly level, when my heart was racing like an express train.

Jim answered. 'The schematics of a device that uses magnetic waves to pinpoint the position of German bombers. When it is placed in the noses of our planes it enables our RAF night fighters to greatly increase the numbers of planes they shoot down.'

I threw Jim a triumphant smile. 'I knew it wasn't carrots.'

'No, not carrots,' said Jim, with a laugh. 'That information campaign served a dual purpose. We got rid of a glut of carrots by convincing people eating heaps of them would help their eyesight, and we were able to provide an explanation for the sudden increase in German bombers being shot down at night.'

'Very clever,' I said.

'We shared the invention with the Americans, partly in gratitude for Lend-Lease. They have fine-tuned the process and are mass producing the items for use in our aircraft and in their own,' said Jim. 'It's technology that the Germans don't have and obviously it's crucial that they don't get it.'

'Someone with a very high security clearance at the American Embassy gave Egan the microfilm,' whispered Temple, 'knowing he would hand it to a British fifth columnist.'

'Was it Lowell?' I asked, almost whispering myself. 'Casey?'

Jim shrugged. 'Harker thinks it is one or both of them, but there are a few other possibilities. Harker doesn't trust anyone at the embassy any more. It was a risky strategy for him, speaking to me about it, but he was desperate.'

'Miss Halliday, I cannot emphasise enough how serious is the threat of information such as this falling into Nazi hands,' said Temple. 'We need to know that we can safely share our secrets with the Americans. Our ability to defend this country would be severely compromised if we cannot. We must be able to uncover the traitor at the embassy.'

His face was grim, and I believed every word.

I said, slowly, 'But isn't it just as important to find out who Mr Egan was meeting that night? The name of the German spy or British fifth columnist who was going to give the information to Berlin?'

Temple and Jim exchanged looks. Temple nodded.

'Egan thought he was meeting a British fifth columnist who had contacts in Berlin,' said Jim, 'but he wasn't. It was one of Captain Temple's men. We set up the operation months ago, after the conviction of the embassy clerk. Egan contacted our agent, saying that he had important material that should be sent to Berlin. We didn't know what it was. Like Harker, we thought it was probably correspondence.'

'Why didn't you tell Michael Harker what you were doing?'

'Just as the Americans keep secrets from us, we need to keep secrets from them.' Temple was unapologetic. 'We intended to gather the evidence and present it to the ambassador, exactly as we did last year with Mr Tyler Kent. We weren't aware that Mr Harker had found out about Mr Egan.'

'The problem we're facing is that we thought Egan was the only Nazi collaborator who remained at the embassy,' said Jim. 'Now Harker tells us that someone higher up must also be involved. We need to find out who it is and expose them before they can do real damage to this country.'

'Mr Harker would have been the best person for that job,' said Temple. 'Unfortunately, he has been sent away.'

'Can you get him brought back?' I asked, trying to mask the hopeful note in my voice.

'We're working on it,' said Temple. '

'I don't understand why you're telling me this,' I said. 'What do you want from me?'

Temple frowned and sucked on his pipe. 'If I had my way I'd have properly trained you, but we need to act quickly.'

Train me? The conversation was rapidly becoming bizarre. It was as if I had slipped into a twisty, unfathomable world and I wasn't sure how I would escape from it.

'I don't understand,' I repeated.

Captain Temple leaned closer. I resisted the temptation to move back, away from that unsettling gaze.

'Miss Halliday, you have one great advantage over trained agents.'

'What advantage do I have?'

'You are already on good terms with Dan Lowell.'

'I detest Dan Lowell.'

'Hide your contempt. He appears to like you. What we want you to do is to become a closer friend of his.'

'A closer friend,' I said, on a gasp. 'What do you mean. How close? Mata-Hari close? I can't do that. I *won't* do that.'

Temple shook his head and seemed pained. 'A common misconception about secret service work is that women must use sex to gather information,' he said, on a puff of pipe smoke. 'I am no believer in what has been described as Mata-Hari methods. I am convinced that more information has been obtained by women agents if they keep out of the arms of the man than was ever obtained if they sink too willingly into them.'

'So what exactly do you want me to—'

'I do *not* want you to attempt to seduce Mr Lowell. What is required in this case is a clever woman who can use her personal attractions wisely.'

'My personal attractions? I'm not sure what—'

'Nothing is easier than for an attractive woman to gain a man's confidence.'

I gazed helplessly at Jim, who shrugged. It was *Ambulance Girls At War* all over again. They wanted me to do something I was not able to do, thinking that my assets would be enough to get me through. Only this time no one could dub over my voice when I was with Lowell.

'Captain Temple, I'm the worst actress imaginable.'

'All the evidence points to you being an intelligent and resourceful young woman. Brave, too. Patriotic.'

I broke in forcefully, 'And a terrible actress. I'd probably just make things worse.'

'If the Nazi collaborator is Mr Lowell, then he is not sure where the microfilm is. There are four alternatives: you have it, Mr Harker has it, before he died Mr Egan managed to give it to the man he was to meet that night, or it was destroyed in the explosion. He knows that Mr Egan slipped the fob into your pocket after he saw Mr Harker. That makes it much more likely that you removed it from the fob, or Mr Harker did after he took it from you. If he thinks you have it then you may be in danger. We intend to use Lowell's lack of knowledge to our advantage and we need your assistance to do so.'

'Casey threatened me yesterday. He thinks I have the microfilm. Doesn't that make it more likely that it was Casey who gave it to Egan?'

'Leave Casey to us. We need you to deal with Lowell. Will you help us?'

My throat felt very dry. Was I in danger? Could I act the part required? I looked at the floor and thought about it. I was used to flirting with men, being thought desirable, using my assets to make men desire me when I was onstage. I was able to be friendly to the most odious of men; you have to, when you work onstage, and I'd been doing so for years. I was also used to rejecting unwelcome advances, so I knew how to stop Lowell getting too amorous. *Maybe I could do this*.

Temple and Jim were both watching me. I took a deep breath and let it out slowly. If doing this would help my country, if it would help Michael, then how could I hesitate?

'What exactly do you want me to do?'

'We want you to meet Mr Lowell and be friendly to him. We need you to give him certain information, but discreetly in the course of a seemingly innocent conversation.'

Jim spoke up. 'In a nutshell, you need to make Lowell think that Jack Moray is a sympathiser to the fascist cause, and that

Moray has the microfilm. Moray's been briefed and he knows what to do.'

Flabbergasted. That was the word. *Flabbergasted.*

'Jack Moray?' I said, weakly. 'My station leader? Moray's a bank clerk.'

Jim smiled. 'He's a bit more than that, but as we said earlier, all of this is top secret. It is crucial that Moray's activities are kept confidential.'

His activities? Moray was a spy? Again my head seemed to spin. Was anything what I had thought it to be? Anyone?

I blew out a breath. 'What you're saying is that Mr Egan was going to meet Moray that night in the Café de Paris?'

Temple shook his head. 'No. He was meeting another agent. The bomb detonated before our man could make contact with Egan. I now think that it was a stroke of luck, because otherwise we'd not have been able to be informed by Mr Harker that Egan was simply the man in the middle.'

I stared at him. *Luck? Did he know how many people had died?*

'What if it isn't Lowell?'

'If he doesn't act on the information you give him, then we'll know to look elsewhere, probably John Casey.'

'Perhaps you'd better explain the plan to me,' I said. 'In simple words, please, and in detail.'

So they did.

CHAPTER THIRTY-FIVE

Dan Lowell picked me up in the same showy black saloon as before, and drove out of London, just as he had before. I'd dressed carefully, in a light summer frock with a lacy cardigan. After a cool start to summer, the weather had been gradually improving and that day was sunny and fairly warm. Fluffy white clouds drifted over the fields ahead of us. I imagined myself back in the south of France, tried to remember how I used to flirt, in the French way. Lightly and delicately.

'It's so lovely to breathe air that's not scented with brick dust,' I said, smiling and tilting my head slightly.

'They seem to have stopped bombing London.'

'The tip-and-run raiders still cause us problems. Even one raider can do a lot of damage, injure a lot of people. We were very busy on Thursday night. It gets you down after a while, all the damage and injuries. So it's lovely to escape to the country. Thanks ever so much for inviting me.'

Lowell smiled. 'Thank you for agreeing to come out with me. Our last meeting was tense.'

'Because of Michael Harker?' It was surprisingly pleasant to say Michael's name to this man, who hated him enough to wrongly blame him for Egan's death. A secret thrill ran through me to use such an off-hand tone in speaking of Michael.

'Yes,' said Lowell.

I shrugged, dismissively. 'Is he still in England? I've not heard from him for weeks.'

'No. He was sent away.'

'What you told me about him shocked me, but I did feel sad for him, losing his wife like that and I can understand why he might want vengeance.' I stole a look at Lowell. 'He came to see me that night – after you and I met for lunch – and he was very angry at me indeed. We argued and he stormed off. It was horrible.'

Lowell shifted down a gear to drive off the main road on to a smaller, country road. 'I'm sorry to hear that. I got the feeling you really liked him.'

'I did. I thought he was a nice man, and I was sorry we had such a nasty row. Anyway, he never contacted me again, so that's that.'

'Stupid of him.' Lowell smiled. 'Do you think I'm a nice man?'

I gave a laugh. 'I hardly know you, Mr Lowell. So far, you seem very likeable, but I'll – hmm – I'll reserve my opinion.'

Lowell laughed as well. It was all very jolly, but I itched to slap him.

We pulled up at the same pretty country pub as before, and sat in the garden until lunch was ready. As before, I had a sherry and Lowell had a beer.

'I'd love to visit the United States some day,' I said. 'It's such a fascinating country. Of course I only know what I see in the movies. You, Mr Casey and Michael Harker are the only Americans I've really met.' Which was a lie, but made me sound naïve and unsophisticated.

Lowell gave me a lazy smile. 'I'll head back to the States next year, probably.'

'Lucky you. Escaping the bombing. Where are you from in America?'

'I was born in Columbus, Ohio.'

'Pretty name. Columbus.'

'It's a great place, but I haven't lived there for years. I was living and working in DC before I came here.'

I smiled at him. 'I have no idea what that means.'

'Washington DC. Our nation's capital.'

'Oh, I suppose that makes sense, if you were working for the embassy. What do you do there?'

'I'm involved with security.'

'Important work,' I said, sounding impressed. 'Mr Harker never told me what he did, but I thought it must be that sort of thing.'

'Because he searched poor Harry Egan's body?'

I nodded, hoping he hadn't invited me to lunch for the sole purpose of trying to obtain more information about Michael Harker, wanting to discredit him further.

We were called into lunch, watercress soup ('from our own stream'), baked rabbit ('trapped the coneys yesterday') and peach cobbler ('with our Daisy's cream').

'I really do like you a lot, Maisie,' he said over the soup. 'I know you blame me for making Harker mad at you, but honestly, I was just trying to warn you about him, stop you from making a mistake with that guy. You're too nice a girl to get your heart broken by someone like him. I hope you can forgive me.'

He sounded sincere, and I wasn't sure how to respond.

'I don't need looking after,' I said, with my best French pout.

'I know that, but I think Mike Harker's bad news. I really do, Maisie. He caused us all sorts of trouble. And then he got you to lie for him. A man wouldn't do that if he really cared about a girl.'

I looked down. I'd never been sure why I hadn't told anyone about Michael searching Egan's body, but Michael had never asked me to lie for him. He'd allowed me to make my own decision.

'I suppose you're right,' I murmured, and looked at him, again through my lashes.

Lowell was a handsome man and the smile he gave me lit his face. It still didn't affect my breathing or heart rate in any way. I had to face facts; I was besotted with Michael Harker. And that meant I had to get him back to Britain. The best way to do that was to expose Lowell or Casey or whoever was the traitor.

As we drank coffee, spy Maisie made an appearance as I performed the first of the tasks that Temple had given to me.

'It was interesting,' I said, 'what you were saying the other night about the communists in Russia being worse than the Germans.'

Lowell gave me a cool look. 'Why was that interesting?'

'I met a few White Russians when I was dancing in France, and their stories about what happened in Russia during the Revolution were chilling. They hated the Soviets much more than the Germans. That was before the invasion of France, of course. But Moray also says that Communist Russia is a much more dangerous enemy to Britain than Germany and I respect his opinion on such things.'

'Did Michael Harker discuss any of this with you?'

'Not really. He said that we Londoners were very brave and he had a lot of respect for us.' I screwed up my face, as if thinking. 'No, we didn't discuss politics really. He said that he supported Roosevelt and was pleased that he was helping us.' I looked at Lowell. 'I am, too. Although I really don't understand Lend-Lease at all.'

I sounded like a five-year-old, which annoyed me. But Temple had instructed me to act as if I was young, inexperienced in political matters and uninterested in them. He also told me to slip in a few interesting 'facts' about Moray and what he believed in.

I leaned in towards Lowell and whispered, 'Moray even visited Germany a few years ago. Before the war, of course. Sometimes I wonder if he might have German blood, but Moray isn't a German name.' I had decided to throw this in, just to see if Lowell took the bait.

'You don't need a German name to be from German stock,' said Lowell. 'My mom's parents were born in Germany.' He shrugged. 'Germans make up the biggest immigrant group in the States. John Casey's name was originally Classen but they changed it in the last war.' He laughed. 'Your own Royal family changed its name from Battenberg to Mountbatten. It's not sinister. Being of German blood doesn't automatically make you a supporter of Hitler.'

I smiled, and said, 'Well, Moray says that Hitler is absolutely right about one thing.'

'And what's that,' said Lowell, sounding bored.

Again I screwed up my face as if thinking. 'That the survival of the white race is the most important thing. More important than anything. And that's why he hopes the government makes peace with Germany and then we both turn on Russia.'

Lowell nodded. 'That Mr Murray – is that the name? – he sounds like a fella with some common sense.'

I gave a gurgle of laughter. 'No, it's Moray. M O R A Y. He's awfully brave, and very good as a station leader. We all think the world of him, although he was horrid to David Levy, who used to work with us. Moray really doesn't like Jews.'

'Levy? Celia Ashwin's new man?'

'No, that's Simon Levy. David was his brother, who died.' I shook my head. 'Isn't it scandalous? Her and Simon Levy, I mean.'

He nodded. 'Her husband, Cedric Ashwin, will be turning in his grave.'

'Ugh,' I said, with a delicate shudder. 'I hate that expression.' *Ugh indeed!* Spy Maisie was such a chuff.

'It's a strange pairing, that's for sure,' said Lowell.

'I just think it's *wrong*. But it's her life, of course. Moray is upset about it, I can tell.'

Spy Maisie was a chuff and anti-Semitic. I detested spy Maisie, who was pretty much everything I loathed.

'Because he hates Jews?'

'Probably. And I think he has a bit of a thing for Celia. Most men do.'

'I prefer brunettes,' said Lowell, with a smile.

He got a flirty glance through my lashes for that remark, and a simpering smile. Inside I was becoming worried. I had one more task to carry out, but I wasn't sure how to introduce it.

'Mr Egan's locket certainly caused a lot of trouble,' I said artlessly. 'Gosh it scared me when the police thought I'd stolen it. Moray said I wasn't to worry and he'd support me. When I showed it to him, he told me it wasn't in the least valuable, but I suppose the photograph might have had sentimental value to Mr Egan's widow.'

Lowell gave me a considering look. 'When did Moray see it? I thought you told the police that you'd left it at your club. You told me and Casey that Harker tricked you into giving it to him the following morning, before you could take it to Scotland Yard.'

'Oh, yes. What I told the men from Scotland Yard was absolutely true. I *had* left it at the club because I never expected that the police would turn up at the station that day. But after they left, I was so worried about it all that I had a long talk to Moray. He said he would support me if any charges were brought against me for looting, but he said he wanted to see the locket first. So I popped back to the club and picked it up to show him.'

Lowell was now staring at me. 'You didn't mention any of this to Casey and me.'

I opened my eyes widely. 'Didn't I? I told you I'd wanted to discuss it with Mr Moray.' I frowned. 'Or did I tell the police that?'

He said, in the measured tone people used when talking to small children, 'You told the police that you wanted to discuss it with Moray, but you'd forgotten to do so and you didn't have the locket with you because you'd left it at your boarding house.'

I nodded vigorously. 'Yes. That's right. And after the police left I *did* discuss it with Moray. He told me he wanted to see it. So I dashed home to get it.'

'And he examined it thoroughly?'

I shrugged. 'I suppose so. I left it with him while I went to an incident.'

'What did he say when you got back?'

'He said that it was not very valuable, and I shouldn't worry about being charged with theft for not turning it in immediately.'

Lowell nodded, but his mind was obviously elsewhere. I'd done the two tasks I'd been appointed, made it clear that Moray sympathised with fascism and let Lowell think that Moray had probably taken the microfilm. *Well done, spy Maisie.*

'I wish I knew why Mr Egan gave it to me,' I said, hoping I wasn't over-egging the pudding. 'He seemed upset to see Mr Harker. Perhaps that was it.'

Lowell nodded vacantly. 'Perhaps.' He seemed to collect himself. 'Mr Moray's right,' he said. 'Don't you worry about being charged. I'm sure no one thinks you're a thief.'

The date went steadily downhill from then on. Lowell was obviously distracted, worried. He stopped trying to flirt or to obtain information from me, except for a few moments just before we returned to London.

'So this Moray fella, what does he do in peacetime?' he asked.

'I think he's a bank clerk.'

When he dropped me at the club, Lowell didn't get out to open my door straight away.

'Thanks for a lovely day, Maisie,' he said. He didn't suggest another meeting, for which I was grateful. Temple had made it very clear that I was to have nothing to do with Lowell after I'd done what they wanted me to do.

'And thank *you* for lunch,' I said, simpering.

'We should do this again soon,' he said. He made no attempt to pin me down to an actual date. I was no fool. He was giving me what the Americans called a brush off. I gave him the feminine equivalent.

'That would be lovely.' There was no hint of enthusiasm in my voice.

To make it perfectly clear, I leaned across and kissed his cheek, in the sexless sort of way a maiden aunt would kiss a schoolboy nephew.

We both now knew where we stood. Lowell saw me to the door of the club, returned to the car and drove off.

When I was alone in my room I thought about all that had happened that day. I'd done what I'd been instructed to do by Temple. I'd told Lowell about Moray being a fascist, and I'd led him to think that Moray had taken the microfilm. Whatever game Temple had in mind was now in play.

Jim had said that he would telephone me at the club that evening, so I went downstairs to the telephone to wait for the call. When it rang I picked it up immediately.

'Hello?'

Jim's oh-so-upper crust voice answered. 'Hello. This is Jim Vassilikov. May I speak to Miss Halliday please?'

'It's me.'

'All went well?'

'Very well, I think.'

'Excellent,' he said. 'Now forget all about it.'

But how could I do that?

CHAPTER THIRTY-SIX

Moray gave no indication that he knew that I knew about his other career when I arrived at the station early on Sunday morning. He waved at me through the office window when I entered the common room, as he always did, and made no effort to speak to me alone.

When we were sitting in the common room having elevenses Moray came in with his hands full of envelopes. He shook them at us.

'These have been forwarded from the Crown Film Unit. Looks like our Ambulance Girls have got themselves some fans.'

The letters bore a range of addresses: 'The girl who was Mary in *Ambulance Girls At War*', 'Miss Maisie Halliday (Mary) from *Ambulance Girls At War*'. Lily had used her maiden name in the credits, so her letters were addressed to: 'Miss Lily Brennan (Little Sheila) from the *Ambulance Girls* movie'. Somewhat surprisingly, Celia, who was addressed as 'The girl with the wool from *Ambulance Girls At War*', or 'Miss Palmer-Thomas (Lovely Linda) from *Ambulance Girls At War*, had ten letters, as many as me and Lily combined.

I ripped one of mine open and read it aloud:

Dear Miss Halliday,

I hope that this letter reaches you. Wow! You are gorgeous. I cannot describe my feelings or dwell on your beauty sufficiently without using every piece of paper for sale in the local shop.

You are an absolute stunner. I don't suppose you'd care for a pen pal? I'm in essential war work and can't make it to London, but we could write.
Your devoted friend,
Yours faithfully,
Stanley Evans

Lily opened one addressed to her, which said:

Dear Miss Brennan,
I saw you in the wonderful short movie, Ambulance Girls At War, last week and was I blown over by you. You are some sheila, Sheila!
I am a lonely digger over here in England and I'm probably your most devoted fan. I don't suppose we could meet?
Yours sincerely,
Charlie Williams

The others were all in a similar vein. Celia opened one of hers and burst out laughing.

Dear beautiful wool girl,
What a vision of loveliness you were in Ambulance Girls At War. Your white hands holding the wool, your expression of utter concentration, and your perfect Madonna-like features. Then you smiled! If you want to make a lonely airman happy, all you need do is to reply to this letter,
Yours sincerely,
Flying Officer Harwell

'Are you going to reply?' asked Powell.
The three of us exchanged glances and burst out laughing.
'Of course not,' said Lily.

*

The man was waiting outside our ambulance station when I went off shift the following morning. Average height (about an inch or so shorter than me), civilian clothes, grey raincoat and a shabby hat, standing stiffly in the early morning sunshine.

I waved at Celia, who raced past us on her bicycle. The man gazed at her until she disappeared around the corner, with an expression of what I could only describe as sheep-like devotion. When she was out of sight he turned and stared at me with an intensity in his eyes that I found off-putting. Especially when he stepped towards me.

'Miss Halliday?'

'Yes. Do I know you?'

'I think you do. I'm Albert Lee.'

I searched my memory, but the name was not one I recognised. 'I'm sorry but I don't ...'

'Was that Miss Palmer-Thomas? On the bike?'

'Um, I don't – oh, Celia? Yes, it was.'

'I wrote,' he said eagerly. 'I told you how much I admired you and Miss Palmer-Thomas. In the ambulance girls film. You were wonderful, Miss Halliday. And so was she.' I had no memory of reading his letter and wondered if it had been addressed to Celia.

'Thank you for the letter, Mr Lee,' I said. 'It's lovely to meet you and I'm glad that you enjoyed the film, but I really must go now. It's been a long night.'

'I'll walk you home,' he said.

I shook my head. 'No. Thank you but I'd rather walk alone.' He seemed about to remonstrate and I said quickly, 'Mr Lee, I'm engaged to be married. Please don't make a fuss.'

'Is there a problem?' Moray had come out of the station.

'Mr Lee is a fan of our film,' I said. 'I've explained that I don't want him to accompany me home.'

Moray stood, looking at the man, who scowled.

'It was a civil request,' he said to Moray. 'Young women like Miss Halliday shouldn't walk home alone. Anything could happen to her.'

'But it won't,' said Moray, with a scowl of his own. 'Be off with you. Miss Halliday has asked you to leave.'

The man strode off, but after walking about fifty yards, he stopped to frown at Moray. He spat on the ground, turned and walked off quickly before disappearing around a corner.

'And that's the problem with being famous, 'said Moray.

'Do you think he'll come back?' I asked. He didn't frighten me, but it would be tiresome having to deal with him again.

'Let's hope not.' Moray looked in the direction the man had taken. 'Like *me* to walk you home?'

I shook my head. 'I'm not afraid of someone like him. He'll be easy enough to deal with if he gets too annoying.'

Moray frowned. 'You're probably right, but try to keep to where there are people around, and if you feel worried, ask someone for help.'

I laughed. 'Men used to follow me down the street in Paris. I know what to do with annoying males. I've learned a few tricks over the years.'

'Got it. You can look after yourself,' he said, with a smile.

'You know that I showed you the, um, locket?' I said, with some hesitation.

Moray's smile faded. 'I know that. I had the thing for an hour or so when you were out at an incident. That's all you know about it, and let's not discuss it again.'

'Sorry.' I silently cursed myself for my stupidity. 'I'll be off home, then.'

I also silently cursed Mr Albert Lee as I trudged towards Soho in the early morning sunshine. For the first time, I felt apprehensive. I'd walked those streets in pitch darkness without any concerns, and now one strange man who thought he knew me because he'd seen me on film had destroyed that easy confidence.

My intuition was proved right. He reappeared when I was in the narrow alleyway leading to Oxford Street. I increased my pace. So did he.

'It's not safe for a girl as pretty as you to walk alone,' he said, in a hissing whisper as he came up close behind me. 'You're so pretty, Maisie Halliday. Drives a man to distraction.'

His arms came around me from behind, pinning my arms to my side. I froze, then instinct took over. I wished I was wearing high heels rather than sensible brogues as I brought my foot down hard on his instep. When he flinched in pain I elbowed him hard in the midsection, ducked down and brought my head back to connect with his jaw. He let go of me with a howl of pain and I ran, screaming loudly, towards Oxford Street. At the corner, I looked behind me. My heat was thumping and my breaths were hard and fast. Albert Lee was doubled up where I had left him, gasping for air.

'You aw'right, love?'

Two women had appeared from Oxford Street, street walkers from their outfits. I was so keyed up that it took me a couple of seconds to recognise Edna and her friend Rosie. They didn't need to be told what had happened.

'Did that bastard bother you?' said Edna.

In the alleyway, Mr Lee slowly got to his feet, scowling at the three of us. He flinched as Edna ran up to him, swung her handbag high and brought it down on his head. From the loud thump it made when it connected with his skull I surmised that it contained a bottle. Gin, probably. He fell to his knees and wrapped his arms around his head to protect it from further blows.

Rosie was close behind. She shrieked at him. 'You leave respectable young girls alone, you bastard,' and kicked him in the ribs. He cringed away from them, whimpering.

They ran back to me. 'C'm on love, let's get out of here 'fore the rozzers come.'

I shouted to Mr Lee. 'Don't you ever come near me again, or I'll have the law on you. I mean it, Albert Lee.'

We turned into Oxford Street and I marched home triumphantly with Edna and Rosie on either side of me.

CHAPTER THIRTY-SEVEN

'There's a man been asking about you,' said Lorna, when I came down to lunch at the club on Wednesday. It was two days after my run-in with Mr Lee and I had just risen from my morning nap after returning from my shift.

'What man?' I asked, hoping it was Michael.

'An old man. He asked for Miss Maisie Halliday, who was in the film about the ambulance girls.'

I sighed. 'Another fan. This is really becoming annoying. Is he still there?'

'No. He said he'd be back at teatime. He had a thick accent. Seemed nice enough.'

I didn't care how nice he was, I had no desire to meet another man like Mr Albert Lee. Should I slip out after lunch? On reflection I decided that it would be better to confront him and discover how he had found me at the club. A nasty thrill ran up my spine, like a thin shard of ice, because the most likely answer was that Mr Lee had followed me here and told his friends. It would be best to face down this mysterious old man on my home ground. The girls and Mrs King would support me if he became troublesome.

And so, after lunch I sat in the most comfortable armchair in the common room and read *David Copperfield* and waited. At four o'clock Millie put her head around the door.

'Man to see you downstairs, Miss.'

I jumped to my feet and prepared to do battle. 'It's so annoying,' I said to her. 'Just because you're in a film they think they know you. Think they can—'

'But miss,' said Millie, 'he says he's your granddad.'

He looked very much as he had eight years ago, the last time I'd seen him. Then he had stood beside Nannan, red-faced and shouting that Mam and I would be going straight to the Devil if we went to London.

Granddad was still a powerfully built man, although he was now close to seventy and the hair that showed under his cloth cap had turned pure white. The only concession to his age seemed to be a slight stoop, because his shoulders were as broad as I remembered, his blue eyes still blazed with intelligence and fervour and his moustache bristled just as ferociously as it had done when I was a child.

'Granddad?' I said, and was shocked when his eyes filled with tears.

'Maisie,' he said, and dashed a hand across his eyes. 'It's right good to see you. How are you, Maisie?'

'I'm fine, Granddad. How did you get here?' And then I remembered my manners. 'How are you?'

'Train. I'm not but middling.' He had always been a man of few words, unless he was in a pulpit. I knew the Sheffield code. His last answer meant that things were not going well for him.

'I'm right sorry to hear that,' I said. 'Come upstairs, Granddad.' He followed me to the common room.

Most of the girls were able to see from the expression on my face that I needed privacy, and those who didn't were soon shepherded out by Lorna. But Miss King insisted on making an appearance, and was introduced.

'Maisie never told us she was from Sheffield,' she said.

'Not ashamed of us, lass?' he asked me.

'No, Granddad. Sheffield's home and always will be.' I looked at Miss King, who took the hint and left us alone.

He sat very upright in the chair facing me, looking like a caricature Yorkshireman in his Sunday best, clutching his cloth cap like a lifeline.

He swallowed, took a breath, and said, very quickly, 'Your grandmother – she's dead, lass. She were gathered in last month, on May eleven.'

I stared at him, open mouthed. *My grandmother was dead?*

'Now then, say nothing, lass. Sarah were hard on you, I know. She were hard on us all. It were the lead, it poisoned her body and her mind.'

Somehow I found my voice. 'I know it was the lead, Granddad. I know it was her work as a file-cutter made her breathe in the lead. She was ill. I don't hold it against her.'

'But you thought me wanting in not helping you more. Protecting you, like. But if I'd been kind she'd have been worse on you. D'you understand that, lass?'

Tears flooded my eyes. 'I understand.'

'She were right bad since your mam died. Been at Middlewood these past two year.'

Middlewood was the Sheffield Mental Asylum.

'I didn't know,' I whispered.

'You were a good lass, to send us money. Meant she had some treats. She didn't know me at all at end.' He stared into the distance, and said, quietly, 'She weren't always like that. She were sweet-natured when she were a young lass. And she were a beauty. Hair black as raven's wing. Like yours, lass. Skin like milk. Aye, a real beauty she were, and sweet-natured with it. I counted myself lucky to win my Sarah.' He looked up at me and his suffering showed in his eyes. 'It were the lead, and the loss of our bairns. It took her senses.'

I leaned over to put my hand on his. He flinched, then took my hand between both of his. 'You've a real look of her about you,' he said. 'Fair stole my breath away when I saw you on doorstep, looking the spit of Sarah when she were young.'

'Do I?' The idea was shocking, somehow. When I knew her, my grandmother had hair of steely grey, and her skin was sallow.

'Aye. Beauties, both of you.' For the first time, the pain left his eyes and he gave me a shy smile.

'How did you find me?' I'd never let him know my address.

'Your man wrote me.'

'My man? Do you mean Michael? Michael Harker?' I said, astonished.

'Aye. Told us he were courting my granddaughter. Wanted my blessing. It were just after your nannan ...' He swallowed. 'I wrote and told him she were gone and asked him to tell you, but he never wrote back until this week. Said where I'd find you and sent money for train.'

'Granddad, I—'

'Told me to explain why I'd not come to London for your mam's funeral.'

I looked down at my hands, gripped tightly together in my lap, and said, 'Why didn't you come? I had to do it all myself. I was sixteen, and I had to bury my mother alone.'

'Ah, lass.' It was a moan. 'I wanted to come, but I couldn't leave Sarah. Not for so long. And she couldn't come. She were right bad by then.' I looked up and again saw tears in his blue eyes; they were same colour my mother's eyes had been.

I stared at him. 'You should have told me that when you wrote? Why didn't you?'

'Pride, lass. And anger, too.'

'Anger? Why?'

'My only bairn was dead, and so far from home. I were angry at her for leaving and at Sarah for being so poorly she could not be left. And I were angry at you. Our Lizzie came to London for you. She'd have done anything for you.'

'I know,' I whispered.

'I wrote you,' he said, fixing me with his gaze. 'Later, when I thought better of it. Letter came back. Never knew where you were, all these years, not until your man wrote.' He pulled out a big handkerchief, wiped his eyes and blew his nose.

'I was angry too,' I said. 'I'm sorry, Granddad.'

'Lass, it says in Bible we must forgive those who trespass against us.' He stood up. 'You're all the family that's left to me, Maisie.' His voice cracked. 'Forgive me, lass?'

I went to him, and when his arms wrapped around me I thought I could feel Mam there, in the room with us. And I thought she was happy.

I woke up in a sudden panic, but did not open my eyes. My internal clock, which was very reliable, told me it was around three in the morning, and my intuition told me that someone was in my room.

It came again, the slight, hesitant sound that had awoken me. A footstep on the wooden floor? My mind whirled with possibilities. Granddad? Had someone let him in? Surely not. I'd taken him to his lodgings in King's Cross, at Rowton House, where a shilling a night bought him a clean and roomy cubicle in company with hundreds of other men, access to a reading room, smoking room, restaurant and shop. He'd declared himself well content with the accommodation, and we'd made arrangements to meet again on Thursday. It couldn't be Granddad.

Albert Lee? But how could Mr Lee have got into the club? Once the door was locked then you could get inside only if someone let you in, or you could scale a drainpipe. Some of the more athletic girls could do that, but not stringy little Mr Lee.

Lowell? Possible, but why? Surely he didn't really think I had the microfilm, not after I'd practically told him that it was with Moray.

Another sound, this time a slight scraping movement. The legs of my chair? Had my visitor sat down? I kept my breathing soft, shallow and regular. A red haze flicked over my closed eyelids. He'd shone a torch on my face.

Then he sighed. My eyes flew open and searched the darkness.

'Michael,' I squeaked.

A laugh, and he shone the torch on his own face. 'At last you've woken up. I thought you'd snore all night.'

I sat up, indignant. 'I don't snore.'

'Wanna bet?'

'Yes. Apart from this room, I've shared a bedroom since I was born. I *know* I don't snore.'

'You really want to talk about snoring when I've risked life and limb to get to you?'

'Why are you here? How did you get here?' Then it dawned on my sluggish brain that it was *Michael* and I hadn't seen him for weeks. I flung back the covers, flew out of bed and threw myself on him, nearly toppling the chair he was sitting on in the process.

He laughed and stood up and hugged me so tightly that I found it difficult to breathe. I pushed away and lifted my face to him. In the darkness he used his fingertips to find my lips, then he covered them with his own.

Some time later he was sitting next to me on my bed with his arms tightly around me. My head was on his shoulder and I felt perfectly happy as we conducted an intense whispered conversation, so as not to wake anyone else in the house.

'But how did you get here?'

'Scaled a drainpipe to the first floor and got in through an open window.'

'I can't believe you're really here. And that you broke in. Why would you do such a daft thing, you barmpot? You can knock at the door, you know. Between six a.m. and eleven p.m.'

'A couple of reasons. One, I wanted to see if I could breach the walls of the harem. A matter of professional pride. Two, I'm here in England in secret, and I wanted to see you.' He laughed. 'I met two girls sneaking up the stairs – your friend Bobbie had come down to let in your friend Lorna. They remembered me and guided me here. Bobbie said that if you didn't want me she had first dibs.'

'Wretches,' I said, laughing. 'You could have been a sex fiend.'

'I am,' he said, kissing my hair, 'just not at the moment.'

'When?'

'When the time is right.' He ran his fingers through my long hair. 'I've never seen your hair down before.'

'You can't see it now.'

He buried his face in my neck. 'I can imagine it. It's long and midnight black. Like Bess, the landlord's daughter.'

'What?'

'*The Highwayman.* I loved that poem as a kid. Had a real crush on Bess, the landlord's black-eyed daughter, who plaited her long black hair as she waited for her lover, and gave up her life for him.'

I drew in a shaky breath and smiled at his romantic idiocy. 'So that's why you came to me by moonlight tonight.'

He breathed a laugh. 'Perhaps it had something to do with it. You know, first time I saw you properly, in that crummy little cafe after I'd almost knocked you over, all I could think of was that you were just how I'd imagined beautiful Bess. You blew me away.'

I snuggled closer. 'You hid it well.'

'Not any more.'

'My granddad came visiting yesterday.'

'So he came.' Michael laughed softly.

'Came by train all the way from Sheffield. He said you'd written to him and given him my address and sent him the fare.'

'You annoyed?'

'No. It was lovely to see him. We talked for an hour, and cleared the air about a lot of things.'

'That's swell news. It just felt wrong, that you didn't have anything to do with your only kin. You need to be loved, Maisie, and not just by me. You deserve to be loved.'

I gave a shaky laugh. 'He's still a gruff old man. He didn't say it, but I really think he does love me.'

'Of course he does. You're lovable. You catching up with him again?'

'Day after tomorrow. He goes back home the next day. I wish you could meet him.'

He held me closer. 'I wish I could, too. And I will, just not at the minute.'

'When?'

'Honey, I don't know, but it's looking hopeful that I'll be back at the embassy real soon. I can't talk about it but things are looking up for me.'

'It's about time.'

'Hey, I saw your film yesterday. Your voice sounded—'

'That's because it wasn't my voice,' I said bitterly. 'Your friend Mr Denbeigh put in someone else's voice instead.'

I felt his chest moving as he laughed. 'Want me to challenge Denbeigh to a duel or something? For insulting my true love?'

'No,' I said, giving his arm a playful punch. 'Just share in my indignation, please.'

'I do. Denbeigh's a bum.' Michael paused, then said in a less playful voice, 'I hear you've been doing a little sleuthing. I don't like it and I told them so.'

'It was pretty harmless. Has my tryst with Lowell borne fruit? I mean, has he contacted Moray?'

'I can't tell you that. Can't tell you anything.' His voice changed. 'Tryst? You enjoy yourself?'

'Jealous of Dan Lowell?' I said teasingly. 'I'd better convince you that I'm not interested in anyone except—'

When we reluctantly drew apart I said, a little shakily, 'Michael, you're going to have to leave. You can't be here when the girls get up or I'll be thrown out on my ear.'

He laughed. 'And you need your sleep if you're on duty at seven-thirty. Okay. You stay here in chaste repose and I'll slip quietly downstairs and get out the way I came in.' He loosened his grip. I grabbed his arm.

'When will I see you again?'

'Don't worry about that. Soon.'

'Should I watch for you by moonlight?'

He laughed. 'I won't try this trick again, but you'll see me soon, I promise.'

Another long kiss that left me reeling. 'I love you, kid,' he said. 'It'll all work out, don't worry.' And he was gone.

'I love you, too,' I whispered, into the empty darkness.

I managed to fall asleep for a couple of hours after he left, but when I awoke at six my first thought was to wonder if it had been a dream. I found his gift when I sat down in front of my dressing table to put my hair into its usual chignon. On the table was an exquisite Spanish hair comb in filigree silver. It looked antique and expensive. I put it into my hair and preened a little, before tucking it carefully away.

The Spanish comb led me to think that they'd sent Michael to Spain. Why was he back in England? And why secretly? I hoped he wasn't in any danger. Then I told myself not to be silly. This was England in wartime. We were *all* in danger *all* the time.

I was soon to find out, however, that danger was closer for some than others. And closest of all to me.

CHAPTER THIRTY-EIGHT

'Maisie dear,' said Miss King, as I came down to lunch a few days later, 'a man left this note for you yesterday when you were on duty. A very pleasant American man.'

She held out a note, and I took it with a smile, thinking it must be Michael. 'Thanks so much.'

I tore open the envelope without checking the writing. It wasn't from Michael. Dan Lowell declared that he would be delighted if I would agree to dine with him on Saturday, which was the following day.

I have a feeling that I was distracted towards the end of our date, and I'd sure like to meet up to explain it all. Our friendship means a lot to me. Please say you'll meet me.

He gave a telephone number and asked me to call him.

I had no idea how to respond. Captain Temple had said I was to have nothing more to do with Dan Lowell, but if he was intending to explain things to me, surely meeting him was a good idea.

Jim agreed, when I telephoned him.

'He may want to confide in you, which would be very useful. Look, I'll telephone Captain Temple and let you know what his views are about it all.'

'Michael won't be happy,' I said. 'He told me he didn't like my last meeting with Lowell.'

Jim breathed a laugh. 'So you've already seen him. There's been a lot of subtle pressure applied about your Michael Harker. He's

310

not here officially yet, and Lowell doesn't know. So if you meet him, for God's sake don't mention it.'

'I won't.'

Jim phoned back an hour later.

'Captain Temple wants you to meet Lowell.'

My heart began to thump. 'I'm not particularly fond of spy Maisie, you know, Jim. What if she's not up to the job?'

Jim laughed. 'She'll be fine. We think the world of, er, spy Maisie. Captain Temple wants you to say as little as possible but listen a lot. I'm sure you'll do that well. He said to remind you, and I quote, that Man is, on the whole, a conceited creature, and his conceit will often lead him into indiscretion in an attempt to impress a woman. In other words, a sympathetic hearing goes a long way.'

I made a face at the receiver, but replied calmly enough. 'Tell him I'll do my best.'

'Stout fella. He wants you to meet us on Sunday morning to go over what Lowell said.'

'I'll be on duty Sunday morning.'

'We'll fix it with Moray. I'll pick you up outside the club at nine.'

I walked to the Soho gardens with my book the following morning. It was a warm morning of bright sunshine and I was looking for some peace and quiet to take my mind off my date with Dan Lowell that afternoon. John Casey had been wrong when he said I was a champion liar. I thought I'd got away with it all at my last meeting with Lowell, but the more he spoke to me, the harder it would be to keep up the façade.

I had just opened my book when John Casey sat down on the bench beside me.

'What do you want, Mr Casey?' I said coldly. Then I had a thought. 'Are you still on about what you thought I took from Mr Egan?' I stared into his eyes. 'He gave me the locket without me knowing. There was nothing in the locket except a picture.

Moray searched it thoroughly and said it was empty except for the picture.'

He grabbed my arm. 'Moray? Your station leader? What would Moray know about it?'

'Didn't Mr Lowell tell you? After the police had spoken to me I went back to the club and picked the blasted thing up because Moray wanted to see it. I left it with him when I went out on a job, and when I got back he said that it was just a cheap piece of jewellery and I needn't worry about being charged with stealing. Didn't Mr Lowell tell you? I told him last week and he seemed to think it was important.'

The pressure on my arm increased. I'd have a bruise tomorrow, but it was worth it to get this annoying man off my back.

'This is the truth?' he said. 'And you told Lowell this?'

'You're hurting me.' He released my arm and I made a point of rubbing it. 'Yes. I had lunch with Mr Lowell last week and I told him.'

Casey glared at me. 'If this is a lie, you'll be very sorry indeed, little lady.' He stood up and strode away from me.

I continued to rub my arm as I watched him go. It was interesting that Lowell hadn't told him what I'd said. Did it mean that Lowell didn't trust him? I wished I was better at this whole spying business, and I wished I didn't have to meet Dan Lowell in a few hours.

Dan Lowell was waiting outside the club at one, leaning against the big black Bentley. He smiled when I appeared. I had taken some trouble, and was wearing my pretty blue linen frock.

'Maisie, you look lovely,' he said.

'Thank you.'

'Surrey again?' I said with a smile.

'Nah. A nice little place in Mayfair.'

It was a glorious June afternoon. The big car seemed to glide along; London's bumpy, potholed, blitzed roads were no trouble to the suspension of a fancy Bentley. Even with the usual detours, it wasn't a long drive. He pulled up outside a restaurant in Conduit Street. The walls may have been sandbagged and the windows covered in plyboard, but it was clearly very exclusive.

Inside it was dark and discreet. I thought of my dinner with Michael at the bright Victory Restaurant, where he hoped he wouldn't be tempted to be mushy, and I smiled. Dan assumed it was a smile of appreciation.

'I thought you'd like this place,' he said. 'It has class. Just like you.'

Only an American would say such a thing. I smiled again and excused myself to go to the ladies' room to tidy up.

The wine was delicious. Although I was sure to ration myself and drink plenty of water as well, it wasn't long until I felt happily relaxed.

I toyed with my cutlery, wondering if I should mention a news item. Some devil made me say, 'Weren't all the German and Italian consulates in America closed last week and the staff expelled? Does that mean America's views on being involved in the war are changing?'

'They were caught spying,' he said. 'It doesn't mean that the States wants to come into this European war.'

'So you're still an isolationist?'

'More than a hundred thousand American soldiers died in the last war, including my father. I don't want the same thing happening in another European war that's nothing to do with the United States.'

'I'm so sorry about your father,' I said.

'Yeah. I was five years old. It was tough.'

I frowned at him, trying to marshal my thoughts. 'But, don't you see? If Hitler defeats Britain, he'll come for America. Only by then you'll have no allies left. It'll be America against the Axis powers.'

He shook his head. 'It's not our war.'

'It wasn't Ireland's war, either,' I said, heatedly. 'What about that terrible raid on Dublin last month? Eire is neutral, but it didn't stop the Luftwaffe from bombing it. The same thing will happen to America if you let Britain fall to the Nazis.'

'It won't happen to America,' he said.

That made me angry. I knew I needed to calm down. I had to keep the conversation light from now on, and listen, not talk. No more wine, I decided.

Lowell gave me an indulgent smile. 'Do you like the wine? Why don't you have some more?'

I picked up my wine glass and had a sip. 'It's tasty,' I said. Then, annoyed at myself, I had a long drink of water.

We moved on to small talk. The weather got us through soup and rationing through the fish course. During our main course – filet mignon and goodness knows where they got the meat – we began to discuss war issues again.

'You must be pleased at the drop in air raids,' said Lowell. 'You'll be complaining of boredom soon.'

'Never,' I said, laughing. 'They still come over occasionally, as you know. Just not every night, thank God. I think it's the English summer, because there's not enough darkness to protect them.'

'Maybe,' said Lowell. 'Although it hasn't stopped your RAF from carrying out bombing raids into France and Germany.'

'Yes, it's marvellous news. What are the papers saying? That the RAF now has the ascendency in the air war.'

'Otherwise, the war news isn't good for Britain,' said Lowell.

'You mean the loss of Greece and our retreat from Crete?'

He nodded. 'And the attacks on Malta.'

'There's some good news,' I protested. 'My friend Lily is thrilled at the Australian victories in Syria and Lebanon, for instance.'

He shrugged. We were silent as the plates were removed.

'I'm meeting your Mr Moray early this evening,' said Lowell.

'Oh? I suppose you'll have a lot in common.'

He gave me a sly smile. 'Because we doubt Hitler is the monster you make him out to be? Or because we think Russia is a worse enemy than Germany?'

'Well,' I said lazily, on a stifled yawn, 'as Simon Levy said, it's not Stalin who's bombing Britain.'

'Give him time. Stalin's a dangerous enemy.' Lowell looked at me over the side of his glass. 'Quoting Simon Levy. I thought you didn't approve of him.'

I had been right to ration the wine, because I felt as if I was melting into a state of sleepy relaxation. I shook my head in a vain attempt to clear it, and found that I was laughing. 'Don't I?'

Lowell leaned forward towards me. 'You can't tell me it's carrots that makes your night fighters suddenly so effective,' he said.

His remark seemed terribly funny and I gave a peal of laughter. 'Who knows?' I leaned in towards him, so that our faces were very close. 'You should eat a lot of carrots, just in case,' I whispered. I shook my head again. *Why was I so tipsy?* I'd not drunk that much.

'You don't think it could be some sort of secret device?' said Lowell.

I gave an exaggerated shrug.

'Of course it is.'

His face became intent.

'Yes?' he said.

I touched the side of my nose. 'It's secret carrot pills. That's what Powell says.'

I felt extremely light-headed, intoxicated. I took another drink of water.

He leaned closer and barked at me, 'Do you like Simon Levy? Approve of him marrying Celia?'

'Yes, of course I do. He's lovely.'

I sucked in a breath, thinking that I shouldn't have said that. My body felt tingly, fizzy. Lowell leaned back and took a sip of his wine. I forced my eyes open. 'What's happening to me?'

'I put Pentothal in the water. New wonder drug from the US. You'll feel a bit woozy for a while, then sleep. In the meantime you'll be loquacious – that means you'll talk a lot – and you'll be very cooperative in answering questions. Doesn't last long, unfortunately.'

'Oh,' I said, dreamily. 'Loquacious. I like that word. Loqua-a-acious. Nice word.'

'What do you know about the microfilm Egan was carrying, Maisie?'

'Microfilm? Maisie had a microfilm, microfilm, microfilm.' I said the words in a sing-song voice, to the tune of *Mary had a Little Lamb*.

Lowell broke in. 'Does Harker have it?'

'Have what? Sex appeal? Yes he certainly does.' Again I began to sing, this time to the tune of *Yankee Doodle Dandy*. 'Michael Harker came to London just to ride a pony, stuck a feather in his—'

'Moray?'

'In his Moray?' I giggled.

'Does Moray really hate Jews?'

'Yes. We all know he hates Jews and doesn't hate Hitler.' I began to sing an old folk song. 'Down Sheffield Park a maid did dwell—'

He said, sharply, 'Who has the microfilm, Maisie? Does Moray?'

'Don't know,' I said, because I didn't. Then, again in sing-song, 'Haven't a clue. Someone. Maybe it's gone. Gone for ever. For ever and ever, amen.'

'Tell me about Moray.'

I found myself saying, very clearly, 'Moray shouldn't have been so mean to David Levy. David was nice. He died. Lots of people die. I hate Hitler. I says me prayers. To hell with Hitler I says. And then I goes to sleep...' My voice faded.

Lowell squeezed my hand. 'What about Moray and the watch fob?'

316

'He had the thing for an hour or so when I was out at an incident. That's all I know about it, and let's not discuss it again.' My eyes drifted shut.

He squeezed my hand again. 'He had what?'

'The locket, you chuff. And let's not discuss it again.'

'Have you heard of the cavity magnetron?'

'No.'

'Had you met Egan before the night he died?

'No.'

'Did you know he had the microfilm?'

'No.'

'Who has the microfilm?'

'I don't know. Maybe Hitler does. I bet he wants it. I feel sleepy.'

I tried to stand, but my body felt weightless, as if I were spinning in space.

'My dear Miss Halliday,' said Lowell, in a louder voice, 'it looks like you're under the weather. I'd better take you home.'

I could walk, although I was unsteady. Dan Lowell assisted me out of the restaurant past the disapproving eyes of the other diners. Outside, I rested against the side of his big black car and I had a few amused glances from passers-by.

Lowell leaned in close. I tried to shrink away, but he slipped his arm around me to hold me fast as he pressed his mouth down on mine. It was difficult to breathe, and I struggled weakly. He pulled back and his grinning face was only an inch or so from mine, unrecognisable, almost obscene.

'I've wanted to do that for a while,' he said.

'Leave me alone.' I said. It was the slurred voice of a drunkard.

He laughed. 'In five minutes I could do anything I wanted with you and you'd have no idea.'

'Wha'ya mean?' I tried to move, but my body refused to cooperate.

'Don't worry.' He grinned again. 'I'll act like a gentleman. I'm not a heel, but I do like to be on the winning side. And, my dear Maisie, Britain is doomed.'

'Wha'ya goin'a do?'

'Get back the microfilm. Thanks for all the information. *Gute nacht schatz*. Sleep tight.'

The world was fading. Lowell's grinning face now resembled a fleshless skull. I closed my eyes against the nightmare vision. He laid me on the cool, soft leather seat and closed the door behind me. I knew I should be doing something, but I really couldn't work out what. I leaned back in the seat, tranquil, without much thought. I felt the shuddering purr as he started the engine, and the slight jerk as we moved away from the kerb.

A curtain of black velvet enfolded me. I tumbled into it.

CHAPTER THIRTY-NINE

I woke slowly in near-darkness, lying on a narrow bed, knowing I'd had a nightmare. The horror began when my eyes opened on a blurred scene where nothing was where it should be. My dressing table had disappeared, along with the other two beds in my room. The bed I was lying on was too hard, the sheet felt slimy, the blanket smelled, and the pillow was too thin. My foggy brain wondered if I was still dreaming, but I knew. Somehow I knew that I was in danger.

I tried to get up but my body refused to obey me, staying slack and heavy. An attempt to lift my head caused a violent throbbing in my forehead. So I let the heavy lassitude take me, shut my eyes and drifted away into the darkness.

When I opened my eyes again the alien environment came sharply into focus. I was fully awake, unsure how long I'd slept after I'd first tried to wake up. I no longer felt dizzy, but I was terribly hungry and there were other, more basic, needs that I had to attend to. I pushed myself up into a sitting position, fighting nausea as I did so. It was then I realised, to my fury, that I was dressed only in my underwear. *Some gentleman.*

Once I'd quickly checked myself over I was satisfied that he'd not taken any further advantage of me. Apparently the man had some scruples. Stockings were useless without shoes, and they were one of the precious silk pairs Michael had given me, so I slid them off and undid my garter belt. I pulled the sheet off the bed and wrapped it around me like a toga, then stalked across the room to the door. It was locked, unsurprisingly. I switched on the light.

As well as the bed, the room contained a tallboy, a washstand, lamp and a chair. A china jug stood in a large bowl on the washstand. Those items usually had a companion piece that sat discreetly under the bed. I checked and it was there. I used it and felt a lot better.

The blackout blind was in place over the single window. I stumbled over to it and tore down the blind. Two strips of plyboard had been nailed across the window frame. Grunting with the effort, I managed to prise one loose, then rip it off completely, only to find that the glassless window was barred. The sun was still high in the sky and with the double summer time, it would be light until around eleven-thirty. My watch confirmed that it was nearly nine o'clock, so I must have slept for seven hours. I wished I could sleep for another fourteen, but I forced myself into a semblance of alertness.

A stone wall faced the window, around five feet away. Below the wall, filthy paving stones covered in broken glass led to a stone staircase. The footpath or street was at least fifteen feet above me. No railings, but I knew they would have been taken down for scrap at the beginning of the war. I was obviously in a basement flat, but I had no idea where.

I turned away from the window and went to the tallboy. The wash jug held water. I poured some into the bowl and splashed my face, then quickly splashed the rest of me because the thought of Dan Lowell's hands on my unconscious skin was almost unbearable. I used the sheet to dry myself.

It was a warm day, but I did not favour the idea of escaping barefoot and dressed in brassiere and scanties. Wrapped in my now damp sheet, I made a fruitless search of the room for my clothing. My blue linen frock – a favourite of mine – and my best pair of shoes were nowhere to be found. Nor was my handbag. 'Nazi scum,' I muttered.

I sighed. I'd have to wear the dirty sheet. It was old and wafer thin in parts and easily tore in half. I tied one half around my waist like a filthy sarong, and felt like a cut-rate Dorothy Lamour.

The corner of the tallboy helped me to tear three holes in the remaining half. I pushed my head and arms through the holes *et voilà*, a sort of blouse. Not a fashionable ensemble, but I would be decent enough if I managed to escape. My main concern was having to go barefoot when the streets were covered in so many little shards of glass.

I returned to the door and rattled it, then gave it a shove with my shoulder. It didn't budge. Barred window, locked door. Bare feet and barely legal outfit. It wasn't looking promising for an escape attempt. I returned to the window, pulled off the other plyboard and stared forlornly at the wall opposite.

Tippy tappy footsteps sounded on the footpath above me.

'Hello,' I called through the bars. 'Whoever is up there. Please, I'm locked in. Help me, please.'

The footsteps quickened and faded away.

'Thanks for nothing,' I muttered.

I stared at the wall opposite and pondered my next move. Lowell had obviously left me alone in the flat, or my rattling and yelling would have brought someone in to shut me up. Lowell had said he was going to get back the microfilm. Presumably from Moray. Which was exactly what Captain Temple wanted him to do. Why did it all seem so wrong then?

Because what he had done to me was madness. We were in Britain. Lowell couldn't get away with drugging and kidnapping a girl. Would the new ambassador grant Lowell diplomatic immunity? I doubted it. Kidnapping me would be such a scandal, a diplomatic incident. Was Lowell intending to leave the country? Maybe that was exactly what Captain Temple wanted him to do. In the meantime, I did not want to be in the flat when Lowell returned.

I got up and went back to the window. 'Help,' I screamed again. 'Help me.'

A tentative voice came from above, a woman's voice. 'Wassa matter, love? This a joke? Or you really in trouble?'

'Yes, I'm in trouble,' I bellowed. 'I've been kidnapped. Help me.'

A face appeared over the side of the wall. A woman's face, with a feathered hat perched above it. 'What's up?' she said.

'I'm trapped in here. A man kidnapped me. Could you get the police?'

She jerked back, saying, 'I don't mess with no rozzers.' I could see from her face that she was re-thinking her impulse to help me.

'Wait, please don't go,' I said. 'Where am I?'

She gave me a surprised look. 'Soho, of course. Archer Street.'

What was Dan Lowell doing with a Soho flat? This whole escapade was becoming crazier by the minute. I looked as closely as I could at the face that peered down at me from the street above. She was heavily made up and the hat was awfully gaudy.

'Do you know Edna?' I ventured. 'Or Rosie? Edna's patch is on Greek Street; Rosie's usually to be found in Soho Square.'

Her look sharpened. 'You one of us then? I don't know yer face.'

'No. I'm a theatre girl, from the club in Greek Street. But Edna and Rosie are my friends. Would you get one of them for me? Tell them Maisie's in trouble.' I put more urgency in my voice. 'I really *am* in trouble.'

'Saw Rosie a while ago,' she said, uncertainly. 'I'll see if she's still there.'

She disappeared and all I could do was hope that Rosie had not found a punter and disappeared with him.

After a long fifteen minutes a new face appeared, peering down at me from the street.

'Maisie, love?' said a tentative voice.

'Yes,' I shrieked. 'Yes it's me. Is that you, Rosie?'

'Wotcha doing down there?'

Rosie scrambled down the steep stairs and stood outside my barred window. 'Is that scrawny fella still bothering you? Is it him whats got you locked up?'

'No. It was another man. I'm locked in. Could you get the police?'

She shook her head. 'No need for the rozzers. I'll get Edna.'

Frustratingly, Rosie then ran up the stairs and disappeared before I could ask her to bring me some clothes, and more importantly, some shoes. I spent the next half-hour pacing my room in increasing desperation until I heard a familiar voice at the window. 'Maisie love, you there?'

Edna's face was peering in through the bars.

'Rosie says a madman locked you up in here. That right? He hurt you, love?'

'I'm fine, but I need to get out of here before the man who drugged me comes back.' I grabbed the bars and gave them a tug. 'The window's barred and he locked the door to the room I'm in. Could you get the police? A friend may be in trouble.'

'I'll do better than that,' she said. 'I'll get Ned Jenkin.'

'What?' But she'd already disappeared.

Rosie's head appeared at the window. 'Ned'll know what's what.'

'Who's Ned Jenkin?' I asked.

'One of the Tolmer Gang. Do anything for Edna, would Ned Jenkin.'

'The Tolmer Gang?'

I'd heard of the Hoxton Mob, the most dangerous gang in Soho. But not the Tolmer Gang. Tolmer's Square was at least a mile from Soho, across the Euston Road.

'Yeah,' said Rosie. 'Ned's a screwsman. Best in the business, they say. He can get into any house, anywhere. Thinks the world of Edna, does Ned, and he'll have you out in the wink of an eye.'

It all sounded right dodgy to me, but who was I to judge? I spent another frustrating half-hour waiting for Edna to return. It was after ten-thirty when I heard the sound of a motorbike pulling up on the street outside. Edna came down the stairs with a man in tow.

'Hullo, Ned,' said Rosie, and he smiled at her.

'Maisie,' whispered Edna, 'this is my friend Ned. He'll get you out.'

Ned Jenkin was a small, slightly built man with bow legs and a cheerfully wrinkled face that reminded me of a wise monkey. That is, if a monkey were to wear a leather motorcycle coat, leather helmet and tool pouch. He gave me a grin and a wave.

'Have you out in a jiffy, Princess. Any friend of Edna's ...'

He was as good as his word. I couldn't see exactly what he did, but the front door opened in less than a minute.

'My word, you're a tall one, Princess,' he said, as he threw wide the bedroom door. He looked me up and down. 'Interestin' outfit. A sheet?'

I nodded.

'I'd a brought some schmutter if I'd known the asterbar what left yer here had nicked yours. He put the hocus on yer?'

'Something like that,' I said.

'No ones and twos neither?'

I'd been in Soho long enough to know my slang. Schmutter was clothing. The hocus was drugging someone. As for asterbar, well, it's a backwards word, more polite than bastard. Ones and twos meant shoes.

I shook my head.

Ned frowned. 'Yer too big to carry and there's glass all over outside.'

He disappeared, and I remembered to grab my precious stockings and garter belt. Ned chatted to Edna. She removed her shoes and sat on the top stair as he brought them to me. They were high-heeled and a couple of sizes too small, but I shoved my feet into them and minced painfully across the glass-strewn path and up the stairs.

Edna and Rosie stared at me. 'Whatcha wearin'?' asked Rosie.

'The remains of a sheet. He took most of my clothes.'

Edna frowned. 'Did the blighter take advantage?'

I shook my head. 'No. Really, he didn't. He drugged me to get information and left me here to sleep it off.'

Ned stroked his chin. 'It's an old trick.'

'It's a dirty trick,' responded Rosie.

'It's not right,' said Edna, 'Maisie here is straight-cut.'

Ned looked at Edna, then at me. 'You want me to put out the word on him?' he asked me.

'No, please don't bother. But thanks for the offer.'

He gave me a wink. 'If you change yer mind, I knows people.'

'I can't thank you enough for getting me out,' I said.

'It were a pleasure, Miss. I appreciate the chance to keep me hand in.' Ned leaned closer and said in a confidential tone, 'The trouble with this here Blitz is that no one needs me special skills no more. No need to screw open doors when the boys can just walk in through broken windows.' He gave me another wink and gestured towards his motorcycle. 'I'd better drop you off home. Yer not dressed for the street.'

Ned had a point. My outfit was ludicrous and the footpath was strewn with glass and litter. I'd not make ten yards in bare feet.

'I live at the Theatre Girls' Club,' I said. 'In Greek Street.'

Once I was up behind Ned on the motorbike Edna gave him a kiss. 'You take her straight home now,' she said to him, then turned to me. 'No need to worry about Ned. He's staunch.'

'Of course he is,' I said with a smile.

Ned let out the throttle and the bike roared off down the road. I could only imagine what we looked like, the scrawny little cockney in his leathers and up behind him a barefoot female of Amazonian proportions, dressed in a dirty, tattered sheet, whose long black hair streamed out in the wind behind them.

He dropped me outside the club. I thanked him with a kiss on the cheek and carefully picked my way on tiptoe through the debris on the footpath to the big front door. It was opened by Millie, whose eyes became wide as saucers when she saw me.

'Costume party,' I said firmly, before she could speak, and pushed past her into the hall. I took the steps two at a time, ignoring the shocked and amused looks I got from girls I passed on the stairs. My luck held. I did not encounter Miss King.

I threw on a pair of slacks, a dark shirt and sensible brogues and then I paced my room, wondering what to do. Moray would have met with Lowell hours ago, but I wanted to know that Moray was all right. Should I visit Moray's secret Soho flat?

I'd first seen Moray coming out of the basement flat in a building on Soho Square in June 1940. When I asked him if that was where he lived, he'd told me that he'd been visiting someone in the flats. I'd spent many years in Soho, and I well knew that those flats were haunts of prostitutes. All I could assume was that he'd been paying one of the girls a visit.

After that I'd seen him quite often in the area. That made me think he might have set up a lover in the flat. So I was surprised when he was alone in the Soho gardens air-raid shelter. Now I knew more about the world of espionage I had a better theory. If Mr Temple could direct his agents from a flat in Pimlico, why shouldn't Moray rent a Soho flat for spying purposes? I'd lay London to a brick that if Moray had arranged to meet Lowell, it would have been at that Soho flat.

Think, Maisie. What if Moray had everything in hand and my turning up ruined a Secret Service operation? But what if Lowell had hurt Moray? I thought I'd at least go to the Soho flat, check if he was all right.

The sun was setting but it was still light as I strode down Greek Street. I had just reached the corner when someone grabbed my arm. I twisted free and whirled around with my hands in fists, ready for a fight.

'Easy, kid,' said Michael.

If it hadn't been a public place I'd have thrown my arms around him. I settled for squeezing his hand very hard.

He was unsmiling. 'What's going on? You were in a real peculiar get-up when you got off that motorcycle. And why were you on the motorcycle in the first place?'

I drew in a breath, wondering how to explain without him wanting to kill Lowell. A few versions of the story ran through my mind, but I had to accept that he would want to kill Lowell no matter how I explained it.

'Lowell drugged me and kidnapped me,' I said.

Sure enough, Michael became very still. His pale eyes were cold as ice. 'He drugged and kidnapped you?' he said, in a quiet voice.

'He slipped, um, pento-something in my water.'

'Pentothal? Sodium Pentothal?'

'Yes.'

'How did he manage to put it in your water?' Michael's voice was very quiet, controlled.

'He asked me to lunch. Jim and Captain Temple said I should go. Lowell must have slipped the drug in my water when I went to the ladies' room, because it took a while to work. He asked me questions and then left me in a flat in Archer Street. I slept for hours there.'

'Why were you dressed in a sheet? Where were your clothes?'

I'd never seen him look like that before, and it scared me.

'He didn't touch me – not like that, Michael. Truly he didn't. But he took my clothes.' I grabbed his arm. 'Not my underwear, just my outer clothes. He didn't hurt me.'

I began to babble, desperate to stop him looking like that.

'I tore up a sheet to wear and yelled out of the window. A – a woman found me and she got Rosie. You don't know Rosie. She's a friend of Edna's. You must remember Edna, you bought her breakfast. Rosie told Edna where I was, and Edna got her friend Ned to help. Ned's a screwsman. He'd do anything for Edna.'

I managed a smile. 'Oh, Michael, it was champion. He opened that door in ten seconds flat. Nice man, too. Said he would have brought me some schmutter if he'd known that the asterbar had nicked mine. And because I didn't have any ones and twos, he offered drive me back to the club on his motorcycle. Edna said I needn't worry because he was staunch.'

As I chattered away, the frighteningly cold rigidity left Michael's face. His expression softened, almost to a quizzical smile. An eyebrow rose. 'A screwsman?'

'He opens doors and windows to let housebreakers in. Ned's part of the Tolmer Gang, from across the Euston Road.'

'Schmutter?'

'Clothes. Ones and twos are shoes. And staunch means reliable.'

'I take it Lowell's the asterbar.'

'A complete and utter asterbar.'

'You're sure he didn't … take liberties, when you were asleep.'

I reached across to touch his face. 'I'm sure. Really, I am sure. He's an asterbar, a Nazi, but he's not a villain.'

Michael took a deep breath and let it out slowly. 'Sounds like you saved yourself, kid. With help from your friends. Remind me to do something to thank Edna and her friend. Rosie, was it?'

'Yes, Rosie. And Ned, too.' I nibbled my lip. 'Michael, why are you here in the street? I thought your return was a secret.'

'As from tomorrow I'm back at the embassy. A word was had in someone's ear and I had a long chat with the ambassador this afternoon. Tell me more about your lunch with Lowell. So he drugged you and asked you questions?'

'Yes. I tried not to answer but I felt as if I had to be helpful, tell him what he wanted to know.'

'What did he want to know?'

I told Michael what I could remember about Lowell's interrogation.

'And when I asked him what he was going to do, he said he was going to get back the microfilm. I'm worried about Moray. What if Lowell hurt him? Can we check on Moray?'

'Do you know where Moray lives?'

'I think he would have seen Lowell at his secret flat.' I explained about the flat, and Michael nodded.

'Makes sense he'd meet Lowell there. But the meeting was probably hours ago, honey.'

I looked at Michael. 'I need to know that Moray's all right.'

Michael frowned. 'All right, we'll go there. But you follow my orders, okay?'

'I will.'

We walked to Soho Square in the deepening twilight. As daylight faded into cool grey dusk, a single star appeared.

Moray's secret flat was in the basement of what once had been a very grand building. Beside a magnificently carved doorway with pillars were stone steps leading down to the flat's entrance door. In the dusk the stairs seemed ominous, enticing us down to gloomy danger.

We slowly descended. Michael knocked on the door and we waited. At last the door opened and, indifferent to the blackout, electric light streamed out into the tiny courtyard. It backlit John Casey, who stepped towards us holding a revolver. He glanced at me, then pointed the gun at Michael, who raised his hands.

And that's when I became very angry. Casey didn't even think of watching me. I was harmless. Weak. A former chorus girl who wasn't even standing close enough to try to grab the gun. Not with my hands, anyway. But my legs were thirty-three inches long and I could kick as high as my eye.

First a little jump to prepare. Casey didn't notice. Then, quick as a wink, the eye-high kick. My foot struck Casey's hand with a satisfying thump. His hand flew up, but he still had hold of the gun. Have I mentioned that a Tiller Girl could do thirty-two kicks per minute? Up again went my leg and this time the gun went flying.

So did Michael. He launched himself at Casey like a steam hammer. They hit the hallway floor together in a writhing mass of arms, legs and torsos. Fists hit flesh with sickening thuds. Raised arms met blows until a knee pushed brutally into the groin resulted in a high scream of pain. Casey was down and Michael had a knee on his chest. He pulled back his fist and slammed it into the man's undefended face. Casey subsided into an unconscious heap.

Very slowly Michael got off Casey. He knelt beside him to check his carotid pulse. Only once he was satisfied that the man was breathing did he look at me.

'Neat trick, kid,' he said.

'You learn to take care of yourself in the chorus,' I replied.

Then I remembered Moray. I leapt over Casey's unconscious form and headed for the living room. On the floor, in a pitiful heap, lay Moray, his face bloodied. I dashed over to him, shaking him, trying to see if he was alive. A puffy eyelid raised and a green eye stared at me.

'Can you get up?' I asked him. A nod. I helped him to his feet and over to the sofa, where he collapsed.

'Would someone please explain to me what happened?' I said. 'Where's Lowell? And why do you look like that, Moray?'

Michael had tied up Casey, and put him in the bedroom. I'd cleaned Moray's face as well as I could, but he was still holding a handkerchief to his bloody nose and lurid bruises were appearing. He tried to laugh, but a split lip meant he winced instead.

'The things I do for my country,' he said, on a sigh. 'Lowell came this afternoon and took what he thinks is the microfilm Egan was carrying, just like we wanted him to. He's off to Germany, via Ireland, he tells me. He also told me where to find you. Said you were safe and he'd give an anonymous tip to the police about your whereabouts.' He looked at me. 'Thank goodness you *are* safe. How did you escape?'

I shrugged. 'Some friends helped me out. So it was Casey who hurt you. Why?'

'Casey's a misguided patriot. Turned up not long after Lowell left and demanded the microfilm. I told him Lowell had it and he wanted to know where Lowell was. I said I didn't know and he spent a while trying to persuade me to spill the beans, as he put it. The rest you know.'

'I take it the microfilm you gave Lowell is fake.'

'A carefully constructed fake. Should confuse their research into magnetrons for some time. With any luck, he'll tell them I'm entirely trustworthy and my work here can move to a new level.' He gave me an admiring look. 'Well done on convincing Lowell that I was kosher.'

I laughed. 'A kosher anti-Semite. The drug he gave me is very odd, not a truth serum exactly. It made me want to be obliging. I think he used it badly. I was compelled to answer direct questions – yes or no questions – but all I really wanted was to be obliging. I let my imagination run riot and I sang a lot. It helped.'

'You did very well. Temple will be wanting to recruit you permanently.'

Michael came across to me and put his arm around my shoulder. 'He'll have to find someone else.'

I murmured, 'Mmmm.'

CHAPTER FORTY

Jim Vassilikov turned up at nine o'clock that morning in a big black car driven by an ATS girl. I'd managed to snatch a few hours' sleep after the night's adventures and felt vaguely human.

'Moray telephoned Temple this morning,' said Jim, who was in a lively mood. 'He told us some of what happened, and I'm longing to hear the rest from you.'

We set off. Jim seemed happier than I had ever seen him. He was usually very reserved, but as we drove through the streets, he kept smiling. In fact, his mood was almost euphoric.

'What's up?' I asked.

His face lit up in a grin. 'Great news for Britain. Last night Germany invaded Russia.'

I stared at him. 'That was Napoleon's downfall, wasn't it?'

'It was, and it could well be Hitler's also. He will not find the Red Army a pushover. At last we have a tough fighting ally in Europe.'

'I thought you hated Soviet Russia.'

'I do, but my enemy's enemy and all that. This'll turn Hitler's attention away from us.'

My heart began to race. 'Do you really think the Blitz is over?'

'I do. He can't afford to send hundreds of planes to bomb London when he needs them on the other side of Europe. We'll still see a few bombers come across, I expect, in retaliation for our bombing of Germany, but no more Blitz.'

I stared out the window at the ruins, and found myself wanting to sing.

*

332

'We are very happy indeed with the way you handled yourself in difficult circumstances,' said Captain Temple, whose blue-green eyes seemed almost to twinkle.

'I made a lot of mistakes,' I said.

'With no training whatsoever, you did wonderfully well. Most importantly, we achieved our purpose.'

'So Dan Lowell is actually off to Germany?'

'Yes. He's long been a supporter of Hitler, we now realise. Of course, the Americans are sweeping it all under the carpet. I doubt we'll hear his name mentioned again.' He handed me a cup of tea and proffered a plate of fancy iced biscuits. I hadn't seen such luxury in over a year.

'What about Casey?'

Jim answered. 'Casey's being sent back to the United States.'

I shook my head. 'So he's not a traitor, and he thought that Lowell discovered Moray was a fifth columnist?'

'Yes, and that Moray had killed or kidnapped him. Hence his attack on Moray. Apparently he's devastated that Lowell is a traitor.'

'I almost feel sorry for him, but he was brutal to poor Moray. And he's a bit of a pig.'

As I sipped my tea Temple gave me a considering look. 'Would you be interested in joining my little crew, Miss Halliday? You could still work with the ambulance service, much as Moray does, but I'd need you to be available when I thought I could use your particular, er, talents.'

I'd been wondering about this possibility ever since Moray had mentioned it. Michael would be utterly opposed, of course. But, as it would be top secret, he didn't need to know. In fact I *couldn't* tell him on pain of ten years' imprisonment with hard labour. The news about Hitler's invasion of Russia had been the turning point in my mind, because if the Blitz was over, I'd not be needed as much driving ambulances. I hated the thought of being bored.

'Yes, Captain Temple,' I said. 'I would be interested.'

*

'You look pleased with yourself,' said Michael, at dinner that night. He leaned back in his chair, took a long look at me and laughed. 'When do you start your duties with this so-called Captain Temple?'

I stared at him. 'How—?'

He smiled and shook his head. 'Kid, you're excited and guilty all at once and you've not said a word about your meeting with Temple. I figure that means he offered and you accepted. I just hope he's going to train you properly, and he's not sending you out of the country.'

I reached across and took his hand. 'Yes, he'll train me. And no, I'm not leaving Britain. I don't speak any other languages fluently, so ...' I shrugged. 'I can't say any more about it, Michael. It's top secret.' I hesitated, then said, 'Are you annoyed with me? For accepting the offer from Captain Temple, I mean.'

Michael smiled and squeezed my hand. 'Nah. I wish I could wrap you up in cotton wool and keep you safe, but I know you'd never let me. You're perfectly able to take care of yourself and I have a strong hunch that you'll be damned good at ... whatever Temple wants you to do. But you be sure to remember your promise, kid.'

'My promise?'

'Our promises to each other after the big air raid. No silly risks.'

'No silly risks.' I gave him a smile and toyed with his long fingers. 'As I recall, you made some other promises to me that morning.'

'I remember.' He curled his fingers around mine. 'Maisie, I always keep my promises.'

I looked up and met his eyes. 'I'm glad.'

But there was a war on, and some promises could not be kept.

It was glorious, that summer after the Blitz ended. Tall grass and wildflowers sprung up amongst bomb-site rubble, as if the countryside were reclaiming London. Someone reported seeing a hawk in the skies over the ruined Temple. Old men sat in the sunshine on the steps of shattered houses under glassless windows now covered with black paper. Women still spent hours queuing for rationed food, but time went quickly, as they spent it chattering and remarking on the weather and what would go under the ration next. It was not peace; German bombers still flew across England's starry skies carrying death under their wings. Houses were still destroyed and people still killed and injured. We remained busy in the Bloomsbury Ambulance Station, but it was nothing like the frantic, heartrending, constant horror of the Blitz.

True to his word, Michael courted me whenever his busy schedule and mine allowed. We planned our wedding for soon after my twenty-first birthday, but then fate intervened. On Sunday the sixth of December the news came over the wireless: earlier that day Japanese bombers had attacked Pearl Harbor.

'That's it, then,' said Michael. His eyes flashed blue in his grim face.

'Your country's at war with Japan?'

'And soon with Germany and Italy. We're all in it together now, kid.'

His voice was surprisingly flat. In contrast, I was filled with hopeful joy. Britain had a real likelihood of winning this war if both America and Russia were supporting us. I was about to say it when I saw the look on Michael's face. I tried to swallow, but there was a lump in my throat, and it hurt.

'You're going back to America, to join up,' I said. It was a statement, not a question.

He glanced at me, then stared at a point on the floor. 'Yes.'

'I'm twenty-one in four months. We could—'

'I'm sorry, kid. This makes it impossible. How can I marry you now? When I'll be leaving right away and I might not return for years? Or at all? When I might leave you with a kid to raise alone.' He looked up at me and now his eyes were blue ice. 'I won't do that to you.'

I leaned in and kissed him, pushing my lips against his, desperately. He submitted but didn't respond and eventually I pulled away.

'I don't care,' I said, staring into his eyes. 'I don't care if I don't see you for years. So long as we've had some time together now, and so long as we're together eventually.'

He shook his head. I stood and began to pace the room, trying to marshal my arguments.

'Don't you see?' I said. 'This is the choice that faces everyone who falls in love in wartime. Ellie Kavanagh married Raymond last month. They both nearly died in the Café de Paris, and they decided that they should – should, um, gather rosebuds while they may.'

At last he smiled. 'That poem is called "To the Virgins, to Make Much of Time".'

I began to unbutton my blouse. 'Then let's,' I said, my cheeks flaming. 'Let's make much of our time.'

He reached up to cover my fingers, stop me. 'No, honey. Not like this.'

I sat beside him in an abrupt movement. 'You promised to marry me when I was twenty-one. I'm nearly twenty-one. Have you changed your mind? Is that what this is about?'

'No. I *will* marry you, if you still want to, when the war is over.'

'But that might be years,' I wailed. 'By then I might be old. And ugly.'

He laughed, and shook his head. 'Never.'

I knew the signs. Michael thought he was right about this and had made his mind up. I blew out a breath and gave him a tremulous smile.

'I'll still hold you to your promise. Even if by the end of the war I'm a shrivelled-up old maid, living with cats and engaged in good causes.'

'And I will keep my promise. I'll marry you, Maisie Halliday, no matter what. Now come and kiss me, sweet and twenty.'

I snuggled up beside him. 'Is that another quote?'

He was too busy kissing me to answer.

CHAPTER FORTY-ONE

Tuesday 21 April 1942

'Happy birthday, Maisie,' said Celia.

She came up to me and planted a kiss on my cheek, then sat opposite me with as much elegance as a woman who was seven months pregnant could manage. Her smocked velvet gown was in a dark blue that matched her eyes. Celia glowed as brightly as expectant mothers are supposed to do and as she looked around at the bright gaiety of dancing couples, the gypsy band and the painted walls she put a gentle hand on her stomach. She smiled at me.

'Twenty-one today,' she said. 'Congratulations.'

'And we're all back at the Hungaria,' said Lily, sitting beside Simon. 'We should make it an annual outing for Maisie's birthday. Would you like that, Maisie?'

'Of course I would.'

'Then we will,' said Jim.

'How are things at the station?' asked Celia. 'I miss everyone like blazes.'

She had left the ambulance service five months before, and now concentrated on working for a Jewish children's welfare organisation while waiting for the birth of her honeymoon baby.

'And we all miss you,' I said.

'Poor Squire's lost both his best friends,' said Lily. 'First Stephen Armstrong gets called up and then you go off having babies.'

338

'Only one baby and I've not dumped Squire,' said Celia. 'He's my mate. Squire and "the Missus" have been around to tea a few times now.'

I smiled to myself to imagine big George Squire in the delicately furnished living room of Simon and Celia's elegant townhouse near St James's Square.

'I wish Michael were here to celebrate with you,' said Lily.

I managed a smile. 'So do I.'

I had waved him off as he sailed for America on the twenty-third of January. Somehow I'd managed to keep smiling until the ship was away and then poor Lily had to take home a blubbering mess. 'Cry it out,' she'd said. 'I know what I'd be like if Jim went away.'

'Where is he now? Do you know?' asked Jim.

'At a training camp in Louisiana. That's a state in the south of America.'

'What's the mail like from the US?' asked Simon.

'Oh, we write regularly, usually once a week. We number the letters so we know if one's gone missing. But so far none have.'

Our letters were mainly mushy stuff, because I couldn't tell him much about what I was doing and he couldn't tell me much about what he was doing and, apart from the mushy stuff, the censor took out the rest. I didn't mind really. I liked the mushy stuff in Michael's letters.

'What else are you doing to celebrate?' asked Lily.

'I'm taking a couple of weeks off – I'm due a lot of leave – and I'm going on holiday.'

'Where are you off to?'

'Yorkshire.'

I caught Jim's eye. It was no holiday. We were both involved in a tricky situation for Captain Temple, my first 'assignment' since I'd been recruited. At least it meant I had no time to miss Michael. Not much time, anyway.

*

Wednesday 21 April 1943

I celebrated my twenty-second birthday at the Hungaria, as usual with the Ambulance Girls. Celia's son, whom they named David, had been born in June 1942, and was a dark-haired cherub with a mischievous streak. During the evening Lily spent a fair bit of time in the ladies' room being sick. Jim didn't need to explain it was because she was pregnant.

'To Maisie,' said Jim, standing to propose the toast when Lily came back, looking pale, but determined to have a good time.

'And to absent friends and fiancés,' said Celia. 'Where is Michael now?'

'Fighting in North Africa,' I said. My tone was brusque, because I hoped no one would ask me anything else about him. I was worried that I might cry.

After being posted to England for four glorious months, Michael had shipped out in November 1942 to take part in the Allied invasion of North Africa. It had not been a successful expedition for the US troops, who had suffered enormous losses. Michael had suffered a bout of dysentery, but no injuries.

At times I felt very down. Celia and Lily were happily married to men who were posted to England; they were having babies and getting on with their lives. I felt as if I were standing still while time and life whirled around me. And always, every day, there was fear for Michael.

'What happened to your arm?' asked Lily. It was in a sling.

'Oh, a work injury,' I said, exchanging a look with Jim. My second job for Captain Temple had had its dangers, but at least it had taken my mind off Michael a little.

Friday 21 April 1944

By the time my twenty-third birthday came around, London was again under attack, what we called the 'baby blitz'. We'd enjoyed two and a half years with few major bombings, when, in January

1944, Hitler decided to recommence the systematic bombing of British cities, and of London in particular. The raids only lasted an hour or so, beginning in the early evening and over by midnight, but the casualties and damage caused were as bad as many of the raids in the Blitz of 1940–41. Once again, Londoners had to seek shelter every night, in basements, air-raid shelters and the Tube.

I waited outside the club for Lily and Jim to arrive in a taxi. In my pocket was Michael's birthday card, which had arrived that morning, together with a long letter containing a great many blacked-out sections and lots of mush. It had been more than sixteen months since I had seen him and (reading between the lines) it seemed from his last letters that after participating in the invasion of Sicily in July 1943, he was now fighting in Italy.

The Warning hadn't yet sounded, and the streets were full of people, including many American soldiers. American troops had begun to pour into Britain, to prepare for what everyone knew would be the second front – the invasion of Europe – sometime later that year. I could only hope that one day Michael would be among them, so at least we could spend some time together before he was sent into yet more danger.

A taxi pulled up and Jim and Lily waved at me from inside. I climbed aboard.

'We're picking the others up on the way,' said Jim and gave directions to Celia and Simon's townhouse.

They were waiting outside, enjoying the fading twilight together. Celia, as beautiful as ever, was dressed in a pale green frock that made the most of her svelte figure.

'Honestly, Celia,' said Lily as she entered the taxi, 'how do you manage to get your figure back so quickly after each baby? It's only three months since Susannah was born and look at you.'

Lily was right, Celia did look remarkably well for a mother of two. Baby Susannah had joined the family in January. Motherhood had given Celia a glow of warmth and contentment that in my opinion, enhanced her looks. Lily's son, also called David, had been born in November 1943, and although Lily hadn't quite regained the almost ethereal slimness that had characterised her before, I thought she looked better for it.

'Do you think it might be confusing, both your sons being called David?' I asked.

'Not at all,' said Lily. 'Once the war is over our Davy will be in Australia and Celia's David will be here.'

'I can't see too many people confusing Davy Vassilikov with David Levy,' said Simon. 'We all wanted to honour David, and so we did.'

'Tell us all the ambulance station gossip,' said Lily, who had left the station eight months before. 'You're the last Ambulance Girl left at Bloomsbury.'

'You'd find it very different,' I said. 'Sadler was transferred in January to an East End station, as deputy station leader, no less.'

Celia laughed. 'So no more cheap black-market goods for you all. I saw Squire last week and he tells me he's most annoyed about it.'

I smiled. 'We do miss his dodgy wares. Purvis has gone also. He transferred to a station in Chelsea last month.'

'Armstrong's still in the medical corps?' asked Lily.

'Yes,' said Celia. 'Squire keeps in touch with him. Stephen's an excellent orderly apparently. He was at the awful battle at Anzio, and was mentioned in dispatches.'

'Harris and Powell? Moray?'

'Moray is the same as ever,' I replied. 'Harris just became a grandmother for the fifth time, and still mothers the lot of us.' I laughed. 'Powell's latest rumour is that Jerry has invented a death ray – you know, like Flash Gordon – and he'll begin zapping us in a week or so.'

'I find ordinary bombs bad enough,' said Simon. 'Do you think this baby blitz is going to last long? The raid last Tuesday was a very bad one.'

'It was, but the attacks have been tailing off,' said Jim. 'We're mauling their bomber force badly and lots of German planes are being shot down. I doubt they can afford to lose so many.'

'It's Hitler's retaliation for our devastating bombing raids on German cities,' said Simon.

'Speaking of babies,' I said, determined to change the subject, 'where are yours tonight?'

'Davy is being looked after by Jim's godmother,' said Lily. She laughed. 'Or, rather, by his godmother's Irish maid. She's a sweet girl. Comes from a family of thirteen and is a dab hand with babies.'

'Our two are with my parents,' said Simon.

Celia smiled. 'David simply adores his grandfather, and Elise is delighted with a girl, after raising four boys.'

'Have your parents formally adopted Leo, then?' I asked. Leonhard Weitz was a ten-year-old Jewish orphan from Austria who had been taken in by the Levys.

There was a martial glint in Celia's eye. 'Yes, but I insist that we share him. I won't give him up completely, so he spends a fair amount of time at our house. He loves David and Susannah, but Bobby is the main attraction.' Bobby was Celia's African Grey parrot.

The Hungaria was as elegant as ever. We had just settled ourselves at our table when Jim stood and looked at me. 'Care for a dance, birthday girl?'

'I'd love to.'

It was like entering a beautiful dream, whirling around the dance floor with a tall, handsome RAF officer. I had just begun to lose myself in the music when Jim smiled at someone behind me.

'May I cut in?'

Jim surrendered me to Michael and bowed out gracefully with a smile.

'When did you get back?' I asked. My voice was calm, although my heart was beating so fast that I felt giddy.

He was very tanned, but I thought he was too thin. His face looked harder; new lines bracketed his mouth and fanned out from the corners of his eyes, but his eyes were as blue and his smile was just as devastating as before.

'Yesterday,' he said. 'I wanted to surprise you for your birthday. So I phoned Jim and here I am.' He twirled me past a clumsy couple and closer to the band. 'Happy birthday, sweetheart.'

'Have you been posted to England? Close to London?'

'Close enough to see you whenever I have leave. I'm here for a few months, anyway.'

'Oh.'

I knew what that meant. Michael was in training. He would be part of the invasion force that would cross the Channel to France in the summer.

The music stopped and we stood together on the quickly emptying dance floor.

'Are you here long enough for a wedding?' I asked.

'Pushy female, aren't you,' he said, smiling. Then he sighed. 'Not yet, Maisie. We'll wait until this business is over with.'

Michael asked the taxi driver to drop us a couple of blocks from the club, and we walked through the streets of Soho together under a shining river of diamonds, bright enough to hurt my eyes. The waning moon was a pale sliver of faded silver, outshone by the glory of the Milky Way in a blacked-out London. It was slow going, as Michael kept pulling me into the shelter of doorways for long, slow kisses as we learned again the contours of each other's bodies after two long years apart.

'It's been hell being away from you for this long,' he said, and gave a mirthless laugh. 'I've nearly gone mad some nights, imagining you in love with some other guy, someone better than me.'

'You're such a chuff,' I said, smiling.

'You're sure you want to marry a chuff?'

'Positive.'

'When it's all over, I'll come back and I'll marry you. I promise.'

CHAPTER FORTY-TWO

It really is a mug's game to fall in love during a war. I never want to know such fear again, especially as Captain Michael Harker had been one of the first on to the Normandy beaches on D-Day. Thankfully, he got through without any serious injuries.

I'd been so busy, that I'd had little time to dwell on his absence. Not long after D-Day, Hitler made sure that London was again on the front line. It was like the Blitz all over again, but in many ways worse. The pilotless V rockets were Hitler's final vicious attacks on the capital. We called the V-1s doodlebugs because of their whining, whirring noise. You could tell from how loud the noise was when it cut out if it was going to land near you. When it did, it brought devastation. Thousands came over, between fifty and a hundred each day and all through the night, causing terrible damage and injuries and loss of life. Our pilots shot them down, and many were caught in the cables of our barrage balloons, but most got through. The V-2 rockets carried a one-ton explosive warhead. Unlike the doodlebugs, there was no warning before they hit, and we had no defence against them. Thousands of Britons died from these twin horrors and tens of thousands were injured, most of them in London.

Saturday 21 April 1945

By the day of my birthday, we'd not seen a rocket over London for a month. It seemed that the city was holding its breath, hoping that the attacks were over, but too scared to speak the hope out loud.

Michael was somewhere in Germany. I hadn't seen him since late May 1944.

The Hungaria was still elegant, and again I celebrated with the Ambulance Girls. Lily had come up from Oxford for the night. Once the V-1 attacks began Jim had insisted that Lily and Davy move away from London to live with his godmother, who had fled the capital to escape the new terrors. Oxford had never been bombed. Powell's rumour was that Hitler had wanted to use the university city as his capital when he invaded Britain.

'Oh, it's lovely there,' said Lily. 'So peaceful after London. But I do miss all my friends.'

'You never thought of leaving London, Celia?' I asked.

She exchanged a look with Simon. 'No. It's a personal choice whether or not to leave and we understand completely why Jim wants Lily and Davy away from here, but we see remaining in London as a stand against the Nazis.'

'Especially with all of the horror stories coming out of Germany right now,' said Simon.

'Any news about your grandparents in Germany?' asked Jim.

'No. Nor about my uncles and aunts and cousins. In all, my mother's family in Austria and Germany number fifteen. There's been no news from, or about, any of them since 1939.' He shook his head. 'We expect the worst.'

'You'll know soon enough,' said Jim. 'We'll take Berlin in days, and I guarantee that in less than a month Germany will surrender. It's nearly over.'

'To peace,' said Celia, raising her glass. 'To Maisie, on her twenty-fourth birthday, and to peace at last.'

Victory in Europe was declared a month later, and victory over Japan came in August. After almost six years of war, London and all of Britain celebrated almost hysterically. I stood with Moray, Squire, Powell and Harris among the crowds who massed in Trafalgar

Square, and followed as Squire's strong arms pushed through to the gates of Buckingham Palace. There we cheered the King and Queen and Winston Churchill when they appeared on the balcony.

But it wasn't long before the reality of our brave new world sank in. It was a world of ruined cities and devastated countryside, of damaged people and bereaved families. It was a world with the atom bomb.

And yet, it was also a world of hope.

Sunday 21 April 1946

On my twenty-fifth birthday I was again at the Hungaria, but this year only Celia and Simon celebrated with me, because Lily and Jim had gone to Australia in September 1945. Celia was pregnant yet again, and looked very well indeed.

'We want a big family,' she said. 'In a way, I suppose, it's to make up for those who were lost.'

Not one of Mrs Levy's family in Germany and Austria had survived the German camps. I began to murmur something trite and Celia stopped me with a smile.

'And anyway, I love being pregnant,' she said. 'What I dislike is how people congratulate Simon, who's done none of the hard slog, when the babies are born.'

'I know I get out of it all very easily,' said Simon. 'So I make a point of accepting all congratulations with appropriate modesty.'

'Any news about Michael?' asked Celia, rolling her eyes at her husband.

I gave her a crooked smile. 'He's still in Europe, but hopes to get back here soon. And then we'll be married at last.'

'When he does come back you might like to drop in on Katherine Carlow. Do you remember her? The fashion designer who lives in my old flats. She's a very good friend of Lily's and is holding a present for you from her.'

Before I could ask for details Simon smiled at someone behind me and I felt a hand on my shoulder. 'Care to dance, birthday girl?' said Michael. It was the first time I'd seen him in nearly two years.

'When did you get back?' I asked, as he held me close and whirled me around the dance floor.

'Yesterday. I pulled in a few favours and got a ride on a plane. I was determined to be here for your birthday.'

I sighed. 'Twenty-five. I'm old.'

'You're beautiful. And speaking of age, I'm thirty-four next birthday. You want to marry such an old man?'

I put up a hand to wipe away my tears. 'Of course I do. I'm not an idiot.'

He pinned me with his cool gaze. 'You're sure, kid?'

'I'm sure.'

'I want to be married here,' I said, gesturing at the pretty church of St Giles-in-the-Fields. It was the next morning and I was determined to get things moving. 'I love this place. They call it the Poets' Church. And anyway, I live in this parish.'

Michael laughed. 'St Giles? The Rookery was in the streets around here.'

'The what?'

'The Rookery. It's another word for slum. This area around St Giles was one of the poorest parts of London, notorious for its drunkenness and debauchery. Dickens wrote about it.'

His arm snuck around my waist, evidently as an example of the latter. I stepped out of his embrace and faced him, hands on hips.

'Is there anywhere around here that is not mentioned somewhere in one of Dickens's books?'

'Nope.' He smiled. 'Let's go inside and ask to speak to the vicar.'

A short while later, as we ate lunch in the Victory Restaurant, I began to make notes on the back of an envelope I'd found in my handbag.

'I think it'll have to be Saturday the twenty-seventh of May. Just over a month. Doesn't leave much time for the dress, but Celia says I can borrow one of hers.'

Michael shook his head. 'No. I want you to wear a dress of your own.'

'I don't have the coupons,' I said, and gave him a cool look as he began to argue. 'Getting the dress is up to the bride. I'm not a beggar maid to be clothed by you, Michael Harker.'

He put up his hands. 'Okay, okay. Getting the dress is your job.'

But he looked so disappointed that I took his hand. 'Leave it to me. I'll have a proper wedding dress. I promise.' I had another thought and made a note. 'Granddad will need money for the train from Sheffield.'

'Check,' said Michael. 'What about the wedding breakfast?'

'Celia has offered her townhouse and her cook. You'll need to supply the food and drinks though. Don't you Americans have unlimited supplies of both?'

Michael smiled. 'Not unlimited, but sufficient, I think. Let me get this straight. All I'm expected to do is make sure your granddad is here and well turned out, arrive at the church on time and arrange for the booze and food.'

'Check,' I said. 'And supply my wedding ring.' I smiled at the sapphire engagement ring he had given me and tried to imagine it coupled with a gold band.

A thought struck me as I sipped my tea. Lily's friend Katherine, who was apparently holding something from Lily for me, was a dress designer and an absolute wiz at making clothes. If I could find some nice fabric, perhaps she'd make me up a wedding dress.

'Would parachute silk do?' asked Katherine.

I gasped. 'Can you get some?'

'Lily did. Apparently Jim was owed a few favours, and Lily asked him to procure a silk parachute for you.' Katherine smiled. 'She left it with me and suggested it would make a lovely wedding dress. Celia said not to tell you until we knew for certain you'd be getting married.'

'Oh, Katherine, a silk wedding dress. How wonderful.'

She went into her bedroom and returned with a large piece of paper, which she smoothed out on her table. The pencil flew across the page. 'Three-quarter sleeves gathered at the shoulder, a cross-over bodice and a ruched skirt,' she said. 'Full length, of course, and slightly longer at the back to form a small train. Side opening with hook-and-eye fastenings, I think.' She looked at me. 'Have you got a veil?'

'Celia says I can borrow the veil of Alençon lace that she wore when she was presented at Court. I think it was her mother's wedding veil.'

'Lucky you,' said Katherine, and sketched in a veil.

'It's lovely,' I said, gazing at her drawing. 'Could you really make it in time? The wedding's only a month away.'

'Piece of cake.'

They say that it's a happy bride the sun shines upon, and the sun shone on the day of my wedding. It made a halo of Granddad's white hair as he got out of the taxi. He turned to offer me his hand, looking very dapper in the new suit Michael had bought him. There were tears in his eyes as he bent towards me.

'You look grand, lass,' he said. 'Beautiful.'

I took his hand and stepped out into the sunshine. After smoothing my long skirt, enjoying the feel of the silk against my hand, I twisted around to shake out the train. The world was sepia, as I viewed it from behind Celia's exquisite lace veil. I held a bouquet of white roses because I was a Yorkshire lass, and I felt as if I were walking on air.

Granddad escorted me up the seven steps to the grand doors that led into the church. The organist played 'The Wedding March' and Granddad and I slowly processed down the aisle towards Michael, who stood in front of the altar looking handsome in his uniform and more than a little nervous.

He turned and saw me, and his smile lit the old church.

EPILOGUE

We Ambulance Girls went our separate ways after the end of the war. Lily and Jim settled in Australia, where Jim became a barrister and then a judge. Lily not only looked after their two boys, but also became quite famous as an author of children's books in her home country.

Celia and Simon stayed in London, raised five children and remained devoted to each other. Their beloved parrot, Bobby, lived until the ripe old age of forty. After a period of intense mourning, they got another African Grey that they also called Bobby. Simon delighted in teaching it bawdy songs, to Celia's apparent fury but secret amusement (as she admitted to me). Simon was eventually knighted for services to medicine, and visitors to the home of Sir Simon and Lady Levy never quite knew what to expect from Bobby the parrot.

I moved to America with my husband. Michael went back to the FBI and for many years I ran a successful dance academy in Washington DC. We are the proud parents of three daughters and our youngest, Venetia, is the shortest, at five foot seven. Michael calls her the runt of the litter, but is enormously proud that she is a principal ballerina with the New York City Ballet. She was considered a giant when they first took her on, but nowadays taller women are becoming more accepted in dance, thank goodness.

HISTORICAL NOTES

Jack Moray is loosely based on Eric Roberts, a former bank clerk and MI5 agent in Second World War London. Using the alias Jack King and operating out of a flat in the Edgware Road, he used a fake Gestapo identity card to pose as a German agent. He won the trust of fascist groups and individuals in Britain, many of whom were actuated by virulent anti-Semitism. They passed on secret information to him in the hope that it would be sent to Berlin. It was a very dangerous and very successful deception that prevented highly secret information from arriving in Germany, including reports about secret research being undertaken to develop a jet aircraft, secret trials relating to a new amphibious tank and secret British tactics to evade German air defences.

Captain Temple is loosely based on Maxwell Knight, a British spymaster, naturalist and broadcaster, who was reputedly the model for the James Bond character, M. He operated out of a flat in Dolphin Square, and his agents – many of whom were women – were very successful in infiltrating and neutralising fascists and fascist sympathisers in wartime Britain. He recruited Eric Roberts. His most notable success was the infiltration of the pro-German and fascist organisation, the Right Club. This resulted in the trial and imprisonment of Tyler Kent in 1940.

Tyler Kent was an American diplomat and fifth columnist. When working as a cypher clerk at the US Embassy in London in 1939–40 he stole thousands of secret documents, which he gave to the Right Club. When Ambassador Kennedy revoked his diplomatic immunity, he was charged with obtaining documents that 'might be directly or indirectly useful to an enemy', tried in secret at the Old Bailey and imprisoned for seven years.

Radar: The development of the cavity magnetron by John Randall and Henry Boot at the University of Birmingham in 1940 has been described as 'the invention that changed the course of the war'. Britain shared the invention with the USA, where it was used it to develop airborne radar (RAdio Detection and Ranging). The technology was far in advance of that used by the Germans and Japanese and it gave the Allies a considerable advantage in aerial warfare. Later in the war, it enabled the destruction of many V-1 flying bombs before they could hit London.

AUTHOR NOTE

Ambulance Girls At War is the third and final book in my Ambulance Girls series following on from *Ambulance Girls* and *Ambulance Girls Under Fire.*

While each book stands on its own there is some overlap between characters and the timing of certain actions. The bombing incident of 9 March 1941 described in this book is a real event, and is seen from different characters' perspectives in *Ambulance Girls Under Fire.*

FURTHER READING

I could not have written the novel without recourse to the work done by others. As always, I acknowledge my debt to the digitised newspapers on the National Library of Australia site, Trove.nla. gov.au. And I spent many happy hours in the Bodleian Library Upper Reading Room in Oxford devouring information about the Blitz.

The following books stand out as invaluable:

Beardmore, George, *Civilians at War: Journals 1938–1946*, London: John Murray, 1984.

Gardiner, Juliet. *The Blitz: The British Under Attack*. London: HarperCollins, 2010.

Hodgson, Vere, *Few Eggs and No Oranges: A Diary Showing How Unimportant People in London and Birmingham Lived Throughout the War Years*. London: Persephone, 1999.

Holland, Irene, *Tales of a Tiller Girl*. HarperElement, 2014.

Miller, Joan, *One Girl's War,* Brandon Book Publishers Ltd, 1986.

Nixon, Barbara, *Raiders Overhead*. London: Lindsay Drummond, 1943.

Raby, Angela, *The Forgotten Service: Auxiliary Ambulance Station 39, Weymouth Mews. London*. Battle of Britain International, 1999.

Willetts, Paul, *Rendezvous at the Russian Tea Rooms*. Constable, 2015.

Ziegler, Philip. *London at War 1939–1945*. London: Sinclair-Stevenson, 1995.

ACKNOWLEDGEMENTS

Thanks, as always, to my wonderful husband, Toby.

Thanks also to my ever-supportive Australian agent, Sheila Drummond, and Anna Carmichael in London. And to the team at Ebury Press, especially Gillian Green and Katie Seaman. And thanks to Justine Taylor for her thoughtful editing.

Thanks to my dear friends in Perth and in Oxford – you know who you are – especially Felicity Davis and Ilse Peterson, who read early versions of the book and gave their usual insightful comments. And many thanks to Liz and Tim Taylor for patiently answering my questions about Sheffield slang.